VEGAS GIRLS

A Novel

Book 2 of The Queenpin Chronicles

L.L. KIRCHNER

For my chosen family, actual family, editors, cheerleaders, and home team readers — this novel is for you. Thank you for the late nights, the wild ideas, the lengthy phone calls, and for making my reality better than fiction.

*It is not our differences that divide us.
It is our inability to recognize, accept,
and celebrate those differences.*
—Audre Lorde

Contents

Prologue

1945

AT THE START OF WORLD WAR II, PRESIDENT FRANKLIN D. Roosevelt recognized the need for foreign intelligence gathering and so tapped General William "Wild Bill" Donovan, a decorated veteran of the first World War, to head up the Office of Strategic Services.

The son of poor Irish immigrants, Donovan was, somehow, an Anglophile. He modeled his agency after British intelligence, right down to recruiting citizen spies. Like Britain's Baker Street Irregulars, his roster read like a Who's Who of cultural elites: film director John Ford, chef and author Julia Child, baseball player Moe Berg, and Henry and John Ringling North, of the Ringling Circus family.

Perhaps this is why J. Edgar Hoover, head of the United States' internal security, found the department a threat. He was all about appearances and playing politics. To undermine the influence of the OSS, Hoover used the news media to leak false allegations that the rival agency was creating an "American Gestapo."

Wild Bill was not in it for the publicity. More content in a war zone than deskbound in DC, he didn't want to see his agents constrained either. With the demise of President Roosevelt, even Donovan could see the end coming. But he would not go down without a fight.

Believing that his agency's ability to collect and analyze intelligence was key to the country's long-term stability, Donovan borrowed from another British technique. To undermine Hoover's influence, he instructed Special Agent Theodore Nelson—on the heels of his success in Florida—to expose organized criminals working openly within the US, unaware of just how deeply they'd infiltrated the system. The OSS was shuttered by the Truman administration less than a month after the war's official end.

His mission in Las Vegas, however, was not a failure. Not if you were Thelma Miles or Kathleen Young, taking up the fight as Vegas Girls. Hired as pawns, they became the ultimate power brokers.

This is their story.

ONE

MRS. KATHLEEN YOUNG, Saturday

Kathleen Young eyed the gray-haired woman in rollers and a housecoat from the driver's seat of the Plymouth Special Deluxe the girls had rented. The woman was trundling toward a Coca Cola dispenser—a simple apparatus, really. One nickel in, one cold Coke out. A slotted crate beside the machine held empty bottles, which meant the deposit money was going back to the Esso station. She would speak to Bertie and Archie about installing one at Sun City Emporium.

"Pepper," she could hear her husband saying. "Florida is the boys' business now. Let's concentrate on what's ours." Not that he'd said any such thing. But after nineteen years of marriage, she knew what he'd say if he was still speaking.

As Housecoat worked the vending machine, impatience rose in Kathleen. What the Sam Hill was taking Thelma Miles so long in the bathroom? That girl had been nothing but trouble since they'd met. She never would have offered her a spot on the Florida Girls war bond tour if she hadn't been coerced. And the girl had only gotten worse since she'd married into money. Why, she couldn't have been married a month yet.

Scanning the empty horizon, Kathleen considered driving

away, abandoning Thelma, the mission, all of it. Her fingers tightened on the steering wheel, but she knew better. There was no road to escape her troubles, with the possible exception of the one she was on. That road, Highway 91, stretched as far as she could see in either direction across a dusty, scrub-ridden plain hemmed by a ring of mountains and nothing else. A vast expanse of nothingness.

"Boys, it's a dull mind that bores easily," she could hear herself chastising her sons.

Housecoat sure was making that soda look thirst quenching.

The door hinge creaked as Kathleen clambered out of the vehicle, and in wafted the stench of gasoline and petroleum oil. Nausea threatened to overwhelm her—she wasn't finding it so easy to be enceinte this time around. A Coke should calm this unborn child—the proof of her betrayal, the secret that threatened everything she'd built.

The older woman didn't move away from the dispensing machine as Kathleen approached. Instead she stood, legs akimbo, chugging down her cola, the bottle held aloft by a hand clad in a workman's glove. She shouldn't be wearing that in this June heat. And why just the one?

Offering a toothless smile, Kathleen dropped her coin into the slot and tilted her face toward the leather mitt. "What's the glove for?"

Raising a suspicious eyebrow, the woman placed her empty bottle into the receptacle, belched, and went back inside the service station. Now that the cabinet door was clear, Kathleen could extract a Coke. She hitched a hip on the machine, staring after the door as she took a sip. She wanted to follow the mystery lady, except she didn't want to give her the satisfaction traipsing after her like a puppy.

Mere moments later however, she succumbed to the urge. As she pushed open the door, a bell overhead jingled. She'd barely stepped inside before a raspy voice called out from behind the counter. "No drinks!"

Her eyes hadn't adjusted to the dim interior when she made out the unmistakable whirring and clicking of a slot machine. Then another. And another. To her left stood ol' Housecoat, gloved hand playing all three one-armed bandits in rapid succession, eyes locked on the spinning circles. Should anyone have tried to horn in on a game, she'd have eaten their young.

Wealth gained in haste soon goes to waste, thought Kathleen.

"No drinks, I told ya," the attendant snarled, his Adam's apple working furiously.

Kathleen turned to face him. Deep lines etched his gaunt face and hawk-like nose. She couldn't tell if the man was frowning or that was his general demeanor.

Casting her gaze across the shop—the pyramids of oil cans, tools of various sizes and shapes hanging on the walls, and a large glass case stuffed with faded merchandise—she wanted to ask, "You think my drink is going to be this establishment's downfall?"

Deciding against making a scene, Kathleen slipped back through the entrance. After placing her half-full bottle in the wooden box, she made her way around the building to the restroom.

"Thelma?" she called through the door. "If you don't come out, I'm coming in." After briefly studying the threshold's peeling paint, she tried the handle. It was locked.

"Open up," she said sharply, fearing the worst—the girl *had* just lost her new husband—before finding the whole situation a nuisance. Did she think her suffering special? Honestly, war widows abounded.

Or was this why she'd insisted I join her?

"Hang on, will ya'?" Thelma croaked. "I'm almost done."

When at last the door opened, Kathleen was overcome by fumes. "What in blazes is that smell?"

"It's a squat toilet. What'd you expect?" asked Thelma as she gathered dirty rags and paintbrushes from the floor.

"Not *that* smell." She backed into the door to keep it wedged open. "I'm referring to the chemical stink."

"I'm coloring my hair."

"With what? Nail polish?"

"Matter of fact, it's radiator paint." With that, Thelma unwrapped the rag around her head and patted her stiffened tresses. "Ta-da!"

"I wouldn't call that an improvement."

"Don't be a sourpuss. Agent Nelson says we're supposed to be Las Vegas big wheels with big bucks to splash around."

"So you painted your hair to match the faucets?"

"It's silver!" Thelma held a rag up to Kathleen's nose. "The latest trend."

Kathleen pushed her hand away. "Precisely. We're here to spy, not draw attention to ourselves."

Keeping her heel against the door, she angled toward where Thelma crouched on the floor and reached for the girl's chin, using it as a lever to move her head left and right to better assess the damage. Though her former employee had managed to conceal her dark locks, there was no hiding her. She had the most striking amber irises Kathleen had ever seen, and in her heels she was nearly six feet tall. 'Course, everyone was tall compared to Kathleen's five-foot two-inch frame.

"It's 'bigwigs,' not 'big wheels.' And your eyeballs look like they've been blasted with Clorox. I also think you've burnt your scalp." She released Thelma's chin and stepped back.

"The color is only temporary." Thelma stood, towering over Kathleen. "Joyce Bryant says she went right to set with no trouble after painting her hair. I read all about it in *Screen Magazine*."

Kathleen raised her eyebrows. "You should be more careful who you trust."

Thelma grunted. "If you don't mind, Mrs. Young, mind your own beeswax."

"Well, Thelma dear, you've made that impossible."

"Mrs. Young, I think you know you're acting in your own best interest."

Sometimes it was hard to tell if the girl was being sincere or sarcastic. "Yes, dear. That's how blackmail works."

Thelma flinched. "Well, you should've thought of that before you got yourself in the family way."

There was no mistaking that remark. Narrowing her eyes, Kathleen considered a smart comeback, but deferred to her mother's cue, "If you can't say something nice, say it in French."

"*Oh la la. Ma pauvre petite chose.* You've gotten paint on your skirt." She tsked. Poor thing indeed. "We need to leave in ten minutes if we're going to make it out of this hellscape before sundown."

Wiping away remnants of the foul air, Kathleen turned heel and headed back toward the car. She took a whiff of her clothes. "Fantastic," she muttered. "Now I smell like a greaser."

A woodie rolled up. The slim attendant leapt from behind his counter to fill the wagon and wipe down its windows, moving faster than he had for the two women. As he went about his work, Kathleen found herself wondering about the driver. Nothing about his family vehicle or smooth face suggested a trip toward a frontier town best known for vice. What was his con?

She really was bored out of her mind. Perhaps the station had the newspaper.

Other than Housecoat at her gambling machines—how

much had she invested that day alone?—there was nothing much to look at but the backs of motor oil cans.

"How do?" interrupted the fresh-faced driver. "What do I owe you?"

Kathleen went rigid. Did it appear she worked in this establishment? "I wouldn't know."

Turning, she saw a large cardboard trunk strapped to the young man's chest. A door-to-door salesman, just like her Lloyd had once been. Her heart softened. All she wanted was to be by her beloved's side.

Brightening, she asked, "What have you got there?"

"Only the finest sunglasses you ever did see," he said, hoisting his case up onto the counter with the cash register and, with a flourish, opened his trunk to reveal rows of divided compartments.

"I see," Kathleen said, peering at his goods. They were the same assortment she'd ordered for Sun City the previous year. "Very nice."

But he wasn't finished. He grabbed the top level and whisked it away to show another layer of his frames. And two more after that. This boy needed help. Kathleen folded her arms across her chest. "Where are the cases?"

He smiled, pleased with himself. "In my trunk."

"Word of advice," she said, patting his arm. "I'd eliminate the duplicates and put the cases in the bottom row. Make the selection appear more exclusive. You can charge more and you won't have to run back and forth."

"Well, aren't you just the sweetest little thing? But I've got a degree in business, ma'am."

That was how this boy had spent his war years? Kathleen shrugged. "Suit yourself." She grabbed a pair with round frames and pink lenses. "I'll take these."

"You see?" he said, clapping his hands. "Praise, Jesus!"

Kathleen's stomach clenched. Though she'd always considered herself a good Sunday Christian, between the Great Depression and two world wars, she wondered what all the fuss was about. Surely God had lost interest in human affairs.

She still wanted the shades.

"Thanks," she said, pointing at her car. "Leave them inside the case on the Plymouth over there. I need to make a phone call."

As she dialed, Kathleen noticed the young man—who'd also failed to introduce himself—toss her purchase through the window on the driver's side. Kids these days. So sloppy. "How's he doing?"

"He's fine. He's actually awake," said Peggy.

She didn't bother to inquire about Miss Holmes. She'd worked for Kathleen long enough that she'd have known if anything was wrong with her. Besides, showing up on her doorstep with Thelma Miles had revealed her true allegiance. She never should have paired those two on the war bond tour.

"Would you like to talk to him?" Peggy continued.

Kathleen looked at her gold bracelet watch—they'd only been gone for four hours. While Peggy held the receiver to her husband's ear, she reminded him that she'd be home in a couple of weeks, tops. She considered complaining about how Thelma was blackmailing her—given his fragile, post-surgery state, he was unlikely to remember—but why take the chance? Thelma had more incriminating information on her than the unborn child, after all. Instead she told him about the traveling salesman.

"He's no Doc Young. Didn't listen to a word of my advice. Just went religious on me. Can you beat that?"

"How many pairs did you buy?"

Hope flickered in Kathleen's chest—those were the first coherent words her husband had uttered in weeks. Hearing the mischief in his voice, that conspiratorial kinship that had bonded them despite everything it had cost, implied they might have a life to look forward to yet.

"Just the one," she said, switching into their easy banter. "The round frames with pink lenses that Archie liked? This landscape could do with a rose-colored view. Besides, I didn't want to mislead him overmuch about his salesmanship."

"That's nice, Pepper. Never resist an impulse to be kind."

He was fading again already. "Listen, Button, I see Thelma. Finally. We have to scoot if we're going to make Vegas by nightfall. You mind Peggy now."

Watching Thelma head toward the car, Kathleen had to admit—if only to herself— the girl looked like a million bucks. Despite smearing silver paint all over her gorgeous, thick dark locks, she still looked like a million bucks. Not that the hair was her sole source of beauty. No. She glowed with the purpose of fury on a mission.

This might not be Kathleen's fight, but she understood revenge. She would, she vowed, be more charitable toward the girl.

TWO

MRS. THELMA MILES WRIGHT,
Saturday

When Thelma emerged from the bathroom, a slight breeze hit her hair.

Her hair didn't move.

For her husband's sake, she desperately wanted the hair not to be a mistake. Something primal had compelled her to color it. Change it. Since George's plane had disappeared, Thelma had not been the same person. She didn't want anyone thinking she was. That girl was dead too.

Tossing the rag still in her hand in the bin, Thelma moved toward the car. Mrs. Young, coiffed as ever, rested a hip against the driver's-side door, staring at the Coke machine. She hoped dragging her former boss into this wasn't ill-advised, but if she'd learned anything from her time as a Florida Girl, it was when to ask for help.

"I'm all ready," Thelma said, trying to sound cheery. They didn't need to be enemies, did they?

Mrs. Young looked her way with a languid air. Maybe it was the pregnancy? Thelma had never known her boss to be in any way slow.

"Here," Mrs. Young said, handing over a pair of sunglasses

and a case. "I got these for you. Not the latest style, we sold these frames at the Emporium two years ago. Bet we could make a killing selling to these yokels. I should have Bertie—"

When she didn't finish the sentence, Thelma asked, "Are you all right?"

"All right?" Mrs. Young looked at her briefly, alarmed, before sealing her face and gripping the wheel. "Of course, just... Well, Thelma, you remember our last trip here."

How could she forget? That trip had shattered her moral certainty. Or was it their time in California, when it became clear that her movie star dreams were a fantasy? Maybe it went back to last fall, when the Youngs first dangled the promise of a Hollywood contract before a room full of hopefuls? By the time Thelma reached Las Vegas, she expected more out of life than just scraps, which meant she'd already made up her mind to work for Sal Giancarlo. Her long-lost mafioso father. Her enemy.

Of course she meant to run his casino above board. Until her father's stroke threatened that future. Her first impulse was to ditch George so she could take over the Giancarlo operations in Tampa. After a lifetime spent dreaming of independence from the mafia, she became a queenpin in her own right. And she was good at it.

Most likely, Mrs. Young's Vegas memory was of the dead man in her room, Diego Gonzalez.

"Thelma? Are *you* all right?" Her former boss pulled a hard-shell case off the seat between them, handing it to Thelma. "Never mind. I'm sure the fumes are getting to you. Until that dissipates, these shades should help those peepers."

"Why, thank you, Mrs. Young." She took the sunglasses case and pressed it to her chest, veering from hardened to innocent. "That's very kind. They do hurt."

"Mmm. Yes. Well, I'm talking about your disguise. Those

yellow eyeballs of yours stand out. Especially in that sea of red, which, frankly, I don't want to look at."

Yellow? Thelma had always thought of her eyes as *amber.* She reached into her bag.

"There's no smoking in my car, remember?"

A shot of indignation jolted Thelma's core. "Oh, I remember. May I remind you, however, this vehicle is rented in my name."

As she turned the key in the ignition, Mrs. Young eyed Thelma. "The only reason either one of us is here is because I saved your life, and this is the thanks I get?"

Here Mrs. Young paused meaningfully, but Thelma merely exaggerated her rummaging, clawing past her cigarettes. "That's not why you're here, Mrs. Young." *I doubt very much that saving lives was on your mind while you were making it with my half-brother.*

Her old boss continued on as if Thelma hadn't spoken. One of her favorite tricks. "And technically, this car is Peggy's since you can't drive." Mrs. Young then put the car in gear and rolled out of the parking lot.

Thelma reached for the rearview. "You don't mind, do you?" she asked, cranking the mirror to her side. She did look a fright. *Please let this not be a reaction,* she pleaded in silence. To whom or what she couldn't have said. "Just powdering my nose."

"Help yourself. It's not like there's anything I want to see back there."

As Thelma dabbed away at the reddened skin on her forehead, her frustration mounted until she could no longer hold her tongue. "Don't act like you're innocent."

"Thelma dear, the only thing I'm guilty of is sleeping with the wrong person, which I dare say you know something about."

Rage punched Thelma in the throat. "George was my husband," she choked. Thelma had confessed to Mrs. Young the real details of the life she'd escaped in Keokuk, and her friends wouldn't have breathed a word. Not that taking on her dying mother's business was anything like her former boss's dalliance with her half-brother. "And I'd dare say *adultery* barely scratches the surface of how you wronged Matteo Giancarlo."

Mrs. Young hit the brakes. "You wouldn't dare."

Thelma hugged herself tightly, seeing Matteo in her mind's eye, lying in a pool of his own blood on the bathroom floor after being struck by Mrs. Young's bullet. "Try me."

"I was acting in self-defense. *Our* self-defense. Do you really think you're less guilty? You failed to notify the police. The only person you called was someone to come and get rid of the evidence."

She was right, but Thelma was in no mood to concede. "Then there's Diego Gonzalez. Taking out Sal's top man while we were in Vegas—"

"I had nothing to do with that man's *accident*."

Though she'd been convinced of her former boss's innocence at the time, Thelma wasn't sure she believed that anymore. "Says you, Mrs. Young."

The woodie from the service station swerved past them, horn blaring.

"Jesus Christ," her old boss muttered, before mercifully resuming toward Las Vegas, her hands white-knuckled on the wheel.

Whether she admitted her role in the mess they were in, Mrs. Young was officially part of the cleanup. Thelma had no intention of exposing her actual friends to this danger. If George were still alive, she wouldn't be going after Salvatore Giancarlo either. No, she'd be with her husband and her old Florida Girls teammates, Peggy and Doris and Helen, starting their nightclub in Cuba.

"Better buck up, buttercup," she could hear her mother's

voice in her head. "Kathleen Young isn't one to suffer fools, and with all the death and terror of this war, she finds your sorrow a bother. Plenty have sacrificed more and not wound up wealthy."

Vivian Miles. Her mother's admonishments had grown, if not less frequent, at least less harsh, as the anniversary of her passing neared. Yet George's voice had disappeared entirely from Thelma's mind.

She sighed. All her life, she'd burned to shed everything about her existence. It had never occurred to her to wonder how that loss would feel.

A silence fell over the pair as they rolled onward. Watching the Mojave drift by, Thelma felt a peace descend. Joshua trees and creosote bush punctuated the arid plains, reminding her it was always possible to beat the odds. But she couldn't fend off her agitation for long.

The stone at Thelma's neck glinted in the slanting sun, sending a beam of light into the car. There hadn't been time to buy proper wedding bands before they said their vows at the courthouse, but George had given her his grandmother's sapphire necklace. It was all she had left of him. Now his family wanted to erase even that. Their lawyer had sent her a registered letter in Havana, demanding an annulment. A swell of despair overtook Thelma. Why had she let him leave without her that morning?

"You go with the girls and have a look at that property," her beautiful new husband had said before kissing the top of her head. "I'll pop over to the bank and be back in a jiffy. You won't know I've gone."

She knew.

This grief was nothing like when her mother passed. Though Thelma was acutely aware of her mother's absence, Vivian Miles had been sick for some time. While standing in the sunbeam of her ma's love was an embrace like no other, ever since she could remember, the want of that love was near as constant. Thelma had spent far less time basking in her mother's attention than she had foraging in the cold dark.

With George it was different. His love had been a solid presence, steady. She felt him keenly at all times, even now that he'd left this earth. Her sorrow could not be contained as he was never far from her thoughts. The pain cast a pall over everything.

Closing her eyes, she touched the gem at her throat to hold back the tears. Her mother was right—Mrs. Young was not the type to abide distress.

Good thing she never had daughters, thought Thelma, sitting upright. Until that moment, it hadn't occurred to her to worry about Mrs. Young's baby. For the child's sake, she hoped it would be a boy.

A new thought wormed its way into Thelma's mind. *Since Mrs. Young is carrying Matteo's child, did that make her family?*

No. They weren't married. Mrs. Young had to be at least fifteen years older than Thelma's deceased half-brother. And of course, she was already married to Doc Young. Still, Matteo's baby would be her nephew. Or—her palms tingled and before she could stop herself, she knew their child would be a girl—her niece. The ache in her heart surfaced like a tsunami. Thelma was jealous. But not over looks.

Mrs. Young carried the years well for a woman pushing forty, and she'd never been shy about using her curves to her advantage, but that was not the source of Thelma's envy. She'd grown up in houses full of women who put their looks to use. It was that she had children. Was still having children. As a widow with a checkered past, Thelma feared she'd never have another chance at a family.

Soothing herself with an open palm over her chest, Thelma considered whether she was being dramatic. She had yet to turn nineteen. It hadn't been long since she'd have sworn she wanted nothing to do with family.

"I don't know about young Theodore," Mrs. Young said, as if they'd been mid-conversation. "Nothing but a cheap suit in need of a haircut, that Nelson is. Was it his idea to rent this automobile? Two women couldn't do that in my day, that's sure."

Thelma snapped her compact shut, slammed it into her purse, and began rooting around for her tube of Fatal Apple. Why did old people love to talk about how much harder they had it?

I'm an eighteen-year-old orphaned widow, Mrs. Young. Do you really want to play that game? She thought, but refrained from saying. Instead, she pressed her back into her seat and glared out the window, unwittingly replaying a scene her former boss was very familiar with after raising two boys.

Mrs. Young tapped the windshield. "Look." She nodded toward a painted sign ahead that read 'Starburst Motel 8 Miles!' "We're getting close." Turning, she squinted at Thelma. "We might consider taking turpentine to that head at this dump instead of stinking up our hotel."

Thelma ran her fingers over her stiff, silver hair, making a mental note to research Miss Bryant's removal method. *Surely not turpentine?* Her eyes burned in her sockets.

"Let's hope that Agent Nelson knows what he's doing," Mrs. Young said.

"Mrs. Young, even if Sal recognizes me, there's no reason for anyone to suspect we're up to anything other than what we say we are." She pushed the rear-view mirror into place, returning her lipstick without applying any color. Despite her bravado, she thought the better of highlighting the red on her face. "I'm rich. You're a businesswoman. Investing is the perfect cover."

"Hmphf," was all Mrs. Young would say.

The casual dismissal made Thelma's blood boil. After all, she'd helmed an enterprise that wielded far more power than Sun City Emporium. Brief as that reign had been, she'd fallen for its lure. Unlike the fleeting prestige of beauty, that kind of authority lasted. Until the money ran out. Surely Mrs. Young knew that.

"You had your chance," intoned the disembodied Vivian Miles.

Thelma clenched her fists, remembering how her father had confronted her in his office. How she'd pulled the trigger. But she'd wavered.

No matter. Thelma would find Sal's books, uncover the irregularities, and turn the evidence over to Agent Nelson. Getting caught was not an option. She would avenge George's death or die trying.

"We're here," said Mrs. Young with the enthusiasm of a cadaver.

As they drove into the Starburst Motel's parking lot, determination rose in Thelma's throat. Of all the turns her life had taken since her mother had died, cooperating with a federal agent managed to be the most surprising development.

"Is working with that spy so different from your recent attempt to conspire with your no-good father?" Vivian chimed in.

Thelma's jaw clenched. Come what may, this time, she wouldn't waver.

THREE

FIELD REPORT

**** TOP SECRET - EYES ONLY ****

SUBJECT: Operation Fricassee
    DATE: June 5, 1945
    AUTHORED BY: T. Nelson, Head Office, OSS

TOPLINE: Scaling back Operation Fricassee

IN BRIEF: Met with on-the-ground field agents Blackbird and Hawk re: Operation Fricassee. Stated purpose of their mission is to gather and expose fiscal misconduct of known criminal Salvatore Giancarlo in Las Vegas. Did not discuss the larger scheme under the Agency's purview: to spotlight the ineptitude of Hoover's Bureau and increase the likelihood our office will maintain standing as the bureau of choice to oversee not only external but internal affairs. Conducted training in record time.

IN DETAIL: Because our agents are known to various among these nefarious characters, no false identities were given. Blackbird, posing as herself—a newly-widowed, wealthy investor—personally selected Hawk to assist. Their first task will be to attend a groundbreaking for Casino Royale, in itself an undertaking that shows gross misconduct with local unions.

Otherwise, we covered in two days what we ordinarily transmit in as many weeks—self-defense tactics, cover stories, and their autonomy in operational strategy. Besides insufficient time for instruction, it is my qualified opinion that the task is beyond this pair. What unfolded during our time together was an over-reliance on chance and emotion to win the day.

Thus it is my suggestion this become a Morale Operation (MO), where our agents will feed the rumor mill, contribute to disinformation, and generally disrupt illegal activities until our office takes charge.

RECOMMENDATION: Limit operational support.

FOUR

IMOGENE FUCHS, Tuesday

IMOGENE FUCHS SCANNED THE MOTLEY CREW THAT HAD assembled for the groundbreaking of Sal Giancarlo's Casino Royale, sizing up her ability to outperform them. They weren't competition for this story. She was on assignment. Still, a byline that took her beyond the confines of St. Petersburg was worth whatever waited at home.

Her attention veered when, through the haze of dust, none other than Kathleen Young and Thelma Miles—no, Thelma *Wright*—appeared. Her first instinct was to duck. But she was a journalist, she reminded herself, and a good journalist ran toward conflict. Anyone should know not to trust one. Besides, in exchange for Thelma's information on Tampa's gangland activity, she'd agreed to stay out of Giancarlo's businesses in Florida only. Any decent ink slinger would've followed Salvatore to Las Vegas.

Imogene tilted her head. The pair of them weren't exactly traveling incognito, that much was certain. In contrast to the small, otherwise entirely male press corps decked in slacks and rolled-up shirt sleeves, they were kitted out in pressed suits with fitted jackets. And it appeared—she narrowed her eyes—Thelma had dyed her hair silver.

"Mrs. Fuchs," her photographer said, interrupting her thoughts.

My *photographer*, thought Imogene. Another perk of scoring those national headlines for her organized crime reporting? A budget. At least for big stories. She'd brought her own camera too, just in case, the Graflex Pacemaker swinging at her neck. Danged thing had interchangeable lenses. She ran her fingers across its pebbled base. "Yes, Reggie?"

"Judging from here..." Reggie motioned around the makeshift bullpen just off Highway 91, cordoned off with timber pilings. "I'd guess they're already in there, watching the goings-on." He pointed to the trailer at their far left. "If you want to have some shots no one else gonna get, I'd like to run that way and see what I see."

Reggie's local knowledge beat all. Better still, his coppery skin often meant his movements were overlooked. They just might scoop this story. The corners of Imogene's mouth formed a near-imperceptible smile. "Excellent initiative, Reginald."

Behind them, on the opposite side of the highway, sat the El Ranchero. A few lots beside them was the ground where Benjamin "Bugsy" Siegel was building his casino. It had taken Bugs a year just to buy up the land. Though Sal's event was billed as a "groundbreaking," construction on his place was well underway. The reporter in Imogene smelled a bigger story—something to explain how it was that Salvatore Giancarlo was besting these boys—and she planned to be first to report it.

"But Reggie, mind you don't look like you're chasing something down."

Her editor, Briggs, would want the standard shots, smiles and shovels and man at lectern—she'd have to make it clear there hadn't been one—but Imogene wanted more. Sell two pieces out of this single event. *Life* magazine was known for appreciating more candid photos, and that byline wouldn't hurt her future prospects for the news she sensed. She had to play her cards just right, though. She wasn't supposed to go scouting other stories when she was on assignment. None of that would matter if she landed a new post. The trickier proposition would be getting Bill to move.

"Quick now, Reggie." She looked back toward where she'd seen Kathleen and Thelma, but they were no longer standing there.

"Imogene Fuchs," cried Thelma, startling the bejesus out of Imogene. "What a pleasant surprise to see you here!"

"Thelma Wright!" said Imogene, wondering if the girl was sincere.

The woman might've turned in more dirt in one sitting than most informants did in a lifetime, but she likely assumed the reporter was there for the grip and grin. The average person didn't think like a journalist. Not that Thelma was average. And yes, her hair was silver. Damned if she wasn't pulling it off. Just like that Joyce Bryant. Except... was that radiator paint?

"Well, well," purred Kathleen Young. "It appears you've done well for yourself."

Imogene looked quizzically at the former Sun City Emporium owner. Nothing about her appearance—petite curves always decked out to the nines; the lady even smelled rich—gave away the fact she was dynamite in a small package. Must still be miffed that Imogene hadn't written a feature when her two sons took over their store, but she stood by her decision. She'd just done the Lloyd "Doc" Young legacy story. Those boys were what, all of eighteen and twenty? If that. They had plenty of life to earn the ink. Let them at least do something first.

"Mrs. Young!" Thelma squeezed her companion's elbow. Imogene couldn't tell if it was a friendly gesture or a warning.

"You of all people should know how much Mrs. Fuchs here has helped us."

"You mean helped the Florida Girls," said Kathleen Young as she looked into the distance.

Odd, thought Imogene. Could she be mad about that too? It was Briggs's call not to label their little swimsuit troupe the Sun City Girls. *What civilians don't know about the news business.*

Or maybe Mrs. Young was denying her role in turning on the Tampa mafia. That would've been the cunning move.

"Well, I...," Imogene began, just before concluding that whatever ailed Kathleen Young, it was not her problem.

She turned to the tall beauty beside her. The Wrights might be denying their son's fate, but Imogene wanted to recognize Thelma's loss. As far as the rest of the world was concerned, after three days missing at sea, the heir to the Wright fortune was presumed dead. And those three days had come and gone six days ago.

"Thelma, I... I'm just so sorry about George."

Imogene couldn't be sure, but she thought Thelma's eyes welled behind her rose-tinted specs. She might have been out of turn. Thelma hadn't been mentioned in any of the press coverage, and if Imogene were a gambler, she'd have bet dollars to doughnuts that family was contesting their marriage.

"Thank you," said Thelma, looking down. Not a moment later she lifted her gaze and smiled. "Here I'm going by Miles. You said Thelma Wright, but here I'm going by Thelma Miles."

Had the Wrights succeeded already? Imogene wondered. Her brow must've furrowed.

"Think of it like a stage name," said Thelma.

"You're dusting the mothballs off the Florida Girls?"

That feature had been Imogene's first big break in the newsroom. "Get down to Sun City, will ya?" her editor Briggs had snarled. "We need pictures and quotes, and Marty's not back from lunch. It's just some girlie contest."

"She's doing no such thing," said Kathleen.

Imogene smiled. *That woman still thinks she's in charge.*

"Oh, Imogene isn't taking notes, Mrs. Young," said Thelma, smiling and rocking between her feet. "We're old friends. Right, Imogene?"

Imogene froze. She would go to the mat to protect the girl, but journalists weren't *friends* with their sources. "Just doing my job, ladies. Reporting on one of Tampa Bay's most prominent businessmen starting a new venture in Las Vegas. "Why *are* you two here?"

Before either could respond, Reggie reappeared. "They're on the move. Show's about to start."

"Did you get the shot?" Imogene asked.

"Not the one I was thinking," he said, a sideways smirk on his lips, a look that could give a gal ideas. "Better."

A thrill rose in the reporter's chest. She couldn't wait to see the film.

Then Thelma dropped a bombshell. "I'm looking for a casino to invest in. And Mrs. Young here is my advisor."

Imogene did a double take. The young woman appeared serious. Was she herself not aware? Thelma had mishandled Sal's books so badly, if the reporter hadn't agreed to let the Giancarlos off the hook in exchange for her intel, someone would've discovered their trail of dirty money sooner rather than later. For God's sake, Thelma had gone and opened a savings account for Cuban investments. International fund transfers were like a signal flare to the Feds.

Or maybe putting her inheritance into a casino was Thelma's way of spending up George's money so the Wrights couldn't get it back.

Imogene wanted details, but just then a hush fell over the

crowd as some nobody started yakking. Suddenly, she became acutely aware of the sun's rays scorching her skull. Doc Young's introduction at the Sun City contest came to mind, so diametrically opposed to this. She had to admit, no one could warm up an audience like old Doc Young. Not that she was there for the press agent's story.

FIVE

SALVATORE GIANCARLO, Tuesday

Sal couldn't take his eyes off his girlfriend's curvaceous ass as she bent over the trailer's portable air-conditioning unit. His mouth went dry, desire momentarily overriding the constant aches in his joints. That girl had done more to revive him in two weeks than Doc Pugliesi had in two months—made him feel powerful again when his body was betraying him daily.

"Benny didn't show," she said while scanning the crowd through the trailer's dirty window. "That's a good sign, right, Harry?"

"I'll say, Francella. Means our Mr. Siegel must be flipping his lid."

Involuntarily, Sal shot a look at Harry Lindholm, the PR man who'd set this whole thing up so the five of them—him and Frankie, Little Stewy, Bongo, and the flack himself—could wait in the trailer while the reporters assembled outside. But Harry hadn't taken his eyes off the window, watching for some fellow from the local radio station, KSXW. A Davis something-or-other.

A PR man. Frankie's idea. Sal would never have gone for all

this, but damn, she was convincing. He'd hired this Lindholm stiff to appease her.

"You wanna be the first to open your casino, you better make sure you bring a crowd. You need the press for that," she'd said.

Granted, she was straddling him when she said it, smothering his face with her unbelievable knockers. She wasn't wrong. He'd been doing the same thing back in Tampa—building himself up in the papers attached to his legit businesses—but without the promoter. Then that damn reporter brought the heat. How he escaped that shitstorm exposé, he didn't know. Salvatore Giancarlo had the biggest racket by far. If retaliation is what got his Lotus Club burned down, he was having the last laugh. For one, leaving town was easier. He sure as shit didn't have to worry about any evidence he'd left behind. His accountant could run the show while he was away.

And he did want to be first to open. Buy the potential, not the pomp. He was doing fine back in Florida, but Vegas would help him clean that money and make more. All of it legal. Besides, he'd already lost out to that Siegel punk on the racing wire. He couldn't let that twerp beat him to opening Vegas's first luxury hotel and casino. No way in hell.

"That's why Benny's got clout like a movie star," Frankie'd said. "He's always in the paper."

What is it with dames and Bugsy? You didn't need to be a wizard. All you needed in Vegas was the upfront cash. You could be crooked as you liked and, at the end of the day, your business was legit. Just like Tampa used to be.

She never called the man by his nickname. Even when he wasn't anywhere in sight. Not that Sal was jealous. Francella was what? Nineteen? Twenty? Had her whole life ahead of her. No matter what happened—he smiled to remember—he'd left his mark on her.

Lindholm opened the door a creak and slapped the wall twice. "Davis is here. Let's move."

As they crossed the parched lot, Giancarlo kept his arm tight around his girl. Doc Pugliesi had told him not to go anywhere without a cane, but leaning on Francella was better for appearances. Wasn't that what this day was all about?

While Lindholm addressed the crowd with a bullhorn from the makeshift stage, Sal made his way carefully to the front, flanked by Frankie and Bongo. This formation helped him conceal the effort it took to traverse the path and keep his eyes on the ground. Even leaning on Frankie, Sal was well over six feet tall. Bongo, his muscle, was a smidge shorter, but his wavy black pompadour added at least two inches. Little Stewy, Sal's driver, being rounded if short, lagged behind.

"Look," Francella whispered in his ear. "They're here."

They came to a halt and parted. Sal looked up. Standing out like a sore thumb, amid a pack of men in shirtsleeves, stood three women—one mannish-looking gal with a reporter's notepad, the shapely broad from that store in Florida, and Sal's beautiful daughter. He wished she'd take off the sunglasses so he could see those golden eyes, his grandmother's eyes. Gorgeous as ever, despite whatever it was she'd done to her magnificent head of black hair. His hair.

The bigger question though, what the hell was she doing here? *Shouldn't she be out hunting for that boyfriend of hers?* A flicker of hope flared in his heart. For sure, the Wrights wouldn't want anything to do with her. Maybe she wanted to make amends. Didn't they say all girls wanted was to marry their fathers? He couldn't blame her for firing at him in his office. If she hadn't taken him down, he would've done her. And he wouldn't have missed.

As Lindholm droned on, Sal released his grip on Francella's ribs. Standing to his full six-feet, three inches, he almost wished he hadn't left his cane in the trailer. *It's sophisticated*, he'd say, *not supportive.*

"Hand me that," Sal said to Bongo under his breath, motioning toward a shovel. Using the digging tool as his walking stick, Sal moved in front of the publicity man. "Thanks, Harry. I'll take it from here."

Harry handed over the bullhorn and stepped adroitly out of the way.

"Look, it's hot, and I know you all wanna get your pictures and make your afternoon deadline. As you know, my colleague, Mr. Siegel, plans to open what he's calling the world's greatest resort hotel. Right over there." He pointed across the lot. "But who the hell comes to Vegas for the hotel?"

Sal was pleased when this snipe drew a genuine laugh, even if it was only from the flat-footed news lady.

"Sure as I stand here today, I tell ya, we're gonna have the world's premiere *deluxe* resort and casino. And we're gonna build it right where we're standing, and we're gonna be first."

He looked out into the crowd, heat waves distorting his vision momentarily before Thelma came into focus. His memory was coming back like that, hazy visions from a distance. Like that day he'd clapped eyes on her in his office with the Wright sonofabitch. All he remembered about her at first was that Matty liked her. *Oh, Matteo.*

His baby.

The traitor.

Pulling his pocket square from his jacket to stall and wipe his brow, he trained his mind back to when he first heard Thelma was in Vegas. How happy the news had made him. Doc Pugliese would be proud. Like everyone else, he'd assumed she was one of the "unnamed" Florida Girls who went down with George Wright's plane. But no. Frankie said she was in town, and there she was, next to the lady from Sun City Emporium.

That was it. Sun City Emporium. He was firing on all cylinders alright. Time to pull out all the stops.

"Thelma?" he called out. "Come on up here! That's right, you!"

Thelma shuffled to the front, haltingly at first but gaining momentum as Sal started the crowd clapping. Just as she mouthed, "What?" he grabbed the girl by the elbow.

"We might as well tell everyone now. Everybody, this is my little girl. Ain't she a looker? Don't you go getting any ideas though. She's going to be busy, if she'll say yes to running the Casino Royale. Gentlemen—and lady—my daughter, Thelma Miles! Let's give her a big round of applause. How 'bout it?"

SIX

GROUNDBREAKING, Tuesday

KATHLEEN'S ATTENTION WAS ON THE TALL, WAVY-HAIRED thug—specifically the splattering of freckles across the bridge of his nose—when Thelma's name fell from Sal's lips. Wild-eyed, she looked at her coconspirator, but the girl had only time to squeeze Kathleen's wrist before heading toward Sal. It took all her willpower not to holler at Imogene Fuchs, "Do something!" as she fought the instinct to flee—the same instinct that had served her so well her entire life.

But what was there to do?

They were standing amidst a group of news reporters, after all. He was not kidnapping the girl. She and Thelma would connect, debrief, and reconnoiter, surely. The bigger issue was that Sal had recognized her instantly, putting a real crimp in their espionage plans.

"I did not see that coming," Imogene murmured.

At least Kathleen wasn't alone in her surprise.

Having made it to the front of the assembly, Thelma was shunted off to the side as a grown man in a suit and cowboy hat offered a few more remarks. It got Kathleen thinking, maybe keeping Thelma on the inside was a better idea than pretending they were there to invest in a casino. Where did that leave Kathleen? Could she just return to Carlsbad?

What if Salvatore knew her unborn child was his grandson? Maeve O'Reilly might well have snitched to him, just as she had to Peggy and Thelma. She'd been a fool counting on Maeve's discretion as a "society" couturiere. If word got out, she wouldn't survive that kind of talk. Worse, it could throw suspicion her way in Matteo Giancarlo's unsolved disappearance.

"This is not why we're here," Kathleen hissed into the reporter's ear. "As Thelma told you, she's here to invest. I'm here to advise her."

"Is she investing in Sal's casino? Or running it?"

"We're exploring our options at the—"

"Shh," said Imogene.

The nerve.

Kathleen looked toward Sal and his henchmen. Now he and Thelma both held the shovel. From this distance, the girl's disguise worked. Between her sunglasses and the hair, Kathleen was shocked Sal had spotted the girl. Though he had called her by her maiden name. Was he unaware that Thelma had gotten George to marry her? That was wartime for you.

Yes, this turn of events was for the best. If Thelma was directly engaged in Giancarlo's operations, they'd be out of this dump that much faster.

A smattering of applause alerted her to the fact that father and daughter had tossed a pinch of dirt with the shovel. As Sal returned his arm to Thelma's waist, Kathleen was struck by how different the gesture appeared now that she knew he was the girl's father. The first time she'd seen them together, she'd assumed otherwise. The May-September romance had been a good disguise.

With a start she recalled that, until now, Thelma's identity as Salvatore's daughter had been a secret. *Why the sudden change?*

"Let's all head across the street. Bar's open at El Ranchero," Sal said, raising the hand not around Thelma into the air. "Drinks are on Harry!"

The crowd let out a genuine cheer before dispersing to their vehicles in order to cross the road. Kathleen stood transfixed. Sal's man had a hold of Thelma's elbow. He and Sal appeared not to be guiding her so much as dragging her along with their group. And was it her imagination, or was Giancarlo having difficulty holding himself upright? This spy business was getting to her.

She missed her husband, even as she knew that going home would not bring the old Lloyd back. Her Button had been missing from her life for years. She'd never have slept with that Matteo otherwise, of that she was sure.

Forcing a curtain of placidity to return to her face, Kathleen turned to face Imogene. "I take it you're off to file your report."

Imogene's nose crinkled. "This piece could write itself. 'Tampa's Cigar Man Bets Big on Vegas. At a groundbreaking ceremony in Las Vegas today, blah blah blah.' I'm off to the bar with everybody else."

Kathleen considered her next move, unsure how to play this from here. Their undercover operation was blown, but they'd discussed this possibility. Their cover story about investing in a casino still worked. What they hadn't talked about was a scenario where Thelma was carted off by Sal.

What was the strategy now that Giancarlo had announced to the press that Thelma was his daughter? What were the two of them doing? Laying out the company chart? Sal did seem diminished. The old coot probably didn't know where he was.

Imogene tapped her notepad with her pen. "I say, I still

don't get why you two are here. Is Thelma planning to invest in the competition while she's running her father's business?"

Surely Thelma hadn't mentioned anything about Matteo to this reporter when she was spilling gangland's dirty laundry. Or had she?

Kathleen crossed her arms. "That wouldn't be my advice."

"You don't say." Imogene scrawled something more onto her damn pad. "How's that?"

Taking in the reporter—her lace-up Oxford flats, mid calf skirt and four-pocket blazer that might have been fashionable for a flicker during the war, and hair that could've been styled by an electric mixer—it struck Kathleen that this woman had ambitions. That either made her dangerous or easy to manipulate.

"Imogene, darling." As a way of regaining her composure, Kathleen forced herself to uncross her arms. "You of all people should know I'm a businesswoman, and Thelma has just inherited a great deal of money."

"Inherited?" Imogene scratched her ball point pen across her notes. "But—"

"And so I'm here to advise her." She looked around the now-empty lot, its desolate landscape the perfect metaphor for Vegas itself. "Why do you care so much what happens to Thelma?"

Imogene whispered something into her photographer's ear before responding, sending young Reggie off. "Like Thelma said, we're, uh, friends."

"Why is that?"

"Why is anyone friends?" A look of bemusement passed over Imogene's face. "Look, you introduced us. I wouldn't be here today without Thelma."

Neither would I. Kathleen pursed her lips.

Time to force a smile and change the subject. "Will you be heading straight back to St. Petersburg?"

"Not now," Imogene said.

Before Kathleen could figure what to make of that remark, a horsefly bit her calf. "Ouch!"

"Are you all right, Mrs. Young?"

Is that what it takes to get sympathy? My blood? "I'm fine dear, but this heat isn't good for a woman in my condition."

"Oh yes, I heard. Mazel tov! You must come for a toast to your health."

Kathleen's head snapped up as two thoughts collided. *How did she hear?* And, *Imogene is Jewish?* The latter won for her attention—she'd never known a Jewish person. Those horrible pictures from the Bergen-Belsen concentration camp in *Life* magazine flashed in her mind. The utter depravity of those Nazis was mind-boggling. She shuddered to imagine what would have become of humanity had they prevailed. She was altogether speechless, and so fell back on her mother's advice: "When in doubt, mind your manners. You'll never be wrong-footed."

"Thank you so much," Kathleen said. "But, I'll skip the drinks."

"Suit yourself," Imogene said. "Knock wood, there'll be some actual reporting to do."

Of course, thought Kathleen. Thelma would be at the bar. Or Sal. Or the both of them. Then the reporter's words landed —Thelma was a story.

"Tell them what they want to hear," Agent Nelson had advised, "then do what you must."

What she needed was to find Agent Nelson, and she sure as hell didn't need this reporter following her. "On second thought, maybe I will join you for that drink."

SEVEN

THE STARBURST, Tuesday

THE THOUGHT OF ACTUALLY FOLLOWING IMOGENE TO THE
El Ranchero's Wagon Wheel for a stiff snort tempted Kathleen
after a hot morning spent standing around in a shadeless desert.
She was staying at the El Ranchero, after all, and the restaurant
was right there. The smarter move was to check in with the
cheap suit at the Starburst—young Theodore Nelson's dismal
little motel on the outskirts of town—but driving straight to his
lodging on the heels of that press conference was as good as
asking to be followed. To throw nosy reporters off the scent,
especially Imogene Fuchs, she had returned to her room first.

Glancing at the bedside clock, she observed that its face was
framed by a horseshoe, only the ends pointed downward. Either
the owner was trying to jinx the casino patrons, or the fool
didn't know that meant bad luck.

Where the devil is that Thelma?

Twenty minutes had passed since Kathleen had last seen
her at that dusty construction site. It troubled her that the girl
hadn't phoned or left word of any kind. Thelma was many
things. Reckless, yes. Stubborn too. But Miss Miles had never
struck her as a person who shirked their duties, especially

considering how determined she was to retaliate. Reminded Kathleen of how she'd felt when she feared she was losing her Lloyd. Given what all she'd done to save him—and was still doing—she could scarcely imagine the lengths that girl might traverse for revenge. Surely, she hadn't frolicked off.

Could she be in real danger? The girl was convinced that Sal had murdered her husband. What if he hadn't? Maybe he meant it when he'd announced that his daughter would run the casino.

In truth, those concerns were tangential. It seemed unlikely that the man knew about his grandson, Kathleen's baby. What she couldn't have was him finding out that she'd killed Matteo.

Idle hands are the devil's workshop, she thought. Time for action.

After running a comb through her hair, cleaning her teeth, and reapplying her lipstick and perfume, Kathleen sat on her bed. Her gaze fell to the floor where the faint outline of a large round stain suddenly emerged.

She jumped, heart hammering as the memory rushed back, finding a man in this very hotel, blood pooling behind his head like a nimbus. How Matteo had come to her rescue and she'd "repaid" him right there. *Was that when this child...?* she thought, looking down at her belly with a shiver. A life created in the shadow of death. These halls had too many ghosts.

She had to get to Agent Nelson.

Young Theodore's motel was a straight shot down the road. As Kathleen slid into their rented automobile, she couldn't fathom how to take a circuitous route there. Spying was exhausting.

Pulling out of the lot and back onto Highway 91, Kathleen hesitated, her thumbs tapping an anxious rhythm against the steering wheel. *I could be back in Carlsbad before supper. Back to Lloyd.* The thought pulled at her like gravity. But then Miss

Miles would expose the truth about her child's father—and the shame would destroy what remained of Lloyd's fragile health. Neither she nor her Lloyd would survive that smear. And wasn't that why she'd come this far already? Not just for Lloyd, but for a child who deserved a chance, however ill-conceived its beginning.

Resolutely pointing her car toward Las Vegas, Kathleen recalled the curious images she'd seen in the papers—military planes gliding through the city. At the time she'd questioned their authenticity. Her recollection was of bustling thorough-fares and neon lights blasting out the night sky. Closing in on Fremont Street now, the photographs seemed entirely plausible. During the day, the streets were deserted. And, unattractive as they were, the signage wasn't dense enough to be an impedi-ment to a plane's wings. If she truly was there in an advisory capacity, she'd recommend sticking to Fremont Street. It would be years before the gamblers wandered down Las Vegas Boule-vard, if ever. El Ranchero offered more than enough beds for the traffic.

Turning off the larger road, she soon found herself on some-thing called Stewart Avenue, a dusty stretch of derelict build-ings. One faded sign read, Arizona Club. "Ha!" she thought. These people couldn't keep a casino afloat within walking distance of the main drag—confirmation that the construction six miles down the road was a poor investment.

A few more turns and she passed a saloon where scantily clad women sat out front on deck chairs. It had to be ninety degrees in the shade, so when one of them waved her over, Kath-leen nosed closer and rolled down her window.

"Come on in, I don't mind. We have refrigerated air."

Kathleen could not crank her window back up fast enough. Her ears burned. She'd heard rumors of such houses of ill repute, but never fully believed them.

Once she'd calmed sufficiently, she realized she'd left behind the paved road and was kicking up an awful dust cloud. And with linens out to dry. The homes here were made of tin scraps and tar paper. Some were mere tents. A group of children was playing pickup sticks while nearby, two women huddled over a bucket, scrubbing shirts. She'd wandered into the town's colored section.

She tsked. How was it so common that such poverty could exist so close to such garish wealth. It was not unlike St. Petersburg, where her own posh downtown home was mere blocks away from some of the city's poorest residents.

This was how she and her Lloyd had succeeded where so many other businesses had failed, by offering discounted goods that appealed across the economic spectrum, their volume making up for their slim margins as they welcomed all shoppers. Why, they alone hired colored workers. The fact that neither their Black patrons nor employees were allowed to eat at their in-store diner did not occur to Kathleen, busy as she was congratulating herself for her forward thinking.

Instead, her thoughts turned longingly to Florida's afternoon showers which, though they made for some staggeringly humid air, did keep the temperatures and the dust in check. Soon she found her way back to Fremont Street, and from there it was easy to find Las Vegas Boulevard.

Boulevard, she thought. *Mon oeil!*

Presently, Agent Nelson's low-budget accommodation came into view. Kathleen hesitated. The Starburst Motel was decidedly lacking in amenities such as bars and restaurants and, she presumed, clean sheets. Its relative cleanliness, however, was unrelated to her failure to turn into its lot. Despite her precautions, Kathleen couldn't shake the thought that Imogene had followed her. It would've been a snap. She drove several miles past the hotel before her heart stopped thudding in her chest and she was ready to circle back.

When finally she pulled into the Starburst, a family was unloading suitcases directly in front of Agent Nelson's room. Soon they were loading them into Agent Nelson's room. Had he switched rooms? Or more likely, *hotels*? She wouldn't blame him.

Still, they'd convened here the day prior, and he hadn't said a word about relocating. How tedious this man was. Veering toward the center building, Kathleen went in search of the manager. She'd get to the bottom of this.

"Theodore who?" asked the only person Kathleen could find, a man in a sleeveless undershirt who was watering the plants in front of the lobby. Sweat stains darkened his armpits.

"Nelson. He was in room 3-A."

"3-A? You mean Buck Rogers?"

Of course. Nelson had been the one to suggest checking into El Ranchero under assumed names, but surely this had sniffed out that falsehood, false identities being so common at such establishments. Or so she'd heard. And what an odd persona for young Theodore to adopt. He didn't strike her as adept with women or—considering he'd shown them the day before how to kill a man with a newspaper—opposed to lethal force.

"Tall, skinny fellow?" she asked. "Oddly strong jawline?"

"That's the one," the man said, turning back to water his struggling plants. "Left early this morning."

"Oh my word, is it Tuesday already? Slap my head and call me silly," said Kathleen, heeding Theodore's instructions to "follow the curveballs," as if anything about this endeavor was straightforward. "Did Mr. Rogers leave a forwarding number?"

"I don't think so," he answered without a backward glance.

Didn't think so? Was that bargaining or was this man just an imprecise speaker? She needed the person in charge.

Stepping around him, she walked through the glass doors and into the reception area—essentially a desk with a row of keys behind—but no one new miraculously appeared. Perhaps the caretaker *was* in charge. She hesitated.

The cool air was a balm. Looking outward toward the road, Kathleen's eyes latched onto the Plymouth. She could be home by nightfall. Forget this nonsense the same as Thelma and Theodore had apparently forgotten her. The rental papers had to be in the glovebox. She could return the car and take a taxicab to Carlsbad.

The jingle bells hanging from the door chimed, the caretaker was back. "I might have something for you. You staying at El Ranchero?"

"I am," she said slowly, wondering how much this was going to cost.

Kathleen's notions of what it meant to be a spy were based on movies, which admittedly she didn't have the time for. On the big screen, the work always seemed so glamorous. In practice, she found it tiresome.

The man dipped his head behind the desk and reappeared with a letter. "Here you go," he said, handing over a crisp white envelope.

BACK AT EL RANCHERO, KATHLEEN SAT ON THE CACTUS-print bedspread and checked the time. Straightaway, she was seized by a desire to slip the horseshoe clock into her luggage. She reached for the timepiece, noticing its heft in her hand. Not generally a fan of Western-themed decor, she could nonetheless tell that the U-shaped metal plate was authentic. Had actually been on a horse. It was scarred, just like ones the horses wore on her grandparents' farm in Virginia. She turned it over to see if it was branded, but it was not. The hotel would send a bill, so it wasn't theft, was it?

She snapped shut her eyes. No, no, no. This was backsliding. She hadn't stolen anything since she and Lloyd first married, when she was thrust from her family's society cocoon and could no longer afford the fashions she preferred. Not that she'd got religion. Her reformation owed less to a change in her desires than an acceptance of her new role in society, salesman's wife. She couldn't very well thieve from the stores where they purveyed their goods. Then eventually, she owned the store.

A rapping at the door roused Kathleen. Looking over at the bedside clock, she saw it was after two. She must've dozed off. Those reporters should be cleared out of the bar by now, filing their stories. And the baby was ravenous.

She'd just pulled back the covers when three raps at the door stopped her. Thelma? She was the only person who knew where Kathleen was. But why would she knock?

Stuffing her feet into her shoes took some doing. Her swelling seemed worse than she remembered with her first two pregnancies, and she wasn't even showing yet. Normally, she'd brew up some dandelion root and call it dinner, but she knew better than to skip a meal.

Now a fist pounded. "I know you're in there, open up. It's me. Imogene Fuchs."

The reporter? How had she even found her? She and Thelma had used aliases to check in. Could she reasonably ignore the woman? Should she? Now that Agent Nelson was MIA, she felt less sure.

This so-called mission was giving her the jitters. The last thing Kathleen needed was a nosy news lady in her business.

Especially not one with a crusader's reputation. She wished she'd never introduced her to Thelma.

Kathleen rushed to the door to dismiss the intruder, very nearly earning a punch in the face for her trouble as the woman launched into more of her infernal knocking.

"Why Imogene, what a pleasant—"

"Save it. I know you checked in under aliases, which makes no sense if you're here to establish yourselves as investors. And Bess Marvin and George Fayne? Nancy Drew's gang? Really."

"*Très calée, madame.*"

Imogene's face hardened. "I certainly thought so. Twelve years of Catholic school and my knuckles will never let me forget French."

Catholic school? Clearly not Jewish, then. Perhaps her husband was? The woman was a puzzle and that alone made her a threat. Dangerous enough to keep close.

"Indeed. Well, I'd offer you a drink but I'm fresh out in this room. I was just about to grab a bite. Care to join me?"

Imogene closed the door behind her, pushed past Kathleen, and pulled out the single chair at the vanity. "You're going to want to sit down for this."

Defeat registered in Kathleen's shoulders. As Imogene perched on the edge of Thelma's bed, she took a seat.

"You know the story of the Bolita Wars in St. Petersburg, Mrs. Young? How the Giancarlos took the gambling game out from under the Suarez family?"

"Vaguely," Kathleen said, attempting not to scowl. What did *that* have to do with anything?

"The part you might not know, that I found out while I was digging up dirt on all the families in town, is that Salvatore Giancarlo didn't win that fight."

What was this woman on about? Kathleen's stomach

gurgled audibly. On instinct, her hands flew to her belly. She looked at Imogene. "I told you I was hungry."

"I won't be but another minute. We don't want anyone to know I'm here anyway." Imogene rose and laid a hand on Kathleen's shoulder.

The gesture was almost maternal. The woman did have a child, Kathleen reckoned, but she was in no mood to be babied. Her typical fallback was to flirt her way into what she wanted. Barring that, she was forced to offense. Wiggling out from under Imogene's grasp, Kathleen asked, "Why are you here? I still don't understand how you found me."

Taking a step back, Imogene squinted. "I am a journalist, Mrs. Young. I'm surprised someone such as yourself would underestimate another woman."

It took all Kathleen's strength not to roll her eyes. In a few short moments, Imogene had managed to home in on every topic she'd been trying to avoid altogether—the Giancarlos, crime, and her declining acumen. She was there to play the cool-headed advisor to young Thelma, but this pregnancy rendered her emotional state to that of a teenager's. She hoped with all her might that didn't mean this baby would be like its father.

"You may be right, Imogene, but I don't know why you'd be looking for us in the first place."

"You and Thelma are in a lot more trouble than you might think."

Kathleen drew a deep breath. "Imogene, dear, Lloyd and I knew Thelma was Sal's daughter."

"Yeah, and the way Thelma explained it to me, she thinks she's safe because she's his blood. But she's not, and by extension, neither are you."

Good lord, did Imogene Fuchs know that Matteo Giancarlo was this baby's father too?

"I didn't think much about it at the presser. Sal was obviously grandstanding when he said Thelma would run the place and then offered to buy a round. When he didn't show up at the bar, and she wasn't here either, well..."

"Well what? Get to the point and be quick."

"Well, Sal's brother won the Bolita Wars. But Sal didn't want to share. He killed his brother to have the whole empire to himself."

Kathleen's stomach soured. Blood filled her ears. Imogene was still speaking, but for the moment she went unheard. For Lloyd's sake, Kathleen had played along with Thelma—in his state, learning of her infidelity might be the thing to finish him off. She hadn't imagined she was in any real jeopardy. Awareness hit like a stone wall—there was nothing that man wouldn't do to win.

"Mrs. Young, are you all right? You're all *flushed*," the reporter said.

"Of course. Yes. I'm just, I'm very hungry with this baby and all. Thank you, so much, for bringing this to my attention—"

"Mrs. Young, I'm not here to bring this to your attention." Imogene looked at her strangely. "I'm here to help."

Help, Kathleen was certain, was the last thing she needed.

"I haven't pieced it all together yet, but it's not just Sal you've got to worry about. There's something going on with these developers. They're all in on it."

"On what, dear?"

Imogene looked at her in disbelief. "The money grab. Same as you."

Kathleen laughed. She sounded maniacal, she knew, but this intelligence failed to be surprising. They'd been brought in by a US government official. Even if she didn't know where he was.

"I still have to eat, Mrs. Fuchs. Would you like to join me?"

EIGHT

KIDNAPPED, Tuesday

THELMA COULD NOT BELIEVE THE GRIP ON THE THUG escorting her behind the dusty trailer, the same one from which Sal and his buddies had emerged. No one had spoken in the few seconds it took to flee the assembled press.

When the shorter, stockier fellow opened the car door and pushed her in by the shoulder, she ground her heel into his Oxford. He winced, and the proceedings stopped momentarily.

"Sal, where are we going?"

"She calls you Sal?" asked the only other woman in the group, whose name hadn't come up.

"It's a long story, Frankie."

From the way Sal held the much younger woman, Thelma assumed she was his latest mistress. *Back to his old tricks.*

"Get in the car, Thelma," said Sal. "I'll tell you everything."

As her father released Frankie and reached for the car, Thelma noticed two things. One, a look of displeasure crossed Frankie's face. And two, Sal had to hold onto something. Beads of sweat dotted his forehead, and a flush swept across his cheeks. Her father was struggling. Tempted though she was to stab him

49

in the foot with her heel, Agent Nelson would've advised against that. "Let them think you're compliant."

He was her father, after all. Surely, he wouldn't try anything funny with this other woman right there. And hadn't he just announced she'd help run his casino?

To Thelma's surprise, the driver turned out of the lot and away from the hotel. "You aren't staying at El Ranchero? It's right across from your new building." Hearing the desperation in her own voice, she reminded herself that Nelson had taught her to disable an attacker.

"We're gonna take Frankie to her place."

Aiming for pliancy, Thelma rested against the roomy Lincoln's back seat. But her mind would not stay. *This is Sal's thing, keeping his women imprisoned?* The pattern was unmistakable now—her mother, Vivian, had been his prisoner in Chicago for at least a decade before they'd fled to Iowa, her childhood shaped by that captivity. Now this Frankie, too? Thelma's fingers twitched involuntarily, George's hand no longer there to steady her. She was alone in the beast's lair.

"Thelma, honey," Sal turned to face her, and she caught a hint of their resemblance in his broad forehead. "I'd like you to meet my lady, Francella."

Frankie had been struggling to sit still, exuding a frenetic energy that didn't match what Thelma could now spot as a well-tailored suit.

"Francella Ava DiGruppo. How do you do?" Frankie asked, like they were in some movie.

"Charmed, I'm sure. Hello, Frankie," said Thelma. It seemed the only appropriate reply.

"You don't call me anything but Francella," she scowled, lowering her voice several notches. "Unless you want a fat one."

Sal's girlfriend had long dark hair swept high off her face, accenting her strong jaw and aquiline nose. Her profile reminded Thelma of emperors she'd seen on Roman coins in library books back home in Keokuk. She didn't doubt that Francella would make good on her threat.

"Never again," Thelma said.

"Francella's expecting," Sal announced. "You're gonna have a brother."

"Or sister," Francella said with a tweak to Sal's earlobe.

In the space of a few minutes, Thelma had gone from shock to anger to... she wasn't sure what. Touched? Disgusted? Or something deeper and more confusing. The stab she felt in her gut was sharp enough to make her breath catch.

Her fight with Mrs. Young over Matteo had nothing to do with sibling loyalty. For the first eighteen years of her life, before Sal revealed he was her father, the only family she'd ever known was her mother—often distant, often unreachable. Until she married George, she'd never understood how she'd longed for such a connection. Was the violent twisting in her chest envy?

No. It was the feeling she'd been had.

"What about...?" She looked from Francella to Sal.

The only thing Vivian Miles had been willing to say about Thelma's father was that he'd forbade her from having his child. When Salvatore Giancarlo had laid eyes upon Thelma, his reaction was to strike her unconscious. This was why she and her mother had fled Chicago. Years later, when Sal told her he didn't want any more children because he feared bringing another innocent into the world like his daughter, she'd believed him.

"You know. What you said before. About the mental deficiencies."

A smile lifted Sal's cheeks. "Nah. Not since I met you. Anything's possible. Or, like Francella likes to say, why not expect the best?"

Thelma had to refrain from asking what this man had done

with her father. Smiling reflexively, the kind of grin that didn't wrinkle the eyes, she wondered if this new explanation could possibly be true. Much as she liked the sound of expecting the best, the idea filled her with a mild panic.

Outside the window, Las Vegas proper emerged, a cluster of buildings and cars and neon signs, all ablaze even during the day. This area was clearly the heart of Las Vegas. Why hadn't Sal built here? They pulled into a semicircular drive—not a house, but a different hotel, The Plaza. Older than El Ranchero, but more glamorous.

The stocky one, the driver, got out of the car to open the door. Francella slid out, then Sal. She murmured something Thelma couldn't hear as Sal patted her shoulder condescendingly. "You take a rest," he said, loud and clear. "I'll have Stewy pick you up." Then he kissed her forehead.

Thelma cringed. Her father's girlfriend had to be close to her age, though her build was more like Mrs. Young's. And Vivian Miles's, now that she thought about it. All three were petite and curvy in all the right places, but Francella was the tallest. She tried to picture Sal's wife—Carlotta, whom Thelma had never met—but couldn't. Since she could remember, she'd believed she must take after her father's side of the family because she looked nothing like her mother.

"Listen." Sal leaned on the frame of the car's open door, hovering menacingly into the space. "I know you're up to something, showing up looking like that."

Thelma paused a beat, remembering another piece of Agent Nelson's advice—let the prey come to you. Considering her foot-in-mouth disease, this was deeply challenging. She tilted her head, looked at Sal, and tried out a silent, slow blink.

"And you should know, I have no intention of letting you run the casino," he continued.

"Then why am I here?"

"That's what I'd like to know."

Just as they were starting to sound like Laurel and Hardy, Sal got in the car and slammed the door. For the rest of the ride they were silent.

As soon as the car stopped in front of El Ranchero, Thelma grabbed for the car door opener, only to realize she didn't have one. Her heart thrashed in her chest. She looked at Francella's side and didn't see a latch there, either. Had her father opened his girlfriend's door? The driver? Thelma was flunking spy school, only this wasn't a test.

Sal turned to face his daughter. "Now drop the bullshit and tell me why you're here."

Swallowing her panic, Thelma looked directly into his eyes. There was no use stalling any longer. Thelma related the story Nelson had coached her on, about how she was looking for investment opportunities now that her husband had passed away and she'd inherited his trust.

"Much to the Wright family's chagrin," she added, the final pearl. He hated her father-in-law Homer almost as much as she hated Sal.

Her father stood upright, his face disappearing from view as he let out a long exhale. He tapped the car's hood. "Stewy?"

The driver alighted from the car, bolting for Sal on the passenger's side as he produced an ebony cane with a silver top. Did her father need the support because of the stroke? Or was it the bullet wound she'd inflicted.

Tightening her shoulders, Thelma steeled her heart. She would not open to this man again. He might have lost most everyone he loved, but so had she. If it weren't for him in the first place, being with George wouldn't have been so complicated. Or so she'd convinced herself, as if the vast gulf in their social standings didn't exist.

"Why not invest in the Royale?" asked Sal.

Invest in *Sal's* casino, as opposed to other random properties? Thelma could not believe her ears—this was better than any outcome she could've hoped for. She could ask all the questions she liked. She wouldn't even have to play coy. She was bursting to tell Agent Nelson. Yet there it was again—not just a tingling this time but more of a burning sensation in her palms. Her whole life, she'd tried to ignore these sensations. Forebodings, if she didn't suppress them. Since her mother had died, they'd only been getting stronger.

Before she could open her mouth to agree, Vivian Miles's voice rang out in her ears. "Don't be demented. You can't trust this man."

"So you'll do it?"

She must've been nodding. The disbelief flickering in Sal's eyes confirmed Vivian's warning. "Right now, I'm considering all my options," Thelma said, which was not untrue. "Why don't we go and discuss this over a drink?"

Prior to Vivian's death nine short months ago, fear of winding up like her mother had kept Thelma from drinking much. Since George's death, however, that vigilance no longer mattered. Besides, the paint smell was giving her a headache.

A wide smile crossed Sal's face. "Attagirl. Stewy, go ahead and get her door. Bongo, keep her company till I'm back."

Had Thelma thwarted fate? Maybe she should try paying more attention to these premonitions instead of ignoring them.

NINE

THE WAGON WHEEL, Tuesday

"Fly me to the moon, ya da dee, ya da dah."

Sal didn't know the words to the tune, but that didn't stop him from singing. Not these days. Not since Frankie. *Francella.* At least, that was what he told himself. Others attributed his personality changes to the stroke and subsequent gunshot wound. Either way, the reality beneath the facade was more complex.

As he turned into El Ranchero's lobby, he saw a silhouette he recognized immediately, Kathleen Young. From that Sun City Emporium place. His heart soared at the easy recall, but only for a moment before his mood dampened. Had they fought? He couldn't remember. Usually, seeing someone he'd bilked successfully for years gave him a jolt. Course, she must've come with Thelma, who'd failed to mention the fact. That was annoying.

Like a rusted-out engine, details chugged to life in his brain. After that war bond tour that he made happen so he could cozy up to some higher-level politicians, she and that showman husband of hers—*Doc Young was it?*—had somehow bought their way out of debt. She musta run shows she didn't tell nobody about. Those two couldn't beat it out of Florida fast enough when it ended. But turning the enterprise over to those two boys of hers...?

Then again, he'd been ready to turn his casino over to Thelma. *The things we do for our kids.* The old broad looked good, he'd give her that. Even in the family way. *Something else he remembered.* All the pistons were firing up there now.

"Kathleen Young," he called out.

She spun around. Sal thought he saw fear in her eyes, but the moment passed before he could be sure.

"Salvatore Giancarlo." Kathleen changed direction, walking toward him with her hand extended.

"Ahhh, don't gimme that," he said, pulling her in for a hug.

She stiffened in his embrace. She didn't know the new Salvatore yet.

Putting his hands on Kathleen's shoulders, Sal held her at arm's length. "Your condition looks good on you."

Kathleen's jaw dropped. Just what Sal wanted—to shock her. Keep her guessing.

"I mean it," he said, smiling. "Did you hear? I'm expecting a son myself."

"Oh, I—," Kathleen started fanning her face. "I think I need to sit a moment."

Without hesitating, Sal helped her over to the lobby's leather club chair. He kneeled in front of her, unsure what more to do. "You want a doctor? Say, where *is* Doc?" He looked around the lobby, but the space was vast and they were the only two people in it besides the desk clerk.

Closing her eyes, she rested her head against the seat. "No, I... I just need to eat."

"You want me to bring you something?" Sal asked, looking for someone, *anyone*, to assist.

She straightened. "I'm fine."

This was, Sal realized, the perfect opportunity. "Let's go to the café, then. My treat."

Kathleen looked around. Save for that clerk, the lobby was empty. "Swell," she said. "That'd be swell."

K ATHLEEN COULD ONLY HOPE THERE WOULD BE MORE people in the Wagon Wheel. Just not press people. At least Imogene Fuchs wouldn't be there. Taking the elbow he offered, she marveled at the courtly man beside her, wondering what he'd done with Sal. She flipped her corded wristwatch to read the time, one-forty.

Sal gestured forward with his free hand as Kathleen sent up a silent prayer that they were still serving food. Seconds after they'd seated themselves, their waitress appeared.

"We serve breakfast all day long, hon," she said, plunking down two glasses of icy-cold water and menus.

Noting the server's Western garb—dungarees and a plaid shirt with pointed plackets and mother-of-pearl buttons, almost the same as last year's spring line at Sun City—Kathleen wanted to ask where they ordered their uniforms. She'd no desire to open a Sun City out this way, but there was money to be made in supplying dry goods. As their waitress turned away, Kathleen turned to the task at hand—ingratiating herself with Sal.

"Congratulations, by the way," Kathleen said across the booth before taking a sip of water. "Will you go back to St. Pete when the baby's born?"

Sal tilted his head back and let out what appeared to be a genuine laugh. Kathleen had never seen him laugh like that. "I'm sorry, what's so funny?"

"Kathleen, my wife and I are the same age. That ship has sailed." He dabbed at his eyes with his napkin, a cloth that resembled a bandana.

This was where themes went wrong. Too much of a muchness.

"My Francella's having the baby."

Mercifully, the waitress returned with Sal's coffee. "What'll it be?"

Kathleen ordered her usual—two soft-boiled eggs in the shell, dry toast, and half a grapefruit, adding hash browns and bacon on impulse. This baby was hungry. Kathleen herself could never eat at a time like this. "And juice, please."

"Fresh squeezed?" the waitress asked.

"Do you have concentrate?"

The server nodded.

"I'd prefer that. Merci!"

With normalcy somewhat restored, Kathleen focused her attention on Sal. Her thoughts flew in new directions. In this latest iteration, perhaps the elder Giancarlo was no longer a threat. Maybe she and Thelma *could* get in the car and go home. "So, you're planning to relocate here?"

He slapped his meaty palm on the table. "Dammit, Kathleen, you're a funny one." But he wasn't laughing. "I'm a married man."

Kathleen could only nod. Looking at all six-foot-three of him, groomed as ever— though he'd traded the musky citrus notes of his Florida Water cologne for something with bergamot and sandalwood—she questioned how Sal had fooled her so. It began with those cigars of his, Cuban imports from his legitimate concern in Tampa. When he'd offered to help secure building permits and contractors for Sun City, it only seemed natural she and Lloyd would agree to host a bolita window; Kathleen's own father had played numbers games. They were harmless.

Or so she'd thought prior to the Florida Girls tour. Now she needed something to incriminate him before he found out about her crimes. The waitress returned with her juice and Sal's coffee.

"Your boys excited for the new addition to the family?" Sal asked.

After a few sips of the juice that arrived, Kathleen let her forehead soften. They were, after all, longtime business associates sharing a meal.

"Sal, please." She smiled, tilting her chin so she had to look up into his dark eyes. "They're boys. Between transferring Sun City to them and Lloyd's surgery, I haven't talked to them about it."

"Surgery?"

"Oh, he's fine. Just a little procedure. I wouldn't be here otherwise."

Sal, she noticed, stopped listening after the word *procedure*. He was at that age where people became either morbidly fascinated with doctor visits or refused to discuss them.

"Well then, what about you? You hoping for a boy or a girl?"

"Me? Oh, I'm happy either way." Another lie. For years, she'd dreamt of a girl, but at this stage of her life she doubted she had the energy for one. Boys she knew.

"A girl might be just the ticket to help run that store."

Now was her chance. "Speaking of business—"

"Now you mention it, I wasn't sure how involved you two still were at Sun City, what with leaving town and all, but I went ahead and loaned your boys some money to get those bolita games back up and running."

Kathleen's heart seized. Bertie's gambling habit was what had gotten her enmeshed with this lot of hooligans to begin with. *All because of those stupid little numbered balls.* Heat rose at her neck as she recalled encouraging his interest as a boy. Back when she'd believed that lottery games were harmless.

"Aw, ya didn't know."

Once more, the waitress provided a reprieve as she arrived with their breakfast plates. Kathleen hadn't spoken to the boys in some time, but she couldn't imagine they had their hands out already. Not even a month had passed since she and Lloyd had cleared the store of its debt and the Giancarlos, and Sal had sunk his claws back in. Could he be lying? Or was he that mercenary?

"As you were saying, Mr. Young and I have been busy. And we did leave the store to the boys. But you know, that's not why I'm here." She drove her serrated spoon into her grapefruit, wedging out a slice and giving Sal a moment to wonder what she meant. "Delicious."

Sal whacked the bottom of a ketchup bottle over his steak and eggs. "You were going to tell me about your business in town? I'm listening."

"More water?" The waitress was back.

"No," Sal and Kathleen said together.

Kathleen looked again at the girl, whose face was flushed with exertion. "Thank you."

She waited for her to leave before continuing. "Certainly are attentive here."

Sal said nothing, merely hacked away at his food.

"I was surprised by your announcement today," she continued.

Taking a break from his food, Sal rested against the Naugahyde booth. "You surprised me today, too."

"I'm sure." Kathleen smiled as coquettishly as she could muster, tapping her grapefruit with her spoon. "There was no time to reach out. We'd only just arrived and read about the groundbreaking. We're here because Thelma wants to consider investment options and she's asked my advice."

Sal returned to vigorously forking his dish. "Oh yeah? What's in it for you?"

"For me?" Kathleen hadn't thought about that. *Is it so hard to believe I might be inclined to help?*

"More coffee?" The waitress was back.

"Yes, please," said Kathleen, grateful for the interruption.

Sal put his hand over his cup. "Scram," he said, motioning with his head toward the kitchen.

The server flinched almost imperceptibly. His casual cruelty reminded Kathleen who she was dealing with. Beneath the courtly veneer, Sal remained a man who broke people for sport.

Still delaying, Kathleen added some sugar—she usually drank it black—and took a sip. The sweetened brew delivered an unexpected punch. "Mmm," she lied, smiling. "Okay, you caught me, Sal. Of course I want to help Thelma, but Lloyd and I thought we might bring the Florida Girls back. To perform here." Now that Kathleen had said it, the idea made solid sense. Hadn't Agent Nelson said that the best lies were based on the truth? "At our final show in St. Petersburg, we announced the team would be back, but then our plans changed."

A lump formed in the back of Kathleen's throat, making it difficult to swallow. Her eyes filled with tears. The waitress appeared in her periphery, hovering again, which instantly quelled her emotions. Kathleen shook her head, discouraging another approach.

"Our first thought was to tour the Girls, you know, continue on promoting Sun City Emporium and tourism for all of Florida. But a regular show will be easier to manage and more profitable."

"Oh yeah?" Sal said, suddenly withdrawing from the conversation as he motioned for the check. "They got girls here already. Do eight minutes a night. Not sure how much money's in it." He frowned, jutting out his lips. "Or, lemme guess. The bigwigs back home weren't so willing to help you out this time around." Sal eased back into his booth.

Kathleen could picture him twirling his mustache, if he'd had one. Time to show this yokel.

"I've something far grander in mind, Sal. With hit songs on the radio and press clippings across the country, the Florida Girls are an act. Like the Rockettes."

Sal hailed the waitress. *The insouciance.*

"I'd wager we can book running performances here," Kathleen continued, "and still tour if we want to."

"Then I'd say you're about as good a gambler as your boy Bertie. That was all for war bonds, and I'm afraid that ship has sailed. The real stars are back from their USO tours now."

Kathleen lifted her cheeks into an approximation of an unforced smile. "Well, I guess we'll see about that. Only, you've gone and absconded with our star performer."

"You mean Thelma?" Sal asked, hoisting himself up from the table and grabbing a polished wooden cane with a black onyx knob for a handle.

Kathleen wondered how she'd missed this accessory, clearly a custom job. Sal *was* a bit long in the tooth for surviving gun play, or so she thought till he leaned over the booth, his Romanesque nose far too close for Kathleen's liking.

"You two both know what it means to put on a show for the newspapers." He straightened, dropping a ten-dollar bill on the table for food that barely cost two. "Anyways, I don't know where she is. Haven't seen her since the press thing. Now I gotta go pick up my Francella."

His vague threat was all it took to push Kathleen over the edge, the careful facade she'd maintained throughout their meal cracking like thin ice. Agent Nelson was missing. Imogene Fuchs was looking for her next byline in the guise of being "helpful." Meanwhile, Salvatore Giancarlo was lying as to Thelma's whereabouts. And those boys of hers needed a talking-to. She was more than ready to leave Las Vegas—to flee this glittering trap before it snapped shut on all of them.

On the way back to her room, she rehearsed what she'd say if she did hear from Agent Nelson. *You're the one who went off-piste*, she thought, then chided herself for thinking young Theodore would have any idea what that meant.

You were gone, and Sal made Thelma disappear. Better. If things went her way, she'd be having the conversation from the comfort of her kitchen table in Carlsbad.

TEN

GASLIGHT, Tuesday

BONGO MARCHED THELMA DOWN A PRIVATE HALLWAY IN El Ranchero, presumably toward her father's suite. Sal's man was tall—almost as tall as Sal—and thick, with skin like an orange peel. His hand was the size of her thigh. She could not wriggle free of his grip.

"Let go of me, you brute."

He said nothing, simply launched her into the hall and left. She tried the handle, but the door merely rattled in its frame.

"You there! Bongo! I can't open the door!"

He didn't reply.

"You can't keep me locked in here." She pulled uselessly on the doorknob. "I'll call the police!"

"Sal's orders."

She hammered on the door to no avail. Her stomach seized with... dread, maybe? Thelma scarcely knew what she felt since George had disappeared—it was as if his absence had left her emotional compass spinning wildly, unable to find true north. The grief came in waves, sometimes drowning her, sometimes receding just enough to let her breathe. This moment was somewhere in between. Swallowing her angst, she turned to search for the telephone and drew a sharp intake of breath. She recognized the view, the distant mountains visible from every window. This was the same suite where she'd met Sal earlier that year. The generous seating area included a bar with two doors on either side—a bedroom and bath, she assumed—and beyond that, an office. This was her opportunity.

Returning to the entry, Thelma held her breath, listening for any movement from Sal's man. Once she felt certain he had no intention of entering, she began rifling through every drawer in the place. When that turned up nothing she turned to the furniture, digging through cushions, under the chairs and, finally, the mattresses. She was scrounging through the pockets of Sal's suits—not a stray bill or match among them, neat as a pin —when the thundering of a murderous step sounded in the hall.

"Thelma!"

Sal. The man knew how to make his presence known.

Quick as a wink, Thelma slipped back into the living area. Rather than race toward the entry, she stopped mid stride. Sal's impatience reminded her of her former client, Asa, a man who liked to blame her for his speedy ejaculations. "Stupid whore," he'd say, as if she minded the rapid conclusion to their business. She knew how to handle unreasonable men, she thought, shaking her head as she began pouring drinks, aiming for casual.

"Right here..." She hesitated, "Dad."

"You came to Vegas with that uptight discount-store owner Kathleen Young because you thought you were going to tour the Florida Girls here?"

What? The question hit her like cold water. She stole a glance at her wristwatch as she handed Sal his whiskey— neat, just how he liked it, the amber liquid catching the light like trapped fire. A sick feeling spread through her chest. When had he talked to Mrs. Young? What game was the woman playing now? And where had that story come from? If Mrs. Young was making deals with Sal behind her back, the entire mission could unravel. George's death would remain unavenged.

He didn't take a drink or a seat.

"If I recall correctly, weren't you an investor in the Florida Girls?" Thelma put his tumbler on the end table next to the sofa, sat in the club chair catty-corner, and took a languid sip of her own beverage, gin on the rocks. Despite her earlier reservations, drinking—like smoking cigars—had proven useful.

Sal's mouth twitched. "You tell me you're here to invest and she's here to help you. She tells me you're here putting on a show. Now which is it? And cut the crap."

So much for the dear-old-Dad routine. Thelma also noted that Sal's cane was missing. Rage invigorated him, a fact she could store away for later use. The first time they met, before she knew he was her father, flirting had worked like a charm. The recollection revolted her.

If not for this man, she and George would be in Cuba, planning their new nightclub. Her mother might not have succumbed to her worst inclinations. With every ounce of her being, she despised Salvatore Giancarlo.

"Both, Sal," she said, leaning forward. "It's both. Why else would you think I'd be hanging around Kathleen Young? I asked her advice on the Wrights. She said investing in your business would be the best revenge."

Sal crossed his arms, considering. He seemed to take pleasure in her ambition, as if he'd something to do with it. The cretin.

"What you don't know is that the Wrights are fighting me and George's marriage. They want an annulment." She watched his face to see if this registered as a surprise. It didn't. Nor did it appear to strike him in any other way. "Hmph. I thought you'd be pleased."

Sal deflated along with his anger. Gripping the couch, he

eased into its seat, then reached for his whiskey. "Honey, you'd have to be an imbecile not to notice you haven't been mentioned in any of the stories around your husband's disappearance."

Thelma fought to keep from throwing the heavy crystal glass in her hand at his temple—his most vulnerable spot, according to Agent Nelson. "I think it's time you answer some questions, Sal."

Her father laughed. "Is that right?" he asked, before draining his drink.

The reaction stumped Thelma. Did he know Kathleen had shot Matteo? Surely not. If that was the case, he would've murdered the woman. Unless he was biding his time until she had her baby. But that would mean he knew his son was the child's father.

Thelma gulped the last of her gin. "Yeah, that's right, Sal. You killed my husband."

Sal snorted.

The bastard.

"Oh. You're serious. Tell me, why would you think I'd want to do that? Because you burned down the Lotus Club?"

This accusation was one Thelma had prepared for. Ever since she'd put a bullet in his leg, she knew if he survived, he'd realize eventually that she'd been the one who set fire to his place of business. The job had all the markings of her work. For the brief period she'd run his desk in Florida, like she was a real queenpin, she'd used the same method to extract money from deadbeats.

"That's reason enough to want to murder me, wouldn't you say?" With that, Thelma drained her gin.

"Like I said, what's that got to do with offing George?"

Slamming her now-empty glass onto the end table, Thelma stood. "Because I was supposed to be on that plane."

"And how would I have known that? With that reporter snooping around, I got the hell out of town soon as I could."

A gurgle sounded as Thelma opened her mouth, but didn't speak. Couldn't. How would Sal have known? Most of his associates were in jail. God forbid he see her handiwork in Fuchs's investigation now. But if it wasn't payback from Sal, who was after her?

"That's right," he said, watching as she processed the information.

Scoundrel, she thought, pouring herself another drink to avoid giving any signals. He's lying.

Even if he was telling the truth, did she care? George would still be alive if it weren't for that man, whether it had been his direct hand or not. *The same could be said of me*, she thought, gulping more of the brown liquid to quell the emotions rending her body—a viscous stew of contempt, distress, and grief. She'd never fantasized about having a cozy relationship with a father figure. And the man was plenty guilty. Someone had to pay for taking George's life.

"As if you'd say otherwise," she finally said before returning to her seat.

"Plus, Thelma, sweetheart," he said, ignoring her jab. "You did me a favor."

Her heart skipped a beat. He knew. And she was still alive? "Do tell, Sal."

"Jesus, you're starting to sound like her now," he said. "Kathleen Young," he clarified, as if she didn't know precisely who he meant.

Thelma refrained from scoffing. *Progress*. Or fear.

"I got quite the cash payout from insurance." Sal downed his whiskey and let out a satisfied sigh. "More than I needed to get started on the Royale."

"So," said Thelma, thinking fast. "You owe me."

A shadow passed over her father's face.

That was one way to make him angry. Forcing herself to smile, she changed the subject. "Fact is, becoming George's widow has made me a wealthy woman. Mrs. Young is just smart enough to have investment advice and dumb enough to believe I'll work for her again if she puts on a Florida Girls revival."

"Yeah, but why'd you ask her for advice in the first place? I could give you better advice."

"What, that I should work for you at your casino?"

"Aww, sweetheart, that was just a dog and pony show," he said with a tsk. "I mean real advice."

Thelma could scarcely keep up with Sal's shifting emotional winds, but this was just the opening she needed. "Would you?" she asked in a voice as filled with gratitude as she could manage.

"I already did. You should invest in the Royale."

She hitched her elbow into her palm and tapped at her chin. "Gee, Sal. What about that insurance money?"

He laughed. "You're something kid, you know that? You want my advice for real? Only thing you can count on is death and taxes. Business is all about whatcha call contingencies."

"I know what a contingency is, Sal."

"Do ya? Cause you just asked like you was surprised we needed more cash."

Wrapping both arms around her waist, Thelma looked her father up and down. He'd lost some weight, but other than the cane, he looked like his old self—manicured, coiffed, and pressed. "You're not really selling it."

Sal chuckled.

"What I'm saying is, I'd need to see your books."

A loud banging at the door interrupted them.

Without taking his eyes off Thelma, Sal yelled, "What!"

Sal's driver entered the foyer. Beads of sweat dotted the

man's forehead, and from the smell emanating from him, Thelma guessed his armpits were worse.

"I can't find Francella," he said.

* * *

SAL GIANCARLO LOOKED AWAY FROM HIS DAUGHTER. His driver was standing in the corridor, a goddamn sweaty mess.

"Whaddya mean you can't find her? Christ, Stewy." He held up an index finger. "You got one job."

While his driver yapped on about how he'd looked for Frankie everywhere, Sal stopped listening. Instead, he breathed in and out real slow. Just like his doc had told him to.

"You've got to stay calm, Mr. Giancarlo," Dr. Pugliesi had said. "An elevated heart rate is disastrous after a cerebrovascular accident. You got to keep yourself on an even keel, Mr. Giancarlo."

And that was before he got shot. Though the doctor didn't argue when he refused his sedatives—he didn't think it was such a hot idea so close to the stroke either. But he didn't like seeing Sal head out to Las Vegas.

"Doc, you just took a bullet out of my leg. Taking action is whatcha call my stock-in-trade."

It wasn't like Sal could control what life threw at him. He'd always run hot. *The man must not have kids*, Sal thought now, crossing himself. *God rest my Matteo's soul, even if the little punk was a deserter.*

"I'm sure it's not that bad, Sal," Thelma said. "She's here someplace."

Sal looked back in his daughter's direction. He'd forgotten the girl was there. It was like that since the stroke. Moments disappeared.

"We'll find her," she said.

Fast as that, the memory flooded back. What a bullshitter, Sal thought. Though if Thelma was a son, he'd say the boy had strength. He didn't know what to call that in a woman. Disagreeable? That couldn't apply to Thelma, she was too easy on the eyes. But wealthy? Pfft. Of course Sal knew George had been in Florida. He'd been there to get money, which meant he didn't have any back in Cuba. And if the family was carrying on about an annulment like he figured they were? She didn't have nothing.

Where the hell was Frankie? For the millionth time, he hoped she was having a boy. He turned to Stewy. "You say they haven't seen her since this morning?"

Stewy nodded.

"Right. But I walked her into her hotel myself." Sal heaved himself up, and Stewy shrank back as he laid a hand on his shoulder. "I ain't worried, Stewy," he said. And he wasn't. Christ, it was so damn near impossible to go against the law in Las Vegas, there was no need to hurt him by hurting his girl. "A Tampa crook is a Vegas success story."

Nobody laughed. The girl didn't even crack a smile. Did no one have a sense of humor anymore?

"She's probably getting her hair done. Stewy, you come with me. Bongo, you stay here."

A woman's voice pierced his consciousness. "What about me, Sal?"

Right, the girl. Thelma. That was why Bongo was staying. He'd take care of her later.

Without so much as a glance over his shoulder, Sal walked toward the door.

ELEVEN

FRANCELLA AVA DIGRUPPO,
Tuesday

"SAY, LAY-DEE!" FRANCELLA CALLED, HALTING THE WOMAN who'd been marching through El Ranchero's lobby like she was on a mission. *Dangerous*, Wade had called her. From where she stood, the old dame spooked like a rabbit in a trap. He could go after her any way he liked—she had her own ideas. This was going to be fun. "You there."

"Yes, dear. I see you perfectly well." The ol' fussbudget reached up and tweaked an earlobe. "And hear you."

Francella had to admit, fussy as she was, that Kathleen Young was quick on her feet. Not even a double take and she had to have recognized her from the press event.

"Hiya!" Francella said, scooping the tiny gal in an embrace like a long lost pal.

As expected, the lady went stiff in Francella's arms. This was one of her favorite ways of taking people off guard, bowling them over with affection.

"Why, hello, dear," Kathleen said, patting Francella's shoulders before pushing her off. "I believe I saw you this morning. You must be Mr. Giancarlo's..."

Francella cut her off. "Yeah, hi!" She stuck out her palm, but the lady seemed confused. So she grabbed Kathleen's hand and shook it for both of them. "Francella Ava DiGruppo. Pleased to meet ya."

Maintaining her hold, Francella dragged Kathleen across the lobby toward its seating area, the same spot where she'd seen her with Sal little more than an hour before. Soon as they'd headed for the diner, she'd hotfooted it back to her pal in the Wagon Wheel to get the skinny. If a Florida Girls redux was in the making, Francella was ready.

"I'm so glad I bumped into you," she effused. "You weren't listed as a guest in the register?"

Releasing Kathleen's hand as she sat, Francella used her coat to fan the woman's body. Partly to comfort her, but also, she wanted this lady to notice how good she looked. She'd dressed carefully for this "chance" encounter, piling her hair high under a leopard turban that matched the trim on her beige car coat, which she wore over her favorite sequined culottes to show off her legs.

"So, listen Kath. I'll get straight to the point. I hear you want to bring your dance troupe to Vegas? You're gonna need—"

Before she'd finished, Kathleen's jaw dropped. "You heard what—"

Francella laughed, brittle and sharp. "Look at your face!" The flash of alarm in the lady's face was delicious, and almost caught her off guard. She needed cooperation out of this pill. Shifting strategies like dance steps, she made her voice softer, more confiding. "Sorry. I figured you'd be telling everybody. That's what that reporter told me. Genie-something I think's her name?"

Ol' Kath looked like she had a board up her backside. That's what Francella's daddy would've said. Sal, too, come to think of it. No matter. She would show her. This lady knew nothing about this town, obviously.

Shrugging off the nagging sensation of always having to prove herself, Francella pulled her tap shoes from her bag, changed into them on the floor, and leapt to her feet. After a few tap ball heel moves, digs and a shuffle, she slid into a double buffalo with a clunk and a clunk to a swing toe stand combo and—

Is that Kathleen Young pawing at me?

"Francella, dear. My goodness. In your condition, isn't it best if we sit and discuss this?"

"My condition? Oh. That. The stork's a long ways away, silly," Francella said, but instantly complied. She didn't need this biddy asking too many questions. Her husband was a doctor or something.

"Yes, well, even so."

This was not a topic Francella wanted to explore. "Thing is, you won't get anywhere with the Florida Girls here. They already got Dice Girls."

"So I've heard. But—"

"But nothing. I can set you up down the road at my hotel, The Plaza."

"You own a hotel?"

"What? No. I'm just staying there. But I know a guy."

Kathleen sat back in the sofa and let her eyelids flutter shut.

"Earth to Kath." Francella bent toward Kathleen's face. Lady's skin was poreless, unlike Francella's. "Leeny…"

Without moving or opening her eyes, Kathleen Young answered. "Dear, you're a wonderful dancer. With the couth of a rhinoceros. I just can't see how you'd manage."

"A rhinoceros? I ain't even showing! I just want a chance—"

"Even if I did agree to include you in the lineup, what if something went wrong?" Her eyes popped open and looked into Francella's. "The last thing I need is for some tragedy to befall Sal's precious offspring on my watch. No."

"I can handle Sal." She didn't add that she wasn't technically pregnant yet. That detail was just a matter of time. To be the star of a show? She was getting a little long in the tooth for opportunities like that. 'Specially if she actually did get knocked up before she could sayonara out.

"Say, you're in the family way, right? Doesn't seem to be slowing you down none."

"But, Francella, you're not a Florida Girl."

"Last time I checked, you only had one Florida Girl with you. That don't make a chorus line. And she's not from Florida neither."

Kathleen bolted upright. "Excuse me. I've got to call my husband." And like a flash, she was gone.

Shock momentarily overrode the rage but soon enough there it was, boiling inside Francella. Then amazement—how easily she'd been dismissed, as if she were nothing. Though she'd only been with Sal a few weeks, she'd grown accustomed to people taking her more seriously, to the way doors opened and eyes lowered when she walked into a room. Power by association. Especially her stupid cousin, who'd once laughed at her dreams. She watched Kathleen Young's frame recede, each step a fresh humiliation. That battle-ax hadn't even bothered to properly reject her—just walked away like Francella was beneath consideration. Her fingers curled into fists, nails biting into her palms. She'd show her. She'd show them all.

She watched Kathleen Young's shapely frame recede.

She'd show her.

TWELVE

MARGARET "PEGGY" HOLMES,
Tuesday

Sunshine cut through the window, bouncing off the Formica table. Dust motes danced in the air. But what drove Peggy out to the patio with her coffee and cigarettes was the hammering sound of the hall clock. The house was a split level and there was no escaping that infernal ticking. Thelma and Mrs. Young had barely been gone three days, and Doc had been asleep most of that time. Peggy was bored out of her skull.

Though she felt vaguely guilty about smoking while Mr. Young was upstairs recuperating from lung surgery, the silence was murder. He'd certainly done better than so many other men had after the Great War—better than her father, who'd returned from France with intact limbs but a shattered mind, drowning himself a little more each day until there was nothing left. At least Doc Young still had fight in him.

No sooner had she lit up than the phone rang. After smashing her butt into the saucer she'd repurposed as an ashtray —'course the Youngs had none, she'd looked everywhere—Peggy raced into the bright-yellow kitchen and picked up on the third ring, hoping it was Thelma.

"Young residence. May I help you?"

"Peggy?"

"Oh, Mrs. Young. Hi," she said, concealing her disappointment just a hair late. "Do you want me to see if Doc's up to speaking?"

"No. I... I'm heading back."

"Already? Wow, Agent Nelson must be impressed. Gosh, I am. Where's Thelma? Could you put her on?"

"No, it's not that."

Peggy couldn't tell if the next sound she heard was a sigh from Mrs. Young or the whoosh of the long-distance line.

"Thelma's not here. I think, perhaps, she's been kidnapped."

For once in her life, Peggy was dumbfounded. At least the day had stopped being dull.

"Sal took her."

By the time Kathleen Young finished her story however, Peggy was skeptical. "Nah. That makes no sense. He wanted Thelma kept secret in Florida to protect her. Even if he was trying to signal a hit, do you think he'd do it in front of a room full of reporters?"

"We were outside, Peggy."

Mrs. Young could be such a stick-in-the-mud. "But she took off with Sal. Her dad. You haven't seen her for—what, three hours? She's fine." Not that she'd any clue. As usual, Peggy was spinning yarn. The moment she said the words though, she became convinced. Had to. In all the years she'd known Mrs. Young, she'd never heard her express doubts about what to do next.

"Pepper?"

Mr. Young was stirring. Poor ol' Doc, couldn't even say her name right. She covered the receiver and yelled toward the door, "It's Peggy. I'll be there in a jiff."

"Was that Mr. Young?" asked Mrs. Young, alarm in her voice.

"I'm sure he's okay. But listen, the way I see it, Thelma needs your help. I should call Lillian."

"George's cousin? Absolutely not. Not Lillian Wright. You'll do no such thing."

"But Lillian's one of us."

"She was one of us. Soon as she took that movie contract she severed her ties."

"Wasn't that the whole point, Mrs. Young? The Florida Girls tour was supposed to be a competition for a Hollywood deal."

"Margaret Ann Holmes, we were raising money for the war effort. Furthermore, you were all well aware we'd extended the tour before we got to California. And then, of course, we lost the contest."

"Mrs. Young—"

"Peggy, are you telling me Lillian knows about Agent Nelson?"

Peggy had to think on that one. How would Lillian know? George had only flown back to Florida after he and Thelma had eloped. Thelma never got a chance to meet her in-laws before becoming a widow. They'd been in such a rush getting out of town, between packing and dishing out the dirt to that reporter lady, Lillian hadn't come up. Come to think of it, Peggy couldn't say if their friend ever made it back to St. Petersburg after the missing plane was announced. They were in Cuba then, and Thelma was so sure it was a hit job aimed at her, the only person she sought out was Agent Nelson. There hadn't been any memorial. Not yet anyway. That Wright family was a piece of work. Luckily, Lillian was nothing like them.

Maybe this was her ticket out. "You're right, Mrs. Young. How about you and I trade places?"

There was silence on the other end of the phone.

While Mrs. Young took a moment, Peggy made sense of her

suggestion, picturing the rooms at El Ranchero, the casino, that swell pool with the swim-up bar service... Pools. She chided herself. At a time like this.

"Thelma?" cried Mrs. Young. "About time. We've got to talk."

The next thing Peggy heard, the line went dead.

THIRTEEN

SAL'S MAN, Tuesday

THELMA LEAPT UP FROM HER SEAT AS THE DOOR CLOSED behind Sal. He hadn't bothered responding, just stormed out with that Stewy. With the search for Francella underway, she was back to being trapped with the human ice box guarding the exit.

This is ridiculous, she thought, lunging at the door handle once more, only this time it swung open, and Bongo fell backward into her, pinning her to the floor.

She gasped. "Aren't you gonna buy a girl dinner first?" There was no telling if she'd made him smile.

He rolled onto his side and sprang to his feet, surprisingly catlike for someone so large. Extending his hand, he deadpanned back, "Guy like me, I don't gotta."

Thelma regarded his pockmarked cheeks and doughy physique. Bongo was not an attractive man. Or was he saying he got his way regardless? Grim.

She took a different tack.

"Speaking of dinner, I could murder a sandwich. How about we go out and grab a bite?"

"Nah. We both stay right here. Strict orders."

"I see," Thelma said, unsurprised. They stood, practically eye-to-eye in the tight hallway. She was ravenous but needed more to get him on side. She looked toward the floor before coquettishly gazing into his eyes, chin tilted just so. "Surely, you'd like to eat?"

Bongo crossed his arms. "You can't play me."

Thelma straightened. "Play you? You must be hungry, no? I'm absolutely famished. How's about I order for us? From in-room dining?"

Bongo raised his eyebrows.

"What would you like? You a steak-and-potatoes man or pot roast?"

His eyes went ever so slightly moist. Not with hunger, she suspected. More likely was unaccustomed to being cared for. This could be her in. It was something they had in common. Barely nine months earlier, she'd never heard of room service let alone imagined suggesting it to someone else.

"Sal's buying, I'll get you both," she said, turning back into the room. "Where's the phone?"

Under the spell she'd cast, Bongo went to the bureau in the adjoining room and fished the phone out from behind the desk. If she'd missed that, maybe she should give the room another once-over.

She put her finger to her lips. *Our secret.*

After placing the order, Thelma handed the phone to Bongo, mouthed *thank you* and walked in the opposite direction toward the divan, implying he could hide the thing wherever he liked. She would not look. Her ears told her he'd returned it to the same spot.

In the hour that followed—ordering, waiting, even eating— Thelma kept up a lively chatter. "Where're you from?" and all that. As she prattled on about living in farm country during the war, how they almost always had spare eggs and potatoes. Even butter. Bongo mostly grunted.

All the while, Thelma was strategizing. Sal might not have taken down George's plane himself, but the crash had only happened because of their affiliation. If she was going to have her revenge, she couldn't go and call the police any more than she could up and leave. That wasn't the game they were playing.

Under the guise of investing in her father's casino, she would find the information that would lock him away for good. She would return to Havana triumphant, ready to build the club they'd planned with Doris and Helen and Peggy, a place focused on the entertainment. The glamor. If they'd still have her. The Wrights had locked Thelma out of George's bank account.

Is that even legal?

Their wedding might've been informal, but it was official. Doris had greeted them at the courthouse with an enormous bouquet, and afterward Helen and Peggy serenaded them as they walked down the steps. The five of them ate lunch at a sandwich counter. Straight after the meal they went their separate ways to make their departure preparations. Helen and Doris had already left for Cuba by the time she met Peggy and George at the airport the following day to make the same trip, with Thelma's new husband at the helm.

That night they consummated their vows. And how.

Sitting across from Bongo, Thelma traced the faint half-moon scar on her cheek, recalling how George had seen it. Seen her. He was the first person she'd ever told the truth to, about how Sal had left that mark behind after laying eyes on her. "Thelma, honey, I'll never let him hurt you again," George had said.

That memory strengthened her resolve. Sal was not a man to bargain with.

"Do you like music?" Thelma asked Bongo, pushing away from the remnants of her club sandwich to crank on the console radio, twisting the knob till she heard Dinah Shore singing "Stormy weather," one of her favorites.

Spinning to meet Bongo, she held out her arms. As a Florida Girl, she'd learned to dance. "Care to join me?"

As she expected, Bongo shrugged her off. Another thing she'd learned as a Florida Girl was how to cajole a reluctant man into dancing, but she didn't want to make Bongo any more suspicious than he already was. Did he think she was trying to seduce him? Would she go that far?

She began to waltz around the room, humming and singing. For once, Thelma was glad she couldn't hold a tune. Only, Bongo didn't take the hint that lunch was over. As far as cozying up to the enemy, it was a good sign. But she needed to make contact with Nelson.

"Say, I need to freshen up," Thelma said, tapping the dining cart and motioning toward the door with her head. "Would you roll this back out there while I excuse myself."

Thelma had a bath going before Bongo reached the entry. Soon as the door closed, she raced back into the sitting area to call the operator.

"Would you connect me to the Starburst Motel, please?" But they had no record of a guest named Theodore Nelson. Of course they didn't. He had to be using an assumed name, just as he'd suggested she and Mrs. Young do. *Think, Thelma.*

"Then would you try long distance, please," she asked the operator. "Carlsbad—"

The phone was ripped from her hand and the wall simultaneously. She swerved and watched Bongo's backside march out the door. He said nothing.

She considered running after him—to either plead her case or say she was calling for dessert—but she knew it was useless. The jig was up when she revealed she'd clocked the phone. She'd just turned to shut off the tap in the bathroom when giggling sounds wafted down the hall. It was Francella and Sal, who spilled into the room like a pair of giddy lovers.

"You still here?" he asked when he laid eyes on Thelma.

She was scrambling for the door when Sal said, "Bongo, take her out, okay?"

This time she did manage to drive her heel into the top of Bongo's foot.

"Jesus! What'd ya go and do that for?" he asked.

Thelma ignored him. "Meet me in the lobby tomorrow morning at nine sharp, Sal. If you're serious about having me invest, you'll show me everything."

Sal looked at Thelma. *Did he nod?*

"Bongo! I said, take her out."

THE LETTER, Tuesday

A WAVE OF NAUSEA RODE OVER KATHLEEN AS SHE FLUNG open the door.

"Those fumes," she growled. "I'd forgotten."

She stood in the doorway regarding Thelma in her perfectly fitted nipped-waist jacket. Except for her striking eyes and height, she looked nothing like the orphan who had turned up at Sun City the previous fall. She'd had a certain poise then, but this was different. Grief had done its alchemy. Thelma was a force.

The girl's hair was another matter.

The silver paint had hardened, shell-like. It had to itch like hell. "We have to get that paint off your scalp."

Thelma's hands flew to her head as she pushed into the room. "I don't smell a thing. I must be getting used to it. Oh. Never mind about that. You'll never believe the breakthrough I've just had."

"Breakthrough? I was sure you'd had your head broken. Why on earth did you not telephone, Thelma?"

"Telephone?" The girl spun around. "It's barely three in the afternoon, scarcely four hours since I last saw you. How much checking in do you need? What did you think Agent Nelson meant when he said we must be prepared to act independently?"

Where does this girl get her boldness? Kathleen marched past Thelma and headed for the vanity to check on her own locks. "It's customary to keep your traveling companions apprised of your whereabouts," she said, slapping her hips in frustration. "More to the point, you were last seen in the company of the gangster we're trying to get over on. Don't be so jeAna."

"Oh, Mrs. Young. You and your French. You're hopeless," said Thelma, as she pawed through the closet.

"Jejune is Latin," Kathleen said, dropping into the seat at the dressing table. "Anyway, you survived the press conference. Huzzah. I'm leaving."

Thelma stopped manhandling her clothes. "Because I didn't call?" She turned and looked pointedly at Kathleen's bulging feet. "Why, you just need some rest is all. Why don't you take a load off, put those dogs up. C'mon."

There was nothing Kathleen despised more than being treated like an invalid because she was pregnant. Maybe it was the summers she'd spent on Grand-père's farm, but she'd always thought there was nothing more natural than producing offspring. Of course, like the old girls at Shenandoah Fields, she was sluggish. But she was scarcely into her second month. Why *were* her feet so swollen? She didn't remember that with the boys.

"I'll have you know I find fecundity invigorating."

Nonetheless, Kathleen allowed the girl to ease her back onto the chair and fetch a footstool as she blathered away about her, the gist of which was that she hadn't called because she'd been so busy snooping in Salvatore Giancarlo's room.

"So I guess that's why I didn't find anything in the room, he has an office. I still can't believe he invited me to have a look."

"And that doesn't worry you? Desert trailer? No one around for miles?"

"Don't be so dramatic, Mrs. Young."

Kathleen remembered once her eldest wanting to borrow their automobile, supposedly to take a girl to the drive-in. When she reminded Bertie he didn't yet have his license, he'd said the same thing, "Geez, Mom, don't be so dramatic." Lloyd had caved. "Sure, son." Course he'd wrecked the vehicle. Miles from any theater.

"Well, enjoy that, Thelma. I'm off to Carlsbad. I'll send Peggy back with the car."

"But, Mrs. Young, you can't do that. You need to raise a Florida Girls show."

"I have no intention of doing any such thing, and I wouldn't advise you to either." Kathleen rubbed her eyes. This was all so tiresome. It was probably better to leave in the morning, but she was leaving all right. "If there is a Florida Girls revival, Sal's little girlfriend is determined to be part of it."

"That's perfect."

Clearly the fumes were getting to the girl. "Says you. Tell me. How are we supposed to coordinate investigating Sal if that little hussy is hanging around all the time? Also, isn't she in the family way?"

"Didn't you just say how rejuvenating that is? Besides, we don't need to snoop."

As Thelma prattled on about having gained access to Sal's books, Kathleen remembered—she'd neglected to mention the biggest news of all.

"Agent Nelson is gone."

"*Gone* gone? As in, kablooey?"

"For heaven's sake, he's not dead if that's what you mean.

Why must young people insist on reinventing language? No." Mrs. Young reached into her handbag and extracted an envelope. "He left this note."

After she'd unfurled the single sheet from the envelope, she began reading aloud. "If you are in possession of this letter—"

"How do you know he's not dead?"

Kathleen began again. "If you are in possession of this letter, you'll have discovered that I've checked out. After our training, I realized this operation is in competent hands and so have moved on to connect with other operatives. As discussed, this is a perilous time for our agency. Your task—"

"For the agency?" Thelma interrupted. "What's that supposed to mean?"

"That's the only reasonable question you've asked so far."

"Gimme that," said Thelma, snatching the letter from Kathleen. She read on in silence, mouthing the words Kathleen knew by heart.

Should you uncover spending discrepancies, clear evidence of bribery, and/or labor racketeering, leave word for me at John Lee's Chinese Laundry on Freemont. Otherwise, remember your training. You are working in service to your country. Godspeed.

Then she got to the end.

"Burn after reading?" Thelma looked up in disbelief, then around the room. "Where'd I set my purse?"

"There," Kathleen pointed, having noticed the smart patent leather bag that matched the buttons of her form-fitting suit. "Next to the bed."

Thelma dug into her handbag. "Ouch!" she said, yanking her hand out to suck on her index finger. Glancing at her broken fingernail, she reached back into her bag to withdraw a pack of matches, then turned toward the lavatory.

"What are you doing?" asked Kathleen.

Thelma didn't stop. "What does it look like? He's given us our orders. That's all. Nothing's new."

Different as the girl was now compared to when they'd met, Thelma Miles could be just as maddeningly juvenile. But Kathleen had changed too.

"*Orders*," she spat. "Like I said. First thing in the morning, I'm out."

* * *

THE THICK PAPER IN THELMA'S HANDS CAUGHT FIRE IN seconds. When the flames licked her fingertips, she dropped what remained into the toilet, flushed, and returned to their room.

"Do I need to remind you why you don't want to abandon your post?"

Mrs. Young shrugged. "I don't believe you'd hurt Doc by telling him anything, but suit yourself."

When Thelma didn't reply, the woman continued. "Wouldn't you rather Peggy was here? Least she wants to be here."

This was no bluff, Thelma could tell. Mrs. Young's ordinarily tidy appearance was coming undone—her hair tousled, skirt wrinkled, and blouse partly untucked. On another woman, this might've belied the steely resolve. On Kathleen Young, the frazzled look only underscored her determination.

In that moment, Thelma couldn't have cared less about hurting Mr. Young, but she wasn't about to put Peggy in danger. She couldn't let anything happen to the one living person who always had her back.

If she still had that revolver, she would've killed Salvatore Giancarlo herself. Not that she was keen to wind up in jail. She doubted Mrs. Young would spring her—Thelma could vanish, and no one would be the wiser. *No.* Sal should suffer, and for far longer than a bullet took. He might not have been the one to tamper with George's plane, but she didn't believe he was innocent. Thelma was through accommodating men, and seeing her father rot in jail would be endlessly gratifying.

"I'll tell him about Matteo."

"Who? Agent Nelson? He'd hardly care. Another criminal off the street." As if remembering herself, Mrs. Young smoothed her hair.

Seeing she was nervous, Thelma pounced. "No. I'll tell Sal you shot his son."

With a sigh, Mrs. Young stood, tucked in her shirt, and went to the windows. As she opened the curtains to let in the afternoon light, her back still to Thelma she replied coolly, "I don't think he'd take your role in that too kindly."

Thelma glimpsed the spectacular red sandstone formations in the distance before turning back at Mrs. Young. "That's the difference between you and me. I've nothing left to live for."

"That's this hellhole talking." Mrs. Young kicked off her shoes and reclined on her bed, eyes closed. "Please. You're young, beautiful, and rich. You've got everything to live for."

"I'm not."

Mrs. Young snorted. "Don't play poor ugly me, Thelma. It doesn't suit you."

"It's not that. The Wrights are trying to get our marriage annulled. I have some money from him, obviously, but they've frozen the assets in his trust."

Jerking upright, Mrs. Young glared at Thelma, gears turning behind her eyes. "I was saving your life, you may recall. And this is how you repay me? You brought me here under false pretenses."

Thelma nodded, amused. "You think I need this more than

you? Think about it. Sal had George killed to get to me. What makes you think Mr. Young is safe?"

Mrs. Young hoisted her legs over the bed. Her feet didn't touch the ground. "I don't see what we've got to do with it."

Thelma took a seat at the dressing table, saying nothing. Waiting.

"What good will it do to have the Florida Girls here? I only made up that story for Sal," Mrs. Young continued. "And what Florida Girls, anyway? We have you and exactly no one else."

Thelma smiled. "I thought you'd never ask."

Though Francella did figure into her plan, Thelma hadn't thought much about her condition, nor the half-sibling it portended. Having relatives pop up at every turn didn't fit with anything she knew about life and worse, it complicated the current situation. Her reason for being in Las Vegas, she vowed anew, was to make Sal Giancarlo pay for taking her beloved George. The Florida Girls were the perfect decoy.

FIFTEEN

SURVEILLANCE REPORT

EYES ONLY

FROM: WADE DAVIS, NEVADA SPECIAL AGENT
TO: INTERNAL, D.C. OFFICE OF THE DIRECTOR
IN RE: PLAN "SAFEGUARD"
DATE: June 6, 1945

Plan "SAFEGUARD" is designed to eliminate the OSS and establish the primacy of the FBI, as approved by the Director's office. Any news outlets or their assigns, concerned with objectives of Labor, Civil, and Women's rights may be considered agitators and thus SAFEGUARD targets.

Atrocities committed by the Soviets during wartime have continued unabated since, even as the ETO has been secured.

In general, this deception policy is aimed at securing our borders by thwarting the American Communist Party, which, thanks to lapses on the part of the OSS and our internal shortage of manpower, possesses unparalleled strength with plans to expand.

Targets will be subject to our interference as is necessary to root out the influence of Communism.

In Nevada, our object is to induce OSS field officers currently operating on home soil to make faulty strategic movements in relation to their investigation of the so-called "national crime syndicate" in Las Vegas.

The campaign extends to both their field operatives and the general public, inducing them to understand that the mushroom cloud of atomic weaponry hangs over the mirage of a world at peace. Implementation of 'SAFEGUARD' protocol includes: diplomatic engagement with identified agitators, strategic dissemination of misinformation, and cultivation of general tumult and turmoil.

Though we have no evidence to suggest any successful outcomes of OSS operatives' fieldwork, we do have reason to believe that a left-leaning reporter has become involved with their activities.

In anticipation and to monitor, we have numerous operators in place, including one inside girl. Contacts have also been made with our counterparts in the DFS for further disambiguation.

I will keep you informed.

SIXTEEN

SAL'S DESERT TRAILER, Wednesday

Looking at herself in the hotel's bathroom mirror the following morning, Thelma turned her chin slowly from left to right. "Now you look like a boy," Mrs. Young had declared the night before.

Thelma disagreed.

Cropping her tresses had made her eyes stand out more than ever. But really, what choice had she? Her scalp had itched something awful under that paint, and she could not pick or shampoo the silver out. She'd managed to crack some of the silver off, but, often as not, ended up taking the hair with it. Why tolerate the nuisance? If there was one thing about this operation she had absolute control over, it was her hair. She'd taken a pair of nail scissors to her hair. Now, having slicked down the sides and finger waved her short bangs, she thought the new cut lent her an old-school Josephine Baker air.

Better yet, she felt cleansed. Battle ready. She'd chosen her outfit carefully—a fitted off-the-shoulder leopard-print dress. Now for the final accessory.

She picked up her red-labeled bottle and paused to sniff the stopper. The Mademoiselle Chanel No. 1 in her hand had been a gift from George. "From Coco Chanel's salon in France," he'd said. But its rose and jasmine notes were too cloying for this occasion. *Or any*, she thought, feeling a pang of guilt. She'd never liked the smell.

Atop the counter also sat Mrs. Young's perfume, Bandit. The bottle reminded Thelma of nail varnish. She considered wearing it—woody and almost masculine, the fragrance carried with it an air that brooked no dissent—but decided against it. Though she felt less armored up without it, Thelma could hardly face her mortal enemy wearing the signature scent of his grandchild's mother. Even if Sal was unaware of Mrs. Young's role in his progeny's issue, she could not forget.

Stealing a glance at her watch as she hustled to the bureau, Thelma extracted a sheet of the hotel's parchment-colored paper embossed with a horseshoe logo. "That old hen has a point about overdoing it on cowboy culture," Vivian Miles piped in. Or is that me? wondered Thelma as she placed the stationery atop the writing blotter.

N,

MESSAGE RECEIVED. NEW LEADS ARE PROMISING.

—BB

THELMA REREAD THE PAGE AS SHE TAPPED THE DESK WITH her pen. Perfect. No names, no dates, no real discernible information. She hadn't even included her full code name, Blackbird. Agent Nelson would know it was her. And he'd be pleased.

She folded the stiff paper into an envelope—which also resembled old-timey parchment—and nipped down to the lobby, beating their appointed assignation by eight minutes. There, she hid in a phone booth at the far end where she could keep an eye out for Sal, then watch him squirm. Not for too long, but long enough to enjoy.

When Sal appeared trailing Bongo and Stewy moments later, Thelma could not suppress her smile. He was early too, but she'd won this round.

Sal whistled appreciatively as Thelma approached but cut himself short. "What happened to your hair?"

Thelma smiled wide and patted the sides of her head. "Isn't it marvelous?" she asked, batting her eyes as she'd rehearsed. After retrieving her sunglasses from her pocketbook, she perched them on her nose then reached for Sal's arm, taking care to grab the one not attached to the cane.

"Let's go, shall we?"

Soon as they stepped outside Thelma regretted forgoing her hat. It was barely ten in the morning and already the sun was unforgivingly searing. When she opened the car's window, it felt like she'd opened a furnace. Mercifully, they weren't going far.

Sal was humming, "On The Good Ship Lollipop," the old Shirley Temple tune. He was either cheery or delusional.

"How'd it go with Francella?" she asked once they'd settled into their seats, Sal up front with Stewy, she and Bongo in the back.

He looked at her strangely.

"Last night?" she asked.

Catching her meaning, he threw his head back. "Oh yeah. Fine. Got our wires crossed is all. I'm surprised you didn't see her on your way out. She came back almost right after you left."

They fell into silence as Thelma worried over Sal's mental

state. He might not do his own dirty work anymore, but that didn't make him less menacing. There was no telling what he'd do if she corrected his version of events, and there was too much she preferred to leave unsaid. The night before, he'd been apoplectic about the case of the missing lady friend. Now he was blasé. An unstable Salvatore Giancarlo was not someone to be trifled with.

"We're here," said Stewy.

It had taken approximately three minutes to cross the street, but she was just as grateful not to walk in this dusty heat.

The trailer was next to where the groundbreaking had been. A semi-circle of blue-tinged mountains formed the horizon. *How many flowers must that take*, she wondered. *How far was it to the hills? Were the peaks ever capped with snow?* Nevada had a wild beauty that stirred something in her heart. If pressed, she'd have said it felt like freedom. Like anything was possible.

Leading the way, Stewy mounted the three metal steps to the door and let them both in. For a moment Thelma feared boiling alive inside, but Stewy flipped on a window air-conditioning unit. There was so much she hadn't noticed the day before.

Sal gestured toward his bureau. "There's the desk, some file cabinets." He looked around. "Am I missing anything, Stewy?"

Stewy shook his head—not much of a talker—a quality that likely endeared him to Sal.

"I got some business now, but feel free to look around. We got sofa cushions here too."

"Oh," Thelma said, to cover that her chin had practically fallen to her chest. *What was going on here?*

"What about your advice, Sal?" She moved to the desk and rested her hip, curling into a smaller version of herself. "Gosh, I wouldn't even know what to look for."

"No?" Sal was smiling, not a care in the world. "From what I can tell, you're handy with a bankbook."

A cold chill seized Thelma's core. There was no way he could've seen what she'd done with the books at The Lotus Club. Besides, erasing Bertie Young's debt was a rounding error compared to how much she'd brought in. She'd burned the ledgers along with the club.

"What were you thinking, opening a bank account?" he asked.

The bank account? Thelma wanted to pelt him. She looked down at the floor. Of course she'd opened an account. It had been his idea to make Vegas legit.

"Gosh, Sal, I had to do something with the money that was coming in, and the casino was on the up and up."

"Course you did. Course," said Sal. "We could run you back now, couldn't we, Stewy?"

"Sure, boss."

This was a test. "That's okay, Sal. I'll stay. Do my best. Thanks so much."

"Attagirl," he said, grinning ear-to-ear. "That's my girl."

Before the door could swing shut, he'd resumed his tune.

For a while after they left, Thelma rummaged through the files. The neat script surely wasn't Sal's, she'd seen his handiwork back in Tampa. Though the actual scribe hardly mattered. She didn't recognize anyone on the roster, but the corruption and graft was clear—Sal was skimming from the union's construction *and* pension funds to pay people off. It was all there in front of her, barely under lock and key, with entries like, "Judge Renney, extras and tips...$2000."

Thelma's first instinct was to call Agent Nelson, but as she pulled the desk phone close, she recalled his emergency instructions. The way to contact him now was to leave word at the laundry and wait. Not her strong suit.

Then it struck her—there was one person she could call—the original queenpin.

She dialed the long-distance operator. "Queenie?" she said into the receiver. "It's me, Thelma."

She hoped like hell Madame St. Clair remembered her, as well as the way she'd insisted on being called by her nickname, Queenie. They hadn't spoken since New York. Thelma would have to play this just right. Madame St. Clair was the only woman to best the mob, ruling over Harlem's numbers racket for years. She'd not only escaped with her life, she'd kept her money besides.

"I'm calling you from Sal's office in Las Vegas." Thelma leaned on her elbow, holding the phone to her ear as she stared at the calendar blotter, silently tapping the desk with her middle finger. This could be an overreach.

Then again, much as Queenie had taught her that she could face her father head on, Thelma might not be in this mess if St. Clair hadn't sprung Sal on her back in New York. "I'm in a jam. And you owe me."

SEVENTEEN

CONSUELA PÉREZ, Wednesday

ON HEARING THE PURPOSEFUL CLIP-CLIP OF HIGH HEELS moving toward her desk, Consuela Pérez slipped into her shoes and steeled herself. For once, she more than matched the height of the woman heading her way in the peplum suit. The woman, whom she'd tracked in the lobby a number of times, had given the name Miss Marvin when she'd checked in with a Miss Fayne. Like Consuela didn't see through that, even without the silver paint on her companion's head. Comely pair. Didn't look the type to travel unaccompanied, but you never could tell in this town.

Before Consuela could squawk out the required, "Howdy pardner, what can I do you for?" greeting, the lady started right in.

"Good morning, Mrs...," she squinted at Consuela's chest, "Pérez. I'm Mrs. Young. I wonder if I might trouble you for your manager."

How could she have forgotten? This was the woman who'd been through with a bunch of girls just last spring. They did some kind of war bond benefit out by the base. Real snooty. She owned something she called an emporium, some department store in Florida, only instead of trunk shows they put on fighting alligators. Something like that. That was when Consuela's dad was still alive, before watching the customers was part of her remit.

"Of course I remember you. How do, Mrs. Young?" said Consuela, grateful to be spared the rest of the hokey script. "You're in luck. Manager's right here. You're looking at her."

The woman's face registered disappointment, but only for the briefest moment before she started in on some hare-brained idea to bring a variety act to El Ranchero. It never ceased to amaze Consuela, the schemes these people came up with. What must this place have been like during the gold rush days?

It was too early in the morning for all this.

"Mrs. Young, we always appreciate hearing from our esteemed guests. And I do remember your Florida Girls performing in town. Tremendous crowd that night. But you know, a lot has changed. These aren't servicemen flush on furlough pay. These crowds don't come to Las Vegas to think about the war, they come to escape it. We do a quickie show three times a night between meals we serve so the high rollers don't get so loaded they can't stay awake at the tables. For that we got the Dice Girls. People love 'em."

The woman across the counter grinned at Consuela like the Cheshire cat, lowering her voice. "Well, in that case, what do you say we have a chat about your uniforms? I just so happen to represent a concern that I know can get you better quality duds at a lower price, in all the latest Western styles."

EIGHTEEN

LILLIAN WRIGHT, Wednesday

THE PHONE CALL FROM PEGGY CAME AT THE ABSOLUTE peak perfect moment. Lillian was on set filming Fuller Brush Man, and Red Skelton had just mentioned he was heading to Las Vegas for the weekend. Of course he let her join him in his helicopter. She didn't mention she wouldn't be joining him in his hotel room, and Lillian didn't care if that meant her role landed on the cutting room floor. It was a horrid little film. Besides, if Thelma was missing, the girl needed someone who would actually look for her. In other words, not Mrs. Young.

No sooner had Lillian arrived at El Ranchero than everything went topsy-turvy. No one at the check-in desk had heard of a Thelma—Miles or Wright. Then she turned and there was—

"Mrs. Young!"

Until they quit her father's pharmacy to start their own store, the Youngs had been a fixture of Lillian's childhood. Not long afterward, before she was fully aware the pair was gone for good, Lillian had a vivid memory of seeing Mrs. Young at Wright Drug. She must've been eleven or twelve then, this was just before she'd left for boarding school.

It was a muggy Sunday, so she'd stopped by the pharmacy to collect her allowance before hitting the movies with her chum Prissie. Her cousin George was there, sweeping the floors. Ever since his mother died, he was always around. Lillian hadn't thought much about his behavior back then, but now, after studying Jung she figured it was displacement. She ignored him so Prissie wouldn't get distracted—he had that effect on girls.

No such luck. The moment flashed in her mind.

Prissie and George were chatting away in the corner—that girl could talk your ear off—while her father was fishing in the register's change drawer. In burst this tiny torrent who Lillian didn't even realize was Mrs. Young. Not till she slammed her bag on the counter and started speaking to her father in a low tone. All Lillian could tell was that her father was afraid. She felt embarrassed for him, fremdschämen, as the Germans would say.

Trying out to be part of Sun City's war bond tour was meant to be a lark. She was still sore at her folks for bringing her home from Ro midway through senior year. *Because of the war.* How was she to know Mrs. Young would be so involved? Now she wondered what that woman must've had on her father to get back the rights to her husband's stupid Forever Young formula. *Doc* Young indeed. Not that this lady was someone you wanted to cross, but Lillian knew how to handle her type.

"Lillian?" Mrs. Young screwed up her face. "What on earth are you wearing?"

At that moment, Lillian became aware that she was still in her costume from set, essentially a negligee with a chinoiserie robe. But Red had wanted to leave immediately.

"Something to change out of, Mrs. Young. Come. Let's go shopping."

· · ·

THE LOBBY BOUTIQUE SOLD ONLY GOWNS, BUT LILLIAN always needed more of those. "Bring me your latest for summer. I'm a size six, but you'll need to take in the waist and let out the bust."

With the shop girl dispatched to fetch styles and sizes, Lillian turned on Mrs. Young. "Where's Thelma?"

A faraway stare came over Mrs. Young's face. This was new behavior. And troubling.

"Mrs. Young! Are you quite all right? Have you tried Desplex? Everyone says it's a wonder drug for women in your condition. It's just flying off the shelves at Dad's pharmacy."

From the way Mrs. Young looked at her this was unwelcome news, though Lillian wasn't sure which bit. A competitor's record sales—which on second thought *was* thick-headed to mention—or the reference to her diminished state.

"I can have him send some," Lillian continued.

"Lillian," Mrs. Young chirped, starting at a high-pitch that dropped low.

Or maybe she was the old-fashioned type who pretended babies came from storks.

"I don't believe in taking medication for every ail."

"That's rich coming from a drugstore owner," said Lillian.

"I'm merely an advisor now, and I think we both know your father owned the drug store."

"Oh, too right, Mrs. Young. You ran the—what was it? The world's most bizarre bazaar? Was that it?"

"Certainly the most successful," she said, looking into her clutch and extracting a hankie. After mopping her neck, Mrs. Young let the cloth fall back into her purse and snapped it shut. "Anyway, I'm quite well, thank you. So tell me, what brings you here?"

Thelma had come to Vegas on the warpath for Sal Giancarlo, and Kathleen Young wanted to know why *Lillian* was in town. Before Lillian could answer, the shopgirl was back with three satin gowns with voluminous skirting, all in rich jewel tones.

"Marvelous," Lillian purred. "Would you mind?" She pointed at her own handbag. "Be a love and find me some shoes to match that?" Lillian let her boudoir slipper drop from her foot. "These won't do at all."

Now that she had the salesgirl suitably delighted by her impending commission, Lillian could buy more time. The shop was too small.

"Yoo-hoo!" she poked her head through the curtain. "Do you think you can locate a few smock dresses so I have something to wear right away? And I'll need shoes for that too. Also a size six. Ta!"

"Of course, Miss Montgomery. But I'd need to step out to get daywear."

"Why, that's perfect. Thank you ever so much. You're a peach. I am absolutely desperate!" said Lillian as she ducked behind the dressing room curtain.

"Back in a jiffy," came the muffled reply.

"Montgomery?" Mrs. Young asked.

"My stage name. Haven't you heard?"

"I've been busy. Haven't you heard?"

"I know you moved to California, your husband had surgery and, oh! Yes. *Le bébé*. You must be so happy. At your age."

Mrs. Young looked Lillian over. "I suppose the Wrights didn't want their name sullied by having an actor in the family?"

Lillian tsked. "What a fuddy-duddy you are. No. The opposite, in fact. My manager didn't want my reputation diminished by all the family business."

Mrs. Young reached for the girl's hand. "Yes, my poor, dear. I was so sorry to read about your cousin. Si terrible nouvelle!"

Snatching her hand back, Lillian pushed aside the pile of

satin and dropped onto the bench across from her quarry. She crouched to Kathleen's eye level. "All right, save it. Peggy told me you let that thug Salvatore Giancarlo abduct our Thelma. Why do you think I'm here?"

Mrs. Young rested against the dressing room wall, crossed her legs, and ticked her foot up and down. "Why did you come to Thelma's rescue? Honestly, I'm surprised you care. The rest of the Wrights don't appear to want to associate with her at all. Shouldn't you be out looking for your cousin with the rest of them?" She straightened in her seat. "You're not here on their behalf, are you?"

That was a low blow even for Kathleen Young. Plucking a gown from the pile, Lillian jammed the fabric over her head. "I think the way my family is treating Thelma is appalling." She snaked the dress the rest of the way down and returned to face the mirror. "All they care about is money."

"Hardly makes them unique." Mrs. Young snorted. "The fact she's Sal Giancarlo's daughter can't help."

No way was Lillian going to let it slip that until yesterday, she hadn't known about the Giancarlo connection. She doubted her family did either. Since openly opposing Thelma Miles's erasure from the story, Lillian had become persona non grata at family discussions. She knew what Peggy had told her—which, now that she thought about it wasn't much—and that Thelma must be hurting something awful.

"I think if my uncle knew she was out here trying to put Sal Giancarlo behind bars, he'd help."

"Sal Giancarlo." Mrs. Young snorted. "There is something wrong with that man. Did you know he told the whole press corps that Thelma was going to run his casino?"

It didn't surprise Lillian that Sal would want Thelma around. She was beautiful and dreadfully smart. She could be on the impetuous side, but weren't all the best people? Or maybe that explained why Sal was keeping her close. Loose lips and all.

"Then he buys me lunch and acts like she's enemy number one."

Lillian realized something—the less she said, the more Kathleen Young talked. Finally, some inside dope. She smoothed the crimson satin at her waist.

Mrs. Young nattered on. "Then she turns up, insisting I have to stage a Florida Girls show. How? I asked. Of course she doesn't have a clue."

"She? You mean Thelma's back?" Lillian turned to face her companion. "Why didn't you say so? Where is she?"

"Thelma doesn't know you're here? She didn't ask you to come?"

"Ask me to come? We have to go. I have to speak to her." Lillian stuck her head through the curtain. "Where's that girl?"

"She's not going anywhere. She's been back since yesterday."

Yesterday? Lord, this woman was aggravating.

* * *

KATHLEEN WATCHED AS LILLIAN'S RED DRESS POOLED AT her feet, bringing to mind the image of Matteo, face-up on the bathroom tile as the lifeblood drained from the back of his skull.

"Is it warm in here? I think I'm going to be ill," she said.

Before she could stand, Lillian's hand clamped onto her shoulder. "No you don't. You just told me you're the picture of health, Mrs. Young. Now, tell me why you two are even here. And together, of all things."

Once Kathleen started, she let Lillian have it. She wanted the girl to know how she and Lloyd had helped Agent Nelson in the war effort, how Lloyd's cancer had necessitated their speedy move to California for competent surgical care, and how she was here because Thelma needed her help.

"We're here on behalf of the government to deal with Sal Giancarlo once and for all," she finished, having left out that she'd been coerced into action—first by Theodore Nelson, who'd used her son's gambling debt as a bargaining chip, and now by Thelma, who'd threatened to reveal that Matteo was her baby's father. *And worse*, she reminded herself.

The pink chiffon cloud billowing at Lillian's head stopped mid-pull, the dress still overhead. "You're here to kill Salvatore Giancarlo? On behalf of who?"

"Hush! Lord have mercy. Why would you even say such a thing?" Once more, Kathleen retrieved her hankie from her bag and began fanning herself. "Arrest him, just like you said. We're here to put him behind bars."

"By putting on a show? You two?" Lillian shook her head as she slid a stunning sapphire rayon crepe number over her head. She turned to face Kathleen. "Listen, I'm here to help Thelma. That girl has a fine heart. You can either accept my help or get out of our way. In fact, why don't you just switch places with Peggy? She'd love to be here."

Kathleen closed her eyes. She was going to have to be more convincing as a willing part of this scenario. "Forgive me for saying, Lillian, but you seem awfully enthusiastic about this situation."

The girl paused from admiring her reflection and looked squarely at Kathleen. "There's a saying I've learned here, Mrs. Young. If you climb in the saddle, you best be ready for the ride."

"Well, I couldn't have said that myself," Kathleen deadpanned. "Touché."

Why had Peggy called Lillian? She was going to murder that girl. Though there was something lovely about seeing her come into her own. Before Lillian had left for that boarding school, she was a wilting lily. Now in her full bloom, the girl would make a powerful ally.

"Don't misconstrue my motives, dear. I merely want to be sure you're aware of the unsavory aspects of this undertaking."

Lillian—now back in the pink chiffon, the only outfit that could passably be taken for daywear—scrambled to retrieve her bag amidst the piles of clothes. "Be a love and tell the lamb I'll take them all. I've got to go and get myself a room. You are staying here, yes?"

Kathleen nodded.

"Bon. Au revoir, ma cherie," said Lillian before sailing out of the dressing room.

Of course, thought Kathleen. The girl would speak perfect French. Merde.

NINETEEN

JOHN LEE'S CHINESE LAUNDRY,
Wednesday

"Why of course he let you see his books. That town so crooked you couldn't cross the law if you was a jaywalking cock." Madame St. Clair's rich baritone laugh burst through the receiver, though Thelma couldn't find anything to laugh at.

The air-conditioner kicked on and Thelma could've sworn Sal's entire trailer rocked slightly. She gasped.

"Aye now, girl. You have got to lighten up," Queenie said, her sing-song accent making the advice more palatable.

"Sorry, I... I just can't figure out his game. According to Sal's ledgers—and by the way, he never used to write anything down—he's got everyone from beat cops to judges on his payroll. There's even clergy."

"That's right. These ain't no sawdust joints. They making so much money, everyone want a piece. And if someone makin' money, it dirty. Whole town on the take."

That did explain why Agent Nelson wanted them there in the first place. G-men on a mission would tip off the locals. They'd never get anywhere. This job needed civilian boots on the ground.

The door burst open, surprising Thelma. She covered the phone's mouthpiece.

"Who's there?" she yelled, even as her father's mistress came into view, clad in a white midriff top and a long black skirt, belted with a gold chain, more muted than the day before. *Only a day had passed since they'd met in Sal's car?*

"Well, look who's here," said Francella, snapping a wad of gum in her mouth. "What happened to your hair?"

Turning away from the door and speaking quietly into the phone, Thelma thanked Queenie profusely. Though she didn't have advice, Madame St. Clair offered money. "That man change, that's sure," Queenie went on. "But you don't wanna be at his mercy for no money." Thelma had tried to refuse, but the New York City queenpin wouldn't hear of it. "Consider it a loan if it make you feel better. Till you on your feet. Is not that much." She tsked. "You gonna wanna work fast. I hear Sal tell everyone you was his kin."

Thelma was shocked to hear the news had traveled so quickly—the press conference had only been the day before.

After saying her goodbyes, Thelma dropped the receiver into its hook just to hear the satisfying clang of the telephone's bell. Turning to square off with Francella, she remembered Agent Nelson's training. "Find out as much as you can about your opponent. And never let him know he's your opponent."

Or she.

Smiling sweetly, Thelma patted the sides of her head. "Very modern, don't you think?"

"Mmm." Francella frowned. "And I hear you're in mourning," she said, placing a hand over her heart. "My condolences."

This caught Thelma off guard. First, because she wouldn't have expected to be a topic of conversation between Sal and his mistress, and that was the only way this girl could've known George was her husband. Second, her tone. Was it a callous disregard for other people's feelings or—and she winced to remember how cavalier she had been when her teammate Millie had died—did she just not know any better?

Now was not the time for such distractions. As Madame St. Clair had made clear, Thelma would have to find dirt on Sal in some other way. And pronto. Maybe that other way was through Francella? In a voice husky with emotion, she thanked Francella. Swallowed. And got back to business.

"Is Sal with you?" Thelma asked.

She should've known better than to let herself wonder. The memory of her own experience with a man Sal's age came on like a freight train. Suddenly, Thelma was transported to a greasy mattress, no sheets, being smothered beneath a heap of aging flesh and sweat.

What magic had brought her George? He'd made that past less menacing, like something surmountable. "I've seen plenty of men and women do worse, love. War is hell, don't you know?" he'd said. He didn't dismiss or tolerate. When she could finally speak of the years she'd spent prostituting herself so she and her mother could eat, he'd listened. And when she couldn't speak, he let her be quiet.

Thelma looked up to find Francella glaring, teasing the gold chain at her hip between her thumb and forefinger. "Cat got your tongue? I said I was hoping he'd be here."

What past might she be trying to overcome?

They pretended to be curious about Sal a few minutes longer before Thelma asked, "How'd you get here?"

"My car." She beamed. "Sal got me one of those '42 Plymouths with the coach doors. Good as new."

Thelma wondered who her father might have disposed of to acquire that particular vehicle but only briefly. The opportunity was too prime to pass up. "Very fancy. Take me for a spin? I'm absolutely starved, and I've been dying to try Silver Spurs."

This was—Agent Nelson would be proud—a partial truth. According to El Ranchero's concierge, the restaurant was next door to John Lee's Laundry, Nelson's drop point.

"Mmm. Chinese food? I don't know," said Francella.

Silver Spurs was Chinese? But Thelma wouldn't take no. "Well, I may have an ulterior motive," she said, pushing back from the desk and tilting her chin to look up at Francella with wide eyes. "I was hoping you might teach me to drive."

Francella tossed her head back and laughed. "You're a real DP if you think I'm letting you practice driving on my brand-new car."

Thelma rubbed her forehead. She hadn't been expecting rejection over something so simple. As luck would have it, distraught worked.

"Oh, knock it off. You can find a better driving teacher," Francella said with a definitive crack of gum. "Let's do something actually fun. Let's hit the Golden Gate."

Thelma didn't know what she meant but she was ready to escape this trailer and get on with taking down Sal Giancarlo. "Follow the paper trail," Nelson had said. *Like the deed for a car.*

"Sure, sounds..."

"It's my absolute favorite casino in town." Francella put a finger to her lips and lowered her chin. "Don't tell Sal."

THERE WAS NO WAY OF KNOWING WHAT TIME OF DAY OR night it was inside the Golden Gate casino. Overhead chandeliers lit ribbons of blue smoke that snaked between the patrons clustered at gaming tables. The air was filled with the sounds of dice cracking, chips clinking, and the regular clangs of one-armed bandits. Golden Gate was one of the original Fremont Street casinos, if you could believe their sign.

Before Thelma could protest—*how would she get to know*

her quarry in this environment—Francella steered her directly to the largest table at the center of the room.

"Welcome to Golden Gate, where the real Vegas locals put their money down. It's more crowded than I was hoping but..." She turned to Thelma's ear. "Let me show you how it's done."

"Winner winner chicken dinner. What's it gonna be?" yelled a man with an L-shaped baton.

Thelma lifted her brows at Francella.

"Stickman," she said as they sidled up to the table. After retrieving several chips from her bosom, Francella kissed them and placed them on the rack.

"What'll it be, sweetheart?" asked another man standing opposite, wearing the same white, Western-style shirt with a black Kentucky-colonel tie.

"I'll go six the hard way," she said with a wink.

Thelma lurched as he moved Francella's chips.

"Relax," Francella said. "Watch and learn."

But watching hardly helped. Since they'd joined the table, more players had appeared, ready to get in on the action. Chips and cash passed back and forth mysteriously. Francella's chip stayed on the table then disappeared, and she hadn't yet rolled.

"All the dots we gots, pays double in the bubble!" cried the stickman, his Adam's apple bobbing with excitement as several players cheered.

Francella sighed and shrugged. "Changed my bet too soon." She was speaking to the table in general.

"Don't fret, little lady. Nothing we love like a beautiful loser." The stickman shoved dice in Thelma's direction. "Roller coming out! New shooter, new game!"

Francella turned to Thelma with a gleam in her eyes. "You shoot."

"Shoot what?"

The men at the table laughed.

"Roll, silly," Francella said, elbowing Thelma. "Just watch, boys. This one's my lucky charm." Then she lowered her voice. "Keep your hand in the pit, and hit the far wall when you throw."

The dice felt fiery in Thelma's palm, like the feeling her premonitions gave her. Her underarms lit up, too. Holding her breath, she closed her eyes and rolled. The dice went off the table.

"Happens all the time," Francella said. "Try again. Maybe keep those gorgeous eyes open."

After a deep breath, Thelma tried again. Eyes open. Nine.

"Craps loses. Point to nine. Play the field, get lucky!"

"I won?" Thelma asked.

"Even across the field," Francella said to one of the men in white shirts. "Shoot again, Thelma."

The shooting and betting went on for three more rolls, but Thelma grew no more comfortable at the table. "I still don't get the rules," she said.

"Here." Francella handed Thelma a chip. "It'll make more sense if you have some skin in the game."

Thelma tried handing the chip to the dealer but Francella grabbed it. "Why don't you let me handle the betting?" She turned to the dealer. "Take it down," she said as she pocketed most of her chips. Then she put Thelma's chip on the table below the first chip she'd placed. "That's to increase the odds. Now shoot."

As Thelma's pile of chips grew, longing and fear tinged her throat. She didn't understand the mechanics, only that she was winning. And she wanted more.

"Seven-out!" the stickman yelled. Reactions at the table were mixed, leaving Thelma confused until she saw him swipe away every last chip she'd won.

Francella whacked her on the back. "Time for a real steak-

and-potatoes meal," she said as they left the table, much to the chagrin of the others playing craps.

"Fat lady ain't sung yet, gals? Where ya going?" called the stickman.

"Hey, it's my turn to win your money!" said one of the fellows who'd just joined the crowd.

Putting her hand to the side of her mouth, Francella mock whispered, "They think we're leaving our luck behind. Good luck, suckers!"

"What are we celebrating?" asked Thelma.

"I won fourteen dollars," she said. "And that's with you losing the two dollars I gave you."

This news didn't put Thelma in the mood for eating. Her heart beat like a rabbit's. All she wanted was another go at that game. She didn't like to lose. "Honey, this town is devoted to fleecing tourists," she heard Vivian Miles, loud and clear. "Remember why you're here."

Thelma guessed that death had, at long last, sobered up her mother. Or perhaps her ma hadn't changed at all. Maybe the only thing that had changed was Thelma's ability to hear her. The many failings of Vivian Miles, which she'd cataloged over the years, felt increasingly less important. With a sickening thud, Thelma knew she should never gamble again. The lure was too strong.

It couldn't have been ten minutes before they reached the restaurant. Thelma scarcely noticed the walk before a host was pulling out her chair and saying their waiter would be over directly. Her heart was still racing.

"That was something," she said to Francella.

"What'd I tell ya? Way more fun than teaching you to drive."

Mention of the driving lesson brought Thelma back to earth. She did need to stay on course. Of course she knew how gambling worked, but seeing it for herself, winning and losing money out of nothing, also reminded her how difficult it was going to be to track Sal's finances. She reached into her bag for her packet of cigarettes and lit one.

"Say, listen." Thelma pulled a fleck of tobacco out of her mouth. "We should talk about the Florida Girls. I want you to be part of the team."

"Finally, someone with some sense in their head." Francella's feigned indifference was belied by her broad grin.

"May I get you two ladies something to drink?"

Thelma's gaze swept over the waiter, taking in his gleaming bolo tie and cowboy boots, lingering on the classic cowboy shirt with mother-of-pearl buttons and snap-flap pockets. Mrs. Young had commented on the excess of Western-themed kitsch, and, loath as she was to admit it, her former boss had a point about overkill.

"I'll take a scotch. And..." Francella turned to face Thelma. "Can I bum one of those?"

Her palms lit up and Thelma jerked her head toward her father's mistress. The pieces fell together right in front of her. As she handed over a smoke and her lighter, she looked back at the waiter, so slim he poked inside his getup like a praying mantis. "I'll have an RC Cola, please. Thanks."

When he'd gone, Thelma hiked her elbows onto the table and leaned forward. "How long before you think my dad figures out you aren't pregnant?"

TWENTY

CHAMBER MAN, Wednesday

Absent the stage and press photographers, Salvatore Giancarlo's dusty casino lot could've passed for abandoned. Squinting into the haze, Kathleen's stomach knotted at the thought of being trapped here long enough to see his gambling mecca emerge. Even worse was the growing fear that this forced mission with Thelma would scuttle future business prospects. These Vegas developers were poised to spend a fortune—money she desperately needed.

The trailer door was locked, threatening to stop her day before it started. Pivoting, Kathleen glared at her hotel across the road, huffing in exasperation. She wasn't in the mood to wait for the girl a second day in a row. Besides, the scorched earth was making her thirsty. Surely, it was late enough for lunch and a cocktail.

"Thou shalt drink not wine nor strong drink," she could hear her mother muttering every time she saw a woman drinking. A pregnant woman? Mrs. DeVane would have combusted, her Virginia society sensibilities reduced to ash. That quote, as Kathleen discovered when at last she'd looked it up in the Book of Judges, was meant to ensure Manoah's wife had a son.

Perhaps her craving for a midday cocktail was her body's way of aching for a baby girl, someone to keep her company after her beloved Button was gone. Samson's mother never did get a name—another woman erased by history, just as Kathleen feared she might be.

As she reached for the car's door handle, Kathleen felt a stirring in her belly. She'd have sworn it was the first motions of her baby, but that was madness. She hadn't felt a thing before she was halfway to term with Bertie and Archie, and here she was not even three months along. Yet this baby—this unexpected, complicated legacy—seemed determined to announce its presence early.

Maybe she should swing by the room and call Peggy to see how her Button was doing.

But no. Kathleen slid into the driver's seat and headed toward Fremont Street, gawking once more at the desolation of Vegas during the day, the roads deserted, the signs unlit. A second pang struck. Definitely hunger. King Baby wanted steak.

Kathleen stopped at the first restaurant she saw. Inside, a large wooden bar fronted a dining room where Kathleen made out a sizable room set with white tablecloths and service for, she hoped, lunch. The space was cool and fairly empty, save for a couple tucked into a corner of the lounge, though they should've been at a motel.

Plopping onto a chrome stool that strategically faced away from the young lovers, Kathleen rested her elbows on the bar. Coughed.

"Excuse me? Is it alright if I order lunch at this counter?"

The man behind the counter stopped drying the glass in his hand. "Sorry, ma'am, we don't serve lunch till noon."

His brown boots, she noted, didn't match his black bolo tie. These people could use her help.

She looked at her watch, still forty minutes to go. Though Kathleen had delayed arising until her roommate finally left—never in her life had she heard someone make such commotion while going through their morning ablutions—Consuela at the front desk had dismissed her with speedy efficiency. Likewise, it hadn't taken long to ascertain that Thelma was not at the trailer. Had there ever been a time when the only task she faced was lunch? *Just her own.*

Here she was, though, in Nevada. Unlike California, this place was not for early risers. Kathleen suspected that very few establishments served lunch, forget about breakfast. Pulling a dollar bill from her bosom, she addressed the barman. "I'm only in town a short while for business. Could I trouble you to put in for steak and potatoes now? Medium rare. Meantime, I'll have a Bee's Knees." The honey would help soothe her appetite, she thought as she slid her money across the counter.

Propping an arm on the wooden bar, the man grimaced. If Kathleen was reading him correctly, this barkeep was about to deny her simple request.

"Say, Chuck." A lanky adolescent in a striped shirt with a kerchief at his neck sidled over. "How about you see what you can rustle up for the lady?"

The barman's shoulders tensed. Apparently, he'd been as startled by the boy's appearance as she.

"Sure, Wade." He dropped his rag and snatched her bill from the countertop before heading for the kitchen.

Kathleen didn't know if she should thank the boy or ask why he was not in school. Then he jabbed his hand her way and she noticed a wedding band.

"Wade Davis. Pleased to meet you," he said, smiling wide to reveal perfectly square, if small, teeth. Like Chiclets.

"*Enchantée*," Kathleen said as she put her fingertips into his bony grip and reassessed his age. Early twenties? Who was this man? She patted the seat beside hers and tilted her head. "You wouldn't make a lady drink by herself?"

Three cocktails later, Wade was pointing at a black-and-white photograph he'd pulled from his—God help her—saddle-bag. Thelma's silver hair was looking less eccentric by the minute.

"Is that lady with the gun sitting on a mule?" Kathleen squinted at his index finger.

Wade slapped his knee. "Damn right. That's how we do it up for Helldorado Days. Come next spring, you're gonna see this picture everywhere. Gonna change everything."

Apparently, Wade Davis was with the Chamber of Commerce, and he'd just had a very successful meeting with J. Walter Thompson, the New York City advertising executive even Kathleen Young had heard of way out in Florida.

Leaning forward to show her decolletage to maximum advantage, Kathleen cooed. "And that was all your idea? My goodness."

"Gosh, I wouldn't say that."

"You want some ketchup?" asked the barman as he returned with her steak.

Kathleen opened her mouth to ask for Worcestershire but thought the better of it. "That would be marv... just swell," she said but dug in without commenting that it was well past noon.

She was keen to tell Doc about this rendezvous. These were the salad days of this town's expansion, and anything might be possible. This Davis character had the same quirk of personality that had possessed St. Petersburg's John Lodwick—he could spin a swamp into paradise. Or in this case, a dust bowl into a luxury-vacation haven.

Waving her fork around, Kathleen seized her chance. "So

you're saying all this Western look is your doing?" She thought back to the cowboy-inspired designs Sun City Emporium had introduced the previous year. "Do you think it's glamorous enough for the clientele you're hoping to attract?" Nothing reeled in a prospect like arguing for their point.

"Las Vegas has it all. The prices will tell the whole story. Even the well-heeled like to slip off their fancy shoes at the playground."

This Wade Davis was slick. But Kathleen knew how to play him. "However did you get everyone in town on board?"

Between coos doled out at appropriate intervals, Kathleen slipped her calling card to Wade. He squinted at it. "Sun City Emporium?"

She explained how they'd evolved their business from drugstore to department store by trimming profits in favor of quantity. "We use assembly-line processes wherever possible and buy everything in bulk." She beamed. "Like Ford manu-facturing."

"You don't say."

"Oh, but I do." Kathleen tapped his thigh. "You might have heard of us this past spring? The Florida Girls? We put on a fancy war bond show, but now we're thinking—"

Before she could get out her pitch, she heard the unmistakable call of Francella Ava DiGruppo.

"Leenie!"

Daggers flew from her eyes as she twisted her neck toward the sound. She was leaving the restaurant with—

Was that *Thelma?* What had she done to her hair now?

"I see you've met Wade." Francella barreled on, ignoring Kathleen's icy glare. "But then, who in this town hasn't." She looked pointedly at Thelma. "Except you. Wade Davis, meet Thelma Miles."

"Thelma," said Wade, smiling his Chiclets smile. "I've heard about you."

He had?

"Mr. Davis," Thelma said, extending her hand while that Francella woman stood between the two of them like a proud midwife.

"Please, call me Wade," he said, pumping her arm as he looked into her eyes.

"Isn't this just perfect timing?" Kathleen managed to interject. "I wanted to talk to you about bringing the Florida Girls back for a limited engagement."

Without taking his eyes off Thelma, Wade Davis cocked his head, pursed his lips, and asked, "Florida Girls? Why not Vegas Girls?"

"That's the ticket, Wade!"

It was all Kathleen could do to refrain from grinding her heel into Miss DiGruppo's exposed vamp. Suggesting a name change—the cheek! Not that there was time to dawdle. Wade had his arm at Thelma's waist, with Sal's hussy leading them out. As Kathleen snapped up her bag, her business card caught her eye. It was still on the counter.

"Ma'am," called the barkeep, stopping Kathleen's escape. "Your bill?"

Dammit. She wouldn't make that mistake again, skip out on a bill in a town where you're trying to drum up contracts.

Where could they be heading? And together?

TWENTY-ONE

PECULIAR ALLIES, Wednesday

THELMA'S HEAD WAS AWHIRL WITH PLANS. WITH ONE phone call, Wade had arranged for the Vegas Girls to open that very weekend. Mercifully, Francella—so keen to leave when Thelma had confronted about her pregnancy, or lack thereof—became available to call on her dancer friends, all of whom, she assured them, would do anything for a shot at being onstage. That was the thing about performing, wasn't it? You had to be ready when opportunity struck.

By the time Thelma flung open her hotel room door, her nerves already frayed from the day's machinations, the last person she expected to find was her cousin-in-law. But there Lillian was, resting in her bed on a cloud of dusty-pink chiffon, , looking completely at home.

Almost simultaneously a jolt of panic hit her—she'd lost track of Mrs. Young. One loose end could unravel everything.

"Lills?" she said, her voice tentative, throat suddenly dry. Thelma hadn't seen her Florida Girls teammate since the Hollywood leg of their tour, when her husband's cousin had gotten her big break in the movies. Only, she and George weren't married then—weren't even sure they had a future.

They'd been in Cuba when George disappeared, and the Wrights had made it clear she was unwelcome. Or one of their servants had—the memory was a blur of grief and rage that still made her hands shake when she let herself think about it.

"Thelms!" Lillian squealed with delight as she ran at her cousin-in-law. "Peggy said you'd been kidnapped, but then I saw ol' Sun City Phantasmagoria, and she told me you were back, well, probably before I hopped into the helicopter with Red. Now that I'm here though, why don't we send the old lady back and get Peggy here?"

Relief flooded over Thelma. "You're not mad at me?"

Lillian brushed Thelma's forehead, shushing her as she pulled her back onto the bed. "Tsk. My family. They're touched. They're so consumed with money. It's not like they don't have plenty."

"Easy to say when you've always had it," Thelma heard her mother say.

"Oh, stop it," she protested aloud, which Lillian took as her reply.

"Well, I'm not apologizing for them," Lillian said. "That's who they are, what can I do? But Thelms, you're all I have left. George's younger sisters? They're steps. And they're the pits."

They lay side by side in each other's arms, silent for a time.

"How'd you get in here anyway?" Thelma asked.

"Maid in the hallway," said Lillian.

Why hadn't she thought to bring Lillian?

"My, my. What a lovely reunion," said Mrs. Young, peering down at them in the bed.

Her bed, Thelma realized. She'd missed the sound of the key in the door entirely.

"Where's that girl?" Mrs. Young asked.

"What girl?" asked Lillian.

"I think you mean Francella?" said Thelma. Extricating

herself from the folds of Lillian's dress, she stood, not waiting for a reply. "The good news is, we're booked in. Here!"

"What's the bad news?" asked Kathleen.

"Oh, stop," said Lillian. "That's wonderful news. I think? But how is it that a revival is going to help us put Sal away?"

Thelma smiled. "It's just an excuse to be in town asking questions," she said. "Only, well, there is bad news. Our first show is Friday. The Vegas Girls go on in three days."

"The what?" asked Mrs. Young.

"That's the bad news?" said Lillian.

"Yes," said Thelma, looking from Lillian to Mrs. Young as she remembered why she hadn't asked her friends to be part of this scheme. She didn't want to lose any of *them*. "Wade Davis got us a spot here with one phone call, but he insists—maybe because he runs the Chamber?—that we go by 'Vegas Girls.' It's catchy, no? Anyway, it's all the same to me but, Lills, you should know what you're in for."

"She knows," interrupted Mrs. Young. "I told her all about Agent Nelson."

"Is it true, Thelms?"

Thelma bit her lip, nodding. There was plenty she was sure Kathleen hadn't mentioned to Lillian. She herself had left much out, but she would soon right her omission.

"Obviously, we need to bring Peggy out here," said Lillian.

"We most certainly do not," Mrs. Young said, slamming her comb on the vanity. "You'll do no such thing."

"Oh, can it. We're not your employees anymore."

Thelma gaped in astonishment. She'd never have guessed Lillian had it in her.

"I can hire a nurse till she can get back." Lillian crooked her thumb over her shoulder. "How long are we booked in for, Thelms?"

Before Mrs. Young could protest again, Thelma cut her off.

"You're a dear, but I have to agree with Mrs. Young." Thelma said as she reached for her friend's arm. "Come on, let's go talk about this at the bar."

"Thelma," Mrs. Young called after them. "Remember our training."

She spun to face her former boss, flabbergasted. Remembering their training meant they didn't discuss the fact they'd been trained. She took a step toward Mrs. Young, leaning to whisper in her ear when her nose caught the unmistakable scent of soured alcohol.

"Are you drunk?"

"Aren't you a fine one to talk?" Kathleen rose from the dressing table and kicked off her shoes. "I'm perfectly fine. I just... I need a nap."

Thelma wheeled back around in disgust, exhaling audibly. "C'mon, Lills."

"This jape just keeps getting better," said Lillian.

As they walked the long corridor to the Wagon Wheel, Thelma's mother butted in again. "Jape! Who in hell talks like that?" She shook her head, feeling conflicted. Save for a twinge of guilt about her half-brother's baby, putting Kathleen in the line of fire hardly bothered Thelma. As for Lillian, well, she was here. But she drew the line at bringing in Peggy. Out of habit, she ran her fingers over the half-moon scar on her cheek.

"Oh, excuse me!" cried a woman Thelma had just managed to collide with. "I'm so sorry!"

She was petite, decked out like a cowgirl in spurred boots, a buckskin skirt, and vest. Hair hung in ponytails and bangs, like she was Annie Oakley. Extending her hand, the woman introduced herself as Betty Davis.

"Davis?" The name sounded familiar.

"Not Bette Davis," she said, laughing at her own joke, as if anyone would mistake her for a movie star. "She spells it wrong!"

"Pleasure to..." Thelma stopped, remembering. "Hold on, are you Wade Davis's wife?"

"Well, I'm afraid I'm at a disadvantage," said Betty.

"Me too," said Lillian. "But I'm not surprised Thelma knows half the town already."

Once introductions were made all around, Lillian discovered the Davises also ran the local radio station out of El Ranchero, KLAV.

"Get it? K-L-A-V. Or as I like to call it, *K la V*, like c'est la vie!" Betty clasped her hands in front of her heart. "We'd just love to have you as a guest, Miss Montgomery. I mean Lillian!" gushed Betty, clapping.

The woman reminded her of her old teammate, Doris Jurgen—one of the pluckiest gals Thelma had ever known—and an image flashed in her mind, a photo that her friend had snapped of her and George on the waterfront promenade, the Malecón, not long after their arrival in Cuba. In it, Thelma's hair reaches for the sky as behind them, a wave crashes against the rocks, its upward spray caught the moment before dousing them.

"I got it!" Doris had cried, pumping her fist as Thelma and George shook off the briny saltwater.

"Blame los nortes," Helen had said. The north winds.

Thelma was homesick for all of Cuba. What she wouldn't give to be there again with her love and her best friends, Peggy, Doris, and Helen. She longed to return to that refuge.

As Betty and Lillian were setting up an interview for the next day, Thelma's palms felt as if they'd caught fire. She rubbed them together. *Ignore it*, she told herself. Their plans had nothing to do with her.

"You're both doing the show?" Betty suddenly squealed. "You must both come, then!"

THE SMELL OF FRESHLY BAKED DINNER ROLLS WAFTED OUT from the Wagon Wheel's kitchen as Thelma finished her tale, confessing that, not only was Sal her father, but that she'd run his business in Tampa after his son went missing. She left out Mrs. Young's role in that.

"He caught you and my cousin in flagrante?" Lillian gasped. "What I wouldn't have given to see that!"

Thelma looked at her friend sideways, as if she'd suggested something untoward. "You don't say?"

Lillian laughed. "I meant after. Right before you shot the bastard. You've got moxie to spare. How on earth did you know what to do to have power over those men?"

Thelma's gaze traveled to the enormous wagon wheel still hanging at the center of the restaurant. The place was the same as when she and Mrs. Young had their heart-to-heart there, but Thelma had changed dramatically. She knew in her bones that Lillian should hear the whole ugly truth, if for no other reason than to test her pal's mettle. So far, her cousin-in-law had been shockingly nonchalant. She took a deep breath.

"My mom wasn't supposed to have me, or any kid. Soon as Sal laid eyes on me, I was about ten, he whacked me good." She tapped her cheekbone, knowing right where to point without looking. "She got us out of there fast, and for a while things were okay. Till she got addicted to barbiturates and then, well, anything. To keep a roof over our heads, I took on her gentlemen callers. One of the clients, an accountant, taught me everything he knew about balancing books."

Lillian's mouth dropped, and she blinked rapidly. "I don't know what to say, Thelms. That's terrible."

Thelma shrugged. She didn't want her cousin-in-law feeling *sorry* for her. "Happens all the time. Plenty of women in Europe faced far worse fates."

"How did you know what to do?"

A deep laugh erupted from Thelma's belly. "You mean in the world's oldest profession?"

With the timing of a wrecking ball, the waitress reappeared. "Another round, ladies?"

"I'll have another gin and tonic, but this time, hold the gin," said Lillian.

"I'll have the same," said Thelma. It never occurred to her that once you'd ordered alcohol, you could simply switch to something nonalcoholic. It seemed the wiser course. "But in mine, hold the tonic."

When the waitress left, a shadow crossed over Lillian's face. "Why are you here, then? You ran Sal's business, and almost quit George for him. Why turn on your father now?"

She wonders what I'm capable of. If I'll desert George.

Her heart caught in her throat. There was so much to be done, but first, she had to right this mess with Lillian. How could she put into words what George's love had given her? How it had changed her. How that didn't change just because he was gone.

She reached for Lillian's hand. "I spent my whole life trying to run away. But your cousin loved all of me. I'm still figuring out what that means, but one thing I know is this—I never wanted to put any man ahead of my independence. George knew that about me. Now," Thelma's voice caught, "it's my fault he's dead."

"What? Thelma, no. I understand you're in a state but for Pete's sake, George was a pilot. He loved flying. You're hardly responsible for—"

"No, you don't understand," said Thelma, dropping Lillian's hand. "I think Sal was trying to get me."

"You think Sal Giancarlo caused George's plane crash?" said Lillian, loud and clear.

"Shush!" Thelma flapped her hands. "Honestly! I don't know." Caressing the crescent-shaped scar on her cheek, she calmed herself. "What I know is my father doesn't deserve to be walking around free."

"Here you are, ladies." The waitress plunked their drinks on the table.

Thelma couldn't help but notice how attentive the waiters were in this town.

"Well, I agree with you, Thelms. The man is vile. And I'm not just saying that because he bankrolled Sun City to get at my uncle."

Thelma raised an eyebrow.

Lillian guffawed. "You didn't think he helped the Youngs out of the goodness of his heart, did you?"

"I never really thought about it," said Thelma. "I know Sal and your uncle Homer hate each other."

"Hate is too kind a word, sweetie."

"But Sun City also happened to be one of his most profitable betting parlors in Florida."

Now it was Lillian's turn to lift her brow and they both laughed.

"My point is, whatever you need, Thelms, I'm in."

"First order of business," Thelma said, lifting her glass, "is getting the Vegas Girls up and running."

"I can see it now, just like in '36." Lillian held out her palms like the edges of a sign. "'Showgirls defeat crime lords.' Now, that's catchy."

Thelma widened her eyes. "Say what now?"

"Surely you remember. When Thomas Dewey took out

enemy number one by putting his ladies of the night on the stand."

The Dewey trials did ring a bell, just not in the same way as they did for Lillian. What Thelma had heard, first-hand, was from a woman who'd somehow landed in Iowa, how she'd been groomed through drugs and coercion to say what they wanted her to say. But Thelma reckoned she'd laid plenty on the line for one day.

"We just have to make sure we do all this without alerting Francella."

"Mum's the word!" Lillian swiped her fingertips across her lips, twisted them, and then tossed the proverbial key aside. "I wish Maeve was here. She could whip us up something smart from these linens."

The girls looked down in unison, the tablecloth featured a repeating pattern of cacti and flamenco dancers. "What if...?"

"Yoo-hoo! Ladies! It's me! Francella Ava DiGruppo!"

Both turned toward the hollering headed their way. Indeed, it was Miss DiGruppo. Thelma dared to hope she'd have news from Wade.

"You're gonna love this," she said, smiling ear to ear as she folded into her seat. "We can use the Dice Girls' costumes!"

Thelma wasn't thrilled by the prospect, but it did solve a short-term problem.

"Plus, my pal Gloria is ready to join up. She's got gams for days."

"That's still only four girls." Thelma looked between Lillian and Francella. "Is that enough?"

"Long as we show enough skin, it is."

"I can ask Tina, in the shop here, to make modifications to the outfits," Lillian offered.

"Tina?" Thelma asked.

"Absolutely lovely girl in the lobby boutique. Fitted me for a whole wardrobe this morning. Or was that this afternoon?"

"What about the Dice Girls?" Thelma turned to Francella.

"What about 'em?" she asked.

"Won't they need their costumes back?"

"Kid, you worry too much," Francella said.

"Gotta agree with her, Thelms." Lillian stuck out her hand. "I'm—

"Lillian Wright Montgomery. Budding starlet set to dazzle in Red Skelton's upcoming Fuller Brush Man." Francella grabbed her outstretched hand. "Pleased to meet you. Just read that in the latest Variety."

Smirking, Lillian looked at Thelma. "My publicist will be very disappointed in me."

"You have your own publicist? Gosh. Wow. I'd love to bend your ear sometime."

Once Francella was sufficiently calmed, they agreed to meet the following day to assemble their act. Then she raced off to find Gloria.

"She's got coal to spare," Thelma said as they watched Francella's receding frame.

Lillian pulled a face. "I'll say."

"You go and talk to the lady in the boutique. Tina? I'll put together some show notes. See you tomorrow." Thelma paused. "Wait. Were you able to get a room?"

"Silly goose, of course. Being in the movies does have its advantages," Lillian said, droll as ever but for the excited clacking of her kitten heels as she pranced away.

Would these peculiar allies take down crime in Vegas? Thelma believed they just might. She had to.

TWENTY-TWO

ANNOUNCING THE VEGAS GIRLS!
Wednesday

KATHLEEN AWOKE WITH A START. THE ROOM WAS blisteringly bright. As she sat up, the tousled bedclothes on the empty twin beside hers caught her eye. It didn't surprise her that Thelma had made her bed. *Poorly*. At least she'd been in it the night before.

How am I this hungover?

"Thelma?" she called toward the bathroom, making her own head pound.

No one answered. Just as well. She wanted time alone to piece together a strategy, but first she needed food to calm her queasy stomach. Without rising, Kathleen reached for the phone to order her usual—poached eggs, coffee, and grapefruit, then added, "Ice, please. A bucket of ice."

The events of the previous day settled as her mind groaned to life.

The last thing she remembered was sitting at the bar with that Wade Davis fellow when Thelma appeared. That haircut. *Hideous.* What was she thinking? That look was not going to endear her to the men they were after.

My business card. Plain as day, she recalled leaving it on the bar. Or rather, Wade Davis leaving it behind. That was just as she was finishing her third cocktail. Then Thelma and Francella scurried off with Mr. Davis, which left her to pick up the tab. *Gauche.* Then again, he was a first-class hobnobber. Excellent contact.

A rat-a-tat of knocks accosted her ears. "Room service!"

That was fast, she thought, hobbling out of bed to answer, not bothering to slide into her robe or comb her hair. Once the bellhop left, Kathleen flipped on the Philco cathedral radio, thinking music would be a nice accompaniment to breakfast. *I could be happy living in a hotel.*

...BENNY GOODMAN AND HIS ORCHESTRA'S, "GOTTA BE THIS or That."

Howdy-do, Las Vegas! This is Betty Davis, here live from El Ranchero, proud sponsor of KLAV. El Ranchero, Western America's finest hotel and casino with all the amenities you could ask for. It's the only stop you need in Las Vegas.

I'm here with two of our most notable guests, in town to perform for a limited engagement starting this weekend, right here at El Ranchero's Rodeo Room! None other than the screen siren, Lillian Montgomery, Thelma Miles, daughter of local investor and philanthropist Salvatore Giancarlo.

How's about you give our listeners the lowdown on your Vegas Girls shindig. What are you—

KATHLEEN SNAPPED OFF THE RADIO AND—NOTICING THE sunglasses she'd given Thelma atop the dresser as she ran to the restroom—proceeded to disgorge the contents of whatever was in her stomach.

The *Vegas* Girls. Another mess for her to clean up.

. . .

EL RANCHERO WAS SHAPED LIKE A DIVINING FORK AND HAD two entrances. Highway 91 fed the parking lot for the Rodeo Room and casino, which oddly didn't have its own name, while the service road led to the hotel. The guest rooms ran along the long prongs, separated in the middle by a courtyard with three enormous pools, one with a swim-up bar and floating gaming tables—adults only—a lap pool, and a kiddie pool. The front held the lobby, the restaurant and boutique, as well as the more exclusive suites.

Space isn't at a premium here, thought Kathleen as she trod the endless hall toward the Rodeo Room. If she were managing this group for real, she'd have been heartened to see the setup. It meant the casino and lounge drew audiences beyond the hotel. Likewise, she would've been thrilled to hear the girls promoting the show on air. As it was, all Kathleen felt was nausea, which she hoped was from the drinking and not the pregnancy. She hadn't had morning sickness with Bertie or Archie, and she was in no mood for it now.

Pressing open the steel door, she got her first look at the Rodeo Room's cavernous space—beamed, vaulted ceilings over-head, wooden tables and chairs littering the area in front of the bandstand, and an enormous stone fireplace at the far end. The tables did have coverings, but still, she would've described the interior as barnlike. What sort of show would they put on in this homespun atmosphere?

"Yoo-hoo!"

Francella.

"Leenie!"

God, grant me the patience not to murder her. "Good morn-ing, Francella."

"Good morning," the girl said, emerging from a dark corner

of the room. To Kathleen's surprise, she was sporting dancing shoes, a wrap skirt, and a leotard. Rehearsal ready.

"What's with the sunglasses?"

Ah, there's that charm. Kathleen had snatched them on her way out of their hotel room. Evidently, young people these days felt no need to look after what was given to them.

"The glare, you know? I've quite the head cold this morning. Where is everyone?"

Before Francella could speak, in breezed a stunning young woman Francella introduced as Gloria Martinez. Also clad in a dancer's leotard, she was all legs and long, lustrous hair.

"I probably should not have come since I used to be a Dice Girl. But I couldn't say no to Francella."

"Charming," said Kathleen as kindly as she could muster, considering her state. "But we're still short one Thelma Miles and one Lillian Wright. Montgomery."

Those girls should be done with that show. Wasn't the station *on* the premises?

"We don't need them to get started," Francella said with an aggravating level of cheer. "Just watch, and tell us when we're not in step."

Kathleen was about to protest but then realized this plan was ideal. She was hardly capable of offering guidance. More importantly, the shows would have to be ridiculously simple. According to Miss Martinez, there would be three performances a night, lasting for all of eight minutes apiece.

"The house band plays," Gloria said. "And we show a lot of skin."

"I can sing, maybe one song. Two, tops," Francella added. "Most of it's buttering up the crowd."

Thelma would be good at that part, Kathleen thought as she eased back in her chair and let the girls have at it, grateful that by some miracle, Miss DiGruppo had inadvertently left her tap shoes behind.

Soon enough, Kathleen's throat felt itchy. She was parched. Fanning herself, she looked around and wondered if she might find a Coca-Cola nearby, perhaps in one of those vending machines. She lacked the motivation to look, and before long her thoughts turned to her Button.

What would she do if Lloyd didn't recover from this operation? Her heart clenched. Kathleen had spent so much of her life building the life she used to have, she'd never considered carving out her own path. For as long as she could remember, she'd been too busy to let her mind wander.

If the worst did happen, returning to St. Petersburg was accepting defeat. She'd be a burden to her boys, and she couldn't stand that. Besides, more and more gals these days were talking about making her own way. Instead of starting a health sanitorium, which had been Lloyd's dream, she could provide apparel to Nevada businesses. Make a go of living on her own in California. Anywhere, really. She couldn't retire. Not now. Ancient as she felt, she'd only just turned thirty-eight, and she had another child to think about.

"How was that?" Francella yelled from the stage.

"One more time, dear," Kathleen said, resolving to at least try and watch. For any future to work, she had to make sure this paternity issue was no longer a threat.

With only two dancers on stage, it was difficult to assess the show, but there was no denying they were both more accomplished performers than any of her girls from Sun City. She'd done her best with what she had to work with.

"When will the musicians arrive?" she asked, surprised at how many details she'd abandoned.

"Soon, Mrs. Young."

That Miss Martinez was delightful, she thought, her eyelids growing heavy.

Before she knew it, another blast greeted her ears. A panel of sun cut into the room. Someone was barging in the room from the parking lot, and it was not the band.

"Francella!"

Sal. Without thinking, Kathleen jumped to her feet.

Glancing over her shoulder, she saw that the man trailing Sal was the bodyguard from the opening ceremony, an oafish fellow whose hands resembled nothing so much as slabs of beef. Fear spiked in her belly. None of this could be good for the baby.

"Sir," Sal's man was saying. "Take it easy."

But Giancarlo ignored him, moving with surprising agility compared to his halting walk at the press conference just the day before. He beat her to the bandstand.

"Sal," Kathleen called to him. "We're having a rehearsal here—"

Sal was focused on Francella. "When were you gonna tell me, huh?"

Kathleen noticed a vein popping in Sal's forehead.

"Tell you what?" Francella asked.

If Kathleen were wagering, she'd have bet the girl knew what he was talking about. And where was that Thelma?

"You know exactly what I mean Frankie, you goddamn bitch. I got a call from your doctor."

"Salvatore, please. Calm yourself!" Kathleen said, but no one was listening.

"Go to hell, Sal," Francella said. "And don't ever call me that!"

Sal lifted his hand to cut her off and struck her in the face with the tip of his walking stick. Francella screamed and fell to the floor. Sal hovered over her. "How do you like that?" he asked, punctuating each word by driving his cane toward his girlfriend.

"Sal!" Kathleen gasped.

If he moved any closer, he was going to slam that thing into Francella's belly. Her pregnant belly. Kathleen wouldn't stand for it. Whipping off her sunglasses, she stomped on one of the lenses just as Agent Nelson had demonstrated. Then she picked up a shiv-like piece and thrust it at Sal just as Bongo reached for his cane. The glass sank into the bodyguard's forearm, and blood spewed out.

Kathleen took one look, and for the first time in her life, she fainted.

TWENTY-THREE

SHERIFF DEAN LAMB, Wednesday

By the time Sheriff Dean Lamb made it to El Ranchero's Rodeo Room, Chip was already on the scene, bandaging up a cauliflower-eared fellow lying flat on the floor, his clothes soaked in blood, pale as a ghost. Dispatcher must've called the firehouse first. Smart cookie.

Four broads hovered over him, stage girls in leotards, looking like they were about to bark orders. Lamb would've liked to watch that.

"Quick, Dean!" Chip called. "Help me get him to the truck."

For Chip, a wiry fella who'd been a combat medic at Normandy, that meant the situation was dire. As Dean picked up the pace, Salvatore Giancarlo came into view. He sat facing the goings-on, cool as a cucumber, like he was watching a show. The throbbing pain behind Dean's left eye blossomed into a full-blown headache. He hoped like hell the bleeder had tried to off himself.

Slowing before Giancarlo, he asked, "He one of yours?"

Sal blinked his assent.

"Who am I looking for?"

The shrill cry of a dame on the warpath interrupted. "Excuse me, officer! Sir?"

Dean looked up. Coming at him was none other than the society lady turned movie star that his ex had shown him in some magazine just that morning when she was complaining about something or other. She was even prettier in person. What was her name? Lynn? Lily? And what the heck were these people doing together?

"Ma'am?"

"What about her?" The blue blooded starlet was pointing to the other end of the stage.

Lillian! That was it. Lillian Montgomery.

Following Lillian Montgomery's long slender finger to its target, Dean clocked a fifth girl seated behind the fracas. Her elbows circled her knees, propping her head so he could see drops of blood hitting the floor.

"Ma'am!" Lamb rushed forward with his handkerchief, which she accepted without looking up.

"I'm fine," she said. Or something close to it. Her thighs muffled her words.

"You are not fine, Francella. Sal whacked you good," came another voice.

Lamb looked back toward the action, where the new sound had originated, and caught his breath. The woman who'd just accused Sal Giancarlo of attacking the dancer had also just been in the papers. Amazon tall and regal, what the papers didn't catch was her eyes. Golden like she was shining from the inside. Wasn't she Sal's daughter?

Head throbbing, Dean pivoted back to the injured man. "Ladies, let me help Chip here first. I'll be right back."

A tiny older broad in a skinny skirt stomped her foot and let out a low mewl of frustration, but they all stayed out of the way as he and Chip hauled the beefy guy onto a stretcher and out to the fire truck. For a small fella, he was surprisingly strong.

"This guy's in trouble."

This day was going from bad to worse. "Shit. You saw Sal, right?"

Chip nodded.

"What happened?"

"The little one popped him in his radial artery with a shard of glass. He'd have bled out if I wasn't close by. Still might."

"Well, don't kill him on the way to the hospital, 'kay, Chip?"

"You're never gonna let me live that down, are you?"

"You did manage to land yourself in the emergency room."

The tough on the stretcher groaned as they hoisted him onto the back of the truck. Lamb looked at Chip. "You didn't tranq him?"

"Nah. Sal said not to."

Lamb let a low whistle. The way he saw it, men like Sal weren't the problem. Fellas got in trouble elsewhere doing the same things they did here legitimately. The problem was the laws where they come from.

"What could he possibly say?"

To his credit, Chip didn't respond.

"That girl okay?"

"She wouldn't let me touch her. If I had to guess, I'd say her nose is broken. She's fine."

TWENTY-FOUR

THE AFTERMATH, Wednesday

Thelma looked around the Wagon Wheel as she downed the last of her G and T, the closing strains of Doris Day wafting out from the kitchen—"Sentimental Journey," George's favorite. The melody clawed at her chest. The thought of a home-bound journey made her heart yearny too. The only home she had was sentimental, memories of George's arms around her. She slammed her empty glass on the bar, hoping the sharp sound might drown out the music in her head.

"Nobody said anything and they still carted her off," she said, turning to Lillian. "I just wish I could call him. George would know what to do."

Lillian fiddled with the stem of her martini glass. She hadn't even taken a sip. Tapping her fingers on the bar, Thelma puzzled over the waiters' whereabouts now. *And how dare Mrs. Young comment on her drinking,* she thought, apropos of nothing.

"I wish I could call him, too, Thelms." Lillian's perfect manicure flashed as she reached across the table. "But, come on. I bet you know just what to do."

Her words drove a needle into Thelma's heart—not the

gutting of a stake, but still, the unmistakable pinprick of shame. Lillian, with her moneyed innocence, was obviously referring to the war's well-publicized sting operations, when the government asked its citizens to turn in known prostitutes. As if Thelma's past made her an expert in criminality rather than its victim.

"Well, Lills, if it wasn't obvious from my failure to bail out Mrs. Young, the pokey is one area where I don't have any experience."

Maybe it had been a mistake to tell Lillian about her past. Pervasive as those raids might have seemed to the average citizen, they were limited to areas around army bases. There weren't any near Keokuk and besides, any soldiers on leave nearby would've hit Chicago. Mostly though, the chief of police was a frequent caller.

"What are you talking about?" Lillian pushed her cocktail away. "All I mean is, you're generally pretty good at getting things done."

Thelma looked again for the waiter, no sign. "Yes, well, we still need to get the show on. Do you think Francella—"

"Jesus, Thelma. You're turning into her."

"Turning into who?"

"Kathleen Young, that's who!" Lillian sipped her drink. "I know you're having a hard time, but right now, so's she. She may be the devil incarnate, but Mrs. Young is pregnant and her husband is sick. We can't just let her rot in that jail. God knows how long they'll keep her."

Thelma rubbed her forehead. Was Lillian feeling guilty about something? She couldn't stand Mrs. Young. Whatever her reasoning, it didn't change the fact that Thelma had seen a side of Mrs. Young far more mercenary than whatever version of the store owner Lillian and the rest of their teammates had experienced in their society circles. But that wasn't her story to tell.

"You gotta believe me when I tell you, Lills, that woman can take care of herself."

"Oh, I know she can be a tempest," Lillian said, but her brow stayed furrowed. "But why were the police so hostile?"

Laughter, Thelma knew, was not the correct response, but she couldn't stop her mouth from twitching. Her friend really didn't comprehend what real life was like for most people. As she reached for the blue stone at her neck she heard, "Who's being close-minded now?" This time it was George.

Great. Now there were two dead people in her head.

"Lills, listen. This whole situation is bizarre. You heard that sheriff before we even went to the jail." Thelma puffed up her chest, lowered her voice, and slowed her cadence in an exaggerated imitation of Sheriff Lamb. "Far as I know Sal Giancarlo has always been a gentleman and a pillar of the community. Maybe he caught trouble elsewhere doing the same things he does here. That don't make him wrong. Just the laws where he come from."

Lillian was still laughing when she finally asked, "What in heaven's name did that even mean?"

"What it means is, Mrs. Young may as well have hit a cop."

Twirling her fingers in her hair, Lillian asked, "What about that government fellow? Nelson, is it? Why don't we call him?"

"Mrs. Young didn't tell you?"

"Tell me what?"

Thelma froze momentarily. Keep it on the Q.T., she thought. "I guess Mrs. Young left out, when she told you about Agent Nelson, that he is, ah... he's gone onward. On to another mission."

"We're on our own?" Lillian asked.

"Well, no. We can reach him, but ah, yes. We're basically on our own."

The two sat in silence a moment, the clinking of glass and

silverware the only noises filling the room. Someone in the kitchen had shut off the Zenith.

What was becoming ever clearer to Thelma was that the law was not the way to go after the Giancarlos. And Francella was no ally. She'd left the Rodeo Room with Sal before Sheriff Lamb was back from taking Bongo to the firetruck. The shock of Mrs. Young's arrest had not worn off as Lillian drove to the jailhouse, a one-story brick building just past the town center. Unimposing as the place appeared from the outside, the front desk clerk inside made for an impenetrable fortress. He'd barely acknowledged Mrs. Young's presence.

"Thelma?" Lillian knocked her shoulder. "I said, then what are we even doing here?"

Tears nipped at Thelma's eyes as her mood plummeted from shame to sorrow. What happened to "whatever you need"? If anyone was going to stay true to this cause for its own sake, she'd have guessed it would've been Lillian. She was George's cousin after all.

"Aren't you here for—" she began, her voice cracking. "For George?"

"Oh no, no, no." Lillian reached into her purse for a tissue and handed it to Thelma. "Come on."

After blowing her nose, Thelma absentmindedly returned the hankie.

"Keep it. Or, you know, throw it out." Lillian smiled as she pushed away Thelma's hand. "All's I meant was, what's our plan now? How are we going to take down that rat bastard, Sal Giancarlo?"

Thelma's shoulders fell, releasing tension she hadn't known she'd been holding. Instead of embracing Lillian's friendship, she'd withheld her trust. What could such a creature—who seemed so confident of being loved in this world—want with a friend like her? Now, with renewed resolve,

Thelma knew two things: she would avenge George's death, and Sal would pay.

That, she reckoned, she would have to do alone. She'd need their help, but Thelma would not be sharing the final responsibility for Sal with Lillian or Mrs. Young or Peggy. Not even Nelson. The afternoon with Francella had been just the start.

"To begin," said Thelma. "We have to find out if Gloria or Francella have some more friends."

"We do need more girls, but, why them? Didn't you just say we can't trust Francella?"

"We don't have to trust her." She put her hand over Lillian's. "Look, the women these mafia types date tend to be as close as the men. If Francella brought us to Gloria, my hunch is she's connected too." This was, in fact, a guess, not one of her premonitions. But it was based on long experience. "Besides, we don't need much."

"We don't need much to put Sal behind bars?" Lillian said flatly.

Thelma hadn't meant to say that last part out loud. It was only pertinent to her. So she talked about Francella's car, and how surely, they'd all have stories about their boyfriends, and that would give her enough to tip off Agent Nelson so he could swoop in and conduct a real investigation. "Of course we have to talk to the women. You've seen as well as I have, the men in this town are not going to be any help."

Giggling, Lillian slid a silver pill case from her bag and extracted a red tablet which she drank down with her gimlet. "For pep," she said with a smirk. "Want one?"

Thelma shook her head.

"Suit yourself." Lillian popped the pills back into her handbag. "What we need is Peggy." She raised her hand before Thelma could protest. "I can get a nurse to watch Doc."

Doc had nothing to do with why Thelma didn't want Peggy

coming to Las Vegas. That level of honesty was, however—Thelma was sure—an overreach. Besides, the more time she spent with Lillian, the more she knew she didn't want to drag any of her friends any deeper into this situation.

"Before you do anything, let me try and reach out to Agent Nelson and check in on Francella," said Thelma. "In the meantime, you can head to that shop and see how our costumes are going. Maybe find out what happened to the band. They might be in the Rodeo Room now."

"My God, I completely forgot about them," Lillian said.

"Me too, until now," Thelma said. "If we're going to put on the *shindig* we just told all of Las Vegas about over the airwaves this morning, we've got to keep our noses to the grindstone." Scooting her chair away from the bar, Thelma reached for her purse. Lillian didn't move. "I need you to trust me, Lills."

Lillian plucked the lime from the side of her glass and squeezed it into her drink before finishing it in one swallow. "You did run Sal out of town on a rail once already." She stood. "I'll try it your way. For now."

Thelma would take it.

TWENTY-FIVE

JAILBIRD, Wednesday

KATHLEEN YOUNG REGRETTED WEARING A DRESS TO rehearsal, but her pants were getting tight and she'd been running so hot. Until now. The thin crepe was not keeping her warm inside the concrete block jail. Her room—or cell, she supposed—held only a bench, a bucket, a toilet, and a sink. No window. Not even a blanket. She hoped this was an indicator that she wasn't meant to stay overnight.

Where is that damn Thelma?

Kathleen heard the jingling of keys on a chain, accompanied by the jailer's plodding step—the walk of a man who felt no urgency or ambition in his work.

Finally, someone had come to their senses. Kathleen stood, hugging her elbows and stomping her feet.

"I reckon you can make your phone call now."

He wasn't there to release her? "Surely you don't expect me to stay here. Why—" He wore no name tag that Kathleen could see. "Sir, I'll have you know I'm with child."

"You've made that known, lady." He reached for the lock and swung the door open. "Now, get out here and make your damn call."

Without moving, she looked at him through the bars. He was as thick as his walk suggested and had a gentle, doughy face. Hardly appeared capable of maintaining law and order among the hoodlums she'd seen, but he could certainly overpower a tiny woman such as herself.

"This is inhumane. It's unsafe."

"I guess you should've thought of that before you tried to stab someone," he said, leaning on the open door, unconcerned she posed any threat.

Despite all she'd learned from Agent Nelson, he had her dead to rights. Now she was trapped with nothing at her disposal to fashion a weapon. They'd even taken her earrings, and they were clip-ons.

"I did not stab anyone!"

"Yeah," he said, lifting his arm high and waving her to walk through, "everyone in here's innocent."

Kathleen cast a desperate look down the hallway. The building was shoebox small and appeared to have only one exit. Accessing it meant going through the deputy's office and past the front desk. In other words, there was no way out. She had no desire to find out what would happen if another prisoner arrived.

"Just how long do you think you can keep me here without charges?"

This brought a wide, unsettling smile to the man's face. Kathleen noticed both his front teeth were chipped.

"Judge should be back tomorrow."

As she followed him down the corridor, Kathleen realized that, though ordinarily she'd struggle to match his lumbering pace, she was more keen to avoid returning to her confinement. And she had another outstanding problem—she'd no clue who to call.

He led her toward the deputies' offices. No one manned a

desk but him. Motioning to the chair beside his surprisingly tidy work area he said, "You can use that phone." Then he sat in his chair and began scribbling on a form.

Kathleen could've spit she was so mad. Who was she to call? Young Theodore was as unreachable as her husband at present. There was no point in ringing Peggy. She'd heard Thelma and Lillian arguing with the front desk clerk, they were useless. Imogene Fuchs was a possibility, but she had no idea where the woman was staying.

On reflex, she took the heavy black receiver into her hand and dialed for the operator. "St. Petersburg, Florida, please."

The deputy slapped his desk. Depressing the hook he said, "No long distance."

Turning in her chair for privacy, as if there were any to be had, she spoke over her shoulder. "Then I'll dial collect."

TWENTY-SIX

WHILE YOU WERE OUT, Wednesday

Walking in step, arms linked with Lillian's as she walked from the Wagon Wheel toward the lobby, it occurred to Thelma that the two of them might look like girlfriends on a holiday adventure. The life she'd just allowed herself to hope for might have included just such a trip. Would her life ever look like that?

"I'm going to pop in here and see how Tina's doing," Lillian trilled, squeezing Thelma's arm.

Thelma tilted her head, but before she could ask what she meant, Lillian rolled on.

"Our costumes, you ninny! Tina. Shop girl." She wrinkled her nose. "You're hopeless," she said, dashing off into the boutique. "Ta-ta!"

Those pills must be something, thought Thelma, before turning in the direction of the front desk to ask for a cab into town. Again, she wondered if Mrs. Young had a point. Maybe this area was too far from the action. Maybe Sal would lose his shirt without her help.

But that wouldn't be any fun. No, she wanted to be the one to make him pay.

"Morning, miss," the woman behind the desk said. "Nancy Drew's other sidekick, is it? Bess Marvin?"

Thelma looked up abruptly, impressed the woman could sound so sarcastic and helpful at the same time. Her attitude was a stark contrast to the way other people had treated her at this establishment thus far. Reading the name badge, Thelma felt a pang of dismay to have missed noticing this woman until now. She was tiny, about Kathleen's height, but much sturdier looking. Her eyes were so dark they looked like they were all pupils.

"That's right, Miss Pérez." She smiled. "I'm Thelma Wright. Miles. I mean, just Thelma Miles."

Consuela Pérez lifted her eyebrows. "Okey dokey. What can I do for you?"

"Actually, I was wondering. You wouldn't happen to know Gloria Martinez, would you?" Thelma smiled expectantly, but the front desk clerk was scowling.

"You think every Mexican in this town knows each other?"

Thelma reared back ever so slightly. She hadn't given a thought to their backgrounds, sometimes she just *knew* things.

"She's a performer," Thelma blurted out. "And we're in a bind. I figured you might know her from booking acts and..."

The desk clerk scowled. "Oh, relax. I do know Gloria. But so you know, we aren't related."

"Oh, I— I didn't think..." Thelma began, but she didn't know how to finish. Why did the desk clerk say that?

"First, call me Consuela," she said. "It's about time you come to me."

Thelma looked to her left and right, wondering if Consuela was speaking to someone else.

"Look, lady, I know who you are. It was in yesterday's afternoon edition." Consuela leaned forward, her dark eyes narrowing.

"Then Francella DiGruppo walks out of my lounge with a busted face, then your roommate. Only *she's* in handcuffs. On top of all that, you tell the entire town you're putting on a Vegas Girls show at my hotel this weekend with Miss Lillian Montgomery." She tapped her fingernail on the counter, each measured clacking an unspoken accusation. "That whole time, it never occurred to you I was the person you needed to talk to? You don't think a woman like me knows anything. We're invisible until you need something."

Then Francella DiGruppo walks out of my lounge with a busted face, then your roommate. Only she's in handcuffs. On top of all that, you tell the entire town you're putting on a Vegas Girls show at my hotel this weekend with Miss Lillian Montgomery. That whole time, it never occurred to you I was the person you needed to talk to? You don't think a woman like me knows anything."

Thelma was speechless. She just wasn't used to asking for help. Her hand flew to her heart as she realized how often this was how she reacted, assuming others were ill-intentioned. Suddenly, it was clear how this behavior had worked against her. How her honesty said more about her than anyone she used it on. Yet despite recognizing that she and this woman were alike, Thelma had to refrain from telling her she could handle the situation. She needed her help.

"You're right," Thelma said. "I'm sorry I didn't think to ask. Until now."

"Here you are," Consuela said, pushing a slip of paper at Thelma. "Gloria's number. She's already been in touch with some people. None of the Dice Girls, of course. Stay away from them."

"Oh?"

The smirk found its way to the side of Consuela's mouth again. "Why do you think?"

Thelma was barely aware the Dice Girls existed. Her face must've said as much.

"You don't know, do you?" Leaning forward, Consuela explained how Wade Davis himself had insisted she fire them to make way for the Vegas Girls. "That's going to make some of the boys in town mad."

If Thelma caught her meaning—and she was sure she had—the Dice Girls were who she needed. Their "boys in town" sounded connected. Trying to look nonchalant, she looked down at the paper on the counter. "Thanks for this. You don't think we'll have trouble finding performers, do you?"

Consuela, now facing the wall of keys, carefully peeled a perforated sheet from a ledger. "Almost forgot. You got this today too," she said, turning to push the paper across the desk. "Gentleman called this morning. Long-distance. Asked you to call him back as soon as you got in."

Thelma's eyes traveled to the page—emblazoned with 'While You Were OUT'—which Consuela hadn't bothered to fold. As the desk clerk withdrew her fingertips, Thelma made out the handwritten name, *Homer Wright*.

The earth shifted beneath her feet, a cold sweat breaking across her forehead. Her father-in-law. The man who could take everything from her, declaring her marriage null and void and erasing George from her life completely. Somehow she maintained her equilibrium and, stifling a gasp, shoved the message into her pocket.

"Everything okay, Miss Miles?" Consuela asked.

Her heart bouncing in her chest, Thelma affected a casual attitude. "I'm going to need a car to head back to Fremont Street, after I freshen up. And please, call me Thelma."

"Of course," Consuela said to the back of Thelma's head.

She couldn't get to her room fast enough.

. . .

After initiating the long-distance call there was nothing for Thelma to do but wait. She couldn't leave and miss the long-distance operator ringing her back, and there wasn't time to get a message to Agent Nelson.

She wanted a smoke badly but Mrs. Young had forbidden her from indulging in their room. So she moved to the closet door to consider her wardrobe options. The phone rang and her stomach lurched. What did she even want to say to Mr. Wright?

"What in the heck, young lady?" *Wade Davis?* "I heard there was a bit of a dustup at rehearsal."

Much as she wanted to put an immediate end to the call, Thelma forced herself to calm. How had Wade heard this news already? Who'd told him? Did his wife, Betty, know? Would she announce the story on the radio?

Nothing good could come from a discussion with Wade. She had to dispense with him.

"Oh, you know how women can get." She pointed a finger pistol at her head and watched in the mirror as she shot herself. She assuaged him by agreeing to meet at the Rodeo Room. "You'll have a front-row seat at our rehearsal this afternoon."

She looked for the clock on the bedside table, but couldn't find it. Odd, she thought, checking her watch. No, the odd thing was that it wasn't yet two in the afternoon. She had to hand it to Kathleen—that woman had done a bang-up job of running the Florida Girls tour. Thelma had scarcely been in charge for half a day, and the missteps were mounting.

She sent up a silent prayer that she would be able to find Gloria, and that Lillian would find the band. Still, she was trapped. There was no way she was missing a call back from her father-in-law, Homer Wright. Agent Nelson could wait.

Finally, the phone rang. Not wanting to seem too eager, Thelma let it sound three times. But her father-in-law knew she was in a hotel room.

"Mr. Wright?"

"Thelma?" came a familiar voice. "Is that you?"

It took her a moment to place the sound. This was the man who ran Sal's operations in Cuba, had helped her hide Matteo Giancarlo's body, and then convinced the boys to hold the Tampa operation together.

"Carlos Gonzalez? What a delight to hear your voice," she said, though in truth she hadn't thought of him since well before she, Peggy, and George had flown out of St. Petersburg.

"Is it?" he asked.

How had Carlos Gonzalez found her?

TWENTY-SEVEN

CARLOS GONZALEZ, Wednesday

Carlos held the phone against his chest and looked out the window at the parking lot, where heat waves rippled off the blacktop. His brother always said this was a crummy motel, but to him, it was deluxe—there was air-conditioning and a telephone, and both worked. Plus, the joint was so close to Sal's club they could've walked, though Diego insisted they always drive. "Never walk when you can ride, little brother," he'd say.

They'd last stayed here together just before Diego left for Las Vegas. It felt like a lifetime since then. Sure as Carlos knew he'd never see Diego again, he was sure he'd never really know what had happened to him. Now the room's darkness, the stains on the ceiling, the dank smell of the air-conditioner. It was all getting to him. Because surely, that bitch on the other end of the line had not just said she was glad to hear from him. Hadn't she discarded him in Tampa?

Before he could say anything, she started yammering again. "Of course it's good to hear from you, silly. Where are you?"

Her casual tone cut Carlos to the bone like a switchblade—clean, deep, and intimate. He'd been in love with Thelma Miles since he'd first seen her in Sal's office, those glowing eyes of hers igniting something primal he couldn't extinguish. When she offered him the chance to be the Giancarlos' lead on Cuba, he was so sure she felt the same it almost made him forget the pain of his dead brother. Almost. Until everything went to shit.

"Carlos?"

"I'm in Tampa," he answered, still her dog—the good boy who'd agreed to hold the line against the impending takeover when Sal went silent and everyone in town started gunning for his numbers business. Carlos had kept them in line. Until everyone in town started going to jail. Everyone except the Giancarlo crew.

"Still?" asked Thelma.

That hurt. In the past six weeks, she clearly hadn't given any thought to him at all. Or was she expecting him to be waiting for orders in Cuba?

"I just got in from Havana."

The only response was static on the line. There was so much Carlos wanted to say to Thelma, to ask her. But now that she was on the phone and sounded so genuinely glad to hear from him, he was confused. Hope stirred in his chest. What if they did have a future?

"How did you find me?" she asked.

To Carlos's ears, her question sounded like a compliment. "I read about you in the paper, taking over the casino just like you said. I didn't know you were, uh..."

"You mean that I'm Sal's daughter? I had to keep that under wraps. Sal's orders."

"It makes sense now. What you did."

Thelma caught her breath, a sound that went right between Carlos's thighs. Carlos closed his eyes and pictured Thelma's shiny black hair. Those golden eyes. Her legs. Maybe there were things she wanted to say too. First they had to talk business. If she was running Vegas, was he still point on Cuba?

"You sound well," she said, changing the subject.

"You mean I don't sound high?" *God, why'd I say that?* Carlos didn't need her approval like some kind of sissy. He was losing control of this conversation when what he needed was to find out why she'd been in Havana in the first place.

"Well, no. You don't."

The observation was a kick in his gut. Carlos didn't want to tell her how, after she left town without a word, he spent a week so doped up and out of his mind he blew the meetup with Tampa's Cuban investors. He desperately wanted her to know that he was ready to be a soldier again. Her soldier.

"When the raids started going down, and then Sal's club went up in flames, I needed to be sharp. I quit cold turkey. It was rough the first couple of weeks, but I made it."

He didn't add how it felt like someone had ripped his heart out when, during the worst of it, he found out she'd eloped with George fucking Wright.

"When you went to Cuba," said Carlos, still hesitating too much. "I didn't know, you know, where we stood—"

"Where *we* stood?"

Was she being coy? Maybe she thought he wouldn't have heard she was in Havana. *Married.* He was livid when he found out. He'd never have ordered his boys to take down that plane otherwise. Thank God that didn't work. She was his last best bet for running Sal's Cuban operations. And now she wasn't married no more neither.

"When I heard you was running Sal's casino out in Vegas." Now that they were talking again, Carlos had hope. Maybe his little stunt had worked better than he'd expected. "I thought—"

"Oh, right. That."

"That? I'd say things have turned out pretty well for you."

"Would you?" she asked.

Carlos couldn't be sure, but that sounded a lot less friendly.

"I'd say they turned out pretty well for you too," she added.

It was true that Thelma had hooked him up with some of Tampa's most prominent businessmen, and he was making nice money off them. But how'd she know anything about that? None of that was Giancarlo's business, that man never wanted nothing to do with heroin or girls. If he wanted to leave that money on the table, fine. Carlos wouldn't.

None of it changed the fact Thelma had left him out to dry and married someone else. He hadn't even known she was dating.

Before he could respond, the line clicked. "Hello? This is the operator. I have a long-distance call for Miss Miles?"

"You never got married?" asked Carlos.

"I'll take the call, ma'am," said Thelma. "Carlos, I'm a widow. May I ring you when I'm back in Havana?"

She didn't wait for his answer, but Carlos wasn't going to let her forget this time.

TWENTY-EIGHT

THE SECRET OF THE OLD CLOCK,
Wednesday

AFTER DISPENSING WITH CARLOS, THELMA DROPPED THE handset into the cradle and stood. Her reflection in the mirror gave her a start. Her hand went to her hair—what was left of it— all flecked with silver. She didn't care who did or didn't like it. For the first time since George disappeared, she felt powerful, in control—like a goddess.

The phone rang, and Thelma snatched it up, about to return to her seat on the bed before deciding that standing was the better way to face this phone call with her father-in-law. She'd been wrestling with what to say to this man all week. Agreeing to an annulment felt devastating, like she was giving up on George. But there was no fighting the Wrights. George was not his family or their money. And Mrs. Young had a point —Thelma had only known a few weeks of utter happiness with George. A dream, really.

Time to let go of that dream.

"Mr. Wright?"

"The same." Mr. Wright coughed. "Now listen here, young lady. This has got to stop. Your refusal to agree to an annulment is bullheaded nonsense..."

Tempted as Thelma was to interrupt his now-familiar tirade, she realized the opportunity and waited for him to wind down. She'd only seen her father-in-law in photographs, still, she could picture the lock of hair that often escaped his combed-back style. See him pacing as he delivered this speech, that curl bouncing against a blood vessel popping at his temple. Not that she'd ever seen such a vein, not in a picture. It was his anger, the same righteous indignation that consumed Sal Giancarlo. *How similar they are in temperament.*

As he ranted, Thelma vowed to do things differently. She wouldn't shy away from saying her piece, but she'd take a cooler approach. Like Mrs. Young, but with more street sense.

"What have you got to say for yourself?" her father-in-law finally said by way of winding down.

"Mr. Wright, I know the only reason you've kept up this search is to force an annulment and prevent me—"

"That's not true—"

"Don't interrupt me."

A gasp escaped Mr. Wright's mouth, but he didn't speak.

"You want to be sure I make no claim as his rightful heir." Thelma paused. "And you're right. That's exactly why I've refused. I loved George with all my heart. I can't imagine..." Thelma's voice caught in her throat, and she had to choke back the tears. "Replacing him the way you replaced George's mother."

Another sound escaped Homer's mouth, hastening Thelma back to her point.

"I won't find love like that again, Mr. Wright. I'm sure you know that your son had a heart that was big and true. I don't know what I did to merit his devotion, but I haven't been willing to let go of that. I never cared about the money, but I won't deny our love."

Her plan had been to tell him to send the papers and end

the call, until her eyes fell on the bedside table. The weird-looking clock was no longer there. Had someone been in their room? She was certain it had been on the nightstand. Shifting her gaze to the still-open closet—phone still to her ear—her eyes fell onto Mrs. Young's valise. She flicked open the lid with her toe and found, nestled inside, the horseshoe-framed clock.

After all her carping about the tacky decorations, that thing was Mrs. Young's? Had Thelma caught her trying to abort the mission after all?

"I have to go," she said, not waiting for Mr. Wright's reply as a new resolve washed over her. "I'll sign your papers, but first, I've business to attend to."

Thelma plunked the phone into its cradle and moved to the desk, extracting a few sheets of El Ranchero's distinctive stationery. She held the pen, poised to scratch out a message about their trouble with Sal, up to and including Kathleen's being behind bars, but stopped herself. Agent Nelson had insisted she concentrate on getting information from the men —"the real players," he'd called them—and they'd been no help at all. Why tell him "Hawk's" wings had been clipped if Thelma was about to get her out of the clink? If Mrs. Young might not last the mission? There was no need to mention her at all.

JUNE 6, 1945

N,

We have secured additional inroads to our contacts and work continues apace.

—BB

. . .

She reread her words, pondering Agent Nelson's lack of a code name. Was Theodore Nelson his actual name?

After folding the note into an envelope, Thelma slipped the missive into her wallet and returned to the closet. Her rehearsal duds wouldn't do for a meeting with her father.

By the time she'd donned her favorite form-fitting white dress with rhinestone detailing at the collar, spritzed on her Chanel, and freshened her lipstick, Thelma had mostly forgotten about the call with her father-in-law, Homer Wright, to say nothing of her brief chat with Carlos Gonzalez. She'd put him out of her mind. Her focus was on getting Sal to do what she needed him to do.

As she headed toward her father's room—she didn't call first, wanting the element of surprise—the other person very much on her mind was Wade Davis, head of the Las Vegas Chamber of Commerce. He'd secured their booking at El Ranchero with one phone call and he knew too much not to be as tight with the mafia as the local police were. Still, she needed an ally. She'd promised to meet him at the Rodeo Room, but there were no Vegas Girls to show him. She and Lillian could hardly put on an act for him.

Vivian Miles rang in, "Don't forget that little minx, Martinez."

Oh, Mother.

Thelma hadn't even seen Gloria Martinez perform. By the time she and Lillian had made it to the Rodeo Room that morning—just this morning?—the rehearsal had already ground to a halt. She was probably scared off. "Your idea stinks, Ma."

"Excuse me?"

Thelma must've been speaking to her mother. *Aloud.* A woman walking ahead of her in mules and a bathing suit cover-up turned and stared. She was tempted to ask the gorgeous brunette if she could dance.

"I said, take care in the drink," Thelma said, feeling a flush rise in her cheeks. "The sun's brutal out there this time of day."

"At three o'clock in the afternoon?" she said flatly. "I don't think so."

"Oh my goodness, look at the time. Better get a move on," Thelma said, rushing past. She was starting to sound like Kathleen Young.

"Told you," said Vivian Miles.

Moments later, standing in front of Sal's door, Thelma stamped the ground and rolled her shoulders to clear her mind. She would make her case plain to her father, and once that was resolved, she'd move on to Agent Nelson. No one answered her knock. The room was silent.

Fine. She'd stop by Sal's trailer on the way to John Lee's Laundry. With any luck her father would be there, minus Francella, and she could confront him about Kathleen. Then again, having those two in the room together could be advantageous.

Thelma picked up her pace. Before leaving the hotel, she had to tell Lillian that Wade Davis would be attending their rehearsal and that, somehow, they were going to have to put on a show for him. At least an act.

TWENTY-NINE

ONE PHONE CALL, Wednesday

KATHLEEN STOLE A LOOK AT HER WRIST, ONLY TO RECALL that they'd confiscated her Longines. *What did they think I'd do with that?* Which got her mulling over the possibilities of what she could do. Watches had springs. Not shiv worthy, but perhaps a tool for picking a lock.

Across the room, the policeman occupied himself with fixing a pot of coffee, seemingly unconcerned with Kathleen's existence. She scanned his desk to see what she might find. A stray paperclip. A staple. Anything. But no. And that explained the tidy desk.

On the wall across from where Kathleen sat, the station's schoolhouse-style wall-mounted clock read three o'clock. School would've just let out and Archie would be at the Emporium. Ordinarily, he'd be doing some after-school activity, but she'd lay odds that Bertie had made his little brother work the evening shift, leaving himself free to cat around. Besides, she didn't want to talk to Bertie.

Accidentally or not, if that kid hadn't shot that scoundrel henchman of Sal's, that Gonzales something or other, she reckoned she wouldn't be in this mess. She would not—a gnawing burr in her heart insisted—have flung herself back into Matteo's arms in Vegas.

That was a lie and she knew it.

No. It was that Matteo had come when she called. Immediately and without question. That stood him apart from the other men in her life. She loved her Lloyd, but he was infirm. And Bertie, well, even without the deadly situation, between his gambling problem and general lasciviousness, he'd never been at her beck and call. Matteo, on the other hand—

Stop that this instant, Kathleen DeVane Young. She dared not think such thoughts. This was why she wanted to speak to Archie. He wasn't knight-in-shining armor material, but he was still her baby. His sweetness was comfort enough.

"Bertie?" She gasped on hearing her eldest son on the other end of the line. "What are you doing there?"

"Geez, Mom, is it that bad already? Aren't you a little young yet to be so forgetful? You left the store to your sons. Ring a bell?"

"Ha ha. Where is your brother?"

"I'm doing well, thanks."

"Albert, this call is costing me a fortune," she said, glaring at the policeman's back as he continued to futz at the coffeemaker. He hadn't even offered her a cup. Then again, she'd been the one to turn her back to him. "Now could you put your brother on the phone?"

"He's not here."

Kathleen wished she could reach through the phone line and knock some sense into the boy. He was acting like a petulant child when she needed desperately for him to grow up. Lloyd was right and she'd known all along. Though her twenty-year-old son was older than Kathleen had been when she started overseeing her husband's elixir business, Bertie wasn't ready to run the store.

"Okay. Where is he?" she asked, trying to keep her voice even despite that he was causing her to repeat herself.

"Least halfway to Norfolk, I'd imagine."

A chill ran down Kathleen's spine. "Norfolk?" she said too quickly, with too much vinegar. That could only mean one of two things, either he was visiting her estranged family or enlisting. She couldn't say which prospect was worse. "Whatever for?"

"He signed up with the Navy right after you left."

A vision of Archie in uniform, boarding a ship that might never return, clutched at Kathleen's heart. Her hand flew to her mouth and she began to gnaw on her pinky, mulling over her response as she clamped down on the nail, chewing till the tip gave her the satisfaction of pulling away from the nailbed. She was about to spit it out when Bertie spoke again.

"Said he was going to try to find Grandma and Grandpa before he starts basic."

Instead of spitting out the fingernail, the shock caused her to swallow. "But," she coughed, "we won. The war is all but over."

"No, Mom. Geez, now I am worried. You know the Japs are still killing our people in the Pacific."

Of course she knew that. She also knew those Japs didn't stand a chance. Why, the whole of that country could fit inside California. Aghast as she was, she felt another sensation she could not deny. Pride. Like his father and her dear brother, her son wanted to defend his country. This was also the reason for her panic. The war had killed them both—her brother Thomas, almost immediately, and Lloyd, very, very slowly.

What was behind her boy's urge to see her parents? Was her sweet boy hoping for a dose of familial love before setting off for war? She hoped not. He would be in for a rude awakening.

All she could do now was pray that her son wouldn't be able

to locate his grandparents. Then she remembered, she'd given up belief in any deity.

Her finger was bleeding and she pressed it between her thumb and third finger

"Sweetheart, I'm going to have to go. I'm proud that you're keeping the store together all on your own. I—"

"Oh, I have help."

She didn't like his tone. Not one bit. "Of course you do. We're always—"

"Sal Giancarlo lent me some money."

Kathleen's heart pounded in her ears as the receiver dropped from her grip and clattered onto the floor. She'd put this information so far out of her mind since dining with Sal the day before, only now did she recognize this loan for what it was. Motive. It had compelled her to attack.

The officer turned, narrowing his eyes.

"Oh silly, I didn't mean to do that," she said, keeping her smile plastered on as she reached for the phone and felt her waistband tug at her midsection like a noose. "Pregnancy always makes me clumsy."

Covering her mouth with her free hand, she spoke low and even to ensure her son would do as he was told. "Albert, I need you to put me on hold so you can call Mr. Briggs at the Times. Find out where Imogene Fuchs is staying. Then you need to call her hotel and patch me through."

THIRTY

GLITTER GULCH, Wednesday

As soon as she got in the cab, Thelma leaned against the car seat. The driver's bulbous nose made for a stark contrast to his slender body. "Would you mind popping around to the Rodeo Room first?"

He replied by brushing his fingertips against the brim of his cap.

Thelma was content with a quiet ride. Glad as she'd been to hear that Lillian was in the Rodeo Room, she didn't expect much. Gloria had probably been spooked away, but Lills might have regrouped the band. The two of them plus the musicians would have to appease Wade. She'd find out soon enough.

As she settled into her seat, Thelma heard her mother. "You could've walked there, you know." The admonishment brought a smile to her lips. Vivian would approve. Her mother never missed an opportunity to indulge in luxuries.

After pulling back onto Highway 91, the car turned away from town and then almost immediately into another parking lot, this one defined by a curved stone portal topped by a neon sign that read, "El Ranchero Casino & Lounge" at its apex.

It's no Lotus Club, Thelma couldn't help but note as they

pulled up to the Rodeo Room's entry. No planters. No velvet ropes. Just two sets of ordinary glass doors creating a small vestibule. Then again, the Rodeo Room was no nightclub. More of a casino with entertainment. The crowd would be more interested in gambling in the building across the way than in the free entertainment that came with their free meal. Their set was not to exceed ten minutes, which, now that she thought of it, was a boon—gave her more time to bury Sal Giancarlo.

In this daze of thoughts, Thelma sauntered into the cavernous space, only to find Lillian and Gloria Martinez rehearsing a dance number with three other women, all sashaying in time to the band's rendition of "The Trolley Song." No one sang, but Thelma knew the words by heart.

Thelma felt a pang in her heart. She and George had ironically dubbed this "our song," even if she rejected his claim that she'd fallen for him from the moment she saw him, just as he'd rejected her insistence that he'd fallen in love at first sight. Now she knew she'd been lying to herself, if not to him. She *had* fallen for him from the moment she saw him—not the set of his jaw, or his strong shoulders, or even his capable hands. His pull was something beyond that. They'd teased about it, but now she felt she'd denied him the truth.

Her voice caught as she called for Lillian, her soon-to-be-ex-cousin-in-law. "Lills, would you come here?"

But her friend didn't hear her over the music, so Thelma rapped on the table with a heavy glass ashtray. The crashing sound got the band to stop playing and helped her regain control of her emotions.

"Thelma!" cried Lillian. "You're here!" She hopped off the stage and threw her arms around Thelma. "Peggy's coming. Don't say a word. You need her."

Thelma was too stunned to be angry. How had Lillian pulled together the Vegas Girls in an afternoon? They looked like a real team. Not only that, she was right—Thelma did need Peggy Holmes. If her new plan came off, they'd all be long gone before Sal was any the wiser.

"I talked to your uncle," Thelma began, wanting to tell Lillian that, though she was agreeing to the annulment, she had no intention of abandoning George's memory. Only by then, the other girls had joined them.

"Thelma," a woman who was all legs said as she approached. "We didn't get to meet before. I'm Gloria Martinez."

Lillian put her arm on Gloria's shoulder and leaned toward Thelma. "Let me introduce the other girls." She looked back toward the stage. "Let's take five? Thanks, Stingray."

Thelma's head jerked toward the stage and back. She mouthed, "Stingray?"

"None other. Mr. Ray 'Stingray' Malone and his band, The Fever."

Clever. If Thelma remembered correctly, fever was the name for a group of stingrays.

"And Thelma, this is DeeDee," Lillian said, motioning toward the shorter, curvier of the three new Vegas Girls. "And Mari and June."

The girls murmured excited hellos, and Thelma lost track of who was who, so she thanked them en masse for joining on such short notice.

"Are you kidding?" the taller girl with the long equine face said. "We've been dying for some stage time."

"Thank you, Miss Thelma."

The praise left Thelma too embarrassed to stick around, and the meter was running. She smiled and nodded her appreciation then motioned for Lillian to follow her. "When do you expect Peggy?"

"Tomorrow," said Lillian. "The nurse should be arriving at

the Youngs," she looked at her wrist as if it held a watch, "around now."

"I'm going to get Mrs. Young out of jail," Thelma said. "Then we'll be right back."

Lillian squinted and opened her mouth to speak but clamped it shut and looked at the ground. She was better at diplomacy than Thelma could ever hope to be.

Thelma patted her friend on the shoulder. "Trust me. And..." Again, her voice faltered. "Thank you for all this."

"There it is. Pull over here," Thelma said on seeing the white sign emblazoned with the words "John Lee's Chinese Laundry" in English and, Thelma assumed, Chinese. It was, more specifically, Cantonese.

"Would you mind waiting here for me?" She passed a five-dollar bill over the bench seat. "I won't be long. Thanks."

Before he could answer, Thelma hopped out and pushed through John Lee's entrance. The inside, between a steamy heat and musky smell of damp fabric, was hotter and more unpleasant than standing outside in the June sun. "No wash. Special delivery," she said, tapping the envelope with her index finger.

The old woman behind the register shot out an age-spotted hand to snap up the letter, simultaneously rubbing the fingers of her other, upturned palm.

Money, right, thought Thelma, dropping a quarter into her hand before turning to leave. "Thank you."

She'd barely closed the cab's door when, to her shock, she saw Francella exiting the laundry, carrying the very envelope she'd just left for Agent Nelson. Thelma hadn't seen her father's girlfriend in the shop. Where had she come from? More importantly, what was she doing picking up Agent Nelson's mail? Or had she intercepted it?

"Where to now, miss?"

Thelma looked up. "Hang on," she said to the cabbie as she recognized where they were—in front of The Plaza, where Sal had dropped Francella off just two days earlier. She only noticed the restaurant now because of its weirdly incongruous sign, "Silver Spurs Oriental Restaurant."

"Would you mind waiting here a bit longer," she said as she was getting out of the car again. Francella had already disappeared into her hotel and she didn't want to lose her.

"Exactly what is it you're planning on doing?" she heard Vivian Miles ask.

Thelma's first thought was that her mother always did know how to make her doubt herself. Then again, Vivian made a good point. Lacking a better idea—*or any*—she might do well to take a pause.

Maybe there's a bar in the lobby, she was thinking as she pushed through the grand doors, only to bump straight into Sal.

"What are you doing here?" they asked simultaneously.

"You first," said Sal.

His dark eyes burned with rage and Thelma felt her knees tremble. She wondered at how intimidating Sal could still be despite everything that had happened to him. "I wanted to see how Francella was—"

"Shut it," he said, violently grabbing her arm and shoving her to the side of the vestibule. Once he had her against the wall, he pressed into her, pushing his cane against her neck. "Did you know?"

"Know what?"

Sal pushed hard, the cool stem of his cane tight against her windpipe. "What is this? You're gonna pretend you don't remember this morning?"

"Actually, I was—Sal, you're hurting me," Thelma said, but he didn't move. Thelma had been so distracted to see Francella with what looked like the envelope she had left for Agent Nelson she'd nearly forgotten that she did want to speak with Sal.

She coughed. "I was looking for you."

"You want to gloat?"

Eureka. The last piece of the puzzle fell into place, and Thelma understood what she'd missed while she and Lillian were at KLAV. They'd gone from there straight to the Rodeo Room and found a fireman tending to Bongo. She hadn't given much thought to why Sal would've attacked Francella, simply filed the event under *Sal perpetrating violence against a defenseless woman. Again.*

Now the trigger for her father's rage came rushing to her with unmistakable clarity—he'd somehow discovered Francella wasn't pregnant. The realization filled Thelma with calm. She'd dealt with plenty of men in the throes of humiliation and knew just how to appease their fragile egos. Now she could pounce.

"She didn't..." Thelma lowered her voice. "Did that Francella cheat on you?"

Sal backed off slightly, gears turning in his brain. Her explanation, she knew, was more palatable than the idea that he'd been tricked by a woman. Better still, it threw Francella's virtue into question. This alternative also made it seem like she didn't know about Francella's lie.

Thank God I didn't say anything at lunch yesterday. Or did I?

"Nah, her doctor's office called. She ain't pregnant. Never been pregnant. Made the whole thing up."

Under any other circumstances such a memory lapse would be concerning, but just then all she had time for was relief. The last thing she needed was for Francella to think Thelma had double-crossed her. She bit her lower lip. "Oh, Sal. I'm sorry. I know you were—"

"Shut up!" he yelled, reasserting the pressure of his cane.

What is his end game here? It struck Thelma with stunning clarity—her father had demonstrated he was above the law. He probably could kill her in a hotel lobby with impunity. Why *had* she asked Imogene to let him off?

"Sal Giancarlo?"

Thelma and Sal both looked toward the voice. It was Imogene Fuchs.

"Sal Giancarlo?" she repeated. "Just the man I've been looking for. I wanted to get a quote about the Vegas Girls from you. Specifically, about this morning's incident."

The murderous look in Sal's eyes burned harder, but as he turned, he loosened his grip on Thelma. "I ain't got nothing to do with 'em, and I ain't talking to you."

Thelma took advantage of the opportunity to step away from the wall and reach for Imogene's elbow. "Imogene! Wonderful to see you. I'd be happy to give you an exclusive." She walked the reporter toward the lobby. "Would you mind waiting for me right in here? I'll tell you everything I know. I was there and there's not much to tell. You're smart to come straight to the source."

Thelma patted Imogene on the back, encouraging her departure. If Sal knew Imogene Fuchs better, Thelma's ruse would fall apart. Imogene would never be put off so easily, no *real* journalist would. For most of his life, however, Sal had avoided the press, though he knew enough to understand he couldn't harm Thelma in a reporter's presence.

With this advantage, she turned to face him. "I'll take care of her. But first, I came here looking for you," said Thelma, inventing a way forward, hoping that by twisting the knife of his own rage she'd spur him to action. "Because you should know that putting a pregnant woman in jail is not doing you any favors in this town. If you get my drift."

Sal reared his head and curled his upper lip. "Like you'd know."

Like that, Thelma's pedestal had cracked and she was getting the real Sal. He didn't need anything from her anymore. Maybe he was tired of women needing things from him. Regardless, she had to make him believe her.

Stepping back, Thelma tucked her chin and looked into his eyes, still towering above hers. Despite his health setbacks, his frame was still imposing. She had to play his anger carefully. "All I can tell you is what I heard from Wade Davis, who I'm to meet in about an hour. He wanted to know how a lady took you down."

Sal tensed, and a grin played at his lips. Thelma held her breath. Had she played this wrong?

"What'd you say?" He was practically growling. *Perfect.*

Thelma exaggerated her exhalation. "I told him the truth, of course. I wasn't there." She shrugged. "Anyway, I thought you might want to make a call. I know you have that authority here. And, well, she is with child."

She chose her last words carefully, hoping they didn't call to mind Francella. But she missed the mark. Her father, leaning against the wall, looked askance, deflated.

"Sal?"

Bending closer to Thelma's face, he refocused his glare. "I still don't know why you're here. Investing? To be a dancing girl? You wanna pal around with my girl? How come?"

"Oh, you know Mrs. Young. I had to sweeten the deal somehow. And setting up a show isn't a bad way to get the skinny on the local goings on. Wouldn't you agree?" asked Thelma, almost believing herself. "And anyway, really it was Wade Davis who came up with the idea for the Vegas Girls."

"Wade Davis," Sal spat. "Gets that nose in everyone's business."

"Well, now I'm in a bind. I can't run a troupe of showgirls without Mrs. Young. I need her help." Thelma pouted and looked at the floor—making herself appear more like a child than a threat—tweaking his rage just so. "If you don't spring her out of jail, people will talk. That's the only way to squelch these loose lips."

Sal grunted.

Thelma returned her gaze to him, smiling. "So you'll do it?" Wrapping her arms around him, Thelma recalled how, after his stroke in Tampa, she'd had to prop him up on his office sofa.

"Thanks, you're the best," she said, cutting herself off before the word *pops* slipped out. That would, she reckoned, be a bridge too far. "Now I really must go and speak to Imogene. You know how the press doesn't like to be kept waiting."

She rubbed his tie and pivoted toward the door decisively, hoping he wouldn't sense her uncertainty. As she turned, Thelma noticed that Sal had a new man nearby, a fellow whose head seemed to grow straight out of his shoulders. That's what he does, he swaps us out. This guy was the new Bongo. The same way Francella's baby should have replaced Matteo. Or her?

A pang of longing for George hit Thelma in the throat—she'd allowed herself to imagine their children. Pausing before she walked into the hotel lobby, Thelma brushed away the thought. She spied Imogene, notebook out, scribbling away, her ambition stark.

"You're just who I wanted to see," Thelma said, genuinely glad to see the reporter, plain as ever in her sensible shoes and brown tweed. Not so long ago, Thelma couldn't have dreamed she'd own such a suit.

"Really?" asked Imogene. "I just got off the phone with

Kathleen Young. She wants me to write a nasty story about your daddy."

A splash of leopard print caught Thelma's eye, and she looked up to spy Francella DiGruppo striding through the lobby in a trench coat, scarf, and shades. Outside, she made a beeline for John Lee's. *Is she replacing my note? Or leaving a different one?*

It hardly mattered now. Thelma was going in a new direction.

Grinning, she waved her hand. "Oh, forget that petty gossip. If I play this right, I'll have something much better for you."

THIRTY-ONE

CLOTHES HORSE, Wednesday

KATHLEEN WAS LYING IN WAIT, WATCHING THE DOOR, ready to ambush Thelma as soon as she returned to their room. Her barrage would be subtle if relentless. She would kill her with the motherly kindness she knew the girl craved. How dare that girl leave her to get herself out of jail?

By the time Thelma waltzed into the room however, Kathleen had dozed off. The first thing she saw on waking was the girl's wretched haircut, which threw her off balance. A pang of resentment shot through her—this girl's boldness, her youth, her freedom to reinvent herself. "Took you long enough," she carped as Miss Miles finally entered.

Kicking off her shoes, Thelma smiled brightly. "Oh, it was my pleasure, Mrs. Young. You're welcome!"

Kathleen sat upright. Was that sarcasm? "Welcome? For what? Getting myself out of jail? What have you been doing?"

"You think you got yourself out of jail?" Thelma asked as she moved toward the closet. "By calling Imogene Fuchs? That's rich."

How does Thelma know I called Mrs. Fuchs?

Facing the wardrobe as she struggled with her zipper,

Thelma surveyed her choices. For someone who'd moved all her belongings to Florida in a paper bag, the girl had become something of a clothes horse. Why, Kathleen was still wearing the same outfit she'd had on that morning, but by her estimation, this was Thelma's third costume for the day. Out of habit though, she stood to unzip her.

"Stop fidgeting. Where are you off to now?"

Thelma yanked herself away and finished unzipping her dress. "I have rehearsal."

"Rehearsal? You and Lillian? Not much of a show."

"Don't worry about it." Thelma slipped out of her dress and let it pool at her feet. After moving to the bureau, she turned to Kathleen. "Sit. We need to talk."

Stymied by the impertinence, Kathleen couldn't think of a reply other than to return to her seat. Thelma proceeded to explain how she must be feeling. How she must also be eager to leave.

"You should go home. To your husband," she finished. "Back to Carlsbad."

It was all Kathleen could do to refrain from asking if the girl intended to leave her clothes on the floor like that. Where did all this guff come from? The girl was out of her mind if she thought Kathleen was going to hand over control of this operation. She and her Button had worked so hard to build Sun City. She would thwart that man if she had to do it herself.

Again, she thought. She'd already stolen something precious from him, he just didn't know it. No matter. It wasn't enough. Not if her family was in danger. She'd eliminate all his children to protect her own.

The girl mistook her silence. "You don't have to thank me. I—"

"Thank you? Are you out of your mind? I'm not going anywhere."

Thelma scowled and was about to speak but instead returned to her reflection. "Well, Peggy's on her way."

Kathleen's blood ran cold. "You left Mr. Young on his own?"

"Of course not, Mrs. Young," said Thelma, looking at Kathleen in the mirror. "Lillian hired a nurse that Peggy should be meeting... Well, now. She should've arrived about an hour ago."

"Young lady, what is your plan here? You're going to dig up some financial misdeeds and turn that over to whom, exactly?"

Now it was Thelma's turn to be silent.

Is she weighing her options? Kathleen wondered. This was not going to plan.

"My dear," she began, attempting the maternal approach that had worked well in the past. "I'm here to help you. But also, to do the right thing. I'm not leaving you when you need me."

* * *

Do the right thing? Thelma doubted Mrs. Young even knew what that was. Not that it made a difference, there was no harm in telling her. She couldn't use the information.

"Look, Mrs. Young, nothing has gone quite how we'd hoped since we arrived in Las Vegas. But you should know the only reason you're out of jail is because I shamed Sal Giancarlo into releasing you."

Mrs. Young clenched her arms across her body but appeared to be listening.

Turning to face her fully, Thelma continued. "The problem is, I don't think there's a law you can break in this town. Maybe Agent Nelson figured that out. I have no idea. But I don't trust Francella. Or Wade Davis. There's something off about the both of them."

"I'll give you Francella. But Wade Davis? He runs the Chamber, for Pete's sake."

"Exactly! He represents business interests, and that's all he sees in these gangsters. Big business. You're the one who told me the highest bidder wins. Wade might not be our enemy, but he's not our bedfellow either."

Mrs. Young sat back and lifted her chin, inhaling sharply through her nose, apparently speechless.

"There's nothing we can use in Sal's numbers. Graft is just the cost of doing business in this town. I have to find dirt some-place else. I have to find the Dice Girls."

"The Dice Girls?" Mrs. Young stood and walked toward the window, gazing at the landscape she claimed to despise. When she turned back she sounded perfectly calm. "You mean the dancing troupe we rolled over to secure a spot at the Rodeo Room?

"The same."

"Hmm," Mrs. Young widened her eyes.

Thelma turned back to the vanity and fluffed her locks with her fingers.

"But why do you think they'd know anything about Sal?"

Thelma dropped her hands and looked at Mrs. Young. She'd never told anyone—not her mother, not George—about the tingling in her palms, her hunches. She wasn't about to now. "You just have to trust me. I have very good reason to believe they do."

Returning to her chair, Mrs. Young propped up her legs and smoothed her brow. "And what if I don't?"

"Now you put it that way," Thelma tried not to sound too eager, "this is all very different from where we started. You may as well just go back home and—"

"Hold on." Mrs. Young held out her palm. "Much as I'd love to finish unpacking, you're forgetting one thing."

"Oh?"

"Everyone knows you're Sal's daughter now. No one's going to tell you anything about Sal."

Thelma's impulse was to contradict her straight away, but sure as she knew the Dice Girls had the information she needed, she knew Mrs. Young was right.

"Besides, you can't drive. How long before Sal hears that some driver is taking you to visit women all around town?"

Another excellent point. Thelma sighed. "Well then, get up. We've got to meet Wade at rehearsal, and I want to beat him there."

"You are going to pick up your clothes before we leave though. Right?"

Doing her best impersonation of Mrs. Young, Thelma kept her face implacable. "Oh my gosh, Mrs. Young. Of course." Without rising from her seat, she reached for the hem of the dress she'd left on the floor. "But you just reminded me," she said as she rose to hang her garment. "You're going to have to get another room when Peggy gets here."

Mrs. Young said nothing, but she did start to change. The clock, Thelma saw, was back on the nightstand.

THIRTY-TWO

REHEARSAL, Wednesday

WADE DAVIS WAS SETTLED INTO HIS REGULAR SEAT AT THE Rodeo Room, knees wide, thumbs hooked into his belt loops, trademark toothpick rolling between his teeth, like a man without a care in the world. In truth, he was bored out of his skull. The girls onstage had on far too many clothes for his liking, and he did not enjoy waiting on Sal's daughter.

Not that he had much choice. Keeping an eye on Sal Giancarlo was part of the job, and Wade was lucky to have it. Before marrying Betty, the best he could do was get a job as a mucker on the Hoover Dam. She'd introduced him to Meyer Lansky, who Wade introduced to the Teamsters. Now here he was, babysitting Giancarlo's daughter because his cousin Frankie did something stupid again. He didn't know why his boss wanted to keep tabs on her, but it was just fine by Wade.

A flash of leg onstage caught his attention. *Lillian Montgomery?* What the hell was she doing here? According to Betty, she was a movie star, not a showgirl who had to skulk around for breadcrumbs. She was showing the other girls some fancy kick maneuver, which was at least less boring.

"Excuse me, you there! Mr. Davis!"

He turned toward the high-pitched squeal. That old lady again. What was her name?

"Such a pleasure to see you," she said, leaning close like he'd be tempted by her bosom. Once a looker, sure, but the bloom was long off that rose.

"As you can see," she said, "we have everything under control here."

What a phony.

"Oh yeah?" said Wade, spitting the toothpick out of his mouth while remaining firmly planted in his seat. "Who're the girls onstage?"

Thelma appeared, clapping her hands. "Ladies! Come on over!" She patted Wade on the back, urging him up from his seat. "We have someone here who'd like to meet you."

Wade tugged on the kerchief at his collar, the outfit being part of his job. "A real live embodiment of the town," the LA ad man had billed it. He didn't mind the cowboy boots or the ten-gallon hat—and he rather liked his silver belt buckle—but he was having a hard time getting used to the neck gear.

The introductions were a blur, but from their Mexican names, he knew they were all from the Westside—nickel hoppers who could pass as white, trying to get out of the taxi dance halls and into the casino circuit. Where'd Frankie even meet these girls?

But Thelma? She was something else. He didn't usually care for shorn hair on a woman but on her, it was mesmerizing—dangerous in a way he couldn't quite define. It wasn't just her hair, but the confidence in her stance, as if she knew things others didn't. Maybe it was that combined with the rolled up short pants, tight sweater, and string of pearls wrapped multiple times around her neck, with what looked like a necktie belting her waist.

When the starlet started talking plans, Wade tried to bring

his mind back to the conversation. Movie people were good for business and construction supplies. His job was to fluff them, keep them happy till Frankie could get back.

"We're just gonna have to find a way to keep you around, Miss Montgomery," said Wade, smiling widely as he clicked his heels.

"We'll have to see about that," Lillian said, fluttering her eyelids. "Isn't that right, Thelma?"

He thought he caught her giving her friend a wide-eyed, bail-me-out-here look. Such silly girls. They had no clue what they were up against. Lillian was as replaceable as the rest of them. Except Thelma.

"Of course," Thelma agreed, not as enthusiastically as Wade would've preferred.

"All the tourists make this place seem big," he drawled in his practiced *aw, shucks* manner. "But you'll find we're a small town with small-town hospitality."

"And a lot of money to be made," the old lady said. "Exactly the formula that drew Mr. Young to Florida."

"Mrs. Young, really," said Lillian Montgomery.

Kathleen Young, Wade remembered, chuckling. "Now, now. She's absolutely right."

His wife had said that Lillian came from money. No surer sign than an unwillingness to talk about it. But Wade had his own agenda.

"I've gotta hand it to you gals," Wade said. "I was worried when I heard about Frankie—I mean, Francella. But you lot have made hay in a thunderstorm."

Another look passed, this one between Thelma and the old lady. They better not know Frankie was reporting on their every move. She said she'd put eyes and ears everywhere, but she could be a knucklehead. If calling his cousin *Frankie* tipped them off, it was her fault.

"We have experience," Mrs. Young said. "Why, on our Florida Girls Sun City Emporium tour, we pulled up to army depots with no electricity for the stage. No running water. Can you imagine? But we always found a way to put on professional-quality shows. Isn't that right, girls?"

Wade stopped listening. Of course they weren't suspicious. Like everyone else, they were greedy. Didn't want to lose their spot. The older woman was still talking, but Wade rolled right over her.

"So I hope you don't mind," he said. "I've asked her to join us here."

"Her, who?" asked Kathleen Young, as if he hadn't just shut her down.

"Aw shucks. My Betty accuses me of that , where I'm thinking one thing then just start up like we're in the middle of a conversation."

"Good for her," the lady said.

Unnecessary, and, in Wade's opinion, rude all at the same time. "Anyhoo, I meant Miss DiGruppo." Maybe calling her multiple names would be a good cover. "Francella."

"Oh, that's not necessary," Sal's daughter piped up.

"Can't hurt though, can it?" asked Wade with a wink.

"But," said Thelma. "I'm afraid the show is in two days."

Lillian was nodding and Mrs. Young was swiveling her head between the three of them like she was watching table tennis when one of the dancers inserted herself.

"Her face is busted up pretty bad," she said. "What's she gonna do even?"

"That's an excellent point," Kathleen Young said. "I don't think that's a good look on stage."

Wade nodded in agreement, his favorite trick of all. "Fact is, nobody knows this town better than Frankie, so—"

The door burst open.

"Speak of the devil," said Wade.

In walked Francella, sporting sunglasses she didn't remove, though they did nothing to hide her bruises, which—as he'd seen on plenty of ladies—were only going to get worse. Not that it mattered. The audience would be three sheets to the wind.

"You know what? You're right. Thank you, Wade." Thelma broke away to greet her father's girlfriend by wrapping her in an embrace.

He would never understand women. Betty said as much. Sal was never going to marry Frankie, but she could still have his child one day. Then where would Thelma be? There was something special about her, but she was just a girl after all.

After a moment of confused silence among the girls, one of them asked, "So, Lillian, where do you want us?"

"I'll sit here with Mr. Davis," said Mrs. Young. "Let you know how things look from the audience's perspective."

"Wonderful idea," said Thelma. "You can tell him all about our plans."

Wade glanced at Mrs. Young. Her aghast look brought a smile to his face—she was stumped. Was he smelling a rat?

"When we talked about Wade being here?" Thelma continued, eyes widening. "You wanted to talk uniforms for area businesses?"

Just as he thought. They were in it for the money grab. "Much as I'd love to stay," he reached for the car keys he'd left on the table, "I've got to head out now."

Addressing the room as he left, Wade pointed finger pistols toward the stage. "Looking good, ladies."

"Come on, everyone," Thelma said as he turned his back. "We've only got this place till six, and dress rehearsal is tomorrow, then we're on. Chop-chop!"

It made no difference if the show bombed. He'd done his part keeping them occupied.

THIRTY-THREE

INTERNAL MEMORANDUM

June 7, 1945

TOP SECRET

FROM: William S. Donovan

TO: Agent T. Nelson

It's my understanding that concerted efforts to dismantle our organization so it may be severed and absorbed into separate agencies continue apace. Therefore, I am called upon to seek your return to Washington, D.C., effective immediately.

Report your acknowledgement of this directive posthaste.

THIRTY-FOUR

THE MAYHEM, Thursday

KATHLEEN WATCHED THE FLASH OF LEGS AND SEQUINS from her seat, almost feeling like her old self. Almost.

After last night's rehearsal, they'd all gone out to dinner, where Kathleen had given the girls nicknames to help her tell them apart. There was Gloria Long Legs, their ringleader and by far the strongest dancer. Ana was almost as tall as Thelma and the exact opposite in her reserved demeanor. Kathleen dubbed her Aloof Ana. Curvy and compliant, Smiley DeeDee was easy to remember, as was Salty Mari, always the first to say something off-color.

At lunch, however, the situation took a turn.

Kathleen and Thelma both agreed there was something fishy about the hovering waiters, they were watching too closely. So they chose a diner out near the Starburst to meet up, where Peggy joined them straight from her drive into town. Mercifully, Lillian had the decency to host Peggy in her deluxe suite, which meant that Kathleen didn't have to find or foot the bill for another room. But as they planned an elaborate ruse to introduce Peggy—Sun City's former café manager—as a makeup artist, they spoke over Kathleen like she wasn't there.

Was this what her mother had warned her about? "You'll see, pretty girl. One day, it will be like you're not even there." Kathleen was not prepared for this invisibility, not yet. She touched her stomach briefly—she was about to become a new mother, as sure a sign of youth as any.

A squeal from onstage pulled her attention away from these morose thoughts. Near as Kathleen could tell, the girls had bumped into each other, and everyone but Gloria had landed on their hind quarters.

Forcing her attention back to the stage, Kathleen tried to focus. This performance was nothing like what they'd created for the Florida Girls. More Folies Bergère than war bond show. She had to hand it to Lillian's shop girl, though—her costumes were clever. The girls began in flared skirts that opened when they spun to look like roulette wheels. Underneath that, they wore sequined shorts paired with bolero jackets. For the finale, the girls had enormous ostrich feather fans that, held strategically, gave the impression there was nothing underneath. Once discarded they revealed another, even skimpier shorts ensemble —sans coats—capped off by tiny top hats festooned with aces of every suit. And the seamstress had done it in less than forty-eight hours. If Kathleen did manage to secure any contracts from this arrangement, she'd have to see about hiring her.

The thought pierced Kathleen's heart. She missed the friend she'd had in Maeve O'Reilly, though they hadn't spoken since Florida, when her longtime dressmaker declared they'd never been friends. Now that Maeve had snitched that Matteo was the father of her baby, there was no repairing that rift. She hoped her modiste had only told Peggy and Thelma. That the rest of the Florida Girls were in the dark. They were from St. Petersburg's best families.

But Kathleen didn't want to think about any of that just now. Or ever again, really.

"Gloria!" she called, recognizing that—other than the costumes, which Lillian had overseen—Miss Martinez was the real workhorse behind assembling the team and choreographing the dance numbers. "It's looking blurry from here. What would you think about keeping Maeve in the center, standing still with her arms like so," she stood to demonstrate holding her arms like a flamenco dancer, "while the rest swirl about her?"

"Maeve?" asked Gloria. "You mean Mari?"

"That's what I said," she insisted, though she knew darn well she'd said the wrong name. "Try it, let me see.

"Better. But what if we try Thelma in the center?" That was who she'd meant in the first place. Though she doubted the clientèle would mind if the dances were ragtag, it was always best to hide that girl's graceless high kicks.

She'd barely returned to her seat before the creak of the Rodeo Room's hotel-side door declared Peggy Holmes's arrival. The music had not yet resumed so, as they'd discussed, Kathleen announced her.

Rapping on the table with the heavy glass ashtray at its center, Kathleen made sure to get everyone's attention. "Lillian! I believe your hair and makeup girl has arrived."

Kathleen stood to greet Peggy. Pretending this was their first meeting was surprisingly easy considering she'd known the girl for more than a decade. The young woman before her, with her milky skin and platinum blond bob, was a far cry from the scrawny, pimply pre-teen who'd come to Sun City Emporium, begging for money. Kathleen knew the girl should've been in school, but the Depression was on and times were lean. She'd sensed an intelligence behind her dark eyes—not book smart. Peggy had the common touch. The best thing she could do for the child and her family was to hire her on the spot. So she had.

Kathleen extended her hand. "Hello, Penny. I'm Mrs. Kathleen Young. Pleasure."

Calling her Penny was Kathleen's added twist, to throw suspicion. As if anyone would've thought the two had reason to be acquainted.

"Margaret Holmes," she said, reaching for Kathleen's palm with an unladylike grip. "You can call me Peggy. That's *p-e-g-g-y*."

Lillian rushed forward to hug Peggy and make introductions all around. "I always ask for Peggy Holmes on set. Whenever she's available, that is." She looked admiringly at Peggy. "She studied at Westmore's under Montague Westmore himself, and I've hired her to do all our makeup opening weekend!"

When no one in the crowd took the bait, Thelma piped up. "Monte Westmore! Wasn't he Vivien Leigh's exclusive makeup man on Gone With the Wind? And you brought her here for us? For free? Why, thank you so much, Lillian. That's so generous."

Monte had been Thelma's idea, for his renown and because he'd been dead almost since that film came out, though, apparently, she was the only one reading the Hollywood rags. Fortunately, the fresh bait took.

Crowding around, the girls all spoke at once.

Then Peggy made her move. "Hola, debes ser Gloria!"

"You speak Spanish?" Gloria asked, perhaps too awestruck to reply in her native language.

"¡Sí!" Peggy launched into a back-and-forth that Kathleen could not follow.

This had been part of the plan they'd concocted over lunch. It made perfect sense. No one in town knew Peggy Holmes, and somehow, the girl could speak Spanish.

Peggy was supposed to tell Gloria, in Spanish, that she was thinking about moving to Las Vegas, but first she wanted to see if there was sufficient work. All this had to be on the hush-hush, she'd say, so she wouldn't lose work in LA.

Kathleen had to hand it to those girls—she could not have come up with this plan. She hoped Peggy would remember all the details, especially the part that called for her to join their little outing. Though she wasn't entirely sure why Thelma had agreed to her participation so enthusiastically, no matter what that girl thought, Kathleen was determined to put Sal behind bars. Not that she was opposed to drumming up some business while she was at it.

Dammit. *I bit another nail to the quick,* she thought as she pressed her middle finger between her thumb and third while watching Peggy embrace Gloria. *Seems overmuch.*

Or perhaps she was trying to tell her something. Should they have worked out some hand signals in advance of their night out?

Gloria said something that Peggy responded to with her infernal cackle. She'd spoken to the girl about that laugh at Sun City, disturbed guests in every department. *That was time wasted.*

"We can't just speak in Spanish." Peggy bent toward Gloria, all the while speaking loudly enough to be heard. "We'll meet up later."

"Right-o, Peggy," Lillian enthused. "They want us to clear out of here by six anyway. Why don't we try out a few looks now? That way, we can run a few numbers in our hair and makeup."

"Wonderful idea," Kathleen said, but she was mostly thinking about the fact that she wanted to get this whole affair over with and get back to her Lloyd. He'd managed a few words on the phone the previous night, and finally, she'd allowed herself to think of a shared future in California. It was not a future that included hoodlums.

* * *

Watching Peggy in action, Thelma breathed a sigh of relief. That girl could get on with a brick wall. Her job now was to peel Francella away from the herd for the evening. If Thelma failed, it would be up to Mrs. Young to keep her father's girlfriend occupied and away from Peggy's conversations. Not an alternative Thelma had confidence in.

While she was waiting her turn for makeup, Francella sidled over to Thelma and rested against the wall.

"Still up for Chinese?" she asked.

Chinese? Thelma was stunned. She'd seemed positively repelled by the idea just the day before. Or maybe this was a game.

Crossing her arms, she faced Francella, leaning on the wall to mimic her stance. "You don't want to go out with all the girls?"

"You do?"

Thelma sensed she shouldn't give ground that easily. "Make them come to you," she heard Agent Nelson saying, though he hadn't said anything of the sort during their training. The only person she had new conversations with in her head like that was her mother. Her palms burned and she knew—Agent Nelson must be dead. Should she call off their plan?

"I don't mean anything by that. We're all chums," Francella insisted before looking away. "It's my face."

Thelma didn't buy that—the girl had volunteered to come onstage after all—but it would more than accomplish her goal. Besides, she knew they weren't likely to run into Vegas's connected men at a Chinese restaurant. Whatever fate had befallen Theodore Nelson still awaited. Thelma was in no more —or less—danger than she had been all along. Wasn't that why she was sending Mrs. Young out tonight? She'd seen poor Pegs *wilt* in the face of tough girls in a public restroom. Meanwhile, even pregnant, Mrs. Young had managed a stabbing that landed her in jail. There was no better person to protect Peggy in Thelma's stead.

Smiling, she turned her gaze to Francella. "I have been wanting to try Chinese," she said. "And maybe tonight you'll teach me to drive?"

Francella smirked, "Don't push it."

If you only knew.

THIRTY-FIVE

NIGHT OUT, Thursday

A FINE SWEAT BROKE OUT IN THE SMALL OF KATHLEEN Young's back as she and Peggy followed Gloria toward the green room, where Diamond Horseshoe Saloon & Casino performers readied for their shows. Small wonder, she thought. Between Sal's hooks in her son and the child growing inside her, the stakes were more personal than the usual business deal.

Gloria stopped. "Cool your jets, mija. All right? Most of these girls aren't legal. They might not be willing to talk to you at all."

Kathleen suspected as much, in fact, had been surprised at how easily Peggy talked Gloria into these introductions. But then, how often did these young ladies get free makeovers, let alone from Hollywood talent? So what if, this time last year, Kathleen had just promoted the girl to be the manager of Sun City Emporium's café? The idea was that Peggy, being Peggy, would put the girls at ease and get them talking about their boyfriends. Find out about their lives. Kathleen would cover the expenses. It would be cheap enough, especially if she made good contacts for a garment contract or, better yet, secured an outfitting *deal*.

Ana, Mari, and DeeDee had gladly jumped into the car when Peggy assured Gloria that "the old lady will foot the bill," a pronouncement that irked Kathleen to no end, clever as the idea might have been. She'd have to talk to Agent Nelson about reimbursement, though, considering that food and drink were on the house, it was a bargain. She'd given them each a crisp five-dollar bill and they'd disappeared into the main lounge.

As Gloria spoke, Kathleen took in the cramped, if surprisingly well-lit, space. Boas and hats hung between full-length mirrors. A row of women sat peering into the looking glass that lined the wall, facing light bulbs in wire cages. It could've passed for an interrogation room but for the phalanx of cosmetics they were applying. These women were at once more glamorous than Sun City's Florida Girls had been, yet also rougher around the edges.

"Todo tuyo," said Gloria, tapping Peggy on the shoulder before she looked at Kathleen. "I'll let the manager know you're here."

A broad-shouldered young woman with chipped teeth came forward first, standing to hoist her peep-toe heel onto the chair she'd just vacated.

"Gloria says you do makeup?" she said as she rolled up her stocking. Stopping mid calf, she looked around. She shrugged. "We have makeup."

That pronouncement was all it took to stir Kathleen into action. How many times had she faced something similar in the early days with Lloyd when they traveled the country shilling his cures?

"Not like this," she said, tapping the small valise in Peggy's hand. Lillian had loaned it to her, and then they'd all contributed to the case, stuffing it to the brim with powders and brushes and tubes of lipstick.

"She's a whiz with hair too. Studied at Westmore's with Mr.

Montague Westmore himself. The only makeup man trusted by Rita Hayworth."

Peggy's head jerked toward Kathleen.

"Don't be modest, dear. Here." Kathleen looked at the woman who'd just snapped her hose into place, tapping the top rail of the chair which still held her foot. "Have a seat and let her show you. This is entirely complimentary. And nobody's fast as Peggy."

Patting Kathleen on the shoulder—was that a shove?—before moving front and center, Peggy spoke.

"No le prestes atención," she said, earning a grin from Chipped-Tooth. "Haré lo mejor que pueda, pero si no te gusta, puedo volver a cambiarlo."

Ignoring whatever barb had just been launched, Kathleen pulled up another chair and watched, feigning a deep fascination as Peggy began smoothing out foundation lines on jaws, softening colors that were too harsh, and tightening up hair rolls. She even repaired a nail polish job on one of the girls, chatting amiably in that blasted incomprehensible tongue all the while.

What was really on her mind was Lloyd. Earlier that night she'd only had a minute to speak with him, his new nurse practically hung up on her. "He needs to rest," she'd barked. At least he was being looked after.

Kathleen had just given up on the stage manager turning up —which she'd thought highly inappropriate anyway, a man backstage with ladies all in various states of undress?—when in walked a fellow with rheumy eyes and an unfortunate underbite If he weren't *in* the dressing room, Kathleen imagined his eye might've been pressed against a hole he'd drilled in its wall.

"Mrs. Young?" He approached, hand outstretched. "Gloria tells me you might to have a line on uniforms. I'm Zekeriah Ostrander. Pleased to meet you."

Though Kathleen couldn't fault his manners, Zekeriah's

palm felt so soft and fleshy, so cool and clammy to the touch, it was an effort not to withdraw her own in revulsion.

"Charmed, Mr. Ostrander." This was not an occasion for French.

Before she could begin her pitch, however, one of the girls turned up the radio.

...Advanced level of decomposition had made the body difficult to identify, but sources today have confirmed the identity of the man found on the Nevada border as Theodore Nelson, a government employee agent in town working for the war effort. It's believed that Mr. Nelson's death was accidental, though sources—

"Turn that off," barked Mr. Ostrander, startling Kathleen, who'd been listening intently.

"Why don't you and I go somewhere's more comfortable to talk, eh?" And with that, Mr. Ostrander grabbed Kathleen's elbow and steered her out the back door.

* * *

A SPICY FOG OF GARLIC AND GINGER ENVELOPED THELMA and Francella, teasing them as they stared at their plates. The waiter stood over them, grinning madly as he balanced two slim reeds between his thumb and first two fingers, clicking their ends together. The pair rolled uselessly in Thelma's hand, but Francella took hers and—as the waiter had shown—lifted a stalk of broccoli from her plate. She was either a quick study or an accomplished liar. "Watch. She could be both," Vivian Miles whispered in her head.

"May I have a knife and fork please?" said Thelma.

"Oh, thank Christ," Francella said under her breath to Thelma before smiling brightly at their server. "Me too. Please."

Definitely both.

Francella cupped her hand over Thelma's. "Listen, I wanted to thank you."

Flinching, Thelma tried to cover by shifting in her seat and snatching her hand toward her heart. "Why, whatever for?"

The waiter interrupted with their silverware, and Thelma, her appetite stirred by the new sites and smells, tucked in.

"Oh," she said, her mouth half-full. "It's delicious."

Francella poked at hers, lifting a slice of beef to her mouth, and chewing slowly. "Bit salty, though, no?"

Forcing herself to lay down her cutlery, Thelma turned to her companion. "I should be thanking you. You don't care for Chinese food, do you?"

"I'm not here for the food," she said, dropping her fork with a clank. "We're only at this place because nobody who's anybody ever comes here. So let's cut the baloney."

A knot formed in Thelma's gut. Maybe Francella really had intercepted her note for Agent Nelson.

"I know you brought in that makeup artist for me, and I appreciate it. But I wish you wouldn't keep—" Francella waved her hand in front of her face. "Drawing attention to this."

As she let out a loud sigh, Thelma chided herself for being so jittery and resumed eating. "Don't be ridiculous," she said through a mouthful of rice.

"From what I hear, no one wanted me on the team because of it."

"Come on, Francella. Where'd you hear that?" Thelma paused, aware she was stringing her along too obviously. "Does that surprise you?"

Francella merely cocked her head.

"Look, Lillian brought in Miss Holmes to do her makeup. I guess she's self-conscious about her wealth? Didn't want to stand out."

Leaning closer, Francella looked around the restaurant

before speaking in a low voice. "It's more than just a job for me, you know."

What is she on about? Thelma's pulse quickened. She longed to come out and just ask who Sal's competition was and where could she find them, please—George's face flashed in her mind, fueling her determination—but she wasn't about to tip her hand to Francella.

Forcing her face to go blank, she put down her fork. "What do you mean, more than a job?"

"Sal loves me," she said.

"I never said he didn't," said Thelma, sucking in her cheeks. *They always love you in the beginning, honey.*

"He didn't mean it when he—" Francella sat back and removed her shades.

Thelma startled.

Her nose was swollen, but that was nothing compared to the scratch on Francella's brow and the eggplant-tinged lines beneath her eyes. Either she'd wiped away her makeup or the color was so dark it had seeped through.

"They never mean it," Thelma said, fingering the crescent-shaped scar on her cheekbone. "Same thing he said about this."

"Sal gave you that scar? When? Didn't you two just meet?" Francella picked up her fork. "I never even noticed that before now."

A surge of anger pushed on Thelma's chest, hot as the first time Sal had struck her. How dare Francella make light of her pain? She narrowed her eyes, considering her next words, a tactic she was finding increasingly useful—and hauntingly familiar, like she was channeling her father's calculated coolness.

"Look, all I'm saying is you should be careful. My mother was once in your shoes, and it didn't turn out well for her."

Francella went rigid. Thelma had hit her mark. Or so she thought.

Pushing back her chair, Francella hooked one leg atop the other and faced Thelma. "Sweetheart, I don't think you understand what game you're playing."

"Then enlighten me."

Francella replaced her sunglasses. "I know you're here to try and turn Sal in, but you won't catch him doing anything. He's not bringing that Chicagoland business here."

Sweat broke out on Thelma's brow. Francella was right—she didn't know this game. Not that she was going to let on. "Oh yeah? Are you sure about that?"

THIRTY-SIX

STARS IN THEIR EYES, Thursday

"WHERE ARE WE GOING, MR. OSTRANDER?" KATHLEEN asked, trying to keep her voice calm, though the question revealed she was on edge. They were alone, in the dark. She heard the gravel crunching underfoot as Ostrander shuffled her through the parking lot toward, she presumed, the back of a stranger's car.

Ostrander gave her elbow a squeeze. "I like 'em feisty."

Before Kathleen had recovered from the shock of his words, he'd steered her around to the front of the building and guided her past the hat girl into a small office. A swell of orchestral music burst forth, followed by a surge of hoots and catcalls. Ostrander shut the door, dimming the sound considerably. No one would hear her scream.

"Have a seat." He walked around the desk and indicated the chair opposite.

Catching her breath, Kathleen regarded the battered green filing cabinets and mismatched office furnishings strewn about. She felt unhinged. Maybe he did want to talk business? Ostrander hardly seemed like a man with power to burn, especially not with an office in this shape, fronting a money-printing facility like a casino.

She didn't sit. As her heart rate returned to normal, she remembered the radio report—Agent Nelson, dead. How?

"Thank you, Mr. Ostrander, but I'm afraid I can't stay. Miss Holmes, you see, ah, we've got a number of stops planned—"

"I'll make this brief, then. Gloria says you can help me out."

Good Lord. "Why, I'd be delighted to correspond with your, ah, decision-maker. Do you have his business card or—"

"Decision-maker? You mean like the owner?" Ostrander's eyes darkened. "That enough decision-making for ya?"

Ostrander was the owner? Kathleen had but one move now. "Oh goodness, sir, pardon me. I don't know anything about anything, really."

Kathleen moved toward the end of his desk and sat on it, crossing her legs and hoping like hell she could salvage this gaffe. "I'm here because, well, my husband is ill."

"Sick, is he? Hmm."

Kathleen brushed her brow with the back of her fingertips, relaxing into the role of damsel in distress. "Oh it's just temporary, his illness. But also, you see, tonight I'm supposed to be helping Miss Holmes. I'm just not prepared at all." She fluttered her hands for emphasis.

Ostrander grunted again.

"Mr. Young is much better at this than I am. But I do know one thing. Sun City Emporium can match any price. As my Lloyd likes to say, we work on the same principle as Ford, satisfied with lower margins and quantity sales."

"I don't know about all that," Ostrander said. "All's I need is costumes. You're friends with that movie star in town, right?"

* * *

"SIR?" FRANCELLA RAISED HER HAND IN THE AIR, CAUSING a jacketed waiter to appear almost immediately. "Bring us two Pink Ladies."

Once he was dispatched, she continued. "Thelma, you've been under surveillance since you stepped foot in this town."

Thelma smirked. "Sal did announce my arrival to the media."

"No. Before that. From when you showed up at the gas station."

Thelma shook her head. "I don't know what you're talking about."

"Please, Thelma, we've agreed to be frank here." Francella paused to stuff a cigarette into a black lacquered holder she'd produced from her pocketbook.

Thelma reached reflexively for the lighter on the table and watched as Francella took a long drag, then exhaled. "This is a small town."

"Well, yes, of course."

"No, I mean, a lot of us are related. Wade and I? We're cousins."

Thelma didn't know where she was going with this. "What's that supposed to mean?"

"His mother is my mother's sister."

"Yes I know what cousins are, but—"

"Our other cousin, Slim. Traveling salesman. Sold your friend the sunglasses that almost killed Sal's man. He told us you were here and I told Sal."

Something in the way Francella described the chain of events caused Thelma to believe Sal wasn't fully aware of these relationships.

"So? I wasn't even there," Thelma said.

"Sure, you were. Dying your hair."

Thelma fiddled with her earlobe.

"The woman who owns the Starburst is my grandma. How do you think your father picked you out at that presser right away?" Francella asked.

Her words pierced Thelma. In some small corner of her heart, yet unbeknownst to her, she'd been harboring a belief that she and her father shared a connection—one that cut through the violence, the money, the greed—and that was how he'd recognized her. A mirage.

"Gamma also told me you met with the G-man at her hotel."

Thelma's heart skipped a beat, and a cold chill snaked its way from the base of her skull to her belly. Her palms tingled. She had no defense ready and suddenly she felt like she wasn't speaking but, rather, watching someone else do the talking for her.

"Since we're not playing coy here, Francella, aren't you working for the Man?"

The light reflection moved across Francella's sunglasses as she slowly turned her head. "Are you joking?"

She was going to have to force the issue. "I saw you pick up my note at the laundromat."

"What? The letter Wade asked me to pick up?" Francella leaned toward Thelma. "Are you following me?"

Unaccustomed as she was to following her inner guidance, Thelma felt the jolt of energy leave her. She said nothing.

"You don't get it, do you?" Francella continued.

Get what? Thelma wanted to yell, but she was trying to make her target more agreeable. "You're right, I don't."

"These other guys in town? I'm too much for 'em. I got ambitions too, though."

Somehow, Thelma had backed into the opening she'd been waiting for. "You're very talented."

A faraway look crossed Francella's face.

"That wouldn't scare my father," Thelma continued.

"I know." Francella's lip quivered.

Dammit. She'd gone too far. Sad Frankie wasn't going to get Thelma anywhere. She'd seen this plenty of times in her gentlemen callers. Thwarted ambition turned to anger. Meant she had to take care of them just so, or she was as likely to get punched as paid.

"Hush, sweetheart. Everything's going to turn out fine— you'll see," Thelma said, squeezing her dining companion's shoulder. "Let me help you."

Sagging beneath Thelma's fingers, Francella sighed. "You can't help this."

"Because of the other guys? What guys?"

Francella squinted at Thelma. "You know what guys. Your father isn't the only person trying to build a casino in Las Vegas."

Thelma had to make an effort not to squeal. "I know Mr. Siegel is building something." Her father had said as much at the press conference.

"Everybody knows that—he's a master at the publicity game. Gets that good-for-nothing Virginia Hill into the paper every week."

"I'll say. How does he do it? Are they ever even in town?"

"I thought things would be different when Sal agreed to that publicist," Francella said, looking dangerously glassy-eyed. "He didn't even introduce me at the groundbreaking." She gave Thelma a cold, hard stare.

So that was the play? Francella had used Sal to elevate her status, and in turn, Wade used her ambition to make her a pawn. What had she meant about the *Chicagoland* business?

"Your cocktails?" asked the waiter, who'd returned with a tray carrying two gleaming martini glasses, each topped with a frothy white layer and garnished with a candied cherry.

Desire surged in Thelma's veins. Since George had gone

missing, she'd stopped caring if she ended up like her mother. It wouldn't be a bad way to go. But as she reached for her glass, her mother chimed in. "You'll never catch Sal if you're soused all the time."

In that brief pause, Thelma realized she didn't need Francella. The information had been under her nose all along—the newspapers. All she needed was a library.

"Francella, you're not trapped," she said before tasting her drink. She'd never had a Pink Lady. Never heard of one. Delicious. "I bet Lillian could introduce you to some people in Hollywood. You are talented."

"Oh yeah? And why would she do that?"

For the second time in as many days, Thelma saw herself clearly. It hadn't been long since she would've felt the same distrust, but she'd learned a lot from the Florida Girls.

"Oh, Francella. You can always find men to lick your ass, but women will save it."

* * *

Kathleen had to knock on the back door several times to be heard over the raucous crowd.

"Where ya been?" Peggy demanded on opening the door.

"There's a fine how do you do," Kathleen said, scowling, even as relief washed over her that Peggy was still in one piece and she just might have a new line on business after all. "Now get your stuff and let's get out of here."

"We have to get the other girls," said Peggy as Kathleen marched past, eager to grab her purse and escape the hellhole that was the Silver Spurs.

She stopped mid-reach. "Do we?"

"Mrs. Young! You know we do."

"Fine," Kathleen said, snatching up her clutch and knowing

full well there was no way she was going back inside that building. "We still have to exit through this dressing room or we'll disrupt the show. You go inside and get the girls. I'll warm up the car."

Before she turned away, Kathleen clutched Peggy's forearm. "Did they say anything more? About the report on the radio." She whispered, "The dead man."

"That's why we have to keep going, Mrs. Young. Wait til you hear what I found out," said Peggy, before marching back into the club.

What people won't do with a little power, Kathleen observed.

THIRTY-SEVEN

THE CONSPIRATORS, Thursday

THELMA STOOD OUTSIDE LILLIAN'S DOOR, FEELING SELF-conscious. After that dinner with Francella, she knew without question that she was being watched. But it was early enough, and since Mrs. Young hadn't returned to their room, it was reasonable enough to stop by her teammate's room the night before their debut.

This part of the hotel is usually quiet, she thought. Then remembered how she'd come by that knowledge last spring, when she helped Mrs. Young clean out her room after the Diego Gonzalez incident. Maybe Carlos suspected she knew what happened to his brother? He'd sure sounded sore about something.

As if to clear her thoughts, she knocked resolutely.

"There you are!" her cousin-in-law squealed as she opened the door and drew Thelma into the room. "Tell me everything."

This was the first time they'd been alone since attempting to spring Mrs. Young from jail. Just yesterday? So much had changed since then, she hardly knew where to begin. A warning about Francella? Wade? Her fear about Agent Nelson? Or the way Sal Giancarlo was being kept out of the loop? But no. The latter, at least, was the one risk she had to face on her own.

"I talked to your uncle," Thelma began.

Lillian guided her to the sitting room that faced the pool. "Have a drink."

Thelma rolled her neck as she took a seat in a club chair. "I need a coffee."

"Fresh out. But..." Lillian walked to the bureau for her handbag. "I think you should try this. You seem a bit *twitchy*. These blues will mellow you right out."

Thelma kicked off her shoes and hugged her knees. "God no, especially not those."

"Okay," said Lillian, perching on the desk to face her friend. "But you look a fright."

As if looks mattered for what Thelma had in mind.

"So," Lillian slid her pill case back into her bag, "what did dear old Uncle Homer have to say?"

"It's what he didn't say, Lills. I finally understand why he hasn't called off the search for George. He wants me to agree to the annulment before my husband is declared dead. I guess so I won't have any legal rights as his widow? Whatever that means. All I know is, fighting won't bring him back. I'm not going to contest the annulment. I'll—"

"Thelma Miles Wright, you take that back this instant!"

Her mouth gaped. "What? I thought—"

"You thought nothing." Lillian dropped her clutch and pulled an armchair up to face her cousin-in-law, taking her by the hands. "Don't be a fool. Of course that money won't bring George back, but it will change your life."

Dumbfounded, Thelma pulled away from Lillian and rested her chin on the rough wool of her slacks. "Don't you want them to call off the search so we can honor his memory?"

"I do, yes. But, sugar, that's a lot of money."

Thelma sat a moment, unable to make sense of Lillian's words. The only reason she hadn't agreed to this annulment already was so the crooks in Las Vegas wouldn't know she was broke.

"You, of all people, should know that I didn't marry George for his money. Besides, you told me George wasn't getting any money. After you and I had that conversation, I was surprised to find out he even had a wedding trust. A lot more money than I've ever seen, and good to start the club. But I'm afraid that a lot of that cash went down with him. What is there to fight for?"

Lillian stood, gesticulating as she paced. "No, no, no, Thelma. Death is different. In the case of George's demise, his family would be entitled to his share of the Wright businesses."

"You're saying there's *more?*"

"Yes! It's loads more than his puny wedding inheritance. There's an increase every year, and you'd get it all. You must take it. Why wouldn't you?"

Thelma sat motionless, afraid to confess the truth while also burning to unburden her conscience.

"Sweetheart, you've had it bad enough," Lillian went on. "You've no family. I'm certain George would've wanted you to have the money. And I'd love nothing more than to see you on that Board."

"Don't you see? It's my fault George is dead," she blurted out. "I was supposed to be with him on that plane, but we got a call about a property that was going up for sale. He said we should go look at it. That he'd be right back..." Overcome, Thelma paused, gasping for air to keep from crying.

"So let me get this straight." Lillian curled her legs underneath her hips, resting her cheek on her palm. "You go off with Helen and Doris to look at some real estate for your club, and George goes to get the money you've all agreed you're going to use to help fund said club."

Thelma could only nod, her face too contorted to speak.

"Then his plane goes down, and that's your fault? Thelma, you didn't make him do anything. He loved flying almost as much as—"

"No, you still don't get it." Thelma reached for her pocketbook and extracted a cigarette. "They were after me."

Standing, Lillian put a fist on her hip. "I hate to tell you this, but it's still not your fault. Did you make him fall for you? If I'm remembering correctly, you tried to push him away."

Thelma didn't have an answer for that.

"Just tell me, did you sign anything? You—"

The door flung open and in walked Peggy Holmes. "Chickadees, I'm home," she called out, practically skipping into the inner chamber. "What happened here?" she asked, but her curiosity didn't last. "Whatever it is, it can wait. You won't believe what I found out. Lills, you might wanna sit down for this."

Once Thelma and Lillian were settled on the divan, Peggy told them about her visit to the casino.

"We couldn't have been luckier. As soon as the boss man left with Kathleen, they turned the radio right back on, but they didn't have anything more on Nelson."

Thelma frowned. "I knew he was dead."

Peggy and Lillian both turned toward her, disbelief in their eyes.

"I mean, I had a feeling something was really wrong," she clarified.

"Anywhoos, I'm just about to ask what landed that guy in a ditch, when they start talking rapid-fire about how glad they are this G-man's out of the picture, because their men can get back to work. So I ask, 'Hey, not to change the subject but, well, I'm thinking about moving here for work. Isn't there enough work?' And then they say not to worry. This place is gonna pop. So then I ask, 'What's the holdup?' And they tell me there's no construction materials. I mean, of course not. Supplies are still jammed up from the war.

"Then they tell me how, every once in a blue moon, a shipment comes in off a Hollywood lot. They deliver in the morning then come back and steal it at night. Sell it back the next morning. Tiles, piping, copper, steel, fixtures. You name it." Peggy made a circle with her index finger. "Same stuff just keeps going around." She leaned against the bureau, wiggling her half-moon brows and giving a wide, gap-toothed grin. "Pretty good dirt, huh?"

"I'll say," Lillian said, in genuine awe.

Skipping ahead several steps, Thelma almost surprised herself. "We need Mrs. Young. Just for the next two hours or so, but we can't let her know or she'll be a real demon."

"You sure we'll be able to tell?" asked Peggy, and a wave of mirth overtook them.

* * *

THE SMELL OF FISH AND PUNGENT SPICES ASSAULTED Kathleen as she entered the Pearl Dragon. Taking in the paper placemats and metal chairs, she made a silent vow not to use the restroom. She looked at her watch, nine o'clock precisely. The exact time she and Peggy had specified. Thelma better have refrained from getting herself kidnapped again. No sooner had she seated herself than a waiter rushed over and muttered something incomprehensible.

"I'll have lobster bisque and a cheese sandwich." She could barely understand his reply. Not that she failed to smile and nod. Heaven forfend they spit in her soup, something she herself might have done a time or two when pressed into service at Sun City's lunch counter.

Pointing at the mug-shaped ceramic on her table she said, "Coffee?" She picked up the cup. *No handle?*

The girls arrived before her food, walking arm in arm like college chums. A spike of envy flared in Kathleen's chest. She'd been a girl when she and Lloyd had married, younger than any of them. She'd gotten the man of her dreams, but she'd missed out on those golden carefree years. Out from under the shackles of the DeVane household. No obligations holding her down. Save for society's expectations of what she could become as a Richmond debutante.

These girls looked like a bunch of ragamuffins. Thelma with that mannish hair. Lillian sporting trousers she'd clearly borrowed, she absolutely swam in them. And Peggy in peep-toe platforms with dungarees.

"What on earth are you all dressed for?" Kathleen asked. "Or were the mirrors removed from your room?"

"I said to put on pants, Mrs. Young," Thelma said, her eyes aglow. "Tonight, we're going to do some exploring."

She looks touched, thought Kathleen. Though for once she hadn't felt the need to change clothes. Weirdly, her wide-legged-trouser look managed to be stylish. Certainly compared to the other outfits in the group.

"Exploring? It's eleven o'clock at night."

"It's now or never, Mrs. Young," said Peggy. "I already told these two—Sal's men are skimming off the construction sites, and we're gonna catch 'em. These yuks got no idea."

Kathleen knit her brow. Perhaps her sons did a better job articulating their thoughts than she gave them credit for. She had no idea what Peggy was talking about.

"Stealing, Mrs. Young," Lillian said, putting her perfectly manicured hand over Kathleen's thoroughly destroyed cuticles. "Peggy found out that Sal's men are stealing building materials, keeping some—it's still difficult to come by wood and metal—

and then selling it back the very next day. The supplies they just purchased!"

The restaurant's ambient sounds dimmed. All Kathleen could hear was her heart beating in her chest. She knew Sal had his hooks in the unions. Had he created those cost overruns at the Emporium to keep her family in constant debt? Was that what he was doing to her sons now?

"... will bring him down, Mrs. Young," Thelma was saying. "The other wise guys in town? They'll never let him get away with this."

Kathleen gaped in disbelief as the girls picked up their menus and proceeded to calmly discuss their order. Thelma had just implied that she planned to divulge this information to the other hoodlums in town personally.

"This is what you meant earlier? You intend to—" Kathleen stopped herself before she said Salvatore Giancarlo's name aloud. "You're going to take matters into your own hands and simply abandon Theodore's plan?"

"That's something else you should know," Thelma said. "Our mutual friend is, well, dead. Agent Nelson is dead."

"I am aware. I heard the radio report, same as the rest of you." Kathleen was scrambling for ground.

"So how are we abandoning his plan? Last time I checked, he abandoned us."

"Fine, Thelma. You are correct. Perhaps not his plan, but *the* plan. Our plan."

"What plan? To feed Nelson the intel we found? That went out the window when he left town."

"What makes you think exposing yourself like that is a good idea?"

"You don't have to be cagey, Mrs. Young. Look around. This isn't the Ritz. Wise guys don't come to places like this. That's why we're here," said Thelma. "But to answer your question, yes. We are moving on, just like Agent Nelson would've wanted us to."

Just then, the waiter returned, depositing what looked like a cup of warm urine in front of Kathleen. She sniffed at it.

"It's green tea. You must've ordered it. Try it. You'll love it." Thelma then proceeded to order for Peggy and Lillian.

It was all starting to feel like a dream—one minute cloak-and-dagger, the next, girls on holiday—when in walked Imogene Fuchs, sporting her sturdy orthopedic shoes.

"There she is," said Thelma. "Imogene's going to document everything."

Kathleen knew the girls had thought they were being very crafty when Lillian telephoned Imogene Fuchs and, speaking in French, arranged this rendezvous. But bringing a reporter into this situation? These girls had lost their minds.

As their chatter rose, Kathleen sipped her tea. She did, in fact, like it. Holding the cup in both hands, she let the steam rise to her face. Perhaps there was another way out of this mess. Preferably one that did not involve double-crossing the head of the Tampa mafia while making themselves very visible to the rest of the criminal underworld. Clearly, the Las Vegas police were in cahoots with these crooks, but if she had more time, she could find another resource. She had to stall them.

"Hang on," said Kathleen. "You don't know your way around the inside of a car, let alone a casino that isn't even on a map. How on earth do you propose we investigate?"

"Oh, I do," piped in Imogene. "I've gotten tours of most of the buildings being developed in town. Folks at the Nevada Projects Corporation were only too happy to show me around."

"The *what* corporation?"

"The Nevada Projects Corporation, Mrs. Young. That's the business entity that owns the casinos. These guys don't own anything."

Kathleen suspected that Imogene had been the schoolroom know-it-all and teacher's pet. She'd been the teacher's pet, too, of course, but she'd had the sense to conceal her intelligence.

"May I just remind everyone," Kathleen said. "Our first show is tomorrow night. It's probably best to wait at least until Miss DiGruppo can perform with us so she's not underfoot. And didn't you two just have dinner? What did you find out?"

"Now that *is* an excellent question," said Thelma, widening her eyes. "It turns out, Francella and Wade are related. He pushed her on Sal—my guess is their family is connected—because she is desperate for fame. And I bet we can get her to work for us, too."

"I've got that covered," said Lillian. "I'll make some introductions for her."

"But, you've never even seen her onstage." Kathleen was incredulous.

"Didn't you tell Thelma she was good?"

"Yes, but—"

"But nothing," Peggy interjected. "There are plenty of people without any talent in Hollywood."

"Introductions are just one part of the currency in the movie biz," said Lillian, nodding. "And as for our show, we don't go on till seven."

"You know you don't have to join us, Mrs. Young," Thelma said. "In fact, it might be better if you didn't."

Kathleen paused for the briefest of moments, collecting all her resources to muster sincerity. "My dears, I'm simply trying to keep us all safe." She didn't have to fake the next part. "No one wants to see Sal Giancarlo taken down more than I do."

She couldn't help but notice that Thelma pursed her lips. Right. Though the financial stress that man had created for her family couldn't have helped Lloyd's condition, if Sal had actually murdered her Button... well, she'd have taken him out with her bare hands. So, though her lust for vengeance might indeed have been second to Thelma's, she couldn't take back what she'd said. The horse was out of the gate.

"Alors," said Kathleen. "Allons-y?"

"After we eat," replied Lillian, raising her glass. "Cheers."

"No, dear," said Kathleen. "You don't toast with water."

THIRTY-EIGHT

TO HAVE AND HAVE NOT,
Thursday/Friday

After their meal, as they drove away from the bright lights of Las Vegas, Thelma contemplated the vastness overhead. The sky was like a great dome of midnight blue, sprinkled with pinpricks of light. She'd never felt so fully alive—in the moment, yet utterly apprehensive about events to come.

Then again, she'd never thought much about how she felt before she left Iowa. The Florida Girls tour had been a roller coaster, but since George had disappeared—died, she reminded herself—nothing but flashes of anger and misery had punctuated her emptiness, as if her insides had been scooped out and replaced by nothingness. This realization pushed the anxiety forward just as the car slowed to a stop.

Mrs. Young pulled the door handle, stepping out into the desert. "Gadzooks, it's freezing out here. What happened? This place is maddening."

"Sand doesn't retain heat," said Imogene.

"That hardly explains—"

Thelma cut their bickering off as she slid behind the wheel. "I told you already—"

"I know, I know. I didn't have to come along. I heard you."

Mrs. Young rounded the car and got in on the passenger side. "You're sure they'll be there, Peggy?"

"Yes, ma'am," said Peggy. "You just be sure you find a spot where you can see the guard *and* the road. We'll see Sal's men when we're coming in, but once we're inside we won't see anything."

None of them wanted Mrs. Young on this adventure, but for Thelma's idea to work they needed her at the outset. They couldn't just pull up to Benjamin Siegel's construction site and start snapping pictures. Especially not at night.

"Can we just get started, please?" said Thelma.

"I know we've been over this, but I want to be absolutely certain everything is in order before we head out since, according to Il Duce over here," Mrs. Young pointed her thumb at Thelma, "it's black ops."

"I, for one, prefer Thelma's plan to getting caught," said Lillian.

"Easy for you to say. You and Peggy are driving right up to the place."

"Mrs. Young," said Thelma, while keeping her eyes glued to the road. "The longer you delay, the less time we'll have to make this happen. We have to get in there, get some pictures, and get out *before* the guards change shift. There's no telling when another shipment will come in, and the longer we stay in this town, the more likely we are to get found out."

"Oh relax, Thelma. I don't agree with you, but I'm here, aren't I?" said Mrs. Young. "Driving isn't hard. Just put the gear into neutral—just like that, yes—now press on the brake and this, the clutch, at the same time. Yes! Now slide the shifter into first gear."

To Thelma's surprise, the car heaved forward. "Oh my God!"

"Very good, dear." Mrs. Young pointed at the dash. "Do you hear that? The engine's struggling. Time to try going into—"

The car lurched to a dead halt.

"Owie-zowie, geez," yelled Peggy, after being thrown against the front seat. "Slower, Thelms. You gotta treat that thing like it's a man's privates."

"Margaret Holmes!" Mrs. Young's head swiveled toward Peggy. "That's actually an excellent way to put it."

Even Imogene laughed at that, distracting Thelma from the task at hand and causing her to stall the car again.

"I hit a pothole!" A grinding, clanging noise traveled from the engine and through her arm. "Dear God," she said, clacking her fingernails against the manual gear shift.

"You're doing just fine. You only need to get this heap across the street," said Lillian. "You'd already be driving if they'd had any Cadillacs for rent."

Mrs. Young shrugged. "Good thing it is a rental," she said, settling back into her seat.

Much as Thelma appreciated the woman's lighter moods, she'd felt more uptight since they'd begun, as if someone had to play the worrywart at all times. Now however, between maneuvering her hands and feet while listening to the engine, she could hardly breathe, forget about dissecting the night ahead.

"Hang on. Let me try again," she said, focusing all her attention on the beam of the car's headlamps. The car lurched, but even so, she made it all the way to third gear before stalling again.

And this was how she'd survive the next twenty-four hours —focusing on what was just ahead. The first thing, according to Imogene, was a forty-minute hike to Siegel's construction site. They should return to the hotel.

"Let's head back to El Ranchero," Thelma said. "When we

get to the lobby, I'll make a big ruckus about driving myself to Sal's office."

Peggy slid forward and draped her elbow over the seat. "If they're paying that much attention, will it seem weird that we're all coming back at the same time?"

"No, I don't think so. Not since you and Mrs. Young left together." She shifted into fourth and immediately stalled, causing Peggy to pitch forward into the back of Mrs. Young's head. Her profuse apology only angered the woman.

"For goodness' sake, I'm fine. How often must I say it? Pregnancy is not a disease. At times it can be invigorating."

Ignoring the non-sequitur as she restarted the car, Thelma reminded herself that they were better off with their old boss in their sights. There was no telling what she'd do if left on her own. "Dynamite comes in small packages," her ma had often said.

"You three just head to your rooms." Thelma looked toward Imogene in the back seat. "I'll hurry. You won't have to wait long."

"You're sure I'll be able to slip through Lillian's room unnoticed?" Mrs. Young asked.

Thelma flicked her head from side to side in disbelief. "You of all people know how deserted the suites are at night." She waited for her words to sink in. Surely she hadn't forgotten about the dead fellow she'd disposed of in her suite just a few short months ago?

"And no one is in the pool at night," said Lillian, oblivious to the tension. Pills did that, Thelma knew.

As agreed, they said their effusive good nights in the lobby—heaping on plenty of gratitude for the driving lesson—before heading to their rooms. Then, as if remembering something, Thelma yelled, "Oh no!" Before declaring that what she needed was in Sal's office.

"Do you need it this minute?" Mrs. Young asked, the picture of weary defeat.

"You don't need to fret," Thelma chirped, refraining from scanning the room to be sure someone was listening. "I'll drive over there myself. Back in two shakes. You go on up."

Not long after reaching the parking lot, Thelma discovered they'd overlooked a critical step.

"Sorry, I'm no help," said Imogene, still crouched on the floorboard in the back. "I only started driving after Bill left for war. He'd just gotten an Oldsmobile with an automatic transmission. How he loved that car."

"I bet," said Thelma. "But I'll get this, don't worry. Honestly, I was more surprised you didn't know where Bugsy Siegel was staying."

Imogene chuckled. "You and me, both. Though I'm still fairly new to this game. Only started working after Billy—that's my husband—was off to war and my Sally started school. And that was just Classifieds. I was basically a secretary with a better title. My first big story was the Florida Girls."

The car stalled out again. "If I ever figure out how to reverse, I'll teach you how to drive a stick," Thelma said.

"That'd be peachy."

After several sweaty minutes, Thelma found reverse. By the time she'd made it across Highway 91, Mrs. Young was already sitting on the steps to Sal's trailer, still in her slim skirt and silk blouse. Her only concession to their trek had been to switch her heels for a pair of oxfords.

"Come on, we need to hurry," said Mrs. Young.

Glaring at her old boss, Thelma clenched her fists and exhaled through her nose. The woman must've known she'd have trouble reversing. *Who does she think is running this operation?*

Imogene clicked on her flashlight. "Okay, everyone, follow me."

Her words made Thelma giggle. They couldn't all three be in charge. She tried but couldn't suppress her laughter, and soon Imogene joined.

"What's so funny?" asked Mrs. Young.

This only made Thelma guffaw. Three women accustomed to being in charge was a rare challenge, and here they were embarking on a mission that required teamwork. When she'd calmed sufficiently, she agreed. "You're right, Mrs. Young. It's not funny. These are long odds we're facing and I want you both to know—I'm grateful that you're here."

* * *

THE UNEVEN TERRAIN AND PITCH BLACK MADE FOR SLOW going, so they walked arm in arm in silence, following the orb of light that Imogene pointed toward the ground. Thelma was glad they wouldn't have to break into anything or scale fences. With the war diverting supplies, developers relied on remote locations and guards to safeguard property. That was where Lillian and Peggy came in. Thelma almost wished she could watch them perform their ditzy-blond routine for the guards.

At last, on the horizon's edge, they could just make out the neon glow of downtown Las Vegas. Pausing, they unlinked arms and Imogene snapped off her torch. "There it is," she said, pointing ahead. "Future home of the Flamingo."

In the distance, Thelma could scarcely make out the rough outline of a backlit construction site. Her stomach took a flip, but she felt nothing in her palms. So much for her guidance tonight.

"I still don't understand what these men see out here," Mrs. Young grumbled.

"It's what they don't see, Mrs. Young," said Imogene.

"And what's that?"

Imogene and Thelma looked at each other and answered at the same time. "Cops."

They picked up their pace as the curved concrete shell that would be Siegel's casino took shape ahead. As they drew closer, they made out pallets of marble tiles and lumber strewn scattershot amid sleeping bulldozers and cranes.

No wonder the competition helped themselves. Thelma glanced at her watch. "We've got a little under five minutes before the shift changes," she said. "Let's find a place to hide."

"Shouldn't we get the picture first?"

"That's the guard's station right over there, Mrs. Young," said Imogene, pointing out a small but distant hut beside a stone archway, just off the highway. "I want to make sure he's looking in the opposite direction. I'm not shooting anything till I hear the honk from Lillian and Peggy."

The entrance was identical to the Rodeo Room's stone portal. Thelma wondered if that owed to a lack of materials or imagination.

"Yes, we have to time this just right, Mrs. Young," Thelma said. Can't have the security guys seeing the flash."

"The guards obviously haven't seen us, or they'd be on us already."

Thelma inhaled deeply through flared nostrils. She wanted to strangle Mrs. Young. Was she turning into her father? "Just find a place to—"

She didn't get to finish before the successive bleating of a car's honking horn pierced the night. Imogene turned and lined up her shot as Thelma ducked into the building's skeleton, where she had a perfect view of the events that unfolded next.

In what seemed like slow motion, Imogene triggered her camera's flashbulb. As soon as the internal mechanism stopped whirring, she turned, collapsing from view as the unmistakable tinkling of glass breaking hit Thelma's ears. Her camera had hit the ground.

Mrs. Young, who'd frozen in place during Imogene's crash, turned to the guard's station. A beam of rapidly bobbing light was approaching. Springing into action, she snatched Imogene's flashlight from the ground, smacked it until it came on, and charged toward the oncoming trouble.

* * *

"THERE YOU ARE!" CRIED KATHLEEN YOUNG, AS SHE SENT up a silent prayer that Imogene, the clod, had the good sense to roll behind something. "My goodness. I thought I was out here all alone and... Oh, look! There they are. Sir, you must help me at once." She grabbed the security guard's wiry arm and marched him toward the entrance, next to Lillian and Peggy's waiting car.

The guard, who looked all of twelve, appeared to have been roused from sleep. What had become of the shift change?

"Ma'am, what are you doing out here? What was that flare of light?"

"I could ask you the same question, couldn't I?" Kathleen said as she reached the girls and threw a protective arm around them, hoping the young man couldn't see Peggy's advanced age in the dark, the girl had to be at least twenty-four. "You young ladies are in big trouble.

"And my God, you're drunk! Give me the keys. I'm driving us home this instant." Kathleen held out her palm.

She was just about to get away with it, too, when up drove the overnight watchmen. Damn.

THIRTY-NINE

ONE NIGHT IN VEGAS, Friday

Even with Thelma acting as Imogene's human crutch, the return trip to Sal's trailer took over an hour. All the while, she could only hope the reporter's film hadn't been ruined. Not that it would do much good even if the celluloid was intact—all they had was a picture of construction supplies. Imogene hadn't dared snap another.

Instead, they'd watched from behind the skeletal hotel walls as Peggy, Lillian, and Mrs. Young were stuffed into a car that sped off. The two men left behind appeared to be arguing before one of them left in Peggy's car, leaving one man who did look in their direction briefly but returned to the guard's station. Within minutes, a truck drove up through the desert, just like Peggy had said. Four men jumped out and started carting off the supplies, leaving behind less than half the pile.

By the time they made it back to the rental car, Thelma had made up her mind to find Benjamin Siegel right away. Better to go to him without photographs than to risk a second try. Once word got out they'd been at the Flamingo, Sal would cover his tracks. There was no telling how long it would be before she'd get another chance to expose him. And the sooner she turned the tables on Sal, the sooner she'd see her friends.

Or so she had to hope.

For now, she had to believe they were alive, if not entirely safe. With Lillian Wright Montgomery in tow, they had to let them go. Sal Giancarlo didn't need the kind of heat that another disappearing Wright would bring, and Mrs. Young would not fail to point that out.

"You just passed my hotel," said Imogene. "Or were you having trouble slowing down?"

A smile crossed Thelma's lips. "No, silly I'm taking you to the hospital."

"What? No," said Imogene as her hotel receded in the rearview. "You can't do that. Whatever lie Mrs. Young is telling will be destroyed if they find out that Tampa's rat fink reporter turned up at the hospital with a busted ankle."

"Didn't they give you a tour of the place?"

"Exactly right. Why would I go back?"

Thelma's mouth fell open. She wanted to protest, but Imogene was right.

"Look." Imogene hoisted her foot in the air and moved it gingerly from side to side. "Just a sprain. I can still move it. The swelling only looks terrible because I've been upright. I'll be much happier in my room, where I have a radio, an endless supply of ice, and won't need a nurse's permission to use the bathroom."

"Yes, but—" Thelma knew it was too soon to ask when she might go back for pictures again. She needed another subterfuge. They wouldn't get away with the beautiful-women-lost-in-the-desert-conveniently-at-shift-change ruse more than once. "Well, if you're sure."

. . .

THE SUN WAS CRESTING OVER THE HOTEL AS THELMA pulled into El Ranchero's lot. Every muscle in her body ached, a physical discomfort she noticed with relief—then panic— followed by the familiar raw pain clawing at her chest.

Good. She wasn't ready to give up the heartache that propelled her. She didn't quite admit it, but deep down she feared that giving up her pain would mean giving up on the love she'd had for George.

"Any messages?" Thelma asked the hotel clerk.

She shook her head.

"Don't mind me." She tried to appear nonchalant. "I managed to fall asleep at my desk."

Why did I say that?

Rather than thrash herself for revealing more than necessary, Thelma thought ahead to her next crucial moves. She would find out from Mrs. Young what had happened and then possibly grab a nap before the library opened. At least shower. The desert trek had left her filthy.

She swung open the door, and her plan came to a halt—Mrs. Young's pillow showed not a dent. She raced to the bedside phone to call Lillian's room. No answer. She shivered.

What now?

TWO SHOTGUN BLASTS WOKE THELMA WITH A START, leaving her in a pool of sweat. The distinct odor of vinyl car seats baking in the sun burned her nose as a woman in cat-eye glasses came into focus. She was smiling and waving at her. Ahead, a sign read, "City Library." There was no gun. Thelma had driven straight to the library and fallen asleep.

"Are you coming in? It's not as hot inside," Cat Eyes said as she reached for the door's handle.

How had she nodded off? Mrs. Young, Peggy, and Lillian

were missing, just like Agent Nelson had been. Just like Agent Nelson had been?

The library's door stood open. Thelma could thrash herself later.

Grabbing her bag, she walked in behind the librarian, the screen door creaking as she entered the cool dark space. Sun bounced off the polished floors. Thelma felt at home. You need the periodicals, she reminded herself.

The librarian practically waltzed through the space, flipping on light switches. "Can I help you find anything?"

"Yes, please. Where are your magazines and newspapers?"

"Right this way." She dropped her bag on the information desk and indicated that Thelma should follow her. "Are you looking for a particular title?"

Thelma's brain was cobwebs. What was she looking for? Her favorite magazines—Modern Screen, Hollywood Stars Parade, and Screen Sirens—were always catching "filmland's elite" coming and going from hotels. All she needed was a snap of Siegel "seen here leaving his hotel in Las Vegas." Then she'd have him.

"Do you have any celebrity magazines?" she asked, feeling shy about asking this smart-looking woman for her gossip rags.

Cat Eyes smiled. "Over here," she said as she walked into a separate room, flipping on another light switch. "We have them all. We're practically neighbors with Hollywood, of course." She pulled wooden racks from a bin and laid them on the table. "These are the latest. If you need anything else, I'll be out front."

Thelma sat behind the pile of magazines. Tempted as she was by a cover shot of Joan Crawford at a fashion show, she forced herself to concentrate. Captioned photos, like she was looking for, were usually in the front section. She began flipping pages. And more pages. Her hopes sagged.

Soon she'd gone through the entire stack on the table. Though Siegel appeared in several photographs at nightclubs and events in Las Angeles, in Vegas there was nothing. *Why would Benjamin Siegel turn publicity shy in Vegas?*

Returning to the front desk, Thelma found the librarian helping a young girl. She felt the tender ache of recognition. Thelma had whiled away many a summer day, alone, asking for the latest Nancy Drew.

But Thelma had to snap out of all this wistfulness. Falling back on one of her old tricks, she forced herself to zoom in on an object in the room. The first thing she saw was a nameplate that read, Dr. Estelle Nettles.

This lady didn't just *look* smart.

FORTY

THEY WERE EXPENDABLE, Friday

KATHLEEN COULDN'T SEE SAL, BUT SHE HEARD THE dangerous snarl in his voice.

"Whatsa matter with you nincompoops? Get in here. All of you."

After tying their hands with rope, the thug who'd pushed her and Peggy and Lillian so unceremoniously into the car had thrown pillowcases over their heads. When the vehicle stopped and Kathleen was ushered out, she was stunned to feel concrete beneath her feet rather than the desert floor. Soon enough, the sounds of clanging dishes and splashing water told her that she was not behind a rock at some undisclosed location, rather, being whisked through the back end of a hotel kitchen. Then it was on to what Kathleen assumed was a service elevator.

"Salvatore Giancarlo!" Kathleen barked, trying to match Sal's forcefulness despite the headgear. "I demand to know what's going on here."

"Judas Priest, take those things off their heads."

"Sal?"

Francella? Dear God. *We're in* Sal's love nest. Those boys are nincompoops.

"Get back to bed, Frankie," Sal growled. "You. Follow me. Not you, you moron. You go wait by the door with Chickie."

Kathleen felt the whoosh of cotton and saw Lillian and Peggy, hair ajumble, blinking in the narrow corridor. She felt a shove from behind.

"You heard the man," their escort said, attempting to assert some authority. "Get in there."

"Hey, watch it, buster," said Peggy. "The lady's pregnant."

Their guard scowled and tossed up a hand as he turned back toward the door.

His dismissal infuriated Kathleen. She marched into the seating area, where she found Sal in a silk robe and a matching set of pajamas, lighting a cigar.

"Put that out unless you want me to vomit," said Kathleen.

A murderous rage crossed Sal's face. He sat back on the couch, took a languid puff, then extinguished his cigar in an exaggerated manner. "Why don't you all sit down," he gestured, "and tell me what the hell's going on here?"

"Really, Sal. Send the girls off, and let's us adults have a grown-up conversation. They have a show tonight at the Rodeo Room."

Sal looked from Kathleen, who'd seated herself in the love seat opposite, to Peggy and Lillian, still standing in the corridor, mute.

Without taking his eyes off them, he yelled, "Chickie!"

An enormous man—presumably the replacement for whoever she'd sent to the hospital the day before—came storming in, only to be stopped in the hall when Peggy and Lillian didn't step aside.

"Lock those broads in the other room."

Chickie grabbed Peggy and Lillian roughly by their elbows and steered them back out the corridor. Kathleen heard a muffled, "Hey!" and, "Ouch!" as they were pushed back out into the hall.

"Where is he taking them?"

"Shut up, now. You're the one answering questions here. What the hell were you doing at Moe's?"

"Who's Moe?" Kathleen lifted her chin, eyes defiant.

"What'd I say about the questions?"

"Tsk. Sal, There's not much to say. You know I'm hoping to drum up some business here in town. The girls wanted to see some of the establishments, and on the way back to our hotel, I guess they thought it would be funny to leave me by the side of the road." Kathleen, relaxing back into her chair, gave a shrug. "But you must release us. This isn't funny. The last thing you need is another Wright disappearing anywhere in your vicinity. And of course, I am with child," she said before unleashing an audible yawn. "I'm exhausted."

Another look of fury marched across Sal's face. "Are you sure? You don't look pregnant."

He lurched forward, fists clenched. "Oh, screw this. I'm going to deal with you same as I did that phony soldier, Nelson. Chickie! Get in here." Sal dug his fingers into the divan's armrest and heaved himself upright.

Panic seized Kathleen. *Did I play the wrong cards?* Typically, mention of anything that sounded like female troubles shut men down. This called for desperate measures.

"Sal, I don't know how to tell you this, but... you need to sit down."

Something in her tone must have done the trick because Sal stopped in his tracks. "Give us a minute," he said to Chickie, then returned to his seat and waited till his bodyguard left the room. "This better be good."

Kathleen had only one option. Perspiration broke out at her temple, and she could hear her heart beating in her ears. If there was any other way to divert his attention from the mess they'd created on this stupid mission that she'd been blackmailed into, she'd have taken it. Her husband needed her home, her boys needed her to fix the mess they'd gotten into by taking money from Sal, and her baby needed her alive. Thelma could go to hell, for all she cared, but she needed Giancarlo put away for good.

"Salvatore, I have a confession to make," she began, shifting uncomfortably in her seat and fanning herself with her palm. She took a deep breath. "You were right to be suspicious when I showed up here in town. I have more of an agenda than just helping Thelma. I've been trying to think of a way to tell you this. You have a grandson. Matteo's baby. I'm carrying Matteo's baby."

* * *

"Excuse me, Dr. Nettles?" Thelma said, addressing the librarian after the young girl had walked away. She felt embarrassed at her failure to find what she was looking for, and that was before she'd discovered this stylish woman was a doctor. "Do you have an archive of the magazines you pulled for me? I can't seem to find what I'm looking for."

"Sure, but please, call me Stella." She slid off her glasses and wiped them with the end of her sleeve. "Do you want to tell me what you're looking for? Maybe I can help you."

"Oh no, thank you, but..." Thelma bit her lip. *Why not ask for help?* If her plan came off, she'd be driving to the airport with Peggy the next day. If she didn't succeed, well, her pride wouldn't matter either. She had to trust someone, why not a librarian? "Actually, I bet you can. I'm trying to figure out where Benjamin Siegel is staying."

Without even a sidelong glance, Stella pressed her glasses

back into place. "I could've told you that an hour ago. Mr. Siegel always stays at the Frontier when he's in town. Books the whole top floor."

Thelma gave Dr. Nettles the first genuine smile she'd offered anyone in weeks. Of course the librarian had the answer. "Thank you." She hurried toward the door, but stopped midway. Turning back, Thelma cleared her throat. "What's the address for that one, Stella?"

* * *

"You must think I'm an idiot, Kathleen," said Sal, who had somehow risen and was now glowering down at her without any assistance from his cane. "Matteo's number came up in December. You'd be—"

A glazed look came over Sal's eyes, as if he was trying to calculate a complex equation. It reminded Kathleen of watching Lloyd read a newspaper article that displeased him. She had to bite her tongue to keep from doing the math aloud, though she'd thought it over many times. After basic training, Matteo was shipped out to Italy. She suspected he'd escaped the country in early March with the help of relatives. Their encounters had ended when Kathleen left Las Vegas, a couple of weeks before Hitler's death at the end of April—she'd never forget hearing that news with Doc at Sun City. She reckoned she was eleven weeks along.

"I know you're aware that Matteo had..." Kathleen paused, unsure how to delicately phrase her thoughts. If Sal had wanted to get his son out of military duty he could have, and she herself had burned with shame when she realized that Matteo was a deserter. But she had to convince him.

"Somehow, your son followed us to Vegas. And, you know I

love Mr. Young, but he's been ill for some time now." Kathleen cast her eyes to the floor, chastened. "I was very *lonely*."

"You dirty, lying whore. If what you're saying is true, I know Lloyd's an older man, but I think I would've heard about this from him. *Unless...*"

Kathleen's heart skipped a beat. She couldn't have this gangster thinking her Button was involved with Matteo's death.

Before he could yell for one of his henchmen, Kathleen reached for his necktie and played her ace. "Sal, Lloyd doesn't know."

"Quit lying to me. This is not helping any of you. Speaking of, where the hell is Thelma?"

Kathleen had Salvatore Giancarlo right where she wanted him.

"Sal, you didn't get where you are by denying the truth when it's right in front of you. The girls were playing a prank on me. I haven't a clue where Thelma is. And Matteo's middle name is Alphonse. After Al Capone. He said you used to tell him he'd never live up to it."

Sal's eyes traveled from Kathleen's bosom to the flush in her cheeks then down to her swollen ankles. Still, he refused to relent. "You coulda found that out from anyone," he sneered.

But she saw the uncertainty lodge behind his eyes. "He also had a small purplish birthmark on his left hip."

This last part was false. In fact, it was her son Archie who had such a mark. She felt confident, however, that Sal hadn't spent any time changing his son's diapers. Come to think of it, she could not recall if that mark was on her youngest boy's left or right hip. But that was beside the point. Doubt bloomed in Sal's expression, morphing into ordinary disbelief. She patted his tie. "Congratulations, Grandpa."

Tears welled in Kathleen's eyes. Actual tears. This pregnancy had endowed her with the emotional reserve of a teenage girl, so her display did not come as a surprise. For once in her life, she was glad to come across as distressed.

"Save the waterworks," Sal said. "I'm gonna have my own doctor check you out to be sure you're even pregnant. You better hope like hell that kid looks like his daddy. Where the hell is Lloyd, anyway?"

Kathleen reached for her handbag, only to realize she didn't have it. She needed to blow her nose. "Do you have a tissue?"

Ignoring her question, Sal stood immobile. Glaring. Kathleen wondered if his walking stick was a ruse. Like his so-called stroke. No matter. She was through anticipating other people's needs in order to mold herself.

"Lloyd's recuperating at our home in Carlsbad. With a nurse. He's just had some of his lung removed. Call the California Medical Hospital if you don't believe me."

"Oh, you can bet your bottom dollar I will." Sal looked at the ceiling and shook his head, but went into the bathroom, muttering, "Jesus Christ, kid. Still killing me." He reached for his pocket square, tossed it at Kathleen, and returned to his seat. "Chickie!"

The bodyguard appeared in seconds. "Have Johnny Torrio take the girls back to their hotel. Get Moose on this one. She doesn't go anywhere he's not with her. That includes taking her to my doctor. Understood?"

"Yes, boss."

Much as Kathleen wanted to protest being stalked around by one of Sal's cronies, she knew they were lucky to be getting out of this situation at all. "Do as you like, Sal. I'm only here for a few more days."

Sal let out a sound somewhere between amusement and derision. "Like hell you are."

Was the man planning to keep her in Las Vegas until she had her baby? It could be years before Kathleen's child came into anything like a family resemblance. Perhaps "Grandpa" was a bit much.

"—and you'll stay on that door till Moose gets back," Sal said, finishing a sentence that Kathleen hadn't heard the start of. Using his staff for support again, he hoisted himself up and tottered after his bodyguard into the hall.

That left Kathleen alone in the room. After a few moments of still silence, she tiptoed toward the hall. She'd no real goal, unsure as to where her handbag and wallet were, but her urge to escape superseded such concerns. She turned the door handle as slowly as she could, cracked the door and peered into the hall, only to face the wall of a pinstriped suit jacket.

After closing the door as softly as she'd opened it, she made her way back to the couch. Sat. She was, in fact, bone-tired.

"Kath!" Sal's mistress emerged from the bedroom in a sheer yellow peignoir and matching dressing gown, her rollered hair secured with a scarf in a clashing tiger-striped fabric. Her face, Kathleen noted, was fully made up. "We need to talk."

Did no one sleep in this town?

FORTY-ONE

THE OUTSIDERS, Friday

THELMA CHECKED HER REFLECTION IN THE CAR'S REAR view mirror. Moving her head side to side, she was again grateful for the low-maintenance locks, though her face was a fright, complete with a smear of dirt on her forehead. The bigger issue was her outfit—the dirty trousers she'd belted with one of George's neckties weren't going to help her case. Not with a man like Bugsy Siegel, a notorious sucker for womanly charms.

She pulled up to the lobby at El Ranchero, planning to race to her room, freshen, change, and hustle over to the Frontier. But the front desk clerk, after plucking her room key from the board behind the desk, turned with them in his fist, midair. After a purposeful look through the lobby's glass front, he frowned. "You can't park there."

"Why," Thelma intoned in the singsong trill she'd heard Mrs. Young employ many times, "I won't be a moment. The Vegas Girls debut tonight—busy day!" Flashing a bright smile, she fluttered her eyelids and snatched the keyring from his hand.

Once she'd turned down the corridor to her room, Thelma thought she was home free. Then she saw a chunk of a man in a pinstriped suit, hair slicked back, standing in front of her room. She stopped in her tracks. That had to be one of Sal's men at the door. Whatever they'd done with her former boss, Thelma couldn't disappear before she got to Siegel.

Turning heel, she dashed back the way she'd come, hoping the man at the door hadn't seen her. She had only one choice left—to go to the Frontier hotel directly.

The Frontier was downtown, like Francella's hotel. "Old Vegas," she'd billed it. As Thelma drove into town, her mind wandered over this and other events of the last few hours. Certain as she was that the thieves were Sal's men, she had no proof. Neither of his involvement or the theft. She wouldn't rat out Gloria's friends, but what would she say? And what if Bugsy didn't believe her?

If she admitted that she'd come to town for the sole purpose of finding such evidence because Sal—wanting Thelma dead— had inadvertently murdered her husband by tampering with his plane, he just might suspect she was playing him. As if Thelma, embittered because she'd been cut out of her husband's money and her father's, was angling for a piece of the action.

Tears welled in her eyes as it occurred to her, again, how she lacked proof she was George's bride. She had no ring, no child, only the sapphire necklace. What did that show? Any documentation was at the courthouse in Florida.

A vibrato blast pierced Thelma's thoughts as she slammed on the brakes and swerved to avoid the oncoming honking truck. The car's engine sputtered and stopped, causing her head to bang into the steering column. Hugging the wheel, Thelma rested her forehead, panting. Minutes passed before she lifted her skull.

Looking at the sun's position in the cloudless sky, she

guessed it was almost noon. The air in the stopped car was stifling so that now, adding to her visible charm, Thelma was drenched in sweat. What choice was there but to plow ahead?

* * *

KATHLEEN STARTLED AWAKE, BUT SHE WAS SAFE IN HER hotel bed. Or safe for now. Sal's goon would still be standing guard at the door, the same spot where he'd dumped her unceremoniously earlier that morning once she convinced Sal's mistress that her talents would be recognized. She rolled to check the clock on the nightstand, only to spot her handbag. Right. She'd put the horseshoe monstrosity back in her valise.

My handbag.

Relief flooded through Kathleen as she reached for her purse, but it vanished immediately when what felt like a hot iron stabbed into her neck. She winced, remembering she'd fallen asleep on that infernal couch in Sal's room, causing her old horsing injury to flare.

Turning onto her opposite side, Kathleen rubbed her neck. It dawned on her then—Thelma was still not in her bed. Hadn't been in the room at all. As far as Kathleen knew, the last person to see Thelma would've been Imogene Fuchs. She had to speak to that reporter, find out what had happened. Kathleen had assumed her ruse at the construction site allowed Thelma and Imogene to escape with the film—neither Sal nor Francella had said anything to contradict this belief—but those two fools could've been found wandering in the desert after she'd left Sal's room.

How had Sal's girlfriend pieced together their plan?

If Miss DiGruppo was to be believed, Gloria had said that she and Peggy "grilled" her girlfriends before "hot footing it out of the club fast." Then, when Francella heard that Kathleen and the girls had turned up at Bugsy Siegel's construction site, she figured they were there to snoop on the supply raid.

Kathleen had no answer. Denied everything. But that wasn't Francella's point. She was convinced that Sal was getting played, as she said, "like every last one of 'em."

Or something like that. Kathleen should have paid more attention, but she'd been dangerously overtired.

Until Francella had the gall to advise Kathleen. "Play your cards right and there's greenbacks in it for you."

She assumed "greenbacks" was some colloquialism for money. She wasn't sure what bothered her more, the insinuation or the drivel that passed for communication these days.

Not that it mattered; Kathleen had no intention of being in business with Sal Giancarlo ever again. And that went double for her children. They could work all their days and still owe. She'd only told him about the baby to divert his attention from their unwelcome appearance at the construction site and put the attention back on Sal. Most men fell for that, but not only had her scheme *not* worked, it had backfired.

That fool Francella. At least when Kathleen had lied about being pregnant, she knew enough to get Lloyd to knock her up right away. Fortunately, Sal's man had showed up, putting an end to their bizarre pillow talk.

Nestling under the covers now, it occurred to Kathleen that this trip to Vegas was the longest stretch she'd had in years with no one depending on her for a meal, a schedule, or a paycheck. The gap left her with time to ruminate.

The health business they'd planned for Carlsbad was Lloyd's dream. Was that what she wanted to do with the rest of her life, carry out another of Lloyd's dreams? Even the best outcome from his surgery would leave all the work to Kathleen.

Flinging aside the covers, Kathleen resolved to confront this gnawing dilemma. After she made sure Sal was out of the way.

Especially now that her little secret was out. Regardless of what path she chose, the last thing she needed was to be known as the mother of some two-bit gangster's bastard.

Hiking her legs over the edge of the bed, Kathleen stared into the closet. She knew they'd never see Sal Giancarlo in an actual courthouse, but she could put her case to the court of public opinion. So long as Imogene had survived the night.

Shaking the cobwebs from her head, it dawned on Kathleen that she'd fallen asleep in her clothes. She looked at her watch but couldn't make out the numbers that early in the morning. At least, that was what she told herself as she reached for the clock she'd stowed in her suitcase. She wasn't about to start wearing eyeglasses.

Past ten already?

After tossing the clock in her purse, she picked up the handset to call Imogene. Thelma's warning came to mind. "They're watching our every move."

If Sal hadn't been keeping a close eye on Kathleen before, the bodyguard at the door erased any notions of privacy. She dashed around the room, flipping on the Philco and opening the bathroom tap so Sal's thug wouldn't overhear her call. As soon as the operator picked up, she recognized that even phoning Imogene would lead Sal straight to the reporter and her camera.

Slamming the receiver onto the hook, Kathleen screeched in frustration.

The bodyguard opened the door immediately. "Everything okay in there?"

Which made Kathleen want to scream again.

"Fine," she said, her voice breaking. She wondered if she'd ever regain control of her emotions.

Taking a deep breath, she called on her better angels to help assess the situation. Thelma was God-knew-where with the car, while Kathleen was stuck in their room, afraid to place a call.

Leaving meant being followed. Of course she was flustered, she was more trapped than when she'd been in prison.

Prison, she thought with, to her surprise, a chuckle. Her mother would have a coronary if she knew her debutante daughter had landed in jail for assaulting a mobster.

Suddenly, the song on the radio pierced her consciousness—Guy Lombardo's "Bell Bottom Trousers," a formerly bawdy tune about sailors that had been sanitized for the radio. It made her think of Archie. *Her baby.*

Had he shipped out to the Pacific yet? How could Bertie have let him go? The stirring of pride she'd felt when she learned her baby boy had enlisted was long gone. All she felt now was the ache of missing him. But it was the song's double entendres that drove a stake into her heart.

Fat tears dripped down her cheeks as the tune's last notes played, and—in a rare moment of seeing her sons clearly—Kathleen recognized that she might never have grandchildren. Archie and Bertie both would likely be lifelong bachelors but for very different reasons. Her only remaining hope that her bloodline would continue was the baby she was carrying.

You are listening to Good Day, Las Vegas! I'm your host, Betty Davis! That was Guy Lombardo & Jimmy Brown, burning up the charts with, 'Bell Bottom Trousers'—

Eureka! thought Kathleen.

She might not be able to telephone Imogene Fuchs since her calls were being monitored, but she wasn't an actual prisoner. She could go wherever she liked. The fireplug out there would just have to follow. There was yet—she double-checked her wristwatch—time to work the public angle.

The jangling phone startled Kathleen. She rushed to answer.

"Mrs. Young? It's Gloria Martinez. I wanted to confirm our call time at four with Miss Holmes, but no one is answering. Are they with you?"

Lillian and Peggy weren't in their room?

Kathleen looked again at her wristwatch. Eleven o'clock. The Vegas Girls were supposed to go on stage in seven hours and she didn't know where her emcee or spotlight talent were. Panic washed over her until she heard her Button clear as day. "Pepper, you thrive in a pinch."

"Everything's fine, dear," she told Gloria, lifting her cheeks as she spoke to convey good cheer. "We're still meeting in Miss Montgomery's suite for hair and makeup at four. Must run now. À bientôt!"

This new information called for a scorched-earth approach.

* * *

Inside the Frontier, Thelma stood, mouth agape, as she took in the large stone fireplace and mounted animal heads. Momentarily thunderstruck by the gun rack and rifles leaning up against the wall, she practically bumped into a leather horse saddle that framed the lobby's seating area. It wasn't much of a stretch to picture a drunken reveler straddling the seat and whooping.

Her eyes landed on the reception desk at the far end of the room. Relief washed over her to find the space empty. She couldn't ask for a Mr. Siegel—he'd never answer for Sal's daughter. Dr. Nettles had let it drop that he always rented out the entire top floor. Amid the visual pandemonium, however, she couldn't spot the elevator.

The unmistakable spicy floral notes of Shalimar perfume

jolted Thelma—it had been her mother's favorite scent. She looked toward its source. A woman was making her way down the now obvious grand staircase, her red-lacquered nails brushing the sideways log that served as a handrail.

"Here to spy?" the woman asked.

Thelma's eyes popped and her hand flew to her chest. "Me? No. I, uh—"

"Oh, relax, sweetheart. I do it all the time." She marched forward, hand extended. "Maxene Lewis, the Frontier's entertainment director."

Between the imposing shoulder pads in her jacket and the frilled top underneath, the lady gave off conflicting signals. *Is she about to make me cookies or kill me?* She reminded Thelma of Mrs. Young in that way, except she was tall and slender.

"The Florida Girls came to see Liberace here earlier this year. Remember?"

Thelma didn't remember the Liberace show because she'd been at dinner with Sal Giancarlo. "How could I forget? He was electrifying."

Or so Peggy had said.

"Mmm," grunted Maxene before returning to her original topic. "What are you doing here? Isn't your Vegas Girls show debuting tonight? Shouldn't you be getting ready?"

Thelma felt heat rise at her neck. She'd cleaned off in the library's powder room, but she hardly looked the picture of a Vegas showgirl. "Oh, but you were here first." She smiled, attempting to regain her composure. "What are you doing here?"

"I already told you—I work here."

Thelma bristled but kept the smile plastered on her face, nodding as she wondered what Maxene Lewis might want and what sort of information she might have. Even if the woman was part of Wade Davis's network of citizen spies, there wasn't time enough for Thelma to get in any more trouble from this. She and Peggy would be boarding a plane for Havana the next day. And if things went her way, Sal would never be a threat again.

"I have a meeting with Mr. Siegel," she improvised. "He's expecting me." Based on what she'd learned about this town, this could plausibly be true.

"Really," Maxene said, her intonation suggesting less a question than a comment.

"Yes, and I'm late. Which way is his—"

"I don't tend to know our guest's room numbers."

"Oh, that's fine. I can—"

"But you happen to be in luck because I know just where Mr. Siegel's room is." Maxene rolled on as if Thelma hadn't spoken. "Come with me."

Thelma was hardly in need of a chaperone, and her first instinct was to insist that Maxene was too busy. But that would be the weak response. Thelma had spent too much time on her back heel in Las Vegas. No more.

"Wonderful, thank you."

"Follow me," she said, before setting off across the lobby. "And I bet I can convince you to bring the Vegas Girls to the Frontier."

As they walked toward a set of moving stairs, Thelma listened to Maxene's pitch. Supposedly, the entertainment director had a direct line to Hollywood that could work both ways for her talent. Thelma had heard that one before.

When she failed to respond to Maxene's offer of four hundred fifty dollars a week for their act—thinking the woman's pause was merely another launching point for a new topic—Mrs. Lewis immediately upped her bid to five hundred twenty-five dollars. "You're right. There're six of you, and you'll need an alternate."

Thelma still hadn't said anything.

"That way you'll each get seventy-five dollars a week."

If Thelma weren't about to set fire to her bridges on the way out of town, she would've had to seriously consider the offer. Seventy-five dollars a week for a half hour's worth of work a day? The money would make the looming specter that was her annulment more palatable. She hadn't allowed herself to consider what would happen in Cuba now that she no longer had anything to invest in their night club, but she hoped that Doris and Helen would still let her stick around. Though Thelma didn't have Peggy's vocal talent, she'd work twice as hard.

When they reached the second floor, Thelma paused. Turning to Mrs. Lewis, she asked, "This is all very interesting, Mrs. Lewis, but why us? Don't you already have showgirls in Las Vegas?'"

"Please, honey, my mother is Mrs. Lewis. Call me Maxene." She rested her hand on Thelma's shoulder. "And Maxene always says, 'Don't underestimate the value of a known act.'"

"You mean Lillian Montgomery? I don't think—"

"Cripes, no!" Maxene guffawed and pulled Thelma down the hall. "Right this way. Don't get me wrong—Lillian would be a catch. But she's on her way to becoming a star. What I mean is," here Maxene paused and held up her hands as if framing a sign, "The Vegas Girls. It's the name."

Crossing her arms, Thelma looked down and let the implication sink in. "Meaning, you don't need me either?"

"No, ma'am."

"Please," said Thelma, putting her hand on Maxene's shoulder. "It's Thelma. No ma'ams here."

The least Thelma could do was give Maxene's information to Gloria and the rest of the girls. That kind of money could change lives.

"This is it," said Maxene, nodding toward the door they'd

stopped in front of before she pressed her card into Thelma's hip pocket. "I'll leave you to it. Don't sit on my offer for too long."

Thelma stood stock still until Maxene turned the corner, then rapped on Mr. Siegel's door. There was no answer, not even a stirring. She banged on it harder. Flipped her Bulova bracelet watch around her wrist. It was after two. Maybe Bugsy was at lunch?

Unenthusiastic as Thelma was at the prospect of loitering in the hallway, the idea of returning to the lobby and having to make up another story for Maxene was less appealing. She turned her back to the door and slid down the wall, marking time.

* * *

The On Air light over the studio door went out, and Kathleen pressed her way in, positioning herself against the doorjamb as she turned to face Sal's man. "You can see the whole room from here, Moose. There's nowhere for me to go."

Inside, the space was far smaller than Kathleen had expected. Just a round table with a microphone hanging overhead and a couple of panels festooned with a series of incomprehensible knobs and meters.

Quick as Betty Davis looked up, the fury that crossed her features softened into a wide smile. "Why, Mrs. Young. Shouldn't you be in the Rodeo Room getting ready for your show?" She looked around the room as if it held the answer. "I'm going back on in just a couple of minutes."

"That's just perfect!" Kathleen said. "I hope you don't mind me dropping by, but I wanted to preview our big announcement for your listeners before tonight's show."

Mrs. Davis lifted her chin. "Your what?"

"You'll see. May I?" Without waiting for an answer, Mrs. Young took a seat at the table. "You look smart in those headphones. Do I need a pair?"

"No, I can count you down. I mean... Mrs. Young, this is highly unusual."

Keeping her tone and smile bright, Kathleen agreed. "I know, it's not every day a town opens up its doors to people like Las Vegas has done for us. We wanted to show our appreciation. Between you and me?" Kathleen leaned forward. "This will be especially thrilling for your Wade."

The light at the door flashed. Mrs. Davis grimaced but held up three fingers. Then two.

Fortunately, on her walk to the studio, Kathleen conjured up the perfect diversion.

* * *

THELMA HAD BARELY BEEN IN THE HALL FOR A MINUTE when Virginia Hill sauntered up, barefooted, an ice bucket resting on one hip and her sheer robe dragging behind her. The visage might've been startling, but Thelma was mesmerized by the tousle of flaming red hair surrounding Hill's head like a diabolical halo. She wasn't a beautiful woman, but Thelma had no trouble understanding why men fell for her. Hill reminded her of her mother that way. Both had the undeniable sex appeal of a siren.

"You again?" she said through the cigarette dangling at her lips when she stopped to open her door. "Are you coming inside or what?" Hill said as she entered without looking back.

Scrambling to her feet, Thelma held the doorknob a moment. If she could handle her mother, she could handle Virginia Hill.

"You remember me?"

In response, Hill banged her ice bucket on the table and marched into the bathroom.

Thelma scarcely recalled their encounter, so it stunned her that Virginia Hill did. Then it struck her like a blow—the day they'd met in Tampa was the same day Sal told her that he was her father.

Returning to the room, washcloth in hand, Hill proceeded to pluck cubes of ice from the pail. "Kiddo, since we met in Tampa you're like a bad penny. You show up at a meeting we're having with that creep you call Daddy. Now my old man's ranting about you. And just now, some lady was on the radio, talking about you and making some movie. So yeah, I remember you. Are you following me?"

A chill ran down Thelma's spine. Bugsy Siegel was looking for her? *Did that radio report mention Lillian or Peggy or Mrs. Young?* Hill, meanwhile, had made her way back to her tangled bed and placed the cold cloth over her face. If Vivian Miles was any indication of what this pose portended, Thelma would be best served by escaping.

"If you're not feeling well, I can come back another time," said Thelma.

"Who said I wasn't feeling well?" Hill sat up in the bed. "You've never done this? This is my morning routine. Gets rid of the under-eye bags. Also terrific for the pores—"

"I was looking for Mr. Siegel," Thelma interrupted. "I have urgent news for him.

Hill rolled her eyes and layed back down, covering her face once more with her ice pack. "Get in line. He don't get up till three o'clock."

Thelma wasn't sure what to make of that news. Brushing her fingertips over the scar on her cheek, she considered the possibility of mining Hill for information. Before she could think what to ask, Virginia Hill snapped to attention.

"Business?" she asked, sitting up again. "Whaddya mean, business?"

"Now you've done it," Thelma heard her mother say. "Virginia Hill thinks you're sleeping with her boyfriend." Vivian would've advised placating Hill, but Thelma was done trying to play small to fit other people's needs.

"I'm afraid that's none of your concern, Miss Hill."

Nestling back into the pillows, Hill hid most of her face beneath the washcloth again. "You're here. You're looking for my man. So you made it my business. Either talk, or get out."

At last, the invitation Thelma needed. She'd gotten all the information Virginia Hill had to offer. If the man didn't get out of bed till three, it was no use loitering around in this hotel. But she could urge his appearance at the show, her next best shot at speaking to Siegel.

On her way out, Thelma barged into Maxene Lewis's office. "So sorry to interrupt. Would you mind," she draped across Maxene's desk, reaching for pen and paper, "passing this message along to Mr. Siegel? Miss Hill wasn't feeling well. Thank you so much."

There was but one person who had the information she needed—Estelle Nettles.

"DR. NETTLES!" THELMA CALLED OUT, RELIEVED TO FIND the trusty librarian sitting calmly at the front desk, reading something. "I'm so glad you're not at lunch!"

Stella Nettles looked up and placed her index finger to her lips, smiling. With her other hand she held up a copy of her magazine, *Silver Screen Confidential*. She whispered, "You inspired me."

Thelma laughed but then covered her mouth. Withdrawing her hand she mouthed, "Sorry."

Dr. Nettles waved her apology away and, in her regular speaking voice, asked, "What can I help you with now?"

"May I borrow your phone directory?" She did *not* need some hotel operator/informant snitching that the show might not include Lillian, but Gloria needed to know. "And, may I use your telephone? Not the public one. *Your* phone."

The librarian tilted her head.

Before she could say no, Thelma had an idea. "I'll send the Vegas Girls over here for a publicity shoot at the library."

As if mulling over a difficult proposition, Dr. Nettles swayed in her seat but couldn't keep the smile out of her voice. "I don't know why you think you can bribe me. But you can. Deal." She stuck her hand out.

What did Hill mean about a movie?

FORTY-TWO

THE SHOW, Friday

"You can't come in here either, Moose. Ladies only." Kathleen offered Sal's bodyguard what she hoped was a quaintly apologetic smile.

After her triumphant appearance on Betty Davis's show, she'd been ravenous. All men were more pliable on a full stomach, so she'd invited her watchguard to eat with her. Turned out, his wife was also expecting. Knowing that did have the effect of making the forced visit with Sal's doctor feel a tad less sordid, but by the time she had Lillian and Peggy's room in her sights, she was late for call time. Not her style. To her relief, peals of laughter wafted down the hall, emanating from their suite.

Thank God. She hadn't thought about what she'd have done if her stunt hadn't worked and the girls were still missing. *How would I explain that one to Homer Wright?* Except that—for this one, incandescent moment in her life—she was no one's chaperone.

Inside, the girls rushed to her, with Thelma first in line. "Oh, thank goodness! There you are, Mrs. Young!" Thelma wrapped her in an embrace that Kathleen returned with an enthusiasm she hadn't thought possible. Or probable. Then

Thelma went and spoiled the moment. "We know nothing about this movie you announced on Betty Davis's show," she whispered in Kathleen's ear, "but we haven't let on that we're in the dark, so help us keep up the act. And who's Moose?"

Kathleen didn't have time to answer before the girls swarmed her.

"When do you start shooting?"

"Are they really gonna let you call the movie *Helldorado Days?*"

"Any big names attached yet?"

"Do you have a part for a lady who can ride a steer?"

"That's not all she rides!"

She'd have sworn that would have been Mari's wisecrack, but the short, curvy one had made the innuendo. *DeeDee?* Her brain hadn't gone fuzzy like this with the boys. Then again, she wasn't twenty anymore, either, as Sal's doctor had scolded.

"At your advanced age, mortality rates increase. You need to begin regular appointments..."

For heaven's sake, my grandmother gave birth to twins at forty-two, thought Kathleen. She said nothing. The fact that the man knew she was thirty-eight was personal enough. She didn't want to give these people any more information about herself than was absolutely necessary. At least he was using that bizarre frog test, so Sal would know by tomorrow that she was, indeed, with child.

Gloria gave three sharp claps. "Ladies! Give her some room so she can tell us everything!"

"Yes," Thelma said. "We told them they had to wait to hear everything straight from the horse's mouth."

Cheeky, thought Kathleen as the girls quieted and backed away. The space allowed her to take in the bedazzling array of tulle, feathers, and satin around the room. Thelma, Lillian, and Peggy stood in the back, arms linked, looking like they'd survived a shipwreck together. Kathleen felt a twinge of envy that she'd been sent away with Moose and missed their reunion. Then again, she'd never have devised their life-saving scheme if they'd been together.

"I'm so pleased you all listen to Betty's show."

"Like we have a choice."

"DeeDee," cautioned Gloria.

So this DeeDee was less compliant once you got to know her. Not so surprising. Still, Kathleen was struggling to stay in the conversation. Lillian and Peggy appeared unharmed. As did Thelma. *Where had they been?* She couldn't ask in front of Gloria and the rest, but perhaps she could glean some of the details. They were all putting up a good front.

"I'm just glad you girls were ah, *awake* to hear it," Kathleen said. "Speaking of, I had some questions for you earlier, Lillian, but couldn't reach you or Peggy. You devilish things. How late did you two sleep in?"

Peggy hung her head and shrugged. "Preshow jitters, Mrs. Young. We barely slept. So we went out and got breakfast and only got back to the room at—" she looked at her wristwatch. "What time did you say you went on air?"

They must have met up with Thelma at that diner. They'd all missed her radio gambit. "Between eleven and noon."

"Just after that," said Peggy, raising her half-moon eyebrows pointedly.

So they'd heard nothing of her radio interview, which, she was sure, had saved the day. Announcing she would produce Wade's little film was a real stroke of inspiration. One that would ensure uniform contracts as well.

"What did you get up to today?" Lillian asked Thelma, tilting her head in that way that made her blond hair fall in waves across her shoulder, just like Veronica Lake.

Had they not spoken? *Oh bother, what does it matter?* Kathleen had her own aims, firstly, asking Lillian for a testimonial about the quality of her clothing. After all, the girl was willing to vouch for Francella.

"Oh, I guess I had a case of the nerves too," Thelma said. "So I went to the library. Always calms me down." She looked at Kathleen. "Who's your friend?"

Was this girl suggesting something untoward? The nerve. "Oh! Moose!" Kathleen offered her most puckish smile. "That Sal. We had a chat about our little misunderstanding and he wanted to be sure me and my baby were, uh, safe. Have you heard about what happened to him?"

Silence fell over the room. She had them right where she wanted them. If Kathleen had her way, she'd have them believing Francella actually had been pregnant. And she needed this lie to work. "Poor Francella lost the baby. She won't be joining us tonight after all."

"Misunderstanding? You practically killed his guy—" Mari began before Gloria elbowed her.

"Aw, geez," Gloria said slowly. "That's too bad."

"We'll have to visit her and make sure she's okay," said DeeDee.

Kathleen's mouth twitched as she suppressed the laugh threatening to erupt. How she loved to rewrite a narrative. "I'm sure you can pass along your condolences tonight. I imagine she'll be in the audience."

"That reminds me," Thelma said. "I met the entertainment director over at the Frontier hotel—I went over there to invite Benjamin Siegel to tonight's show—"

Surely she did not intend to tell Benny about Sal's thievery already. "You did?" asked Kathleen.

"Yes, Mrs. Young. I did," Thelma said evenly.

They weren't getting it. By announcing the film production, Kathleen had not only ensured the girls' release, she'd bought them more time. The only photograph Imogene could've gotten was of the supplies. Such a shot would prove nothing.

"And are we," stammered Kathleen, "picture perfect?"

"Of course we are. We have to be. It's now or never. And Mr. Siegel is one of this town's major developers. But—and this is the big news—Maxene Lewis, she's the head of entertainment over at the Frontier, asked if we'd consider taking the Vegas Girls act over there. Five twenty-five a week to start!"

"Dollars?" asked Mari.

"Yes! As in hundred," said Thelma. "Five hundred twenty-five a week."

With that the girls were abuzz again. There was no point mentioning how such a move might irk Wade Davis now, and there was no time for a debrief. Kathleen would continue apace with her own plans. As Peggy tried to corral the girls for hair and makeup, Kathleen was left to her own devices.

THE GIRLS ASSEMBLED IN THE HALLWAY OUTSIDE THE Rodeo Room. There was no green room, not even a Doc Young makeshift special. A rush of camaraderie overcame Thelma. Before signing on with the Florida Girls, she'd never known the pleasure of working with a team where everyone had their part in creating something bigger. She was happy that Gloria, after watching her sing and dance, had put her right back in the role of emcee. That would make leaving easier. She'd grown fond of these Vegas Girls during the past few days. Nothing bonded quite like performing together.

"Here, let me fix that," said Peggy, adjusting Ana's sequined cowboy hat. "My dad, God rest his soul, would die if I didn't."

Smiling as she recalled adjusting Peggy's hat before a show, Thelma recognized it was her teammate who'd shown her how to be open to others without baring her soul. No one suspected that Peggy wasn't a makeup artist, and they all loved her. It helped that she'd made them all look like a million bucks.

Thelma crept to the door's porthole window to scan the room. "Nice crowd. Mrs. Young's out there nattering away," she said before turning back to her teammates. "But I don't see our, uh, special guests."

"Men like that are always late," said Gloria. "They probably won't come till the last show of the night. No point in waiting on them."

Not wanting to get the show underway without Siegel in the audience, Thelma looked to Lillian, but her friend merely shrugged.

"He'll come or he won't," she said. "You'd better get out there, Thelms."

Thelma faced the Vegas Girls—taking in the evening gowns that covered their cowgirl getups, which showed more skin than most bathing costumes—and gave a big smile. "Ready?" Once they'd nodded, she signaled the band and marched out to the opening strains of Helen Kane's "I Want to Be Bad," a classic tune that didn't rely on a good singing voice.

Though they'd been asked to perform for only eight minutes, they pushed their set to ten. And by the time they finished their second encore—a cover of "I'm Gonna Love That Guy," with an improvised audience sing-along for the men—the show ran closer to fifteen minutes. Still no sign of Moe or Bugsy.

By the eleven o'clock show, Thelma had decided she'd return to the Frontier and wait all night if she had to. She'd ripped her roulette wheel skirt during a costume change, so on her cue she stepped out in her sequined shorts.

"To be, or not—" Thelma began, imitating Kane's singsong vocals, but lost her place when Benjamin Siegel appeared at the far end of the room. With her father.

She picked back up on the next line, knocking Mrs. Young

as she passed her table to be sure she'd seen him and inferred her meaning. Thelma needed her to distract Sal so she could spirit Siegel away. Instead, her former boss jumped to her feet and left the room. Thelma wondered if she'd hit her too hard. *What the hell is Mrs. Young doing?*

Luckily, the show didn't miss a beat as the other girls joined her and danced their way toward the stage as the audience roared. They'd lost interest in the singing part of the song.

Such concern didn't last, supplanted by a new one as she spied Mrs. Young being chased out the door by none other than Bugsy Siegel. There was no going after the old bat now, Thelma was trapped. *The show... it must go on.*

FORTY-THREE

THE CONFRONTATIONS, Friday

KATHLEEN YOUNG BARELY MADE IT TO THE BATHROOM stall in time, her body relaxing as she relieved herself. This was absolutely something she remembered from her first two pregnancies, and it was only just beginning.

After Mr. Siegel arrived with Sal, she'd taken the first opportunity that presented itself to elude Moose, a feat that owed more to the show than her stealth. She wouldn't bolt, not now. This operation had gone sideways enough. If she didn't take charge of things, she might wind up spending the next eighteen years with Moose. It just so happened that the ideal rendezvous point coincided with her bodily needs.

The door swung on its hinges as she stood to smooth her skirt. Hardly adequate preparation for the man waiting outside her lavatory cubicle. Without looking over her shoulder, she walked to the sink and twisted the faucet handles as one.

"So," she said in a measured tone. "We meet again, Benny."

The recognition had been instant. Those electrifying azure eyes hadn't changed in the last twenty-odd years, nor had his thick patch of wiry curls.

"Gotta say, I never thought I'd see the likes of you with the likes of these." Benny leaned against the tile wall beside the door, regarding his perfectly manicured nails.

Vain as ever. Kathleen's mind flashed back to their single meeting back in 1925, a lifetime ago, when she'd fled her mother's side and forayed out into the streets of New York City alone. She prayed her mother's words had faded from his memory like the mark her hand had left on Kathleen's cheek after she caught them sharing an ice cream soda. "Get away from that good-for-nothing, no-count punk," her mother had spat. If only she'd known what they'd been doing in the alley just minutes before.

"Neither did I, Benny. Neither did I."

* * *

Eighteen excruciating minutes later—the ten o'clock crowd was by far the rowdiest—Thelma was congratulating the girls on a job well done in her best emulation of Doc Young, the consummate barker. "I'm so proud of what you did out there," she said, searching for Lillian's eyes. She wasn't doing Sun City Emporium's former owner and professional shill any justice, but she wanted to signal the need for a confab. Peggy had gone to collect their wardrobe from the stage, and Thelma had to find Mrs. Young.

Lillian took the hint. "Ladies, what do you say we head for the casino and let these folks buy us some champagne? I, for one, plan to find a devastatingly handsome man to trifle with," she trilled before leading them back to the Rodeo Room.

More torturous minutes passed as the girls filed by, each thanking Thelma for including them in the show. She tried to make pleasantries but couldn't get her mind off how Bugsy Siegel had appeared to chase Mrs. Young.

Before Thelma could head out to follow their trail, Sal

Giancarlo appeared at her side. "Come with me. Now." His cane was nowhere in sight. Fury was good for his health, apparently.

"Sal, I—"

"Now," he said, grabbing her roughly by the elbow.

* * *

"You look good, Kathy," said Benny.

On his lips, her high school nickname made her feel young again. Rebellious. Had he forgotten? How those many years ago her mother had put him in his place, yanking her by the ear all the way back to their hotel. "Kathleen Louise DeVane, that boy is worse than trash," she'd said.

"That's not why you followed me here," Kathleen said.

"All right. Let's just cut to the chase. If you're making a movie in Las Vegas, you're going to put Virginia Hill in it."

"Am I?" Kathleen finished drying her hands on the hand towel roller before hitching her hip on the sink basin. "And why would I do that?"

"It's either that, or I start talking about what happened to Diego Gonzalez."

Kathleen gasped—*What other secrets did Matteo tell, and to whom?*—but covered her slip with indignation. "I've no idea what on earth you're talking about."

"Aw, Kath. It wasn't even three months ago. You trying to tell me you forgot the dead guy in your room?"

Getting close enough to smell his aftershave, Kathleen murmured, "I'm not trying to tell you anything. You're the one followed me into the ladies. Do you normally spend a lot of time in women's washrooms?"

"Oh, I'm not the one who needs to be answering questions here, Kathy."

Not this again, thought Kathleen, finding it easy to ignore the icy glint in his eye. Her mother, she believed, was right. He was an insecure boy—all front and a sharp suit. All he needed was placating.

She smoothed his lapels and returned to the sink, hooking her elbows into her palms and gazing up at him. "When you're right, you're right."

"So tell me, why'd Sal's men pick you up last night?" Benny faced her, stance wide, hands upturned, and head tilted.

Kathleen shrugged. "Last night, the girls wanted to go out on the town, so I took them. Then they thought it'd be a real lark to leave me stranded by the side of the road."

Her story sounded more plausible with each retelling. She still didn't know why Sal's men had carted them off. *If they were there to steal, why would they have shown themselves to Siegel's guards?*

*   *   *

"Listen to me, young lady," Sal said, his fingers still digging into Thelma's elbow. "You better believe you are in hot water."

"What is it this time?" she asked, yanking her arm from her father's grasp.

"Don't you sass me!" He marched her through the dining hall and out into the parking lot.

Her mother had always treated her like an irksome little sister rather than behaving in this parental fashion. Thelma didn't much care for it.

"Sal," she began as soon as they were outside. "I may be your offspring, but I am not your child."

"I don't know what you're talking about," said Sal, raking his hand through his thick dark hair. Thelma's hair. "But you need to shut your trap and listen up. I haven't been able to find you all day, and Bugsy is mad as hell. What the hell do you think you were doing last night?"

Thelma was still rubbing her elbow. "I was out with your girlfriend, Sal."

"I know that. After that. With Lillian Wright and that diner waitress. Out with Kathleen Young."

"Peggy Holmes?" she asked, truly perplexed. He'd either forgotten the woman who'd nursed him after his stroke or was suggesting she was low-class. "With Mrs. Young and Lillian? Together?"

They'd told him the story about being out on the town—they must have. Key to that story was how they'd left Kathleen in the dust. *What makes him suspect I was with them? Or did they give him a different story altogether?* Her open-mouthed shock failed to convince him.

"I don't believe you for one minute."

Thelma rolled her eyes. "Listen—"

"No, you listen. I could keep you safe in Florida. But here? There's only so much I can do. If Bugsy finds out what's going on under his nose, it's gonna put a halt to half the construction in this town."

"So you admit it. You are stealing from him."

"All of us take from his lot. He's the only one who can get anything in these days." Sal shook his head as he let out an exasperated sigh. "Think about it. If my men were there for the goods, how come they left with the girls?"

Thelma's palms burned, but for once, instead of pushing the sensation away, she let it tell her what it was trying to. Looking deeply at her father, she thought about how he'd offered her the casino—his man had drawn up a contract. He'd kept her a secret to keep her safe. Now that his circumstances had changed, so had his tactics.

He was telling the truth. His men hadn't been there that night to take supplies—though someone had. They were there keeping an eye on the girls.

Like lightning, it hit her—what he'd said a few days before. Her father didn't have anything to do with George's murder. He was telling the truth about that too.

But if it wasn't Sal, who was it?

Before either of them could say more, a knot of revelers tumbled out of the Rodeo Room, heading for the casino across the lot. Sal and Thelma looked off into the distance, in cahoots against outsiders.

When they'd gone, Sal was the first to speak. "Honey, I've been worried sick about you."

His words held the force of gravity, knocking the breath out of Thelma and turning her heart to jelly. She felt as if a dam had broken, releasing years of pent-up longing she never knew existed. The feeling was something like missing George but lived just beside that.

"Come here," he said, wrapping Thelma into his broad arms and barrel chest.

A lump formed in her throat, and she teetered on the edge of tears. In that moment, Thelma realized just how starved she'd been, how much she'd yearned for this simple human connection without ever acknowledging it. She swallowed hard, forcing back the tears, but the emotional intensity lingered, leaving her raw and strangely comforted.

* * *

"WOMEN. JESUS. I DON'T KNOW WHY SAL'S MEN ARE watching you so close. Near as I can tell, it's a waste of their time, so what do I care?"

Kathleen reached for Bugsy's face, swiping her thumb

against the base of his chin. She lowered her voice. "You know just how women are."

From the way he looked at her, she knew he still wanted her, and damn if her libido wasn't rearing its head again. She would not make the same mistake she had with Matteo. She'd long used her sex appeal to get what she wanted, all the while letting men mistake her for harmless.

He shook his head and moved toward the mirror. "Kath, listen to me." He stared at his reflection. "You're going to put Ginny—Virginia—in your movie.

This couldn't have gone better if she'd planned it. Joining him at the sink, she spoke to his reflection. "Why, Benny, I can't think of a better vehicle for Miss Hill than a movie with no script attached. *C'est parfait!*"

Bugsy Siegel grabbed her wrist. "You remembered," he said, his voice registering a deeper tone.

"Of course," she said, though she had no idea what he was referring to, only that he was coming across as less menacing and more like a man in her thrall. She pulled her wrist from his grasp but then clasped his hand with hers. "There is something I need to tell you."

THELMA HEARD THE PURPOSEFUL CLACK OF MRS. YOUNG'S heels before the woman's voice broke her and Sal apart.

"What in the Sam Hill?" Mrs. Young said. "A little father daughter love. I hope."

Only Mrs. Young could make me feel the need to protect Sal Giancarlo, thought Thelma. But that wasn't entirely true. She'd looked after him in Tampa, and now he was trying to warn her about his associates. In his line of work, that was saying something.

"I've heard enough outta you today, Kathleen. I tried to help you girls last night. But Bugsy is fuming."

"What in heaven's name do you mean? I was just with the man. He's fine."

Sal laughed and took a cigar from his pocket. As he rolled the stogie between his fingers, the fine scent wafted toward Thelma. She hadn't had one since she'd been in Sal's office. Suddenly, she wanted one desperately.

"I don't know what that man said to you," said Sal, "but if I was you, I wouldn't believe a word he says."

Mrs. Young planted her fists on her hips and tapped her foot, looking more like a schoolmarm than ever. "But you, I should believe?"

"Okay, everyone," Thelma said, stepping between the pair and placing a hand on each. "Will someone please tell me what happened last night?"

"First, I'd like a word with you, Thelma. In private."

"No one's going anywhere," said Sal, passing the cigar below his nose. "Mom. Yeah, I got the results. You're knocked up all right."

Mrs. Young harrumphed. "Yet you're still planning to smoke that disgusting thing."

This was getting stranger all the time. *What results? Are they referring to Mrs. Young's pregnancy?* Has she—

"After you left, I thought to myself..." Sal looked at Thelma. "That old broad musta been some kind of desperate to say she was having my grandson."

"Thelma. A word," growled Mrs. Young, her lips a straight line.

The words of Madame St. Clair rang in her ears: "Do not cleave to what you think you know about Salvatore Giancarlo. He is a changed man." While Thema had seen the changes herself, she now recognized that advice for what it was. Her father might have mellowed, but she was not about to best him at deceit. There was no use trying to play him.

"No. Just stop. Both of you." Thelma stepped back. "Yes, she's having Matteo's baby. And yes, we were out at Benjamin Siegel's place to see if we could get any evidence of the blatant theft your men are pulling off."

"Jesus Christ." Sal crushed the cigar in his hand. "What the hell is the matter with you?"

"Thelma," said Mrs. Young, still sounding inexplicably impatient.

What is the big rush?

"Good goddamn," said Sal, looking not at Mrs. Young or Thelma but directly through the porthole into the Rodeo Room. "What did you do now?"

Thelma turned to follow his gaze, only to see an agitated Bugsy Siegel dodging between the chairs and people like he was avoiding landmines.

"That screwy bastard is coming after us," said Sal. "Follow me." Without waiting for a response, he turned and dashed toward a parked car. Mrs. Young followed.

Thelma stood her ground.

* * *

Bugsy cursed as he burst through the doors, his voice incongruously high-pitched, almost squeaky. "Where does he think he's going?"

Thelma wondered if that tone was where he'd gotten his nickname. He—unlike her father—was unchanged. Mrs. Young had spilled their intel, but Thelma had no intention of losing the upper hand. Virginia Hill might have taught her that the men never suspected you, but Queenie had shown her that she could be a force in her own right.

"Who? Where is who going?" Thelma asked.

Siegel raised his elbow, and for a split second, Thelma thought he might strike her. Coils of wavy hair, normally slicked back, had sprung around his head. Brushing his elbow with her fingertips, Thelma widened her eyes and folded in on herself. Bugsy was a small fella.

"You're just who I've been hoping to talk to," she said.

Flinching, Bugsy frowned. "What is it with you women? Listen, I got no interest. I'm up to my eyeballs right now. But I'm gonna find your old man, and when I do, I'm gonna kill him."

"Is this about the thefts?" Thelma laughed, a twinkling, merry sound she'd perfected over years of practice.

She'd pieced together the obvious—in a stunning reversal, Mrs. Young had been the one to spout off and divulge their intel on the thefts. Now the situation was different. After hearing Sal, Thelma could not unsee his protective behavior toward her —a pattern she'd possibly been blind to her whole life. What she'd heard about her father killing his brother over the numbers racket in Tampa or sending his son to World War II to toughen up—those could have been rumors. Or they could have been true.

Had Thelma been so different? She'd rejected George, sent thugs after deadbeats back in Tampa, and finally burned her father's nightclub to the ground. George's forgiveness may have absolved her, but his love had changed her. *Could I do the same for my father? Should I?*

At the very least, she could protect her unborn niece or nephew.

"Oh, silly," said Thelma, tapping Siegel's shoulder. "You can't listen to a thing Kathleen Young says. She just wants your business. She'd say anything to get you to buy her uniforms. Did she have any evidence?"

Bugsy stopped. Stared at Thelma. Francella must've been

telling the truth when she'd said the casino was his weak spot. Thelma's only hope now was that this gambit would stall him.

"Though... I do have a proposition for you," she said, her first two fingers crawling up his sleeve before she patted his arm and looked away. "But maybe now's not the best time."

He straightened his tie and adjusted his shoulders. "Your old man isn't going anywhere I can't find him. Shoot."

Bugsy reached into his pocket and pulled out his cigarettes, offering one to Thelma. They stood smoking as she unraveled her plans for the club in Cuba. There would be gambling, of course, but the emphasis would be on the entertainment. The glamor. Something like what she sensed Maxene Lewis had in mind for her club. In addition to the big-name performers who would pull in large crowds, they'd have home-grown house regulars. Dancers and singers would keep the party going between the big acts so that the entertainment wasn't an afterthought to the casino.

"A club like that will attract locals and tourists from all over, not just California," she said, her voice wavering as she repeated what George had said when he agreed to the idea. "It's the perfect time and place to be right now." She didn't add his last words—"with you, my love."

Grinding his smoke under his shoe, Bugsy grimaced. "Sure, sweetheart. But the money's in the gambling." He turned and walked toward the sea of cars.

Queenie had been right when she'd said beating these men at their own game was easy. Knowing she'd stalled him momentarily, Thelma smiled. The victory was fleeting. She marched toward the casino to find the girls.

THE AFTER PARTY, Saturday

THELMA WATCHED BUGSY'S CAR ROLL OUT OF THE PARKING lot before she headed into the casino. She let her eyes adjust to the dim interior. A haze of cigarette smoke hung in the air, mixing with the scent of cologne. Flashes of neon and jewels sparkled around the room, all of it a backdrop to the clack of dice, the shuffle of cards, and the shouts of the players. She was seized by an urge to join one of the tables, knock back a whiskey, and surrender her vigilance to the sickening thrill. There would be time enough to lose herself once she'd defeated Sal Giancarlo.

Peggy's distinctive laugh rose above the noise, and Thelma turned to see her holding court at one of the roulette wheels. No Lillian. Hurrying over, she reached for her friend's hand. "Hate to steal her, boys, but show biz is an unforgiving mistress."

"Hey, that's my money on the line over there," Peggy protested.

Thelma winked at the men as she dragged Peggy along. "Keep the change, boys." When she was out of earshot, Thelma hissed, "The house always wins."

Peggy stopped. "Did you just wink?"

"I did."

"You don't wink, Thelms," said Peggy, her voice wary. "Now I know something's wrong. Spill."

"First, we have to find Lillian."

"Find Lillian? Why didn't you say so?"

They spotted Gloria first, at the blackjack table. One look from Thelma was all it took to convince her to follow. Right behind came Mari, Ana, and DeeDee.

"What do you need?" Gloria asked.

"Can you help us find Lillian?"

The girls spent the better part of an hour searching among the gaming tables, in the ladies, even returning to the restaurant for a look around the Rodeo Room before Peggy finally called it. "My dogs are barking."

"But what if Lillian is in trouble?" asked Thelma.

"But nothing, Thelms. At this point, we should think about expanding our search, and well, you aren't dressed for this."

As if noticing for the first time, Thelma looked down at her sequined short pants and Western-style crop top tied at the bra line. She looked back up—all the dancers were still in costume— and laughed. "Mrs. Young would kill us if she could see us now."

Imagining where their old boss might be just then, Thelma's smile fell. She hadn't revealed the full picture to Peggy yet. "You're right. Let's at least go and change."

"She might be in the room," ventured Gloria.

Thelma stole a glance at Peggy before agreeing. "Let's go find out." Holding Peggy back, she let Gloria lead the way. "We should let them go after they change," she whispered in her friend's ear. "I'll fill you in soon as we get a minute alone."

* * *

Kathleen could no longer see the Las Vegas lights, just the ominous dark outline of the mountain range surrounding the city. At least she wasn't worried about finding a permanent home under a desert rock, even as Sal blathered on.

"I don't think you accomplished what you think you did," he muttered, having produced another cigar he kept clamped between his lips. "Everybody's in on this shit. It's not just me."

The only thing to do was hold her tongue. In Kathleen's experience, once a man got to babbling, it was no use trying to talk sense. Best to let him spin out, then just take the upper hand.

"Bugs is the only one who gets any shipments. I don't know how he does it. He's gotta have some kinda direct line to Hollywood studios. Which, by the way—them's the real crooks. Where are they gettin' supplies? War ain't won yet."

The mention of war turned Kathleen's mind to Archie, her gentle baby, so eager to please. When he was maybe five, he caught a butterfly against his arm, but when he peeled away his hand to show his mother, the little creature was smashed against his palm. Archie was inconsolable, not even ice cream changed his mind. Then Lloyd came home and declared that this was for the best, because the butterfly would soon return and have another chance to live. The child talked about reincarnation all summer, until school started, when his teacher told him it wasn't Christian and to please stop. And so he did. Archie always did the right thing. Still, a patriot? He didn't have that kind of fight in him.

Bertie had probably driven him out. That boy could aggravate Jesus Christ himself. Of course he'd turned to Sal Giancarlo. He couldn't hold down the store without help.

"Sal, what exactly are you—"

The car swerved sharply.

"Sir," Kathleen said as she righted herself. "Must I remind you? Precious cargo and all."

Sal snorted. "Would you rather I hit the pothole?"

"I'd rather you explained why you keep kidnapping women."

He slammed on the brakes. "That ain't funny."

"Am I laughing?"

Lifting his foot from the pedal, he resumed course. "You came of your own free will."

"Because a madman was about to descend upon us." Kathleen wanted to push the gear stick into park. "Now I demand to know where you're taking me."

He looked at her with what might have been pity. "I don't know, Kath. But there's some things you should know."

An icy chill lodged in Kathleen's belly. She hoped like hell there was nothing she should know from Salvatore Giancarlo.

*　*　*

PEGGY HAD SCARCELY OPENED THE DOOR TO THE SUITE SHE and Lillian shared before letting out a blood-curdling scream. Not again, thought Thelma, recalling the deadly incident last spring in Mrs. Young's suite as she rushed to her friend's side. What she beheld shocked her, but in an entirely different way.

"Sir! What are you doing here? And where are your clothes?" barked Thelma.

"Uh, Thelms?" came Lillian's voice. "Just a minute."

Someone slammed the door shut. Thelma and Peggy looked at each other then at the girls.

"No wonder she scrammed outta there tonight," said Ana, who was craning her neck to see the action. "The fella's dreamy."

"I wouldn't kick him out of bed for eating crackers," Mari agreed.

"What'd I miss?" asked DeeDee.

"He could balance on that third leg!"

"Mari!" said Gloria, sounding more approving than admonishing.

Peggy and Thelma were, for once, mute.

A disheveled-looking Lillian opened the door, wearing only a burgundy silk robe with a cherry blossom brocade. Recalling Lillian's plain cotton robe from the Florida Girls' tour, Thelma saw she wasn't the only one who was changing.

"C'mon in," said Lillian, guiding them past one of the unmade beds toward the seating area facing the pool, where the curtains had been drawn. "Ladies, meet Phil Skylar, my fiancé."

The dashing Phil, now clad in striped navy pajama bottoms, stopped pouring his drink and turned, flashing a million-dollar smile. "Well, hi, ladies."

For a moment, everyone was silent. Lillian Montgomery was, according to all the gossip rags, dating Montgomery Clift. Wasn't she? With a pang, it dawned on Thelma that she hadn't even asked about her friend's love life.

Mari broke the silence with congratulations, and soon they were all offering their well wishes, chattering at once. Finally, Lillian addressed the question no one had dared ask.

"Ladies, I must request one thing," she said, looking around the room. "This is strictly confidential. You understand? My agent says it's too soon in my career to marry, and certainly not a stuntman. Monte—Mr. Clift—is a dear friend. Isn't that right, Philip?"

Phil nodded. "It's true."

Now Thelma caught up. Montgomery Clift had to be one of Hollywood's perpetual bachelors. As no one's candidate for marriage, he was the perfect safe boyfriend. Heat rose at Thelma's neck—a combination of sorrow that Lillian hadn't confided in her, mixed with the joy of knowing her cousin-in-law had found the kind of love that had inspired her to marry George. She walked toward the couple, reached for Phil's arm, and gave it a squeeze. A wall of muscle. Wow. Thelma felt an unexpected, dizzying rush. A swoon even. She tamped it down.

"It's lovely to meet you, but... may I steal her for just a moment?" She gestured toward the hall with her head. "Lillian?"

The door had barely shut before Lillian was offering apologies. "I didn't know he was coming. He thought it would be romantic to spring a ring on me."

"You just got engaged? Just now?"

Lillian nodded.

"That's wonderful. Truly. And he's a real dish. But—"

"Oh, he is. I know you'll love him when you get to know him. He's been so understanding."

The bride-to-be was gushing, which Thelma could understand, even as she wanted to interrupt. A crisis was afoot. She touched Lillian's wrist, so lovely and delicate. Vulnerable even. She couldn't let her get caught up in this mess, nor could she ask her to run out on her fiancé on the night of their engagement. She'd give anything now to have had that time with George.

"I know you're right, but right now, can you ask him to leave?"

Lillian blanched.

"Just for a minute. We need to change back into our clothes, and then we're heading back out."

"Oh, of course. I can send him to the casinos. He's fine now," she said with a knowing tilt to her lips.

Thelma tittered.

"Where are we going?"

"We? But—" Thelma wanted to lie, but she was suddenly

unconvinced that was the best way to protect her friends. "You should just stay with Phil. Sal took off with Mrs. Young, and Bugsy is on the warpath, looking for them. She spilled the beans, and now Siegel knows Sal was stealing from him."

Eyes wide, Lillian asked, "You think Sal's going to kill Mrs. Young?"

"I don't know. I don't think so. He knows she's having Matteo's baby."

"She's what?"

"Oh, right. Well..."

"Jesus Christ, Thelma. We have to find them."

"But you just got engaged!"

"Oh, don't be so provincial. So what? I love Phil. But George is my family. That comes first. And Bugsy killing Sal is too easy. After last night, we need to put our heads together to figure out how to catch that bastard red-handed."

"It's more complicated than that now." Thelma tilted her head toward the room. "We need to get the other girls out of here so we can talk."

As soon as they'd changed, Gloria, Ana, Mari, and DeeDee were only too ready to head home.

"You don't want to go out? See your adoring fans?" asked Lillian as they said their goodbyes.

"Our adoring boyfriends will be expecting us," said DeeDee. "Plus, we have a show tomorrow night."

Aware she'd probably never see these girls again, Thelma hugged them each in turn. "Call Maxene, Gloria," she said, squeezing the woman's shoulders. "I mean it."

Gloria promised she would, but Thelma decided she'd contact Maxene too. Make sure she had Gloria's number.

Once the door closed, the three of them returned to the sitting room. This time, Thelma pulled up the desk chair to face Lillian and Peggy on the sofa as she filled them in, all the way from discovering that Francella had intercepted her note for Agent Nelson to what had transpired in the last minutes of the Vegas Girls show. Peggy's wide brow was uncharacteristically furrowed and her platinum waves flat, while Lillian sat back, looking oddly relaxed with her tousled honey locks brushing against her red robe.

Peggy, exhaling a giant plume of cigarette smoke, was the first to speak. "I bet Francella knows where Sal is?"

"Are you mad?" asked Lillian, looking decidedly less calm. "She'll just tell everything to Sal. Or Wade. Then we're liable to end up in the same boat as that Nelson fellow." Lillian reached for one of her friend's Pall Malls.

"Lills, you don't smoke," said Thelma, tapping a butt out of her own pack.

"I do now." Lillian struck a match against its box and lit up. "I have to ask this, and I know how it sounds, but... Do we care what happens to Sal? If Mrs. Young already told Bugsy Siegel everything, isn't it too late?"

"Weren't you listening to what I said? Bugsy thinks Sal stole from him."

"He did steal from him," said Lillian.

"So did everyone!"

Lillian rested her head in her palm and exhaled. "To tell you the truth, I don't care about everyone. I care about avenging George."

"That's just it, Lills." Thelma had to make her see. "Sal didn't have anything to do with George's death."

"You don't know that, Thelma. What do you think he's going to say?"

"That's another reason to talk to Francella," said Peggy. "She'll know."

"Now I've heard everything." Lillian scoffed. "You really think Mata Hari is going to help the people who ratted out her boyfriend?"

"Come on, now, Lills." Thelma tried to sound placating. She understood why Lillian would be resistant. "Francella is hardly a double agent. Wade is her cousin. He pushed her to be with Sal, and she liked having that power."

Lillian's face hardened. "I can see how you'd relate."

Thelma stood.

"Now hold your horses, both of you." Peggy moved between Lillian and Thelma, arms outstretched like she was directing traffic. "We need to work together if we're going to get out of this mess. At least we know what Francella wants, right? Broadway contacts."

"You do make a point." Lillian stabbed her cigarette into the ashtray. "There's no limit to what some people will do for money."

Her words set Thelma's teeth on edge. Was that a dig? But Lillian still believed Thelma's mother had forced her into taking on clients. She had no clue that Thelma volunteered. There was so much unsaid between them, but only one thing that mattered right now.

"I know we can trust Francella." Thelma had never confessed this secret, but now that she had, she saw her premonitions for what they were. Not an intrusion, but something central. A part of her, sure as her amber eyes. A gift, if she let it be. "Because sometimes I get these... feelings."

"Feelings?" Lillian reared her head back. "What is that supposed to mean?"

Thelma spoke in measured tones. "I don't know how to describe it. Sometimes I just know things. I've had these, I don't know... premonitions? All my life. But I've only recently let myself pay attention. That's also how I know Sal had nothing to do with this." Relief flooded her body.

Gripping the back of her chair, Lillian hissed at Thelma. "Tell us then. Where do you feel George could be?"

Thelma's eyes clouded and Peggy reached for her arm. "There's still the issue of Mrs. Young." She looked at Lillian. "Even if we have mixed feelings about Sal, we can't abandon her."

"Now that makes more sense. Find Kathleen Young and we find Sal." Lillian straightened. "But then we're back to square one."

This was too much for Thelma. "Okay, listen up. No one wants to make George's killer pay more than I do. But even if you think Sal is to blame, he is not our biggest problem. Our biggest problem right now is that when Imogene's article comes out, we are all sitting ducks. Us *and* Sal."

Thelma's hands tingled as a thought flashed through her mind. "Peggy and I are heading to Francella's hotel."

"Don't you sideline me."

"I'm not, Lillian. Go and find your fiancée."

"What? I don't see how this is getting us any closer to finding George. And don't tell me you have a feeling about it."

Thelma stood, nostrils flaring. "Then you'll just have to trust me." Without thinking, she reached for the sapphire at her throat and yanked the necklace free. "Lillian, you know how much this means to me. I want you to keep it until we make George's killer pay."

Time stood still as Lillian stared into her palm, blinking. When she looked up, tears pearled at the corners of her eyes. She pulled Thelma in for a hug.

"We'll do whatever it takes," said Thelma. "I promise."

FORTY-FIVE

CONFESSIONS, Saturday

The neon lights of Las Vegas burning on the far horizon took Kathleen by surprise. Either the desert had broken her sense of direction—which she'd always considered excellent—or it was this damn pregnancy. Her grandmother had managed to carry twins with four stairstep children under the age of twelve and nary a washing machine or indoor plumbing to speak of. Mémé would accuse her of going soft.

"I knew Matteo was AWOL," he said. "Back when we were in Vegas."

He wasn't going to ask for details about the conception, was he?

"My associates... let's just say, they knew I wasn't happy about it. I coulda got him an exception. I didn't. That boy was always more worried about how he looked than getting a job done right."

"God rest—"

"The military was gonna fix him. Then he..."

Kathleen had no idea where Sal was going with this and wasn't sure she wanted to find out. *Does he know I killed Matteo?* she wondered, quickly adding. *In self-defense.*

"Being sick has given me some perspective." Sal spoke purposefully. "Nobody's ever betrayed me like my body."

Kathleen worked not to scoff. *If only I hadn't gotten pregnant.* "Well, we all age," she said.

Sal's knuckles went white on the steering wheel. "Not in my business. Here's the thing, Kathleen—"

She gulped for air.

Sal slowed the car. "Are you all right?"

"Fine. Fine," she said as she rolled down her window.

The car stopped, and the only sound was Kathleen struggling to breathe. Once her breathing had returned to normal Sal cut the engine and she turned to face him. Ready to confess.

"I think it's my fault someone put a hit on him," Sal said.

Kathleen gasped in relief. Fortunately, Sal misinterpreted.

"Oh yeah," he said. "I musta said a dozen times how I was gonna kill him. How if somebody else didn't do it first, I'd do it myself."

Kathleen thought back. She hadn't been privy to the details of Sal's stroke and recovery. All she knew was that he had rebounded around the time of their finale—the same night she... the image of Matteo on the bathroom floor flashed in Kathleen's mind before she pushed it aside. No one but she and Thelma had been witnesses. Except for that fellow who was clearly besotted with Thelma. Carlos something or other. They could shuck the blame for Matteo's death onto *him,* she realized.

"Aw, there, there. You mustn't blame yourself, Sal." She slid across the bench and squeezed his shoulder before resting her head on it. They stayed that way in silence a moment before she sat upright. "Do you think someone was trying to take over while you were... not yourself, Sal?"

"He was a sitting duck." Sal shifted to look at her. "Did you love him?"

Kathleen blanched. She had no ready answer, so she went

with the truth. "The only man I've ever truly loved is my Lloyd. That's not to say I wasn't fond of Matteo. I... Well, my husband has been sick for some time."

Sal nodded. "Yeah, I checked on that too. Hospital says you're telling the truth about that surgery. But his lungs are bad."

His words struck Kathleen like a blow. So casual. So devastating. Her vision blurred.

"Aw, c'mere," said Sal, wrapping her in his wide arms.

In that moment, Kathleen had no choice but to go to him. Far from soothing, Sal's embrace reminded Kathleen of the stranglehold this man had held on her family for years. Now was the time to strike. After what she hoped was an appropriate amount of "comforting," she wiggled free and scooted back to her side of the car.

"We all worry about our children, Sal. Which is why... I don't know how to even ask you this, but how did you end up giving money to Bertie?"

"To who? Albert? Your oldest son, you mean?"

Kathleen nodded.

"Did I? I don't think I did. Unless Artemis—he oversees Tampa for me—started a new game up there."

"Bolita? Again? Oh, Sal—"

"What? I thought you guys loved it. 'I don't know why it's illegal—it's just a game,' didn't you always say? Made you a tidy sum, I think."

"True, but..." She sighed. "I worry about Bertie. He has an issue with it. With gambling."

Sal started the car back up. "You know what? I'll check in with Artemis."

"Would you?"

"Of course." He smiled as he pulled onto the road. "You're about to make me a *nonno*."

A nonno? What was *that?*

"A grandpa," he said as if reading her mind. "Which reminds me, there's one other thing I gotta tell you."

THE ROOM NUMBERS AT THE PLAZA, KATHLEEN OBSERVED, were painted on tin plates cut to look like diamonds from a deck of cards. She'd missed that detail on her last visit, what with her head being covered by a pillowcase. At least this hotel's embellishments were geared toward the business at hand.

When Francella opened the door, sans makeup, her appearance was shocking. Kathleen forced her face to go blank as she beheld the violent bruising under her eyes, which had turned a deep aubergine purple. With the swelling receding, Kathleen now saw that the girl's nose had gone slightly off kilter. So much for her dreams of making it in the moving pictures.

Looking at Sal, Francella put her finger to her lips.

Strange, thought Kathleen.

"You're here!" Francella cried, opening the door wide for Sal before enveloping him in a warm embrace. "And you brought Kathleen!"

Gratified as she was that the girl had finally gotten her name right, she was outraged at the brass of these people. After all, it was Kathleen who'd righted this ship, first announcing the film and then getting word to Benny about Sal's misdeeds. Yet here she was being treated like an afterthought. She wouldn't have it.

"Nice to see you, too, Francella. Especially since I've got good news for you. For all of you." Kathleen entered and saw Thelma Miles and Peggy Holmes standing in Francella's parlor area.

Thelma jammed her fists onto her hips. "Good news? Mrs. Young, what could possibly have happened since you decided to talk to Ben Siegel?"

"Decided?" Kathleen glared at Thelma.

It crossed Kathleen's mind that she was jealous of Thelma. Through no merit of her own, the girl was stinking rich with her whole life ahead of her. And she lived on her own terms.

But jealousy was for the foolish and the feckless, Kathleen reminded herself. She wouldn't succumb to it. She was about to produce a movie, for goodness' sake.

"Thelma, my dear, wasn't talking to Benny *your* plan?" Kathleen marched in, took a seat on the divan, and hiked her feet onto the coffee table.

"What plan?" asked Sal.

* * *

THELMA LOOKED AT HER FATHER. HIS CLOTHES AND HAIR were a mess. She hadn't seen him in such disarray since his stroke. "Sal—"

"The plan where we turn you in to everyone in town because our government contact is dead, every cop in this town is on the take, and we wanted to be sure that if you didn't die in jail, you at least died a poor man."

Thelma, Peggy, and Francella turned and stared at Kathleen. During her proclamation, she hadn't moved from her seat. *What is wrong with her?* There was coming clean, and then there was suicide.

Sal tipped his head back and let out a great belly laugh, to the room's palpable relief. Until he spoke. "You're gonna get us all killed."

He wasn't wrong. Nobody liked a rat.

Mrs. Young's mouth tightened, but before she could do any more damage, there was a knock at the door.

"Who the hell's that?" Thelma said to Francella in a stage whisper.

"How should I know," she mouthed back.

"Oh, for Pete's sake," said Mrs. Young, who suddenly rose to her feet and bounded for the door. "Who is it?"

Thelma rushed in behind her to see none other than Imogene Fuchs, her ankle trussed up in a bulky bandage. "I got it," Imogene said, lifting the camera strapped around her neck. "Those bastards are finally gonna pay."

"I thought your camera was broken," said Thelma.

Imogene's face fell. "Not the reception I was hoping for, but no. Just the flashbulb and the arm that holds it. I got my spare to stay on with my hundred-mile-an-hour tape." She tapped the side of her Nikon, which was wrapped in the same silver tape as her ankle. "This stuff fixes everything."

"Wonderful!" said Kathleen before turning to address the room. "While you were all getting ready for your show, I called to make sure she got out there tonight."

"You what?" said Thelma. "Oh, never mind. You have to hold your story. It can't run till we get out of here."

"Hold my story?"

Imogene barged past Kathleen, stopping short when she saw Sal Giancarlo. "What's he doing here?"

"What am I doing here? Who the hell are you?" asked Sal.

"I'm the reporter who just scored the scoop of the century, that's who," said Imogene, lifting her chin.

"Gimme that thing!" Sal cried as he lunged for the camera. Soon he was choking her with the strap.

Before Thelma could react, a metal object sailed past her head just as Imogene unfastened the strap's buckle. Sal fell away from Imogene, and her camera crashed to the floor. Imogene staggered back a few steps as the metal heel of their horseshoe alarm clock lodged itself in Francella's wall.

"Imogene!" cried Thelma.

"Sal!" yelled Francella.

"Get the camera," Sal ordered Francella before slumping onto the floor.

Francella scrambled for the evidence, but Imogene was laughing. In a hoarse voice she croaked, "Too late. I already filed."

* * *

After seating Sal and Francella as far away from Kathleen and Imogene as Francella's hotel room would allow, Thelma pulled Peggy aside as she poured drinks. "This is not good."

"It's not the worst either, though, is it?" said Peggy, accepting a glass. "Won't the attention from a story make him safer?"

"I can hear you just fine, Peggy," said Sal.

So he did remember her.

"Do you have any idea how many people this is gonna put out of work?" he asked.

Peggy and Thelma looked at each other. Neither had thought about that.

"You're both fools," said Francella. "No one dies in Vegas. It's the rule. If they want you dead, they run you out of town. You're safer here than anywhere. If a story's in the paper, though, all bets are off."

Thelma scrutinized Imogene, but the reporter shrugged. "I can't say if that's true, but I could find out."

"I'm telling you, she's right," said Sal. "They'll eighty-six me in the joint. And that leaves all of you unprotected too."

Thelma tapped her finger on her whiskey glass. Despite what Sal had implied, she'd always looked after herself. But that wasn't the same as looking after Peggy or Francella or Mrs.

Young. Then there was the baby to consider. This was the exact mess she'd tried to avoid.

Suddenly, her palms lit up. "If they want you dead, we can make that happen." She looked at Imogene. "But first, you have to kill that story. I can get you a better one." She looked at Kathleen. "You will have to sacrifice."

FORTY-SIX

THE SWITCH, Saturday

THELMA, FRANCELLA, AND PEGGY SAT IN THE FRONTIER'S dinner theater, a proper orchestra room with covered tables set around a stage. Maxene had been only too happy to accommodate, ushering them to the front of the house. It probably didn't hurt that they were each decked out in one of Lillian's boutique gowns, though Francella had felt the need to accent her look with a cheetah-print headscarf. Beside them sat none other than Benjamin Siegel, presiding over the table as if he hadn't a care in the world.

"Everyone's with him," Francella whispered into Thelma's ear, the bow in her hair bobbing. "Not only from the Nevada Projects Corporation—don't look, but that's Meyer Lansky and Frank Costello—but he also brought his people, Moe Sedway, David Berman, Gus Greenbaum, and Moe Dalitz."

It was either very good or terrible.

"Act like you don't see 'em," she advised. "Drives 'em around the bend."

As the band played, Thelma tried to keep up a lively banter, even as she worried that Sal might not show up. What if her father had changed his mind about giving up his life to save the rest of them?

Then the star performer took the stage, and she forgot everything else. From the opening notes—a slowed version of Louis Jordan's "Caldonia"—she could not tear her eyes away from Lili St. Cyr.

St. Cyr teased the audience. Out popped a toe, then a bare leg, then she twirled onto the stage, removing her long slit skirt, then her top, until finally she was down to mesh panties and sequined pasties. All the while moving in such a way as to cover herself, making the desire to see her slip irresistible. When she stepped into a clear bathtub, bubbles began to fly.

Peggy's voice broke the moment. "He's here."

Thelma looked to the rear of the room, where sure enough, Sal strode toward them. She waited till he was less than six feet away before nodding at her father's girlfriend. After scraping her chair back from the table, Francella bounded toward him, speaking in angry tones before pushing him out of the way and marching to the exit. Unfortunately, her performance coincided with St. Cyr's finale, which meant Francella's show was lost to the thunderous applause. As Sal followed her out the door, all eyes were on the stage.

No matter. Time to send in Mrs. Young.

As if racing after Sal, Thelma jumped up and gave chase—behind Chickie, of course. It would not have gone unnoticed if her father hadn't brought his protection.

Francella was in position at the top of the stairs, but Thelma didn't spot Mrs. Young amid the lobby paraphernalia until she was upon her. Her former boss had stunned them all when she'd offered herself as bait.

"I know Benny Siegel," she'd said. "I'll draw him out."

Benny? Thelma would have to ask her about that later. This undertaking was either going to work or get them all killed sooner rather than later.

"You're up." Thelma wondered where Lillian and her fiancé, Phil, were hiding.

* * *

KATHLEEN STORMED INTO THE SHOW, HER ONLY assignment to drag Benny out in such a way that his companions followed. The applause was still raging when she approached him from behind, thinking she'd whisper something suggestive in his ear. Before she'd touched his collar, Benny's security man knocked her to the floor. *How did none of us think of this?*

But her distress worked perfectly. The men at the table formed a protective circle around her even as St. Cyr took the stage for an encore. Her knee was throbbing, but Kathleen felt unharmed otherwise. Her nerves must have saved her.

"Air," she said, looking up from the floor into Benny's eyes. They did mesmerize. "I can't breathe."

This worked better than anything she could've dreamed up. With Benny on one side and a heavily cologned man the other, they hoisted Kathleen to her feet and pushed her forward while someone in front of them yelled, "Make way—we got a lady here!"

They burst through the doors, and on cue, the crack of the wooden rail at the other end of the room preceded the sound of a body thudding to the floor. Francella let out a blood-curdling scream. Kathleen's entourage stopped as they all looked toward the balcony.

"Somebody, call an ambulance!" she heard Thelma cry from deeper within the lobby. "My father, he's... help!"

Another woman—whose voice Kathleen didn't recognize— joined the cacophony. "Go get Doc Miller! It's his shift!"

That wouldn't do at all.

Grabbing Siegel's arm, Kathleen swooned. "Oh, Benny, could you see if you can get that doctor for me right away, please? I'm pregnant."

Before the Frontier's in-house doctor even made it to the lobby, two strapping young men and a woman in a freshly pressed nurse's uniform arrived and rushed to Sal's side. In seconds, Thelma let out a heart-wrenching, primal wail.

That girl had missed her calling in theater.

"Jesus Christ. Did that broad just push Sal over the railing?" one of Siegel's men asked.

"Moe, go find out if that rat fink is dead," Siegel said.

Feigning confusion, Kathleen asked, "What is it? What's happening?"

Benny turned back and looked her in the eyes, causing Kathleen to inhale sharply. Her mother was right—she had a thing for bad boys. How lucky she was to have wound up with Lloyd Young.

"Don't you worry about it." Benny turned toward the lobby. "Where the hell is that damn doctor? You!" He pointed at the nurse attending to the body on the floor. "Get over here."

Kathleen sat up. "No, I'm fine. Really."

Benny ignored her, and soon, the nurse—a woman with an unfortunate nose and mousy brown hair—was at her side. She took a stethoscope from around her neck and listened to Kathleen's heart for all of two seconds. "She's not well. She'd better come with us."

Though the accent was British, Kathleen would have recognized that voice anywhere. Lillian. As the girl helped her up, Kathleen turned to Benny and said, with a weak smile, "I was just trying to let you know I'd be happy to have Miss Hill in the cast."

Bugsy grinned. "Nah, 's all right. She told me she don't want to do it. Crime pays better."

"Goodbye, Benny." Kathleen pressed the dimple in his chin. "See ya in hell."

* * *

A WAVE OF SORROW CRASHED OVER THELMA AS SHE watched a pair of strapping male attendants cover Sal Giancarlo's just as Thelma marched into the lobby behind Moe—Sedway or Dalitz, she couldn't say which one.

"Get back, you monster!" screamed Francella, who'd made her way down the stairs. "Show some respect."

Siegel's associate stopped in his tracks, but respect didn't stop Benny. Before he could reach the stretcher, Thelma threw herself in his way and grabbed for his lapels—such a slight man. "Oh no, Mr. Siegel. What're we gonna do?"

To Thelma's astonishment, tears welled in her eyes. The losses of the past nine months—George, her mother, even her old teammate Millie—sloshed through her body. She dropped her head onto Siegel's shoulder before the moment could pass.

"Aw, sweetheart," he said, patting her hair. "Now—"

"Benny!"

Thelma looked up to see Virginia Hill storming across the lobby, flashing her infamous legs through the thigh-high slit in her cherry-red Grecian gown.

"I told you that girl was a tramp!"

Thelma drew herself up to her full height. She stood nearly six feet in her pumps. Hill hesitated, and Thelma pounced.

"You listen here." She strode straight for Hill. "You think you're clever playing by their rules? All you're doing is living somebody else's life."

Hill curled her upper lip, brow furrowed. "What kinda nonsense are you talking? That's my man. Those are the rules."

"Darling!" Nurse Lillian interjected, stopping as she made her way past with Mrs. Young under her shoulder. "So sorry to interrupt, but you must come with me. We must have someone who can identify the body. I understand you would be next of kin here?"

"Quick, Johnny!" Phil Skylar stage-whispered from underneath the blanket on the gurney, keeping his body inert. "Get out of here before anyone can follow us."

Thelma and Lillian piled into the back with Mrs. Young as the truck peeled away from the casino. "My God, Mrs. Young, you were incredible," Thelma said. "And Phil, I gotta hand it to you—you took that fall like a champ."

"Phil thinks it was nothing because it was only a one-story fall." Lillian peeled away her prosthetic nose and began undoing the clips in her wig. "But you were both brilliant."

"You too, Lillian," said Mrs. Young. "Honestly, I had no idea that was you until you spoke. And how on earth did you get a hold of this vehicle?"

"Oh, you know," Lillian laughed. "Money!"

They drove on into the night, speeding away from town toward the Starburst Motel, where Peggy would be waiting with their car and Sal. Thelma hopped out as soon as they pulled into the parking lot. She raced for the fire truck's back door.

"Mrs. Young? Are you okay?"

Soon they were all in the parking lot, hugging and laughing like survivors of a shipwreck. Until Phil interrupted. "I hate to break this up, but uh, I think Chip's expecting his ambulance back. And we should scram before someone notices us."

"Francella assures me this is a safe spot, but you're right," said Thelma before turning and flashing her eyes at her father. "I'll drive!"

"Like hell you will," said Sal. "Gimme those keys."

The urge to fight him rose. Thelma lifted her hand, ready to spar, but stopped herself. She was an inexperienced driver, after all. And she was tired. As Madame St. Clair had said, she didn't need to fight every battle.

"That's a good idea, Sal," she said.

Snatching the keys from her hand he said, "First, we gotta go back for Francella."

FORTY-SEVEN

LILLIAN'S BIG ANNOUNCEMENT,
Saturday

They hadn't discussed Francella.

Despite Mrs. Young's protest—"But you've already paid for the night"—Thelma had checked out of their hotel, assuming it was understood that they'd hotfoot it out of town from the Starburst.

Lillian was staying through the weekend for her honeymoon and to deliver Thelma's goodbye letter to the girls—reminding them also to call Maxene and take some pictures at the library—and then to turn the Vegas Girls reins over to Gloria. Since Lills had agreed to make a few Hollywood introductions for Francella, Thelma imagined her father's mistress would go on her merry way. Alone.

Clearly, Sal had other ideas. For his role in the evening, or early morning, Sal had freshened up. He looked good for a man who'd just fallen to his death. But that didn't make him any less deluded. Francella couldn't be more than twenty-five. He had to be in his sixties, Thelma guessed. She knew very little about her father other than the fact that he had a son, now deceased, a daughter who resided in a home for the mentally feeble, and a wife. *How will Carlotta Giancarlo feel about this?*

Thelma turned to say something, but... Sal was humming? She recognized the melody.

"'Cause I only have eyes for you," Sal sang before returning to his singsong drone.

"Carlotta knows exactly who she's married to," Vivian Miles piped in. "Just leave him be. I'll enjoy watching this."

In response, Thelma rolled her eyes, thinking how good it felt to let herself go like that as a snore arose from the front. She leaned forward to rouse Mrs. Young.

"Aw, let her sleep," said Sal.

She looked at Peggy, who shrugged. *Could this night get any stranger?*

* * *

KATHLEEN OPENED HER EYES AS THE CAR SLOWED, GROGGY enough to think she was back in Las Vegas. She'd been dreaming about having her baby, but nurses were holding her down. Struggling against their confinement, she tried to tell them she wouldn't be able to give birth until they let go, but even her mouth felt trapped. Then a miracle happened, and the baby came. As they let go to catch the newborn, Kathleen floated from the table, up, and out of the room then higher and higher until her problems vanished.

Noticing they were back in town, she lurched upright. "What the hell?"

"She's awake," said Thelma directly behind her.

Sal shut off the engine and put the car in park in an alley. "You stay here. I'll go get Frankie."

They must be at Frankie's hotel. This had to be the route his thugs had taken to drag three women with pillowcases over their heads into a public place.

"But, Sal," said Thelma. "You're supposed to be dead."

That girl could be as subtle as an elephant.

"Like no one'll notice you? Me, I'm in and out of here all the time. No one'll bat an eye."

"But, Sal—"

"Thelma, you're gonna have to just cool your jets."

Thelma groaned as she jerked against the back seat.

"Sal, I gotta agree with Thelma, here. I mean, just suppose word does get out."

"Stay outta this, Peggy," said Sal, pushing his upper lip forward in defiance.

Such a child. Had he been hoping to have a tryst with his lover before hitting the road? As the grogginess cleared, Kathleen knew what this situation called for.

"Salvatore." Kathleen wasn't speaking so much as purring. She even reached for his thigh. "You have a whole car full of women who are worried sick. Here's the thing. It makes sense for Thelma to go and console your grieving girl. It works for them to leave together. Doesn't she have her own car?"

"I gave her that car."

"Exactly. You're so used to taking care of other people. I understand. It can be hard to let other people take care of you."

Everyone in the car fell silent.

"We'll be able to help Miss DiGruppo pack in a jiff. Thelma?" Mrs. Young reached for her door handle. "I'd advise you two to drive away as quickly as possible."

"Mrs. Young?" cried Thelma. But the woman was already on the pavement.

Thelma was not so confident. She doubted very much that Francella would want to accompany them.

Hastening to follow and talk some sense into her old boss, Thelma had barely made it out of the car before the stench of rotting garbage hit her like a wall. Sal had parked beside a dumpster. A flash of movement caught her attention. At the large bin's base, two rats were fighting over a dark object, the discards of someone's dinner.

The crisp grind of heels exiting the alley roused Thelma. She was about to lose Mrs. Young just as Sal's black Lincoln Continental was speeding off in the opposite direction.

This could not be happening.

Thelma caught up with her former boss before she reached the door. "Mrs. Young! A word?" Grabbing her elbow, Thelma urged her quarry toward the vestibule's wall—just as Sal had done to her, she realized—before dropping her arm. "You've done it this time, lady."

Mrs. Young looked up at Thelma, lines around her eyes creasing as she broke into a smile. "Dear, do you think I don't know what I'm doing? Come with me."

With that, she slipped beneath Thelma's arm and strode through the revolving portal into the lobby. Thelma had no choice but to follow.

When they reached Francella's room, the door flew open. "I thought you'd never get here!"

Mrs. Young asked, "Is she still here?"

"Is who here?" Thelma asked. Up walked Imogene Fuchs. She looked at Mrs. Young. "You didn't—"

"Right here, ladies," said the reporter.

If Thelma understood correctly, and she was sure she did, Imogene had agreed to hold this story for twenty-four hours in exchange for exclusive interviews with Sal's bereaved family, friends, and longtime business associate slash suspected lover—namely, Thelma, Francella, and Mrs. Young—. They'd already given their statements—Francella was innocent, Thelma was beside herself, and Kathleen denied everything but was absolutely ready to work with Sal's successor on their garment contract. Now she was in Francella's room?

"After I sent her back out there this evening," said Mrs. Young, looking sheepish, though she was clearly very pleased with herself. "The least I could do was offer her the bigger scoop about how everyone in town is stealing from Mr. Siegel. I asked Francella to connect her with Wade."

A glimmer of recognition sparked in Thelma's chest. She might not be a queenpin in any ordinary sense of the word, but Kathleen Young was a world-class gangster. This revelation about the theft was not only true and would throw the heat off Sal, but Bugsy would be the buffoon. And Wade would have to see that working with the reporter made good business sense.

"I think I have everything I need. Francella, I'll be in touch. Thelma, Kathleen? Pleasure working with you as always." Fuchs lifted her foot. "Injuries notwithstanding."

No sooner had Imogene limped out the door than Francella raced toward Mrs. Young. "Thank you!"

Thelma was speechless.

After patting Francella's upper arm, Mrs. Young stiffened and backed away. "Of course, dear. It's the least I could do. Grandfather to my child and all that."

Her words didn't convince Thelma.

"Come on, then. Are you packed?" Mrs. Young asked. They'd clearly worked this out already. No wonder Mrs. Young believed her father's girlfriend would come along.

"Almost!"

Francella headed toward her dressing table to finish throwing items into her small case.

"Dear, be sure we can manage the bags on our own."

"You already told me," Francella said.

Thelma turned to ask Kathleen what agreement those three

had come to when the phone rang. She and her old boss looked at each other.

"Would one of you get that?" asked Francella. When neither moved, she stopped what she was doing and walked between them to the phone. "Oh, for Pete's sake.

"Yes, hello? Thelma? Mmm. May I ask who this is? Oh, Lillian! Of course! Thelma, it's—"

But Thelma was already grabbing for the phone.

* * *

"Lillian?"

Relieved though Kathleen was to hear Lillian Wright on the other end of the line, Thelma's hysteria ramped up.

"Slow down! What did you say? Oh my God. I'm coming!"

Then Thelma dropped the handset and looked around the room as if possessed. Kathleen didn't know what to make of it. "Thelma, dear, what is it?" She retrieved the telephone and returned it to its cradle.

The girl ignored her, focusing instead on Francella. "You! Throw that crap in your bag or leave it. I have to get to the airport."

Kathleen's shock only grew as Thelma snatched up the other valise Francella had packed—the enormous one—like it was a box of cereal. Stopped mid stride, Thelma convulsed with tears.

"Honey." Francella raced to her side and put her arm around her. "Whatsa matter?"

"It's George. They found him. Alive!"

MEMORANDUM FOR THE DIRECTOR

FROM: WADE DAVIS, NEVADA SPECIAL AGENT
IN RE: PLAN "SAFEGUARD"
DATE: June 28, 1945

THE NEVADA OFFICE OF THE FEDERAL BUREAU OF Investigation has, on behalf of Director Hoover, utilized all the resources available to it in this country, both clandestine and overt, to suppress reports of so-called organized criminals in Las Vegas.

TOWARD THESE EFFORTS, IT HAS DISCUSSED THESE ISSUES with the following persons, among others: Mr. Moe Dalitz, business developer; Mr. Salvatore Giancarlo, business developer; Mr. Meyer Lanksy, chief financial officer, Nevada Projects Corporation; Mr. Benjamin Siegel, chief executive officer, Nevada Projects Corporation.

. . .

WHILE THERE HAVE UNQUESTIONABLY BEEN INSTANCES OF individual manipulations, extortion, graft, corruption, and other practices which have contributed to the present rise in overall criminal statistics, there is no reason to believe that these have been substantially more prevalent in recent years than in the past, nor is there any evidence to support the suggestion that the recent rise has been the result of an organized campaign.

IN CONCLUSION, AND IN KEEPING WITH THE NATURE OF this report, let it be said that the threat has been neutralized and evidence to the contrary, photographic or otherwise, remains safely under wraps.

FORTY-NINE

BIRD OF PARADISE, January 1947

HAVANA, CUBA

THELMA LOOKED OUT AT THE PALM LEAVES IN THEIR courtyard, a shield from both the sun and their neighbors. Doris had secured them an incredible eighteenth-century mansion in central Havana, where the houses were sandwiched in tightly, making this balcony more private than some of the rooms inside. Unless it was raining, she and Helen and Doris met here most mornings to discuss club business.

José walked out with a fresh pot of coffee, which he deposited on the table before handing Thelma a letter. "For you," he said before retreating.

"Who's it from?" asked Doris.

Thelma regarded her friend, smiling. In Cuba, she'd stopped carrying her parasol everywhere, and her skin had turned a golden caramel. She looked healthier and happier than ever. They all did.

"Imogene Fuchs," she said, tearing open the envelope.

Peggy rose and moved toward the RCA Victor.

"Ooh, see if you can find something romantic to play," Doris said.

"Soon as we hear the news," said Helen.

"Darling, aren't you reading a book already?"

"Sweetie, that's not how news works," said Helen.

"I'm with Doris," said Peggy.

But Thelma—transfixed by the newspaper clipping in her hand—had stopped listening. She couldn't tear her eyes away from Elizabeth Short, who seemed to be staring back at her. Between the girl's glowing stare and wavy black hair, she could've been Thelma's kid sister. And she was dead. Found on the western edge of Los Angeles, according to the report before her, her body cut in half.

Her eyes stopped on a quote Imogene had underlined.

I decided to pick her up and make a test for myself and see if I loved my wife or not.

This was apparently how some fellow had described his encounter with Short, as a way of proclaiming his innocence in her passing. A wave of nausea crashed over Thelma. Her hand flew to her mouth.

The motion caught Peggy's eye as she poured herself a second coffee. "Thelms? What is it? What's the matter? You look like you've seen a ghost."

"I think I'm going to be sick."

"Are you pregnant?" asked Doris.

Without a word, Thelma handed the letter to Peggy, whose mop of platinum hair brushed the page as she read aloud. "Dearest Thelma, blah blah blah." She looked up. "She's doing well in LA. I'm just skipping the pleasantries. Let's see... she's managed to get a spot on the crime desk. Her boss has her reporting on that Black Dahlia case."

Helen looked up from her book. "Imogene Fuchs would sound excited about that. My God, so gruesome."

"I'm just glad she landed on her feet after that debacle in Vegas," said Helen, shaking her head. "I'd be furious."

"That's because you want to write a whole book," said Doris. "This was just one article."

Helen put down her book. "My love, it is the principle of suppression I'm talking about. There is no way in hell *Life* magazine needed to kill that piece for reasons of national security."

"At least it got her to LA," said Doris, grinning.

Peggy read on. "My boss, Aggie, says there's something more to this story. If you ask me, there's a bigger story here. I'm learning so much. No one can get sources singing like Aggie. Yours, etcetera."

"That Imogene sure has a nose for news. I bet—" Doris stopped herself. "Thelma?"

"Did you see her?" said Thelma, holding up the black-and-white image of Elizabeth Short. "She looks like we could be related. And this man, this suspect they just let off the hook, is talking about her like she's a lab rat. Apparently, his wife had just had a baby, so stepping out on her is how he's going to figure out if they should still be together? Course, he claims he didn't."

Thelma twisted in her seat toward the house's French doors. "José!" she yelled. "Do we have any Kahlúa?"

She turned back just in time to catch her friends exchanging glances. Peggy was looking through the doors, drawing her index finger across her throat to signal José.

Helen took the lead. "That story is unsettling for all of us. But what do you say we get our business out of the way before we start drinking?"

Though these friends knew more about her than anyone, Thelma resented how oblivious they were to the similarities between her and the Black Dahlia girl. They certainly knew how she felt about her ongoing inability to conceive, especially since Francella had followed Sal to Cuba and then actually became pregnant.

Of course I'm drinking. That didn't make her like Vivian Miles. "Sure," said Thelma, taking a sip from her mug. "Ew, it's cold."

Doris hopped up, dumped what remained in the cup into a planter, and refilled it. "Here, nice and hot."

"Thanks," said Thelma, though she didn't want to be waited on. She wanted George—couldn't wait for her husband to be home. He visited his family in Florida more than she liked since he'd gotten out of the hospital. She couldn't get enough of him. "Let's get started."

"Wonderful," said Helen. "Let's talk about the business at hand, shall we? We need to make sure customs stays cooperative. Last night was big, wasn't it?"

"Huge," Doris said, eyes going wide. "Bola de Neve was on the keyboard, and everything was *yayaya* until five a.m., when the bus came to take them back to the airport."

Thelma sighed. "We did make a killing. There wasn't time for our guests to sober up while waiting in line, so they arrived at the club raring to go."

"How's about I head to the airport this afternoon?" said Peggy. "I'll make sure Rolando and Anja are, you know, cleared to bring our guests directly to Bird of Paradise without having to wait."

"There's no need to be coy about it, Peggy," said Thelma. "Just be sure you take enough cash."

"Dorr, why don't you go with her?" said Helen.

Doris, whose Spanish was almost as good as Peggy's, had also just become a Cuban citizen. Her father, it had turned out, was what they called black Cuban, a fact her mother had revealed only after the girls called her from Havana. Mrs.

Juergen had visited several times already. Helen's family had been far less forgiving.

"*Perdóname, señora.*" José, in his pressed yellow shirt—the girls had insisted he forego the jacket—looked mortified for interrupting them.

"José, what is it?" asked Peggy, addressing him in English because he wanted the practice.

"There is someone here. She is insisting—"

"There you are!" sounded a familiar voice. "It's me, girls. Kathleen Young!"

Helen's book slid from her grasp and Thelma very nearly released her coffee cup.

"Mrs. Young," cried Doris, leaping from her seat again. "You've brought the baby! Let's see her!" Without waiting, she reached for the sling to uncover the babe in her old boss's arms.

"Meet Cora. Isn't she perfect?" Mrs. Young slipped out of the wrap and handed her child to Doris.

The fabric, Thelma noted, was a batik. Not something she'd have thought of as Mrs. Young's style. And wasn't the toddler a little old for a sling?

"Her name is from the French, *encore*. This is my second act, after all."

Leave it to Mrs. Young to steal the thunder from a newborn.

Peggy rose from her seat and strode to Mrs. Young. "I was so sorry to hear about Doc. I hope you got my condolences," she said, embracing her longtime boss.

Thelma remained frozen. There was the shock of seeing Mrs. Young out of the blue like this, but there was also something more. Maybe it was how she looked. Other than the strange scarf, she was stylish as ever in a pair of wide-legged trousers and a V-necked sweater, but something was different. She was more... mannish? But that wasn't it.

Helen hadn't moved either. "Have you been exercising, Mrs. Young?"

How Thelma loved that girl. Spot on again—Mrs. Young's arms had *muscles*. Still curvy but leaner than before. Sporty even.

"You noticed!" she gushed, pulling away from Peggy to lift her arms and spin around before raising one foot in the air as she folded forward, arms outstretched. "Ardha chandrasana. Standing half moon."

"Say what now?" asked Peggy.

The baby gurgled. Doris looked up, eyes wide. "Um?"

"Oh, she's fine," said Mrs. Young, popping up to swipe Cora and deposit her in Thelma's arms. "Don't you want to meet your sister?"

Still rooted, Thelma looked up from the wriggling infant in her lap. Between her rosy, chubby cheeks and thick mane of dark curls, Cora looked more like Thelma's offspring than Mrs. Young's. Or maybe that wasn't right. Thelma wished her mother would ring in with an opinion on the matter, but she hadn't heard from Vivian Miles in months.

"Niece," said Helen. "Cora is Thelma's niece, Mrs. Young."

"Well, we're all one at the end of the day. Om shanti."

Finally, Thelma found her voice. "Mrs. Young?"

"Oh, my dears, I think it's time you all called me Kathleen, please."

"Okay, Kathleen. I think Cora just pooped."

THE AFTERNOON SUN WAS FADING AS THELMA STOOD AT the kitchen's stone counter, talking with Luìsa about dinner, and heard George's voice.

"What's this I hear? Mrs. Young is here with her baby?"

She looked up to see her husband, still in his tennis whites.

He was a good sight more tan and his hair a shade paler than when they'd first met in St. Petersburg. He took her breath away. *Did he still feel the same?*

"Darling!" She ran to embrace him as Luìsa discreetly left the kitchen. She and George could be a bit much, Thelma knew, but she was still so enthralled with her beloved. Even after discovering she'd brought Sal to the island and his father cut him off, he'd stayed with her in Cuba. He swore she didn't, but Thelma couldn't help but feel she owed him.

So, though they had no ownership stake in Bird of Paradise, she and George and Peggy were paid handsomely to help run the club that Helen and Doris had purchased. Beyond her trifling insecurities, Thelma had never felt so content.

She and George were still wrapped in each other's arms when Helen walked in. "Hey, George. Have you seen *le bébe* yet?"

Turning to the redhead, he hooked his arm around Thelma's neck. "God no. Do I have to?"

Helen snickered. "If you're very lucky, Mrs. Young will show you some yoga postures."

"Yoga? What's that?"

"It's something she picked up from Dale Evans's personal instructor on that movie set," Helen whispered. "A Eugenia something or other."

"Is it catching?"

"Shh, she'll hear you" said Thelma, slapping his chest. "I swear that woman's a bat."

Both girls laughed. "Darlings," Helen said in a near-perfect impression of Kathleen Young. "I swear, yoga is the best thing that came out of that movie. Besides the uniform contracts."

"Jesus, that broad always lands on her feet, doesn't she?" said George.

"Well, I don't know. She lost Lloyd, her husband of twenty-some years. She's just had a baby, and she's gotta be almost forty," said Thelma. "Archie's still out serving the war efforts in Japan. Meanwhile her other son... Well, he's Bertie. Gang, she's kind of alone in the world."

* * *

OVER SUPPER, MRS. YOUNG—KATHLEEN—ANNOUNCED SHE wouldn't be accompanying them to the club that night. "I begin my practice as the moon sets," she said, holding her hand over her wineglass to keep José from pouring any for her.

Thelma kept her eyes trained on her plate to avoid looking at Helen. But it was too late.

"Mrs.—" Peggy stopped herself. "I mean, Kathleen." She cleared her throat. "You gotta admit, you sound about as normal as Harry Truman reading poetry."

Everyone at the table laughed. Even Kathleen Young.

FIFTY

THE MORNING AFTER, January 1947

Thelma woke with a piercing headache. It sounded like someone was screaming inside her head. She was going to have to look at her champagne intake more closely. She rolled over at the same time as George, but instead of seeing his face, she beheld a chunky, squalling baby.

Cora?

Thelma sat upright, her brain ablaze. "Mrs. Young!" She shot out from the covers and—not bothering with slippers or her dressing gown—raced down the hallway to the guest chamber. "Mrs. Young!" she screamed again.

Mrs. Young's bed was empty. Thelma looked around the room. *Where could that woman have gone?*

Back in the hallway, Helen and Doris had emerged. "Thelma?" said Doris. "It's seven o'clock in the morning."

She stopped. Shook her head. The brightness of the sun had fooled Thelma, she thought it was later in the morning. But it was May. The days had been getting longer for some time now. They'd only been home a few hours. Mrs. Young must be out on the veranda, doing her practice or whatever the hell she called it. She probably just didn't want to leave the baby alone.

"Sweetheart?" called George. "I think something is wrong with this kid."

Racing back toward their bedroom, Thelma stopped in her tracks again. The vision of George holding that child in their bed wracked her body with longing. For a moment, Thelma wanted Mrs. Young to have left Cora behind.

The baby was still wailing.

"I'm sure she's fine," said Thelma, reaching for the infant.

Peggy wandered into the room. "Thelms? I think Mrs. Young left. As in, her bags are gone."

"What! She up and deserted her baby?" yelled George, swinging his legs out of the bed. "I'm going to kill her myself."

He stormed out of the room, trailed by Peggy, leaving Thelma with the baby. Hugging her close, she rubbed her little back. Cora's body shuddered, and she began to calm.

"You're a natural at that," said Doris as she walked through the door.

"I can see the family resemblance," said Helen, lifting her eyebrows.

Thelma eyed them both. "This is bananas, right?"

Peggy ran back into the room, holding a piece of paper aloft. "Oh my God." She stopped. "Jesus, Thelms, you could be that kid's mother."

Thelma's heart skipped a beat.

"This," Peggy continued, shaking the letter in her hand, "is from Kathleen."

LATER THAT MORNING, THEY GATHERED AROUND THE breakfast table. Luísa's *abuela* had come to help out, but still, the mood was considerably dimmer than it had been the day before.

"Let Sal deal with the kid," said George.

Thelma rubbed at her temples. She hadn't had a drink all day, and she was feeling it. Maybe she was in worse shape than she thought.

"Aw, c'mon, Georgie. You don't mean that," said Peggy.

"Oh, don't I?" George snorted.

Thelma suspected her husband's hostility was coming from somewhere else. He'd been wanting a baby. They'd certainly been trying.

"She's certainly seen to it the child is well taken care of," said Helen.

"You're not making any sense, Helen," said George. "The way a mother takes care of her baby is by sticking around."

"Leaving Daddy to scoot off under the guise of footing the bills," Helen sneered.

"You know what I mean, Helen."

"I think we all know what you mean, George," said Doris.

Had they noticed how often George flew back and forth to Florida lately?

"Anyway, with her husband gone, Kathleen must be both mother and father. Her note makes it clear that the proceeds from her uniform supply business will more than provide for the child."

George scowled. "And what's that got to do with her traipsing off to India? That sounds more like an affair than a job."

The girls exchanged looks. "Surely you're familiar with the Dutch East India Company, George," said Helen. "Exporting fabrics since the seventeenth century?"

That Helen was a whiz when it came to books, but making George feel small, Thelma knew, was not going to win points. It was just a matter of time—Thelma feared—before a doctor would declare her infertile. Her clients had been none too careful, yet she'd never even had a scare. Until recently, she'd considered this a boon.

"*She* isn't dead," George continued. "If that's her choice, let Sal take the thing."

If she'd been conflicted, her husband's words flipped a switch. "My love, that *thing* is my niece, and a helpless little girl besides. I honestly can't abandon her. It's only temporary."

"Are you sure about that?" George looked at Thelma in disbelief. "And how does a baby work with running a nightclub?"

Thelma squinted at him. "Weren't we going to have to figure that out eventually? Sweetheart, look around this table. Families are..."

Her voice caught with emotion, overwhelmed as she was by the messy, complex, all-encompassing love around the table. Never in her wildest dreams would she have pictured this life. She didn't want to leave any of them behind.

"Families are complicated."

George leaned toward her. "So it's just *my* family you're willing to abandon?"

"Me? Abandon them? Last time I spoke to your father, he was doing his level best to get rid of me."

"And you were only too happy to offer up an annulment, weren't you?"

Thelma was panting now, breathing heavily through her nose, doing her best to suppress what she really wanted to say.

"I won't do it, Thelma. I've had to give up my family to make room for yours. But this?" He pointed at the child. "Is too much. We don't have the money for a kid. Especially not—"

He stopped himself, the lavender-blue glint of his eyes had gone steely.

"Not what, George?"

But her husband stepped back, disengaged.

"Honestly, that's about the dumbest thing I ever heard," she said, immediately regretting her choice of words.

"It's me or that baby. Choose."

"What?" Thelma hadn't said George was stupid, just his word choice. That alone, she knew, could be enough.

He didn't answer. Instead, her husband stepped away from the table, causing his chair to fall to the floor behind him. José rushed out to right it, and George practically tripped over him.

The sound of the door slamming shut caused Thelma physical pain. She hadn't meant for any of this to happen. When she asked Sal to join her in Cuba, she was still under the impression that George was dead. It was a lot to forgive, but he'd insisted he had. *Was there something more behind this?*

"I hate to ask this, Thelms," said Peggy. "But... What about Sal? Why not just hand the baby over to him? Mrs. Young'll be back eventually."

"Are you saying you think this baby would be better off with Sal than me?"

"No. But he's got Francella, and they already have a kid."

"She's always off doing shows on Broadway," said Thelma. "The baby would be raised by nannies."

"Well, yeah, but we have a business too."

"Oh, honestly, Peggy."

"I'm more worried about you, Thelms. Kids are resilient. But I know how you are without George," said Peggy.

A lump formed in Thelma's throat. If Peggy believed George was lost already, maybe he was.

A crash erupted from the guest room. "Is okay!" called Josefa, Luísa's *abuela*.

Thelma caught Peggy's self-satisfied *my point exactly* look and burst out laughing. "We'll figure it out, Pegs," she said, feeling a confidence she hadn't known she possessed, one that had arrived with this overwhelming urge to protect this little girl.

It was one thing to care for herself and George. Even her friends. But a vulnerable child who couldn't fend for herself? For her, Thelma would do anything.

That afternoon, when George still hadn't returned, Thelma worried anew. He'd seemed angrier than when she told him she'd brought Sal to Cuba. But back then, he'd only just gotten out of the hospital, was utterly dependent on her.

Was it really so unreasonable to ask for his understanding now? Why should her brother's child be so different from her own? It wasn't to her.

Before she left for the club, Thelma tiptoed into the guest bedroom to say goodnight to Cora. She was already asleep, content in the bed that José had fashioned for her from sofa cushions. Leaning toward her cherubic face, Thelma spoke in a voice that was barely a whisper. "I'll always be here for you, little love. No matter what."

And there, faint though it was, for the first time in months Thelma felt that tingling in her palms.

* * *

◆ Want more Queenpins ◆
Havana is calling 🔥

What secrets are buried in pre-Revolutionary Cuba? How will they link to 1978 Miami?
Scan to discover what Thelma uncovers next in *Havana Girls*.

Or visit llkirchner.com/books to get the stunning conclusion

* * *

Psst! For access to special deals and bonus content, join LL's *Insiders* list at https://tinyurl.com/llk-insiders

FIFTY-ONE

START READING: HAVANA GIRLS

PROLOGUE
Los Angeles - 1950

THE RATATAT OF HER TYPEWRITER KEYS SLOWED AS LIGHTS across the hillside sparked to life, like a bejeweled cape unfurling. Imogene—usually charmed by this sight—scarcely noticed. Must call Briggs, was all she could think as she absent-mindedly tugged out any curl remaining in her hair. The letter she'd been working on could wait.

She shouldn't be putting off either, really, but Briggs's need to know was immediate. She'd no intention of giving the story of the century to the *St. Petersburg Press*. Not when Aggie had promised her a career-changing byline in the *Los Angeles Times*. She couldn't turn that down for Briggs. Scratch that. *Wouldn't*. She was filing with Aggie the next day.

Tipping her wrist, she checked the time. Three-thirty back home. She could still catch him before the afternoon's editorial meeting. The only task she'd put off longer was the confession in front of her.

Imogene touched the top plate of her Robin's egg-blue Olivetti, tracing its curves. How she loved it. So strange to approach it with anything other than enthusiasm. But this was no ordinary missive for her daughter. Unlike the phone call, she wasn't sure this *was* the right thing to do.

Her source could remain forever confidential. That was how this worked. But she wanted her daughter to know the truth. Sally was only eight, but already she saw the world in black and white. It was up to Imogene to help her understand that, sometimes, the only way to fight a monster was to make a deal with the devil. Otherwise, her reputation as a gung-ho reporter would give the girl the wrong ideas. She would lionize her mother. Until the real story came out. Secrets had a tendency to reveal themselves one way or another.

Besides, her story would change lives.

From a certain angle, the reporting did include her original assignment. If it weren't for the Black Dahlia case, she'd never have done this investigation. She looked down at the newspaper clippings on her desk, her work over the past five years. The 'Beautiful Homes' photo spread of the Juergen mansion was on top because chronological order made sense. Underscored what she was trying to show her daughter. That "story" was essentially a collection of captions. That was all Briggs had ever expected of her. At the start, it was all she'd ever expected of herself, and this was why—she reminded herself—she had to tell Sally the truth.

Shuffling the pile, she found her first big piece. The exposé she had given the *Press*—'Bookie Joint, Crap Game, Houses of Ill-Repute — Tampa's Biggest Crackdown.' Her first investigative report. All because Briggs had sent her out on a puff piece— the Florida Girls beauty contest. That *was* a puff piece. Especially after Briggs got his fingers all over it. Thank heavens for Agnes Underwood.

She had shown her how different work could be. Aggie was her mentor, the first woman Imogene had ever worked for and the only woman she'd ever met who took less care in her appearance than she did. Frazzled hairdos and wrinkled suits aside, Aggie never treated Imogene as anything less than a fully capable reporter. Then again, neither had Sal Giancarlo.

Shame bloomed in Imogene's chest. She'd known all along that while Sal was feeding her stories to take down gangland's most wanted criminals, he was moving in on their territory. She didn't plan to let that happen with Elizabeth Short's murder. Until he told her how vulnerable young women were regularly picked up off the streets for the pleasure of men. Then his motives ceased to be a concern. She had to make Sally understand.

The clock struck the quarter hour. Beads of perspiration formed on Imogene's forehead. She fanned herself with her shirt. She could delay no longer.

Lifting the heavy black receiver off the switch hook, Imogene dialed the operator. She'd just come on the line when a scraping noise sounded at her door.

Who on earth—?

The door knob rattled as she half-rose from her seat. A sudden sharp thud slammed the door on its hinges. Startled, Imogene dropped the phone and turned to face the window, cursing the view. This was no mere interruption and there was no escape down that steep hillside. But she couldn't leave her confession lying about.

Ripping the sheet from her typewriter cartridge as she gathered her clips, Imogene thrust the lot into the Manilla folder she'd prepared. What now?

She made a mad dash for the bathroom and stuffed the envelope into the one place no man would look, where her words could easily disappear—her sanitary napkin box. No matter. After her story about corruption in Vegas was killed, she'd taken steps to ensure that wouldn't happen again. Her story was in her desk at the *Times*. Safe.

The door burst open.

* * *

🔥 *Can't wait to see what happens next?* The secrets of pre-Revolutionary Cuba await... Scan for *Havana Girls* now

* * *

*W*HAT'S *LL* WRITING NOW? JOIN THE *I*NSIDERS TO FIND out first + get exclusive bonus content → https://tinyurl.com/llk-insiders

Also By L.L. Kirchner

FICTION:

Florida Girls

Not everything is sunshine in Florida.

(Book 1 of The Queenpin Chronicles, May 2024)

Vegas Girls

Sometimes what happens in Vegas stays with you.

(Book 2 of The Queenpin Chronicles, January 2025)

Havana Girls

Some revolutions start with a whisper.

(Book 3 of The Queenpin Chronicles, June 2025)

MEMOIR:

Blissful Thinking: A Memoir of Overcoming the Wellness Revolution

A 2023 Pushcart nominee and a Foreword Indies Humor Finalist. The raw and honest account of the search for salvation that took me from university halls in the Persian Gulf to the streets of Manhattan to a sex cult in India, all in an attempt to save my sobriety and maybe even land a second date.

American Lady Creature: My Change in the Middle East. A Qatar Memoir

Re-released in 2022, listed as one of Goodreads's funniest memoirs for women, this book delivers an unflinching look at what it took to redefine myself as a woman after a surprise divorce, the loss of my dogs, and an ungodly early menopause, all while living in one of the world's most patriarchal cultures. New foreword.

* * *

Ill-Behaved Women, my blog

Because history is already littered with women's untold stories.

Sign up at IllBehavedWomen.com and you'll be subscribed to the blog along with separate, insider news—behind-the-scenes on works in progress, and commentary by, for, and about women and those who identify as such. Fear not—you won't be subscribed twice and I can't generate that much email.

Author's Note

The inspiration for this book came from the characters, a diverse group of women all experiencing an awakening. In 1945, Las Vegas was the logical next stop, the perfect backdrop for the radical transformation to come. As with *Florida Girls* (Book 1 of The Queenpin Chronicles), the landscape provided something familiar, reminding me of Qatar, a country where I lived in the early aughts, a time when everything was on the verge of becoming something else. Just like our *Girls*.

My initial ideas for the story, however, were drawn from my rudimentary understanding that the mob built Las Vegas. Not that the place was a blank slate. By 1945, construction of the Hoover Dam, followed by the installation of Nellis Air Force—a gunner school for WWII flyers—meant that gambling and prostitution were already well entrenched. It was during the war that President Franklin D. Roosevelt shut down all prostitution near military bases, which meant lights out on Block 16, Vegas's red-light district, though I couldn't resist having Kathleen Young drive through the area as if it was still up and running.

Kathleen's drive was also to underscore how different the town was, as well as how odd it was that the casinos were built far from downtown, a place that had not yet gotten the nickname Glitter Gulch, even though I used it as a chapter title in the novel.

For developers, the location meant that their buildings were outside city limits, thus exempt from city taxes. Though that exemption didn't last long, the location attests to their business acumen. Though, to be fair, the original gangster to build outside Vegas proper was Anthony Cornero, an LA bootlegger. His hotel and casino, The Meadows, was built in 1931, more than fifteen years ahead of Benjamin "Bugsy" Siegel's Flamingo.

In 1941, the Syndicate tasked Siegel with establishing a racing wire in Vegas, launching a yearslong battle with Chicago rival James Regan for control, an imbroglio that's been linked to Siegel's murder in 1947.

In deference to this story, I took the liberty of moving these Vegas construction projects up a year to just before the war ended. Though construction materials remained scarce, Benjamin Siegel was able to secure a regular supply, largely from Hollywood lots. The fact that other gangland members stole from his site has been well documented. It's even been speculated that *this* was why he was gunned down in Beverly Hills through the wall of Virginia Hill's living room. At least for skimming money off the Flamingo's ever-expanding construction budget.

But the romantic in me is drawn to the love triangle rumor.

As this story goes, somehow Bee Sedway got wind of Siegel's plan to kill her husband, Moe. Bee drove straight to the desert and told him that her lover Moose would protect him. In response, Moe apparently insisted that Moose should—upon his death—make an honest woman of Bee. Yes, you read that right. Whether that protection included shooting Siegel or not, it's a great story. Especially the coda. After years of living together under one roof, when Moe Sedway did at last pass away, Bee and Moose wed.

The biggest challenge I faced when I began to research *Vegas Girls* in earnest was the discovery that, between 1945 and 1949, the mob had weaseled its way into every aspect of functioning society in LA and Vegas—from the police to the government to the clergy. Lots of people were getting rich and very few criminals were going to jail. It's also true these gangsters considered themselves a different breed. They cared about business, and murder was not good for business. Bribing officials merely kept the wheels of the gambling industry moving. So I had to come up with a very different tale.

Originally meant to be a story of justice, *Vegas Girls* became a redemption story. In case you're questioning that leap—*isn't fabrication the whole point of a novel?*— I get it. But I do like my work to conform to true stories and, better still, I found this restriction compelling. It caused me to reimagine the entire plot, beginning with the prologue. Or perhaps this was mostly personal. Shortly before I began writing this book, my father passed away. I just couldn't write a story of a woman taking out vengeance on her father, rotten and absent though Sal was. Don't worry though, justice is coming.

As for that prologue, while there was indeed friction between J. Edgar Hoover, Wild Bill Donovan, and Harry Truman, to my knowledge, no bureaucratic infighting led to a covert operation in Las Vegas or anywhere else. Having worked in my share of offices—including *government* offices—such a conflict felt plausible, while also a harbinger of what's to come.

Another fabrication was the inclusion of Mexican women working as showgirls. Census records from the time indicate that the Mexican population of Las Vegas was quite small. However, when World War II interrupted narcotics shipments from Asia and Europe, Mexico became one of the largest suppliers in the world. Meyer Lansky developed new routes of trade through Mexico and Virginia Hill—being fluent in Spanish—was one of his primary liaisons.

Likewise, Blacks made up a small portion of the Las Vegas population, however they did live in conditions such as the ones described in this book. They also faced extensive discrimination. After reading Billie Holiday's harrowing account of her time in Las Vegas in *Lady Sings the Blues*, I tried to figure out a way to shoehorn Doris Juergen back into this story to do a little magic in the style of Josephine Baker—who not only stayed on hotel property in the early 1950s, but made sure that her contract included a table for her invited guests from Las Vegas's Black community—but I couldn't make it work with the plot. PBS has a few good documentaries available online where you can learn more. However, I was able to include Madame St. Clair, the very real queenpin who outmaneuvered the mob in New York City.

A number of other characters included are a nod to real life people and circumstances, like Dr. Nettles. Her character is an ode to Eliza Atkins Gleason, the first Black woman to earn a doctorate in library science, which she did at the University of Chicago. Maxene Lewis, on the other hand, is directly taken from what little information I could find. The entertainment director of the Frontier, she brought in Liberace and—after seeing the crowd he could bring—supposedly tore up his contract and doubled it on the spot. The idea that a woman had this authority then absolutely had to make its way into the book. And finally, Kathleen's surprise ending owes in part to two women: Dorothy Arzner—the first female member of the Directors Guild of America—and Eugenia Peterson, the woman who brought yoga to the West and eventually became known as Indra Devi, and whom I learned about in a book. You can read more about them all in my blog at IllBehavedWomen.com.

Other details in this book also owe to the nonfiction works I consumed, and though this is by no means a bibliography, this list covers the most-often referred to texts, including *The Green Felt Jungle* by Ed Reid and Ovid Demaris, *Black Dahlia, Red Rose* by Piu Eatwell, 30 *Illegal Years to the Strip* by Bill Friedman, *When the Mob Ran Vegas* by Steve Fischer, *The Money and the Power* by Sam Denton and Roger Morris, *Sex Workers, Psychics, and Numbers Runners* by LaShawn Harris, and *Lady Las Vegas* by Susan Berman—as well as the incredible archives available through VintageVegas.com, the University of Nevada's online archives, the CIA's online records, and countless Facebook groups and Instagram accounts I devoured. As of this writing, I have only been to Las Vegas once. But I'm heading there soon!

All errors are mine.

This book would not exist were it not for the village of writers who have advised, built me up, and supported my madness. I am deeply indebted to communities I've met thanks to my writing coaches Camille Pagàn and Sue Campbell, and I'd also specifically like to thank these writers, readers and supporters: Susana Darwin, Kimberly Diaz, Nicole Fincher, Arin Greenwood, Tamara Lush, Desiree Matlock, Bubsy McDonough, Teresa Thomas, Alsace Walentine, and Alex Villapiano. And a special thanks must go to my indefatigable writing partner-in-crime, Betsy Farber, the crackerjack team at Red Adept Editing, The Author Buddy, and my beloved and most favorite husband, Paul.

And finally, *you.* Books only come alive through readers. Thank you for giving this story life.

Photo credit cover: TFoxFoto

About the Author

L.L. Kirchner is an award-winning screenwriter and Pushcart-nominated author whose life and work as an expat in Asia became the basis of two memoirs that combine humor with "her discerning eye" (Foreword Reviews). As an NPR interviewer said, her memoir is "like *Eat, Pray, Love,* but funny." Her writing has appeared in the *Washington Post, Salon,* and *The Rumpus* among numerous other outlets.

Drawing on her eclectic journalism background as a religion editor, dating columnist, and bridal editor, her work explores female-centered narratives. Read more at her blog, IllBehavedWomen.com or LLKirchner.com.

She lives in Florida with her favorite husband and their best boy, Hartley.

On socials everywhere @llkirchnerauthor.

For Book Clubs

I bet you love your book club as much as I love mine. In honor of that mutual adoration, I've put together a discussion guide. Find it on my website, LLKirchner.com under FOR BOOK CLUBS.

From that page, tap the "let's connect" button. I'd love to join your book club's discussion if at all possible!